# GO GIRL! ™

## Robots Gone Wild!

story **TRINA ROBBINS**

art **ANNE TIMMONS**

cover colors **CYNTHIA MARTIN**

D1534644

**DARK HORSE BOOKS**™

publisher **MIKE RICHARDSON**

editor **CHRIS WARNER**

publication designer **KRYSTAL HENNES**

art director **LIA RIBACCHI**

**GOGIRL!™: ROBOTS GONE WILD!**

Dark Horse Books
A division of Dark Horse Comics, Inc.
10956 SE Main Street
Milwaukie, OR 97222

darkhorse.com

trinarobbins.com

To find a comics shop in your area,
call the Comic Shop Locator Service toll-free at
1-888-266-4226

First edition: October 2006
ISBN-10: 1-59307-409-3
ISBN-13: 978-1-59307-409-8

10 9 8 7 6 5 4 3 2 1
Printed in Canada

# Hi everyone, we're back!

We, in this case, are yours truly, Trina Robbins, creator and writer of *GoGirl!*, and the fabulous artist, Anne Timmons.

A little bit about us: Anne and I both have cats, whom we love fiercely, so we put our cats into this issue. Think you can find them? (Hint: of course we included them with Chatty Catty's kitties—that's too obvious!—but we put them elsewhere in the story, too!)

And here's Anne, at a signing for the last *GoGirl!* The photo was taken by her dad, Archie Timmons.

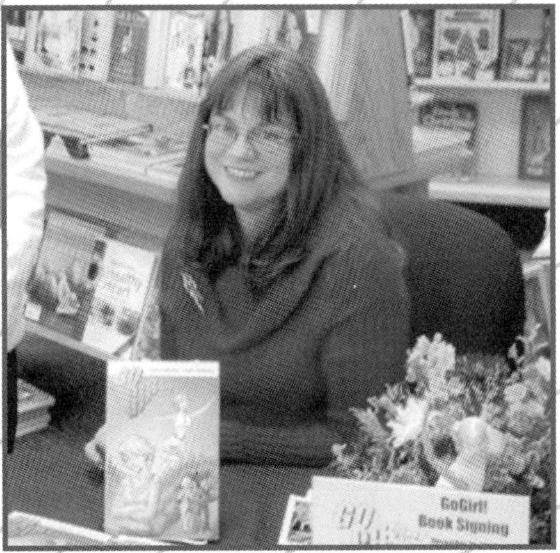
GoGirl!
Book Signing

Finally, what do you think of *GoGirl!*? Do you like her or hate her? Could she be better? Any stories you'd like to see us do? Email me at mswuff@juno.com, and let me know. Send drawings, too!

See you soon!

—Trina Robbins

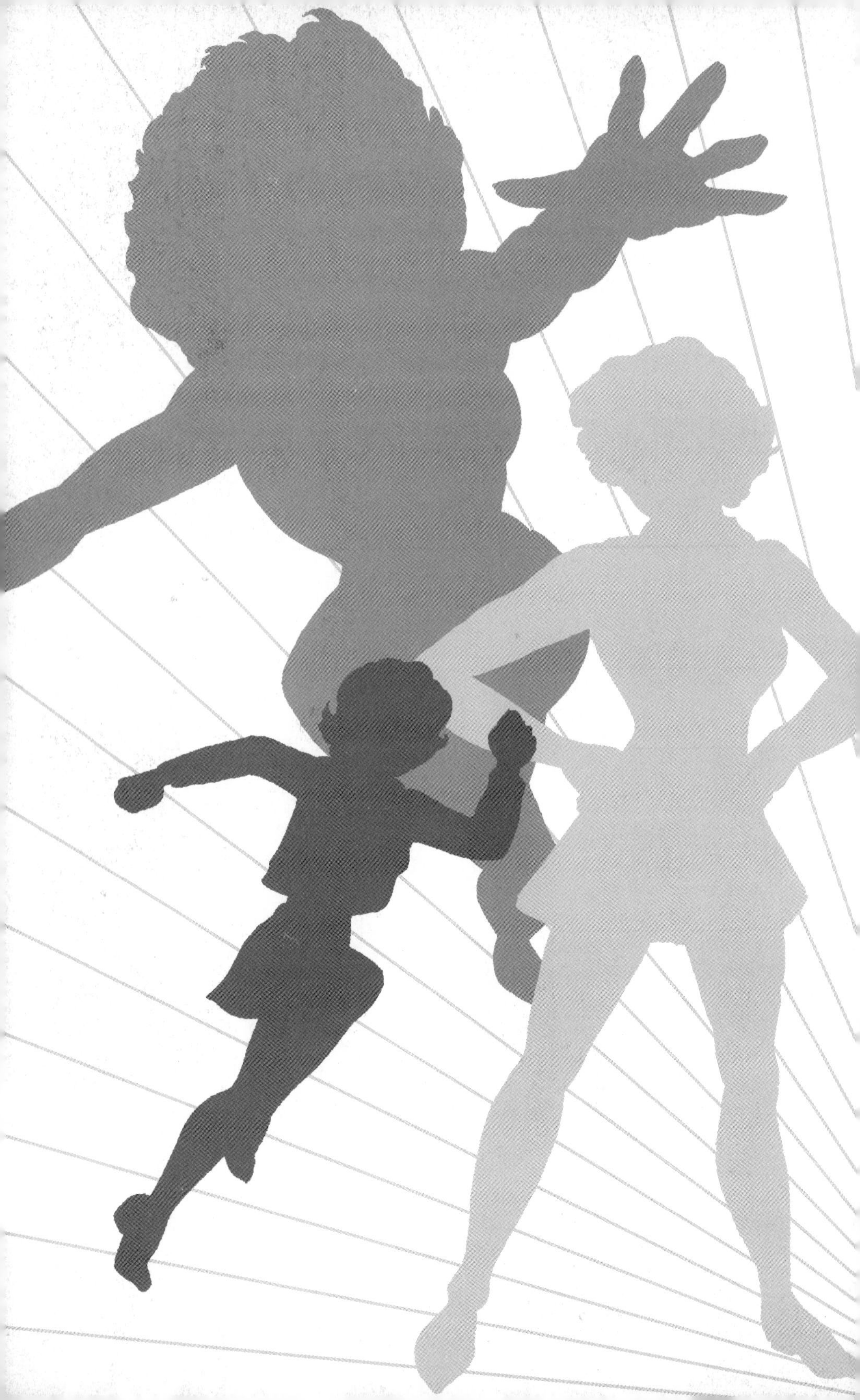

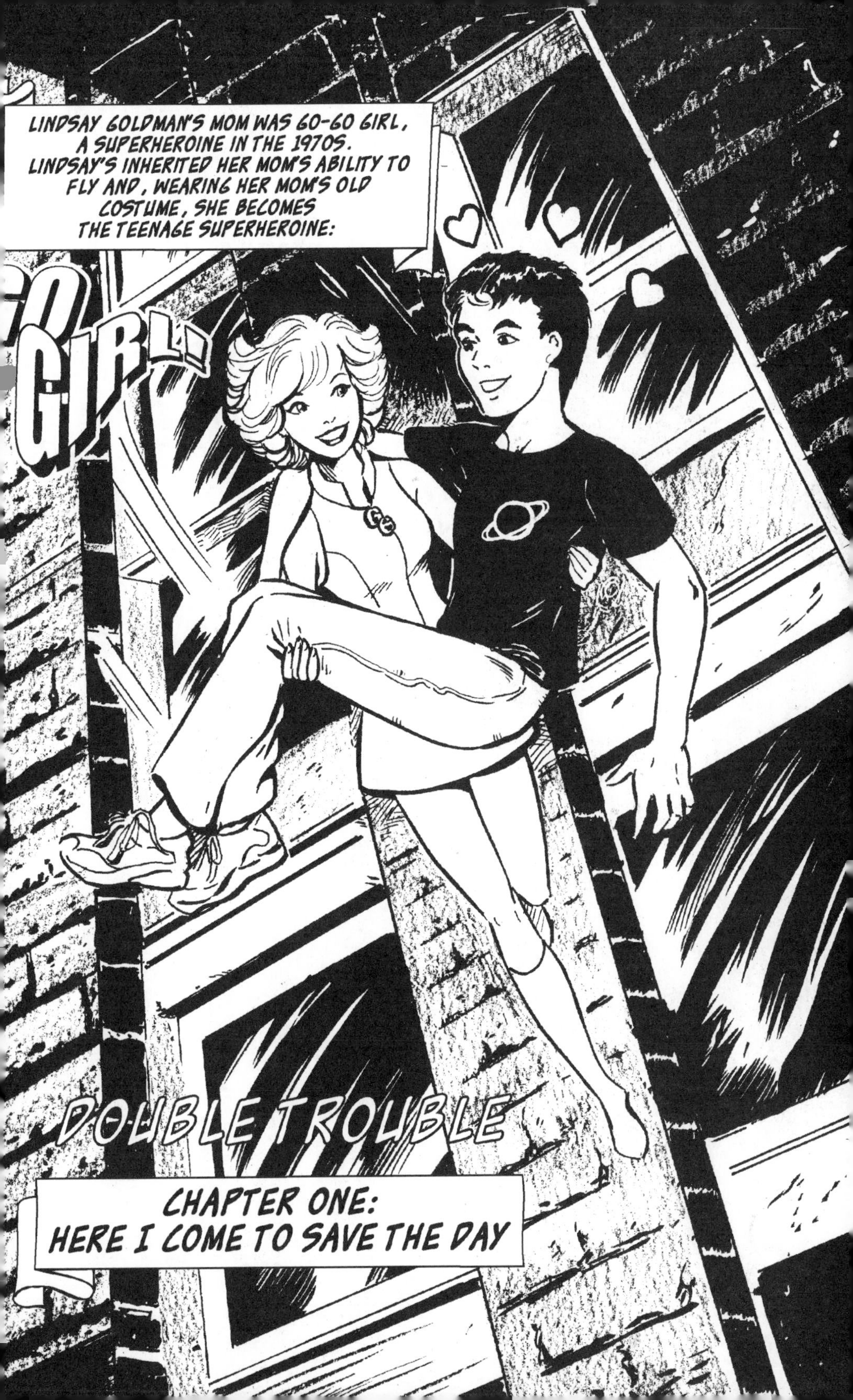
LINDSAY GOLDMAN'S MOM WAS GO-GO GIRL, A SUPERHEROINE IN THE 1970S. LINDSAY'S INHERITED HER MOM'S ABILITY TO FLY AND, WEARING HER MOM'S OLD COSTUME, SHE BECOMES THE TEENAGE SUPERHEROINE:
GO GIRL!
DOUBLE TROUBLE
CHAPTER ONE: HERE I COME TO SAVE THE DAY

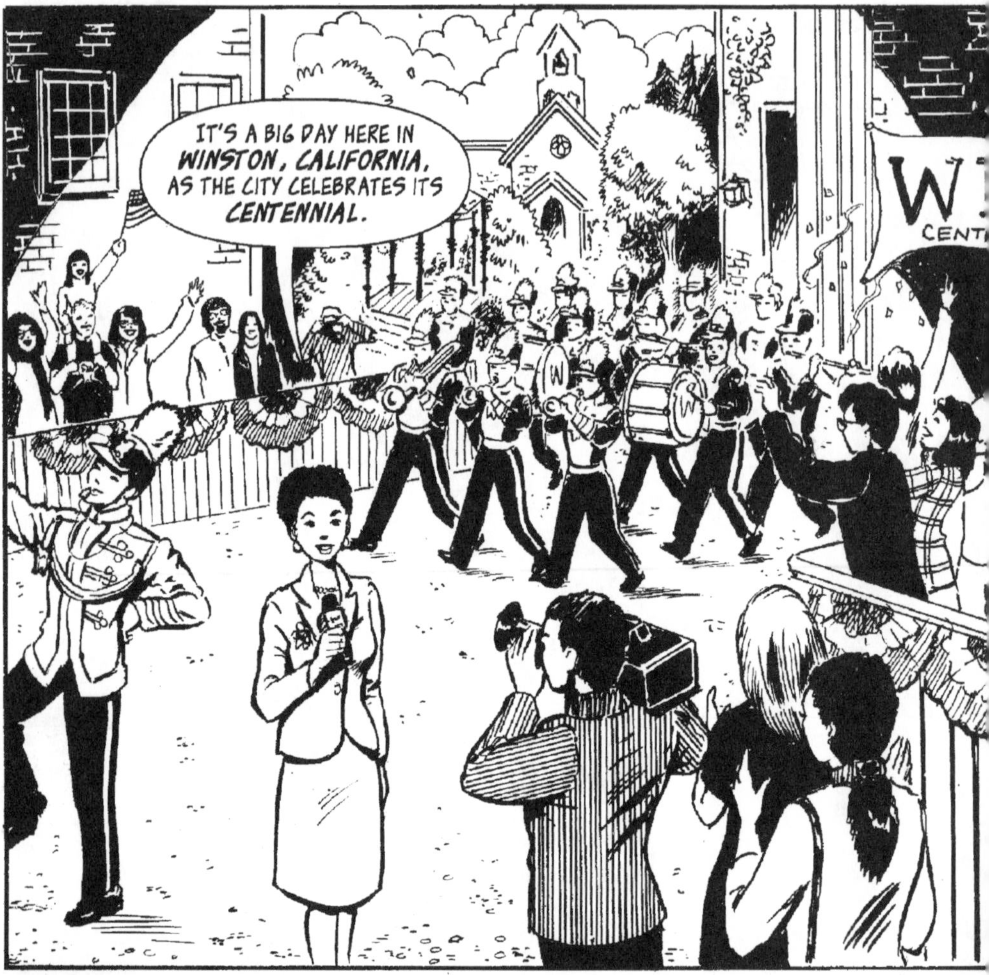
IT'S A BIG DAY HERE IN WINSTON, CALIFORNIA, AS THE CITY CELEBRATES ITS CENTENNIAL.
W
CENT

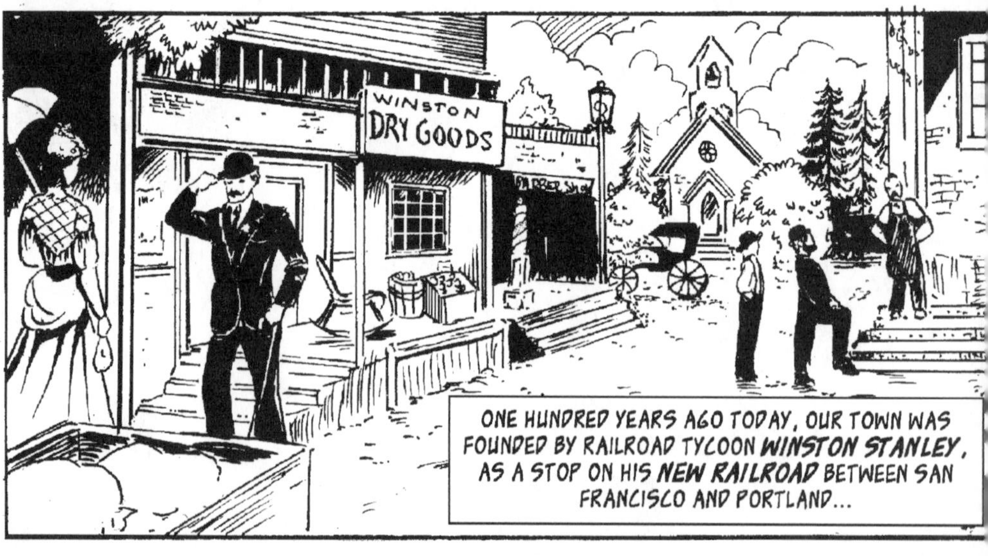
WINSTON DRY GOODS
BARBER SHOP
ONE HUNDRED YEARS AGO TODAY, OUR TOWN WAS FOUNDED BY RAILROAD TYCOON WINSTON STANLEY, AS A STOP ON HIS NEW RAILROAD BETWEEN SAN FRANCISCO AND PORTLAND...

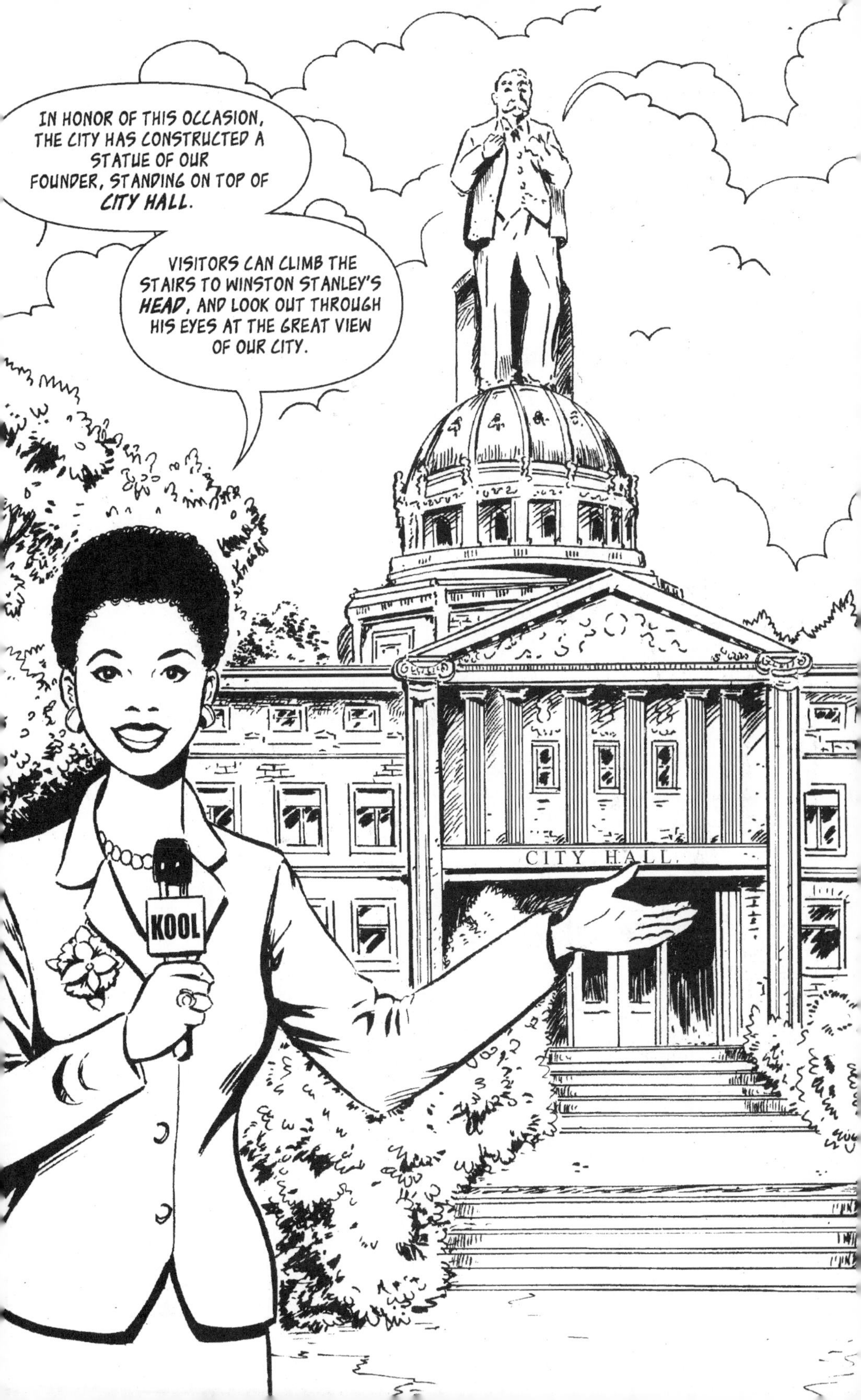
IN HONOR OF THIS OCCASION, THE CITY HAS CONSTRUCTED A STATUE OF OUR FOUNDER, STANDING ON TOP OF CITY HALL.
VISITORS CAN CLIMB THE STAIRS TO WINSTON STANLEY'S HEAD, AND LOOK OUT THROUGH HIS EYES AT THE GREAT VIEW OF OUR CITY.
CITY HALL
KOOL

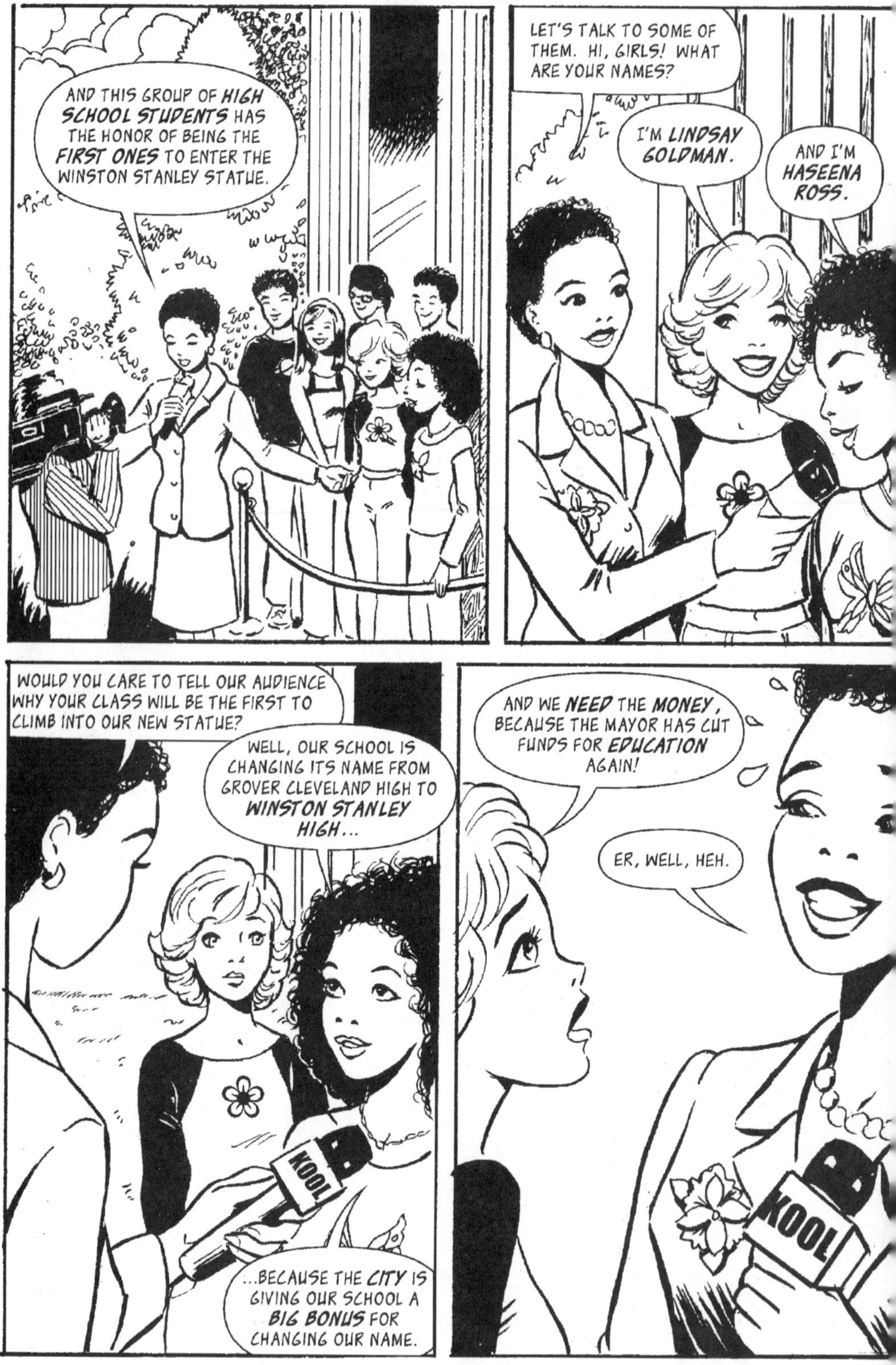
AND THIS GROUP OF HIGH SCHOOL STUDENTS HAS THE HONOR OF BEING THE FIRST ONES TO ENTER THE WINSTON STANLEY STATUE.
LET'S TALK TO SOME OF THEM. HI, GIRLS! WHAT ARE YOUR NAMES?
I'M LINDSAY GOLDMAN.
AND I'M HASEENA ROSS.
WOULD YOU CARE TO TELL OUR AUDIENCE WHY YOUR CLASS WILL BE THE FIRST TO CLIMB INTO OUR NEW STATUE?
WELL, OUR SCHOOL IS CHANGING ITS NAME FROM GROVER CLEVELAND HIGH TO WINSTON STANLEY HIGH...
KOOL
...BECAUSE THE CITY IS GIVING OUR SCHOOL A BIG BONUS FOR CHANGING OUR NAME.
AND WE NEED THE MONEY, BECAUSE THE MAYOR HAS CUT FUNDS FOR EDUCATION AGAIN!
ER, WELL, HEH.
KOOL

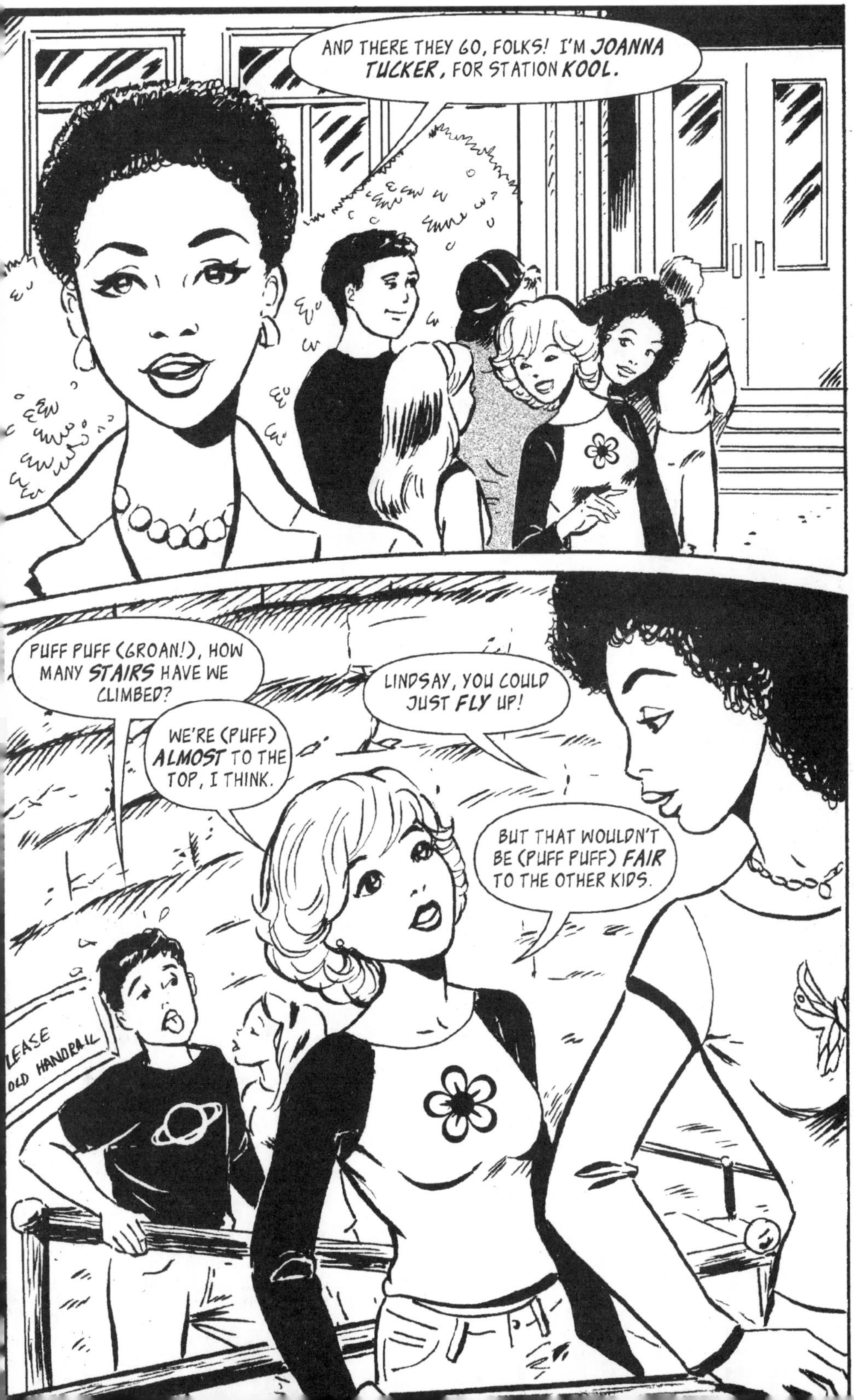
AND THERE THEY GO, FOLKS! I'M **JOANNA TUCKER**, FOR STATION **KOOL**.
PUFF PUFF (GROAN!), HOW MANY **STAIRS** HAVE WE CLIMBED?
WE'RE (PUFF) **ALMOST** TO THE TOP, I THINK.
LINDSAY, YOU COULD JUST **FLY** UP!
BUT THAT WOULDN'T BE (PUFF PUFF) **FAIR** TO THE OTHER KIDS.

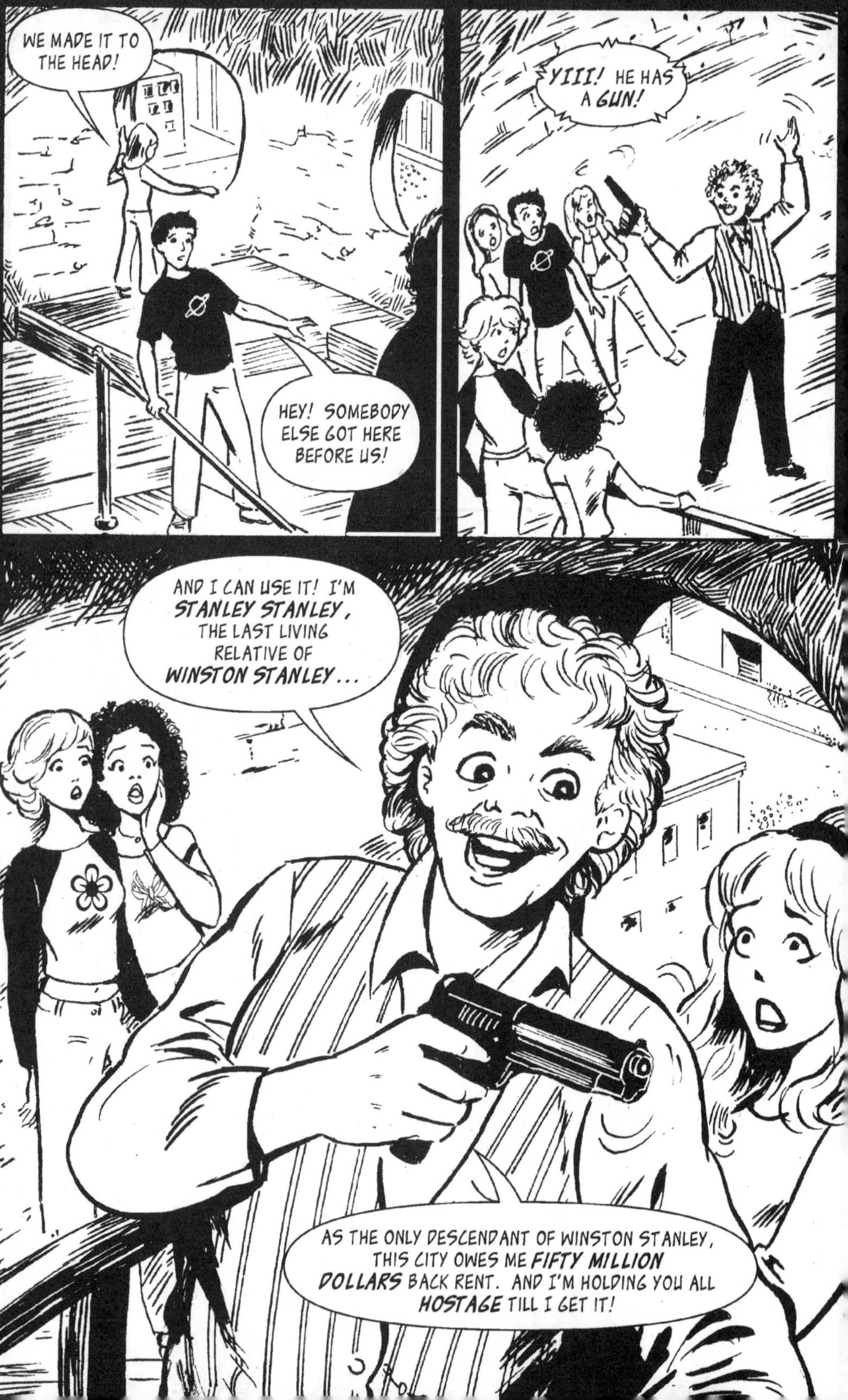
WE MADE IT TO THE HEAD!
HEY! SOMEBODY ELSE GOT HERE BEFORE US!
YIII! HE HAS A GUN!
AND I CAN USE IT! I'M STANLEY STANLEY, THE LAST LIVING RELATIVE OF WINSTON STANLEY...
AS THE ONLY DESCENDANT OF WINSTON STANLEY, THIS CITY OWES ME FIFTY MILLION DOLLARS BACK RENT. AND I'M HOLDING YOU ALL HOSTAGE TILL I GET IT!

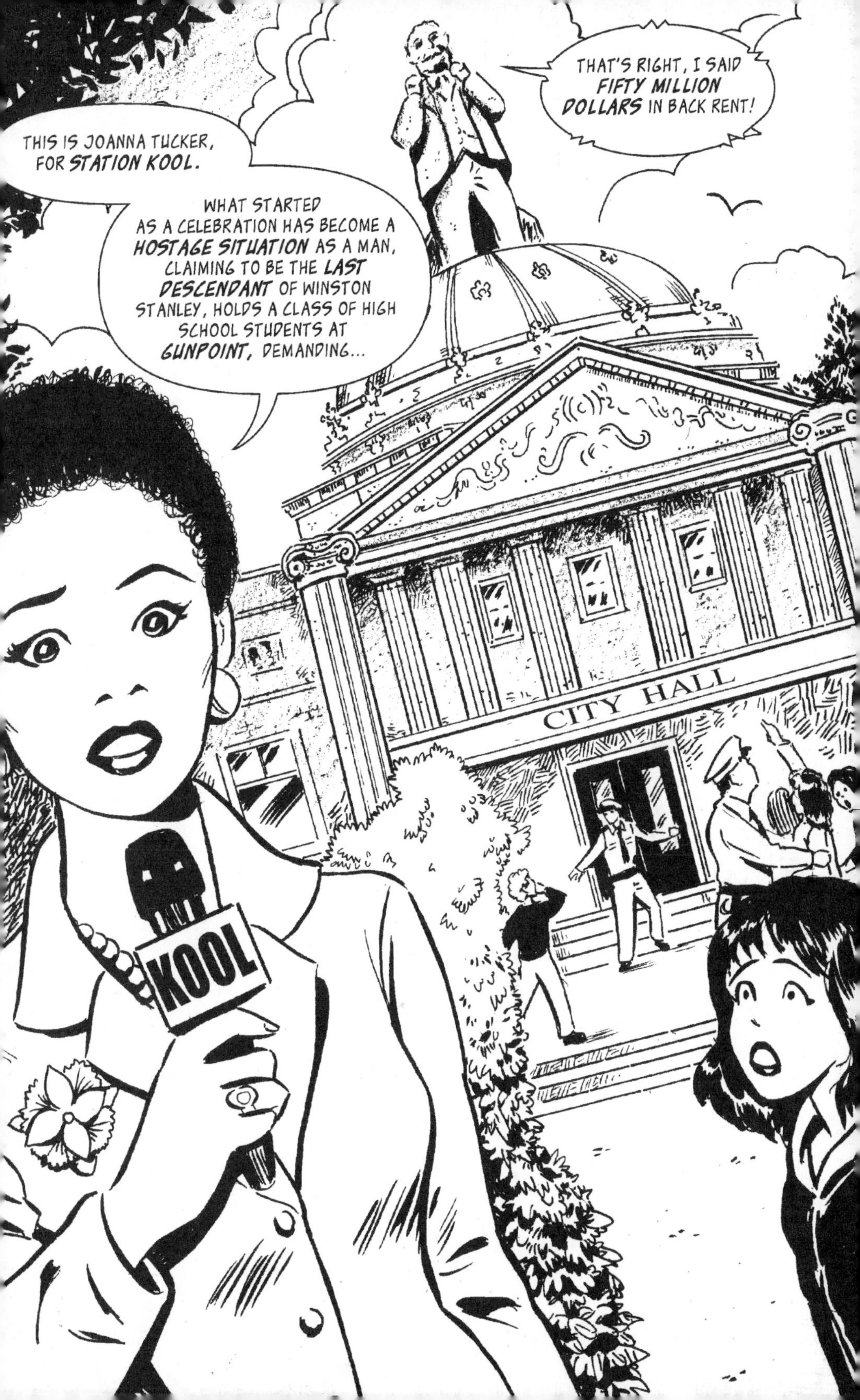
THIS IS JOANNA TUCKER, FOR STATION KOOL.
WHAT STARTED AS A CELEBRATION HAS BECOME A HOSTAGE SITUATION AS A MAN, CLAIMING TO BE THE LAST DESCENDANT OF WINSTON STANLEY, HOLDS A CLASS OF HIGH SCHOOL STUDENTS AT GUNPOINT, DEMANDING...
THAT'S RIGHT, I SAID FIFTY MILLION DOLLARS IN BACK RENT!
CITY HALL
KOOL

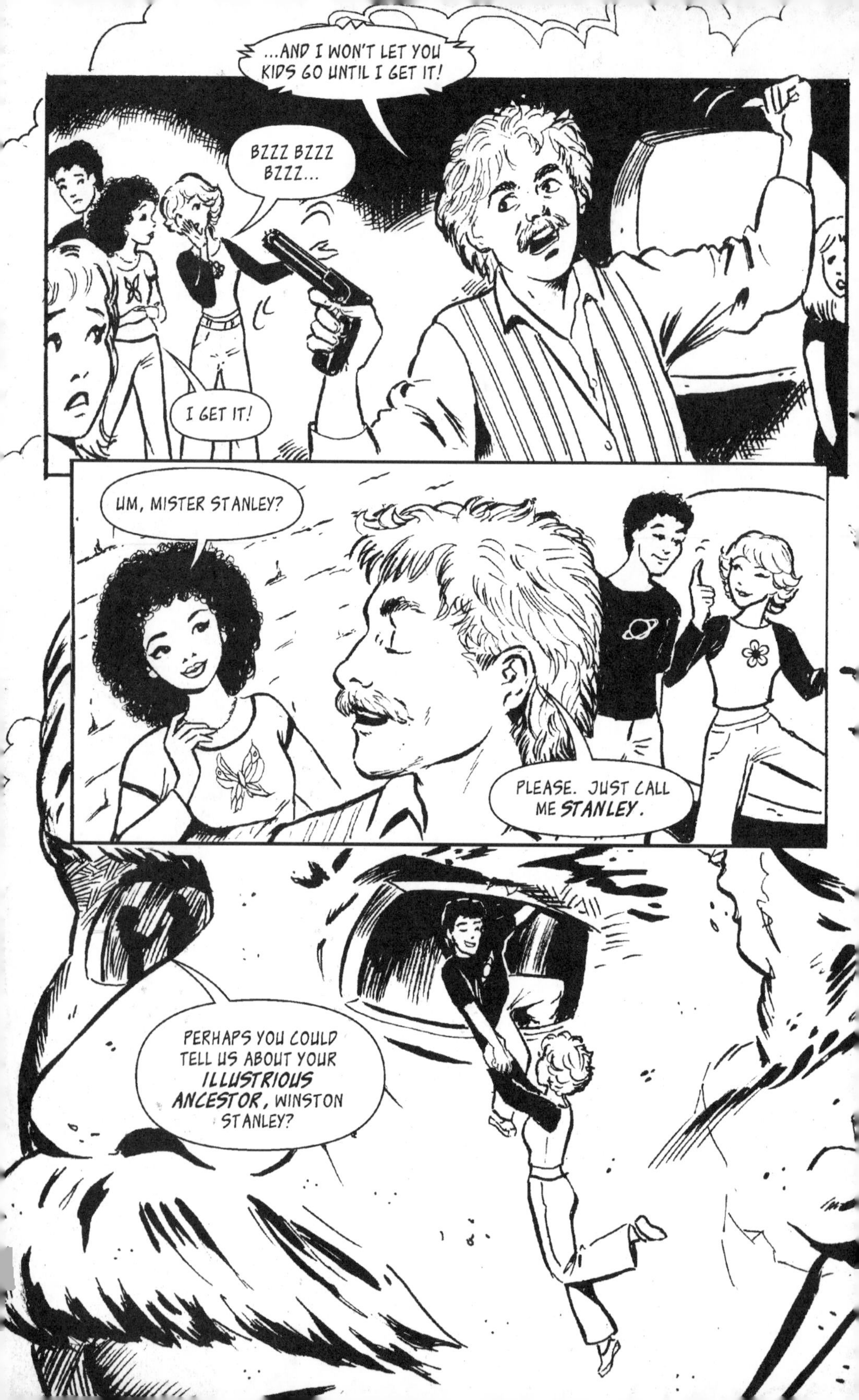
...AND I WON'T LET YOU KIDS GO UNTIL I GET IT!
BZZZ BZZZ BZZZ...
I GET IT!
UM, MISTER STANLEY?
PLEASE. JUST CALL ME STANLEY.
PERHAPS YOU COULD TELL US ABOUT YOUR ILLUSTRIOUS ANCESTOR, WINSTON STANLEY?

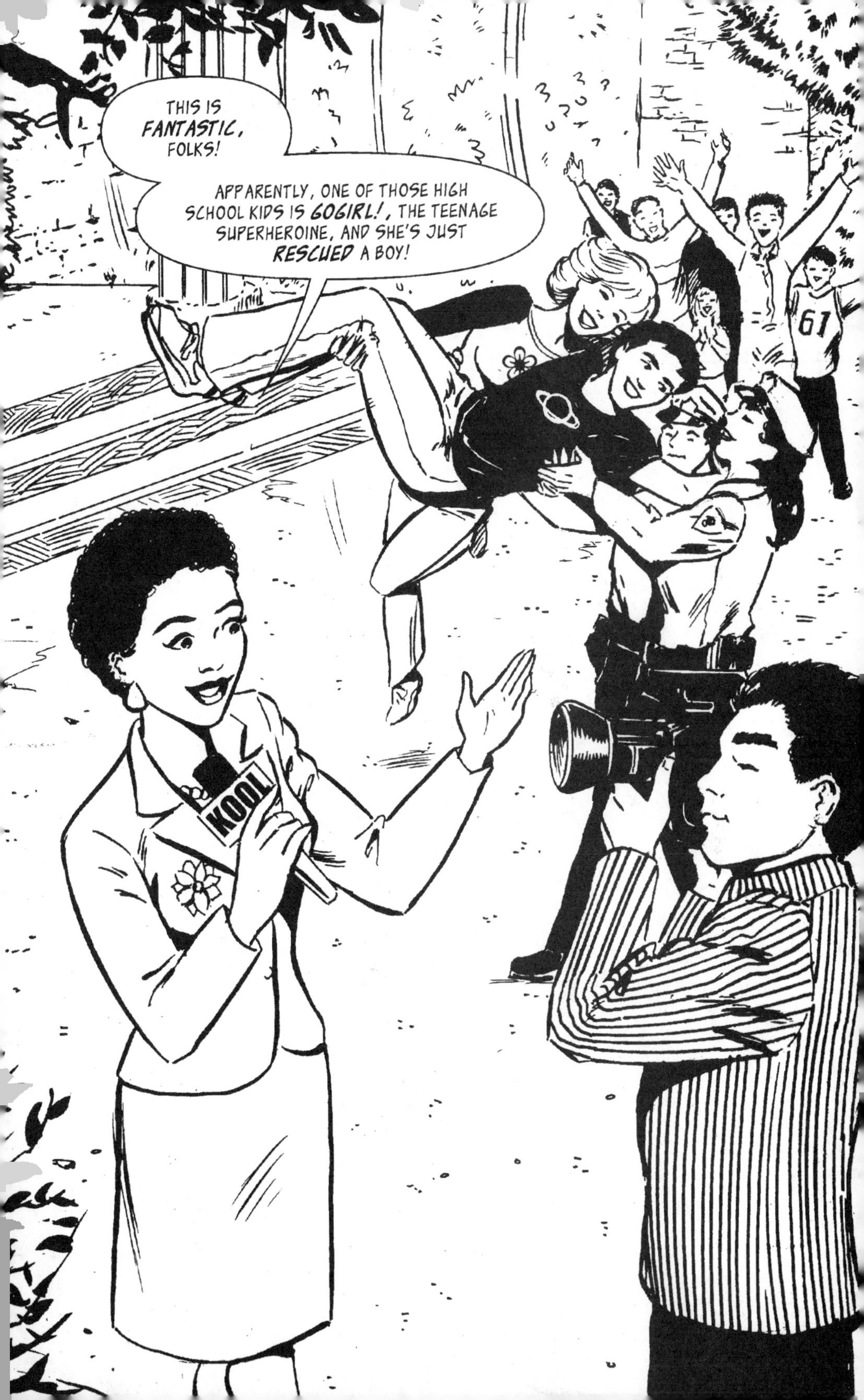
THIS IS FANTASTIC, FOLKS!
APPARENTLY, ONE OF THOSE HIGH SCHOOL KIDS IS GOGIRL!, THE TEENAGE SUPERHEROINE, AND SHE'S JUST RESCUED A BOY!
61
KOOL

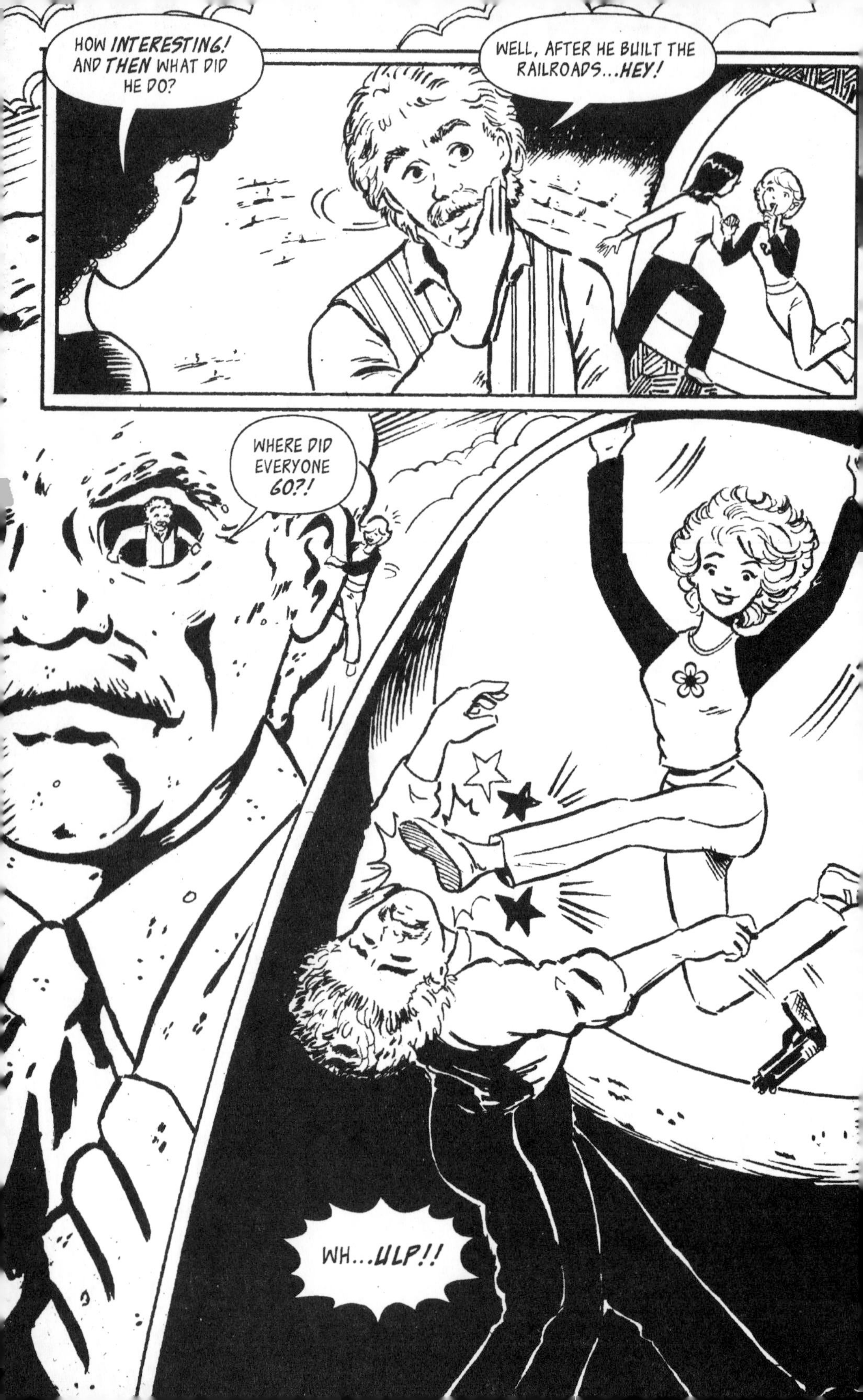
HOW *INTERESTING!* AND *THEN* WHAT DID HE DO?
WELL, AFTER HE BUILT THE RAILROADS...*HEY!*
WHERE DID EVERYONE *GO?!*
WH...*ULP!!*

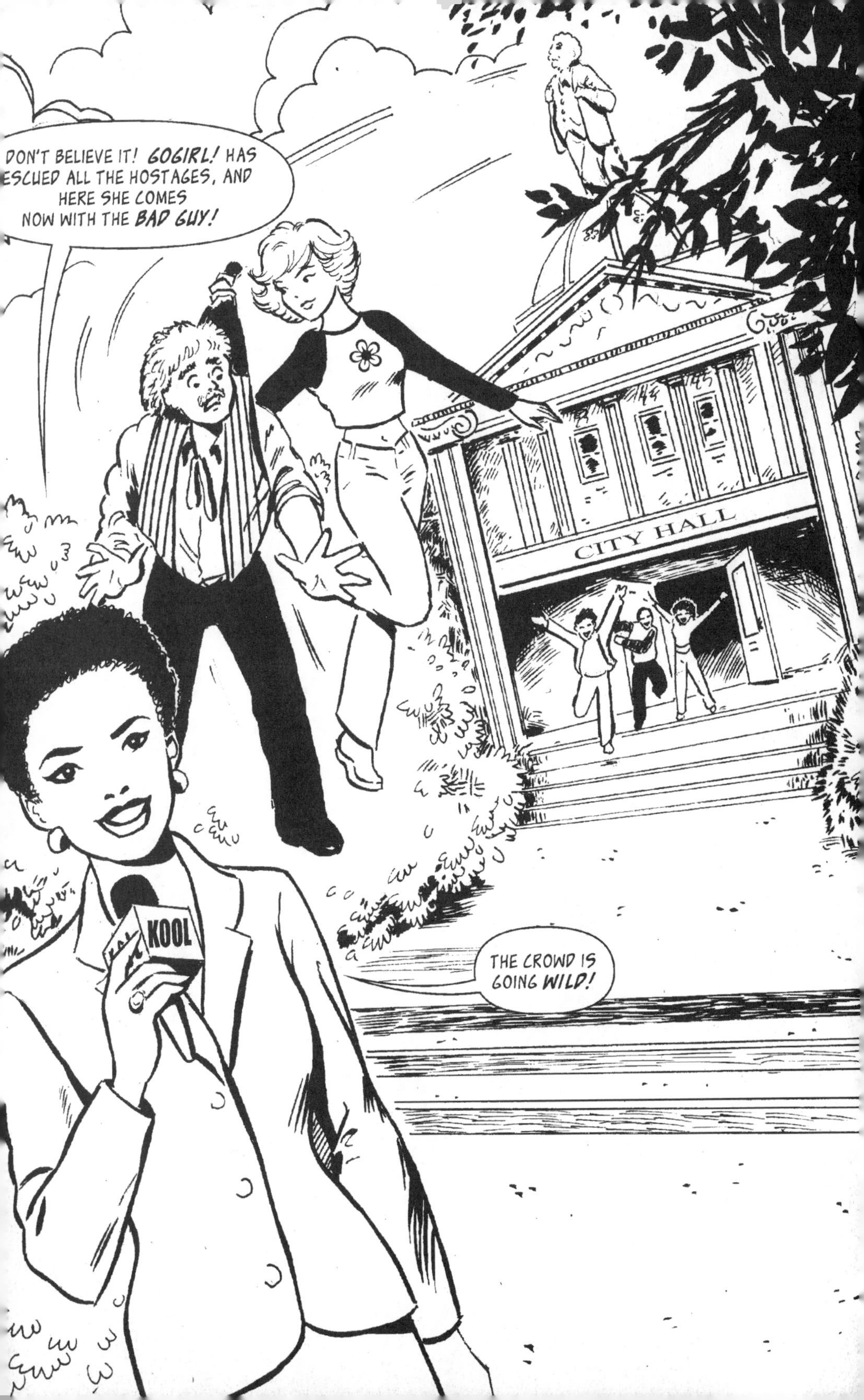
DON'T BELIEVE IT! GOGIRL! HAS ESCUED ALL THE HOSTAGES, AND HERE SHE COMES NOW WITH THE BAD GUY!
CITY HALL
KOOL
THE CROWD IS GOING WILD!

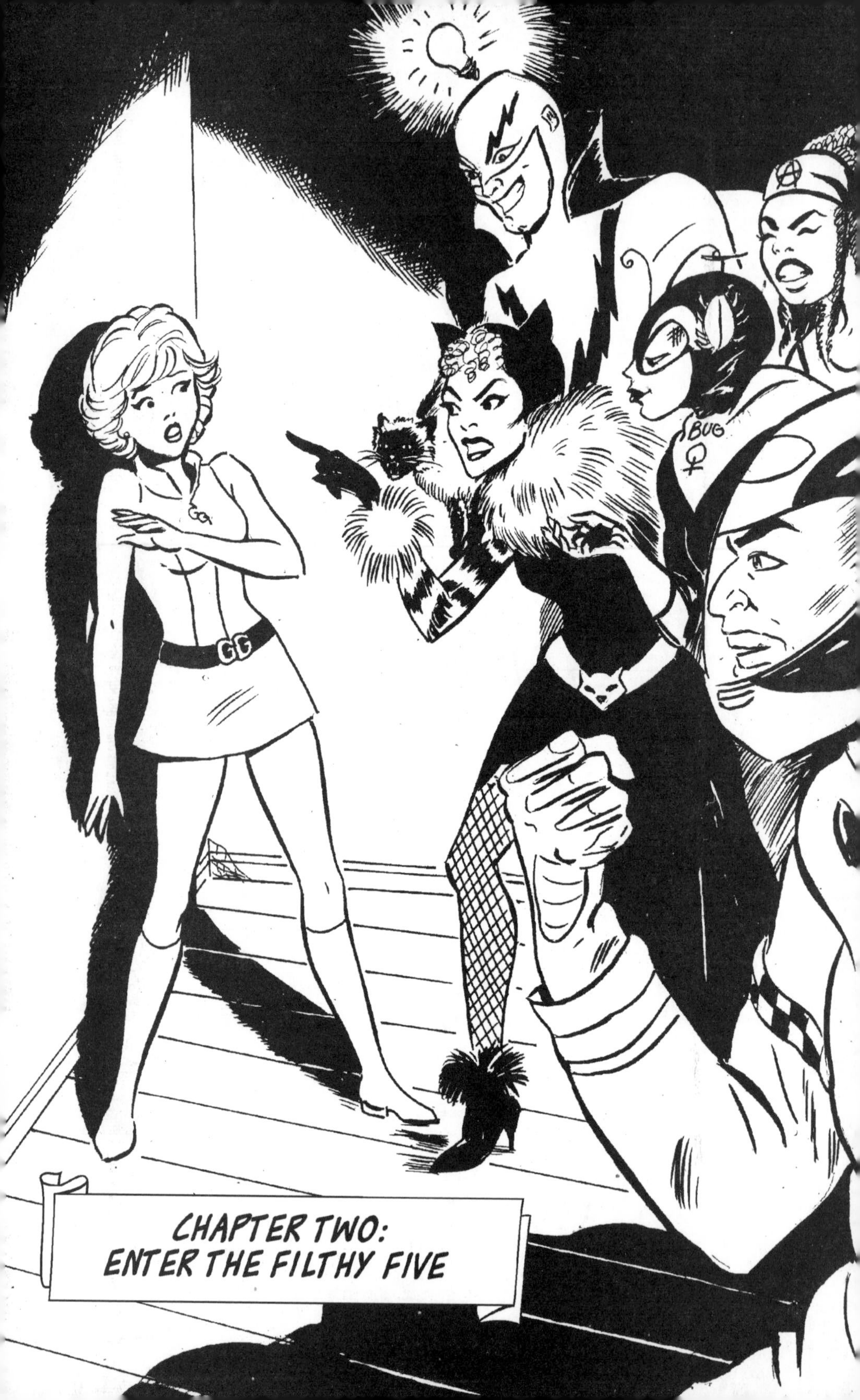
BUG
CHAPTER TWO:
ENTER THE FILTHY FIVE

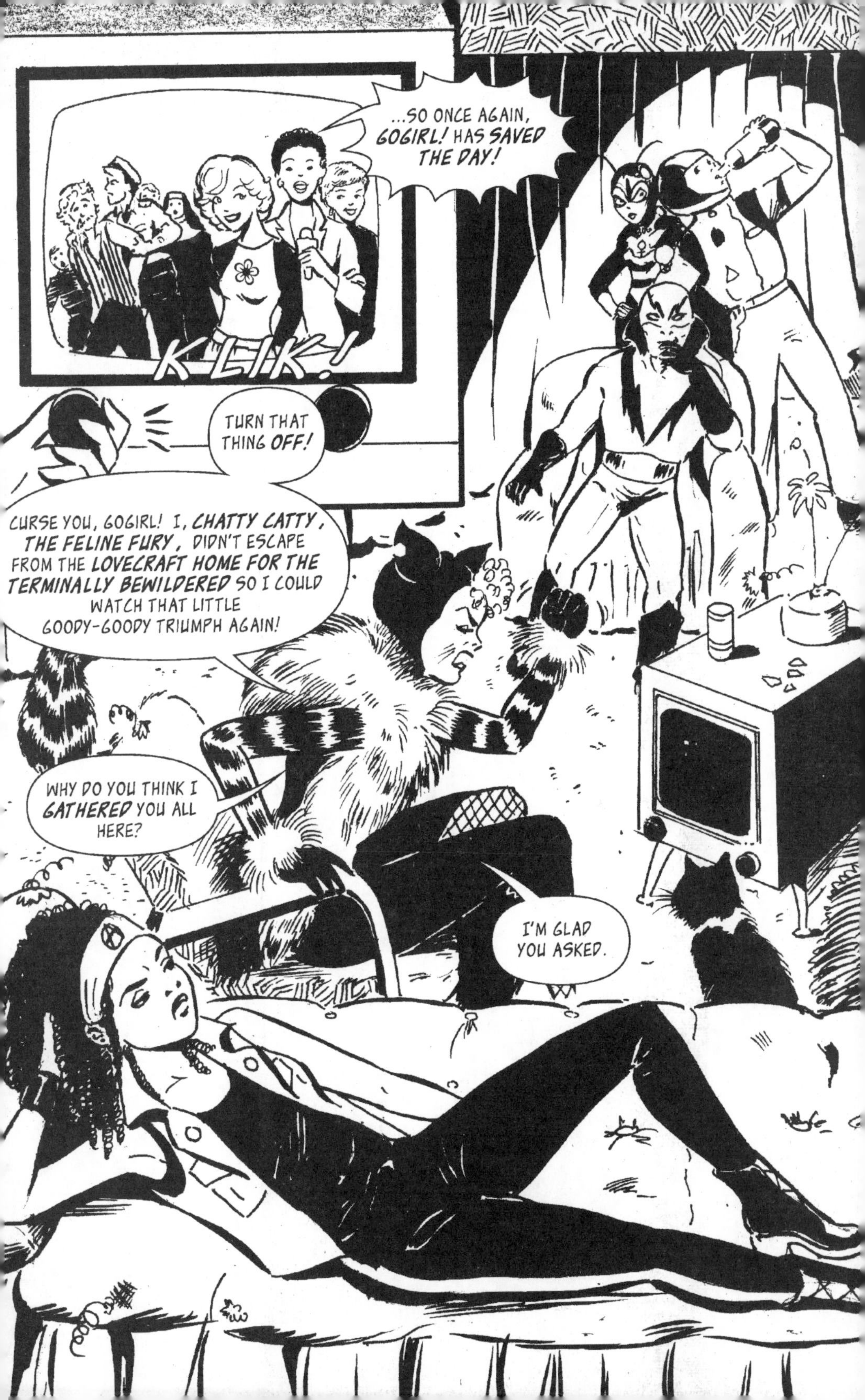
...SO ONCE AGAIN, GOGIRL! HAS SAVED THE DAY!
KLIK!
TURN THAT THING OFF!
CURSE YOU, GOGIRL! I, CHATTY CATTY, THE FELINE FURY, DIDN'T ESCAPE FROM THE LOVECRAFT HOME FOR THE TERMINALLY BEWILDERED SO I COULD WATCH THAT LITTLE GOODY-GOODY TRIUMPH AGAIN!
WHY DO YOU THINK I GATHERED YOU ALL HERE?
I'M GLAD YOU ASKED.

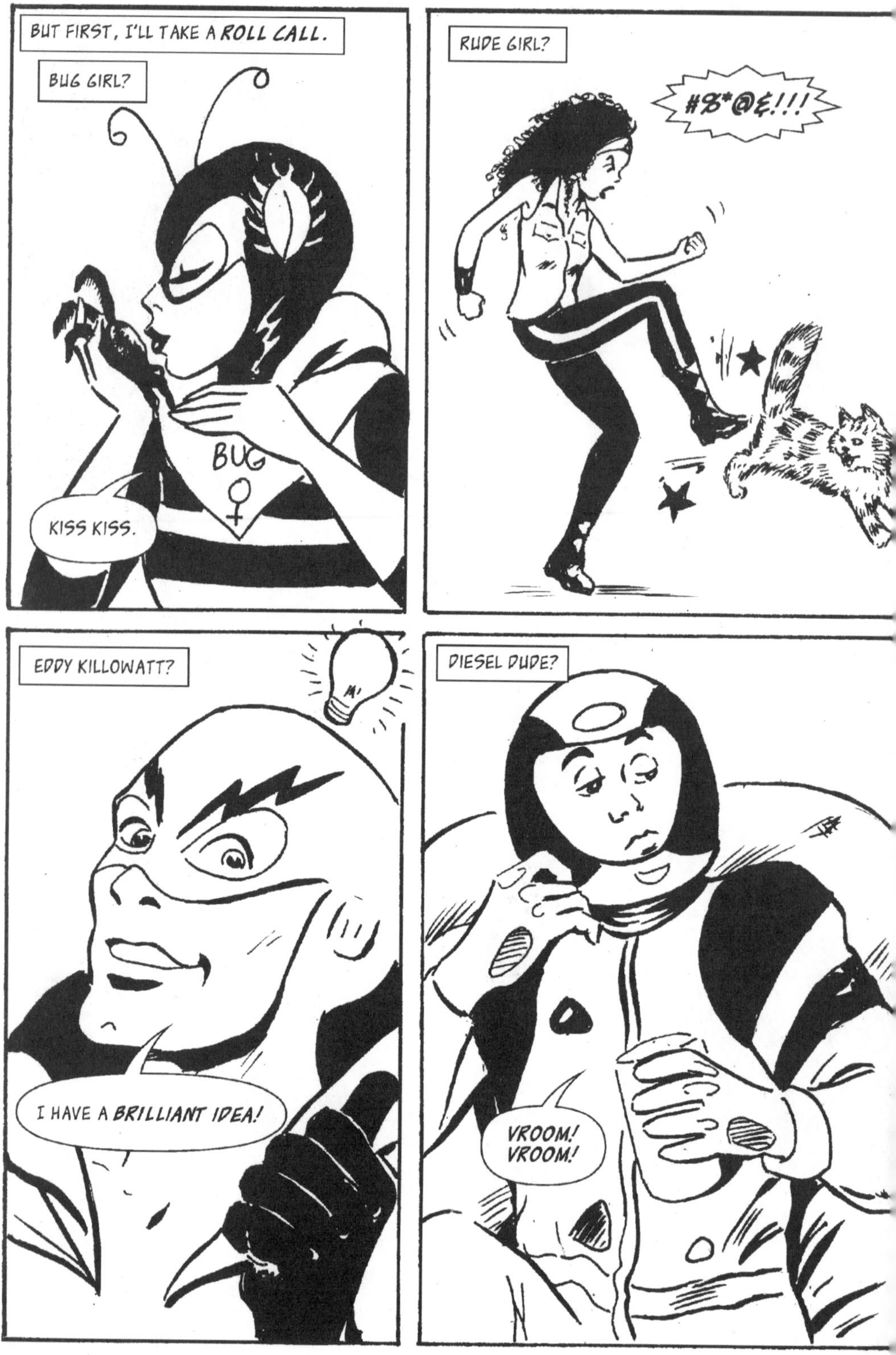
BUT FIRST, I'LL TAKE A ROLL CALL.
BUG GIRL?
BUG ♀
KISS KISS.
RUDE GIRL?
#%*@&!!!
EDDY KILLOWATT?
I HAVE A BRILLIANT IDEA!
DIESEL DUDE?
VROOM! VROOM!

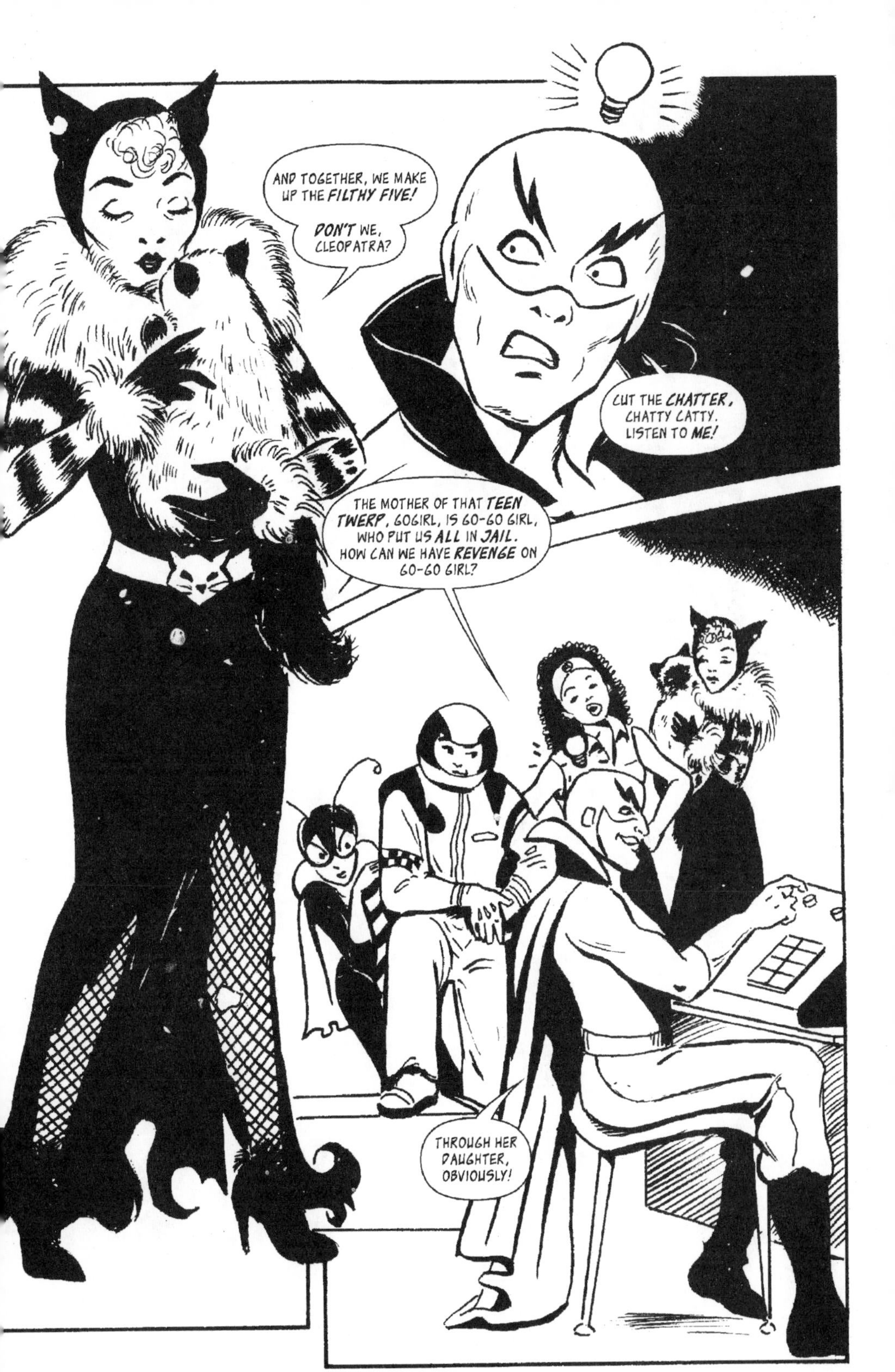
AND TOGETHER, WE MAKE UP THE FILTHY FIVE!
DON'T WE, CLEOPATRA?
CUT THE CHATTER, CHATTY CATTY. LISTEN TO ME!
THE MOTHER OF THAT TEEN TWERP, GOGIRL, IS GO-GO GIRL, WHO PUT US ALL IN JAIL. HOW CAN WE HAVE REVENGE ON GO-GO GIRL?
THROUGH HER DAUGHTER, OBVIOUSLY!

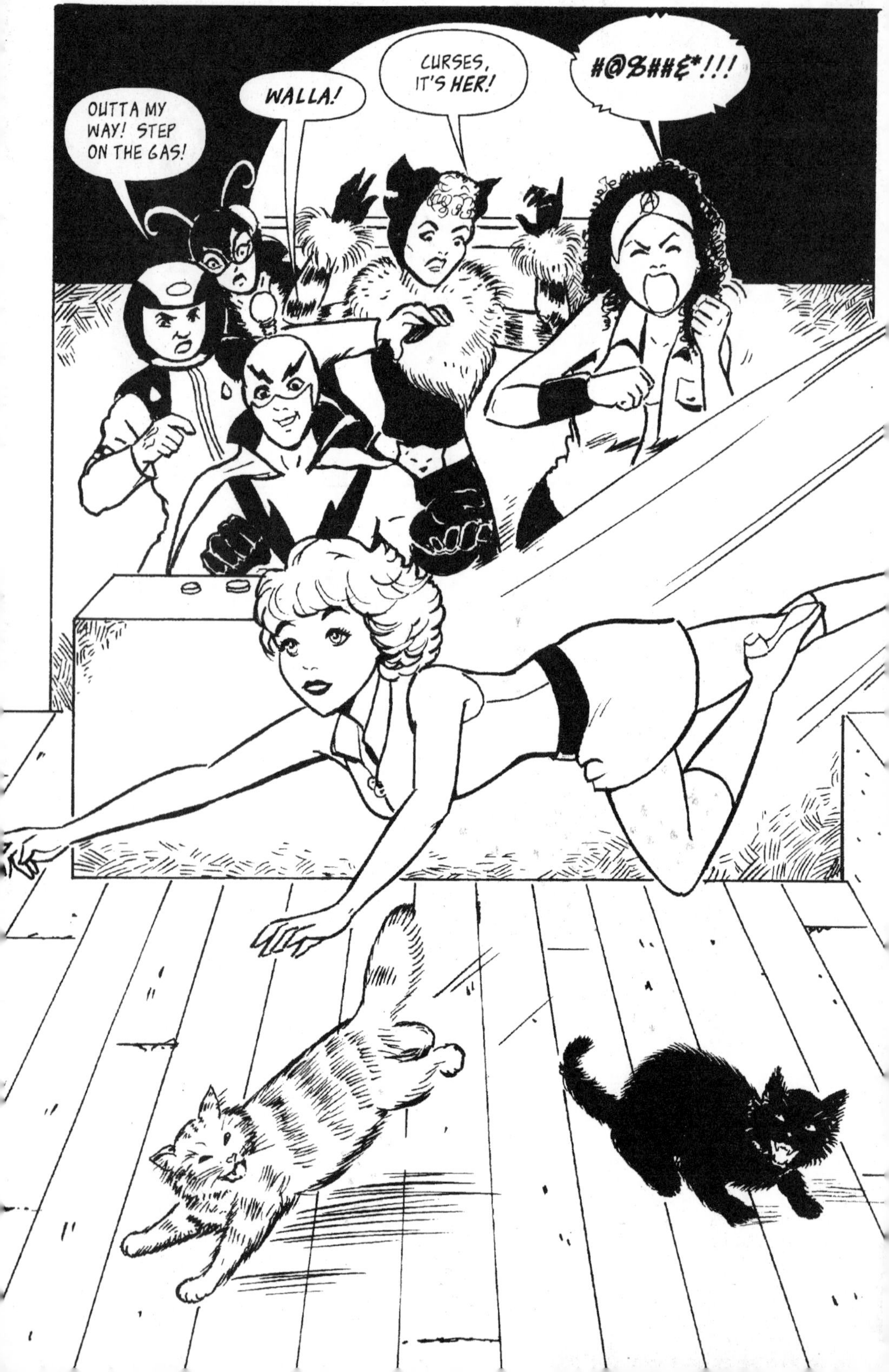
OUTTA MY WAY! STEP ON THE GAS!
WALLA!
CURSES, IT'S HER!
#@$##&*!!!

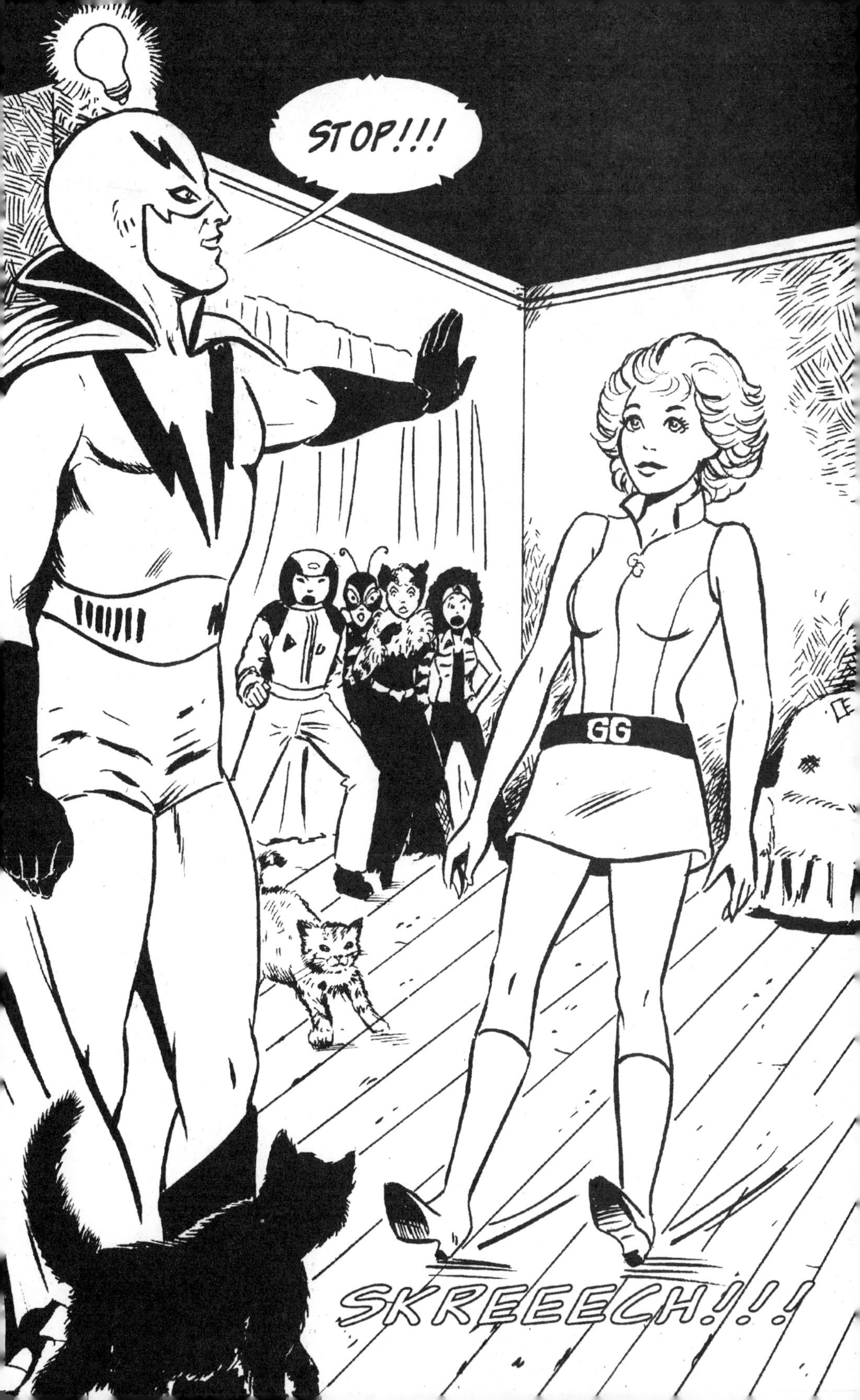
STOP!!!
GG
SKREEEECH!!!!

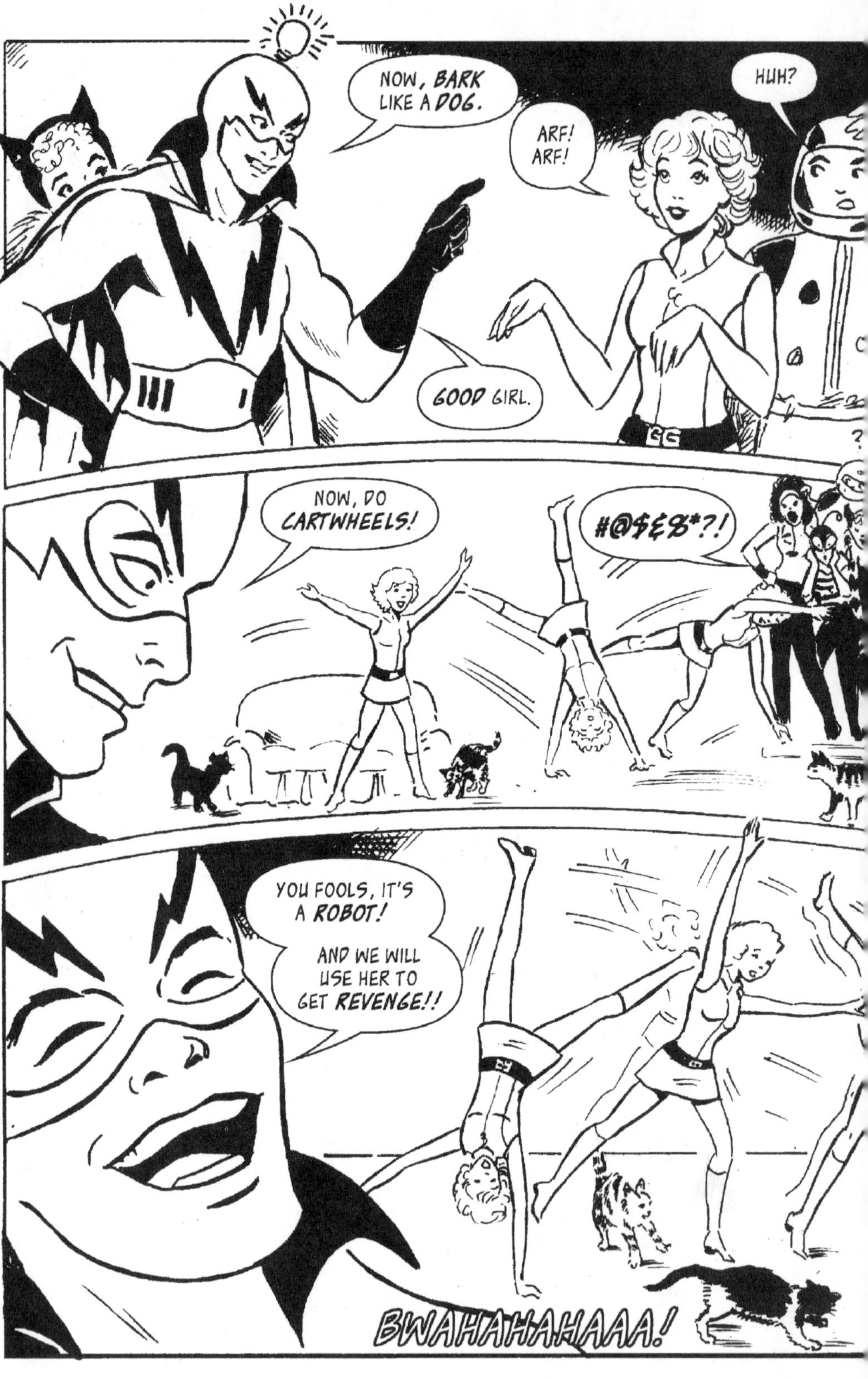
NOW, BARK LIKE A DOG.
ARF! ARF!
HUH?
GOOD GIRL.
NOW, DO CARTWHEELS!
#@$&%*?!
YOU FOOLS, IT'S A ROBOT!
AND WE WILL USE HER TO GET REVENGE!!
BWAHAHAHAHAAA!

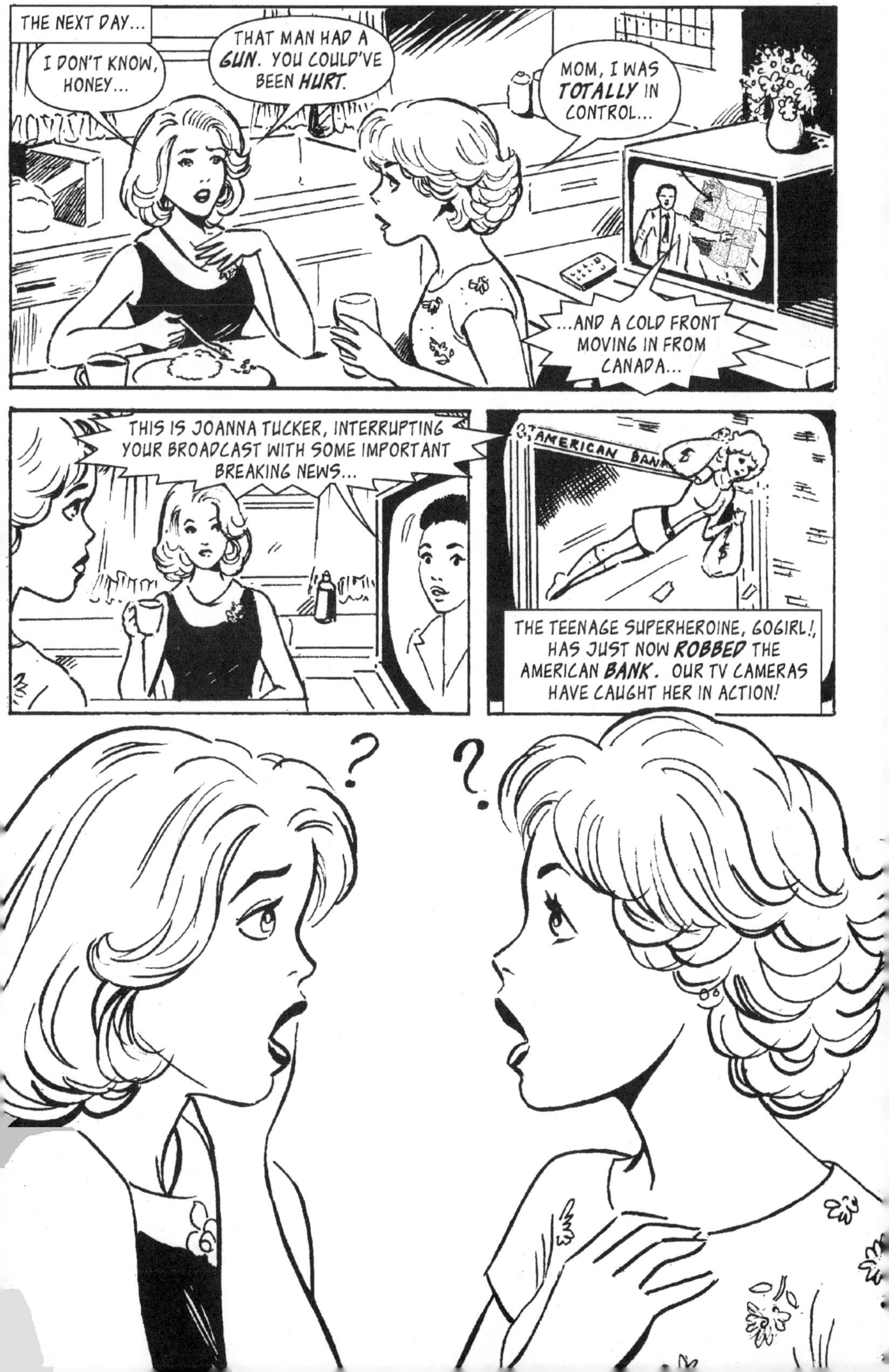
THE NEXT DAY...
I DON'T KNOW, HONEY...
THAT MAN HAD A GUN. YOU COULD'VE BEEN HURT.
MOM, I WAS TOTALLY IN CONTROL...
...AND A COLD FRONT MOVING IN FROM CANADA...
THIS IS JOANNA TUCKER, INTERRUPTING YOUR BROADCAST WITH SOME IMPORTANT BREAKING NEWS...
AMERICAN BANK
THE TEENAGE SUPERHEROINE, GOGIRL!, HAS JUST NOW ROBBED THE AMERICAN BANK. OUR TV CAMERAS HAVE CAUGHT HER IN ACTION!
?
?

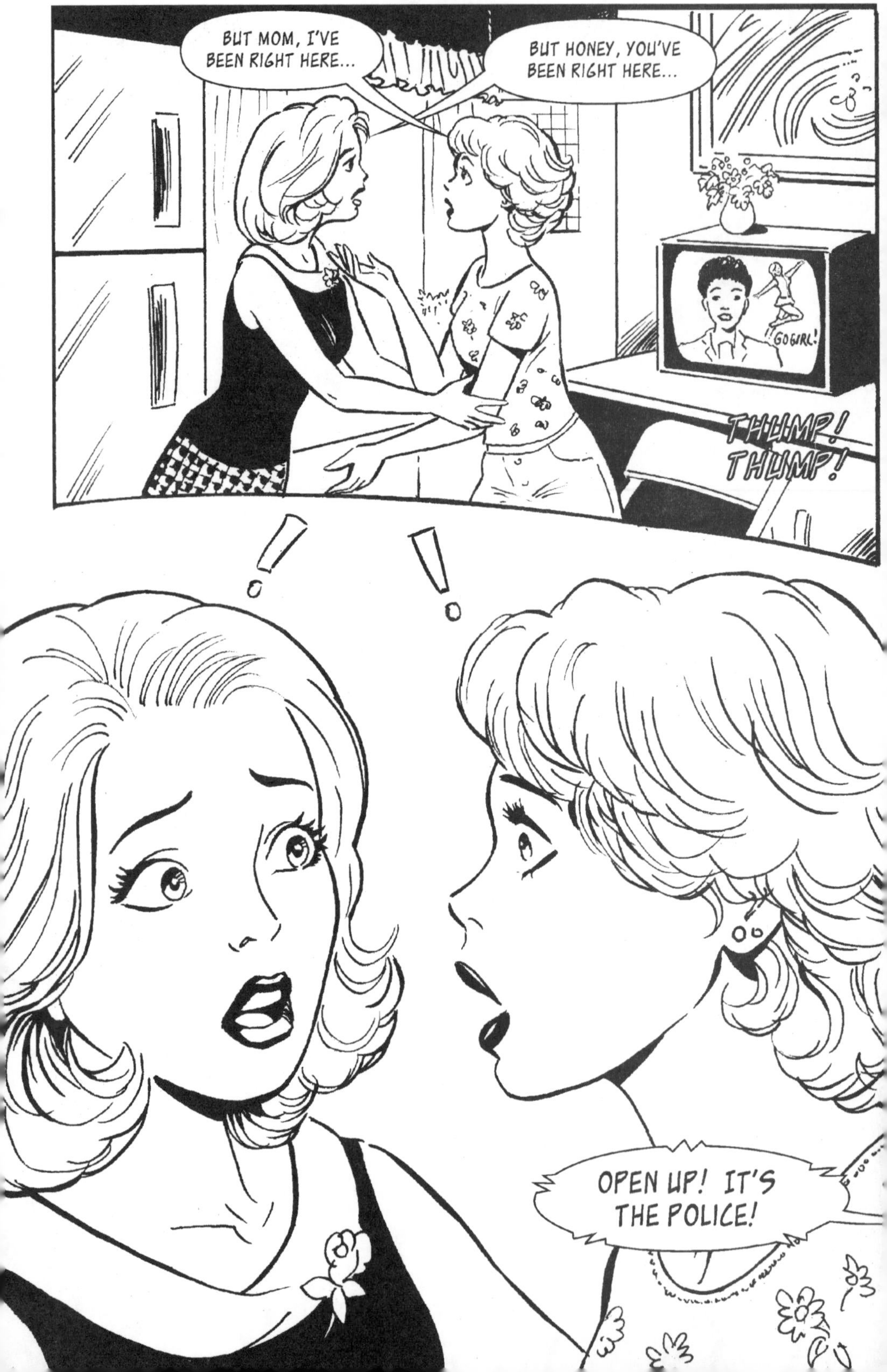
BUT MOM, I'VE BEEN RIGHT HERE...
BUT HONEY, YOU'VE BEEN RIGHT HERE...
GO GIRL!
THUMP! THUMP!
OPEN UP! IT'S THE POLICE!

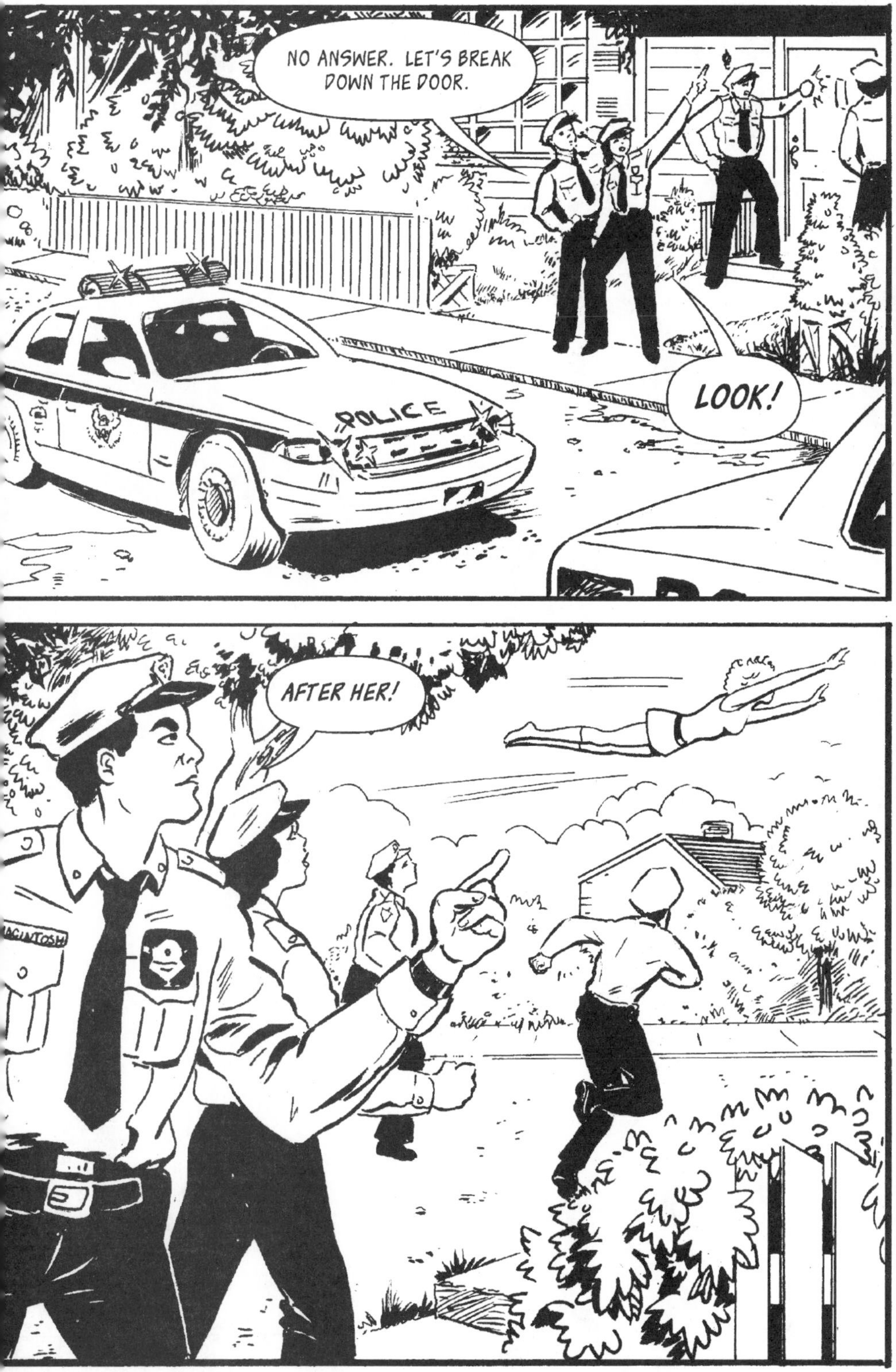
NO ANSWER. LET'S BREAK DOWN THE DOOR.
POLICE
LOOK!
AFTER HER!

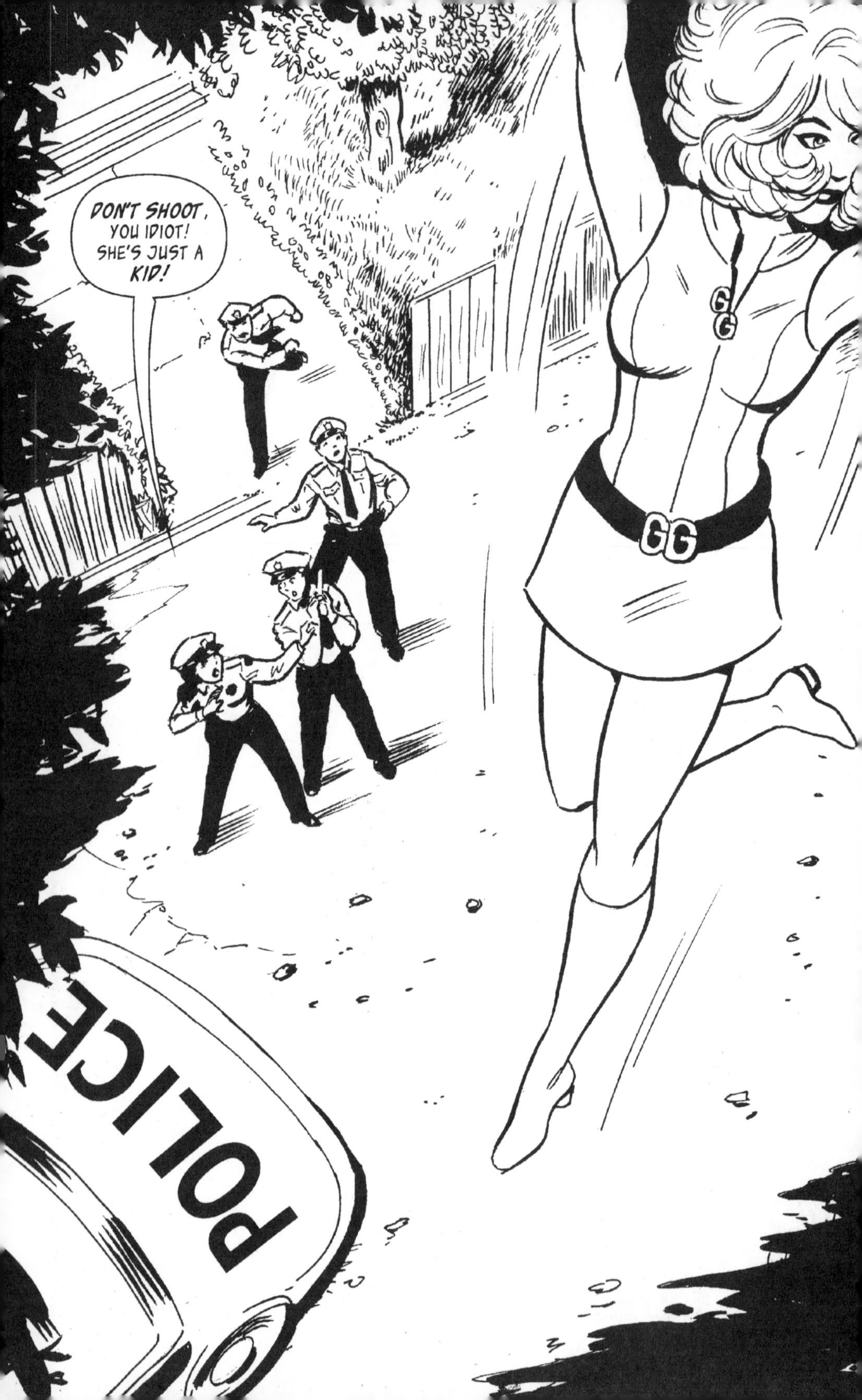
DON'T SHOOT, YOU IDIOT! SHE'S JUST A KID!
GG
GG
POLICE

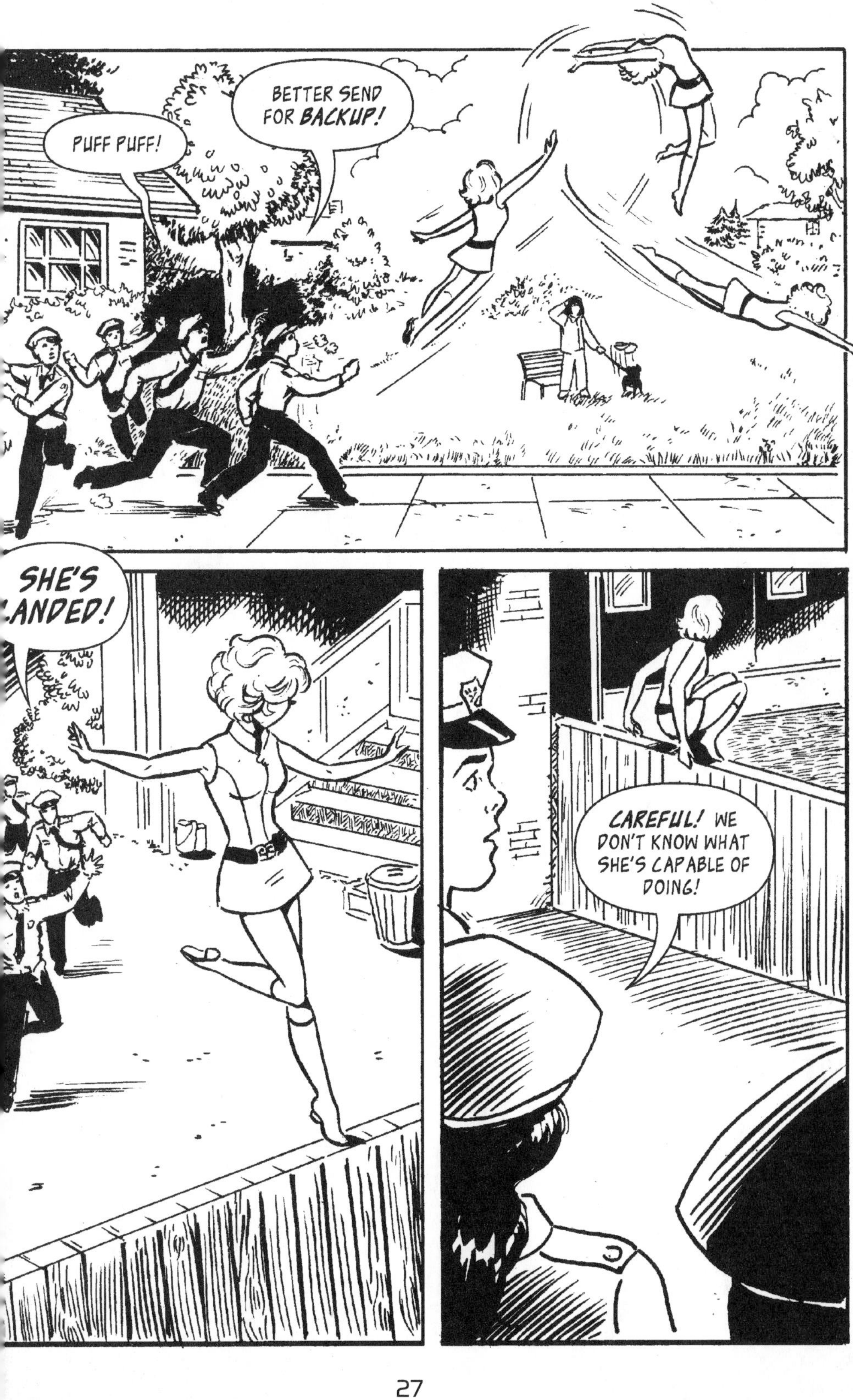
PUFF PUFF!
BETTER SEND FOR BACKUP!
SHE'S LANDED!
CAREFUL! WE DON'T KNOW WHAT SHE'S CAPABLE OF DOING!

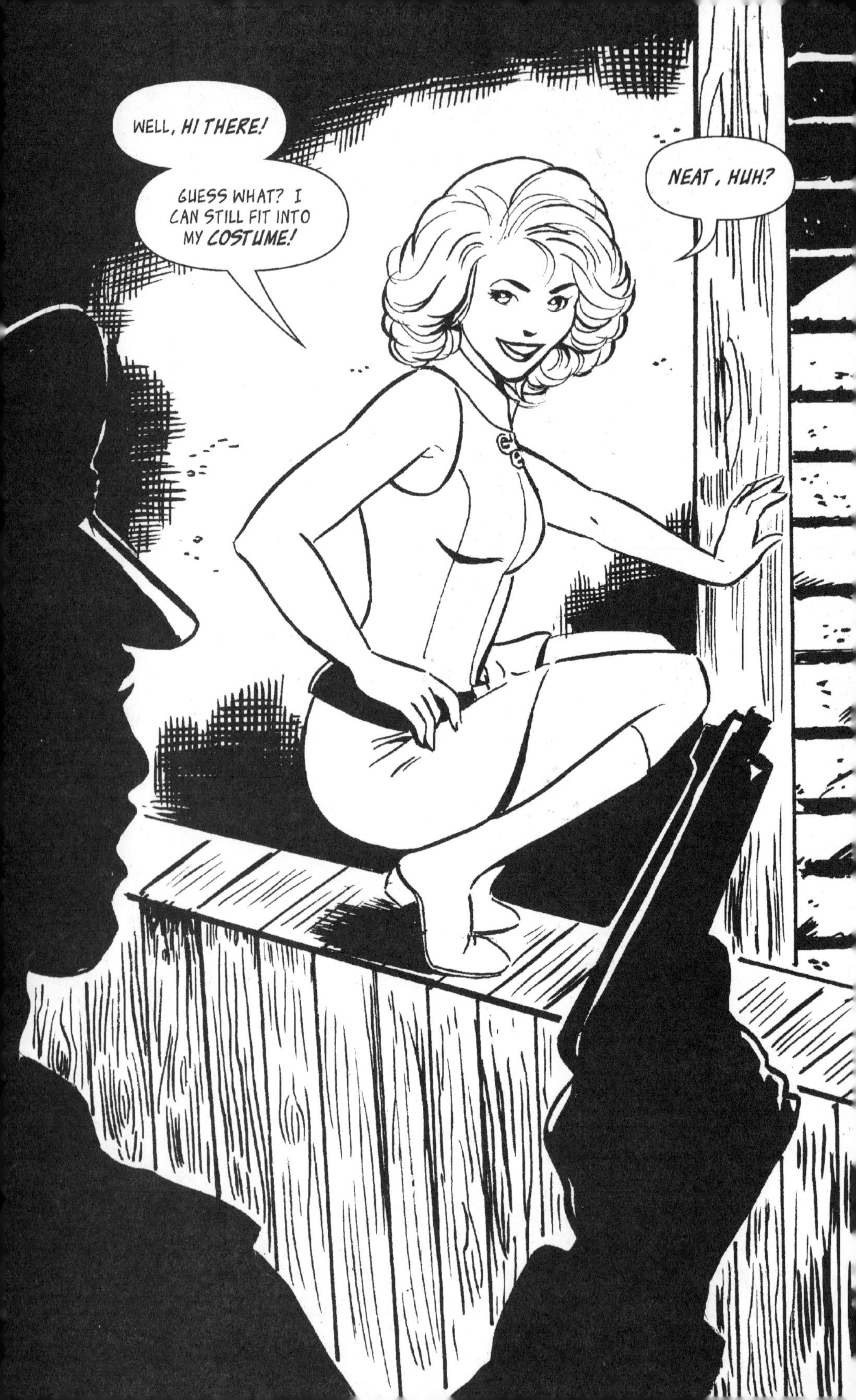
WELL, HI THERE!
GUESS WHAT? I CAN STILL FIT INTO MY COSTUME!
NEAT, HUH?

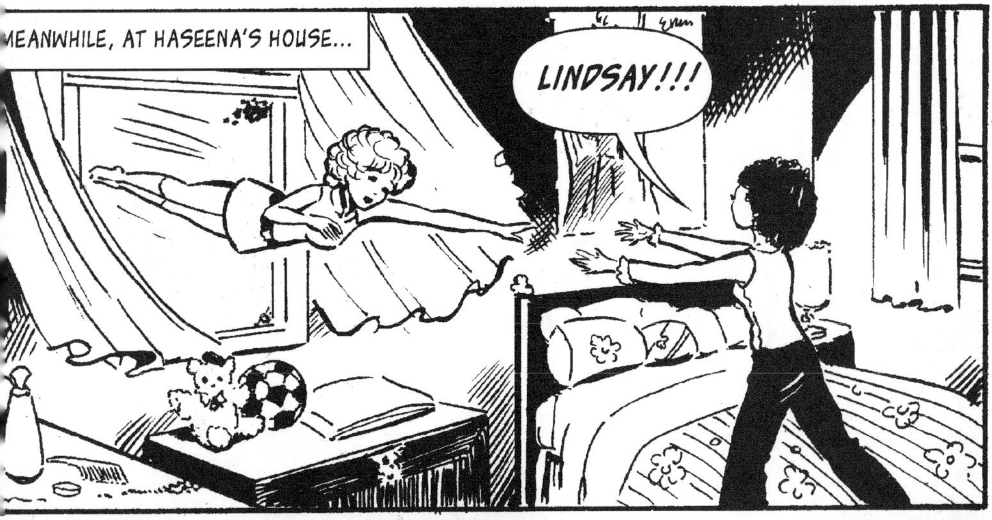
MEANWHILE, AT HASEENA'S HOUSE...
LINDSAY!!!

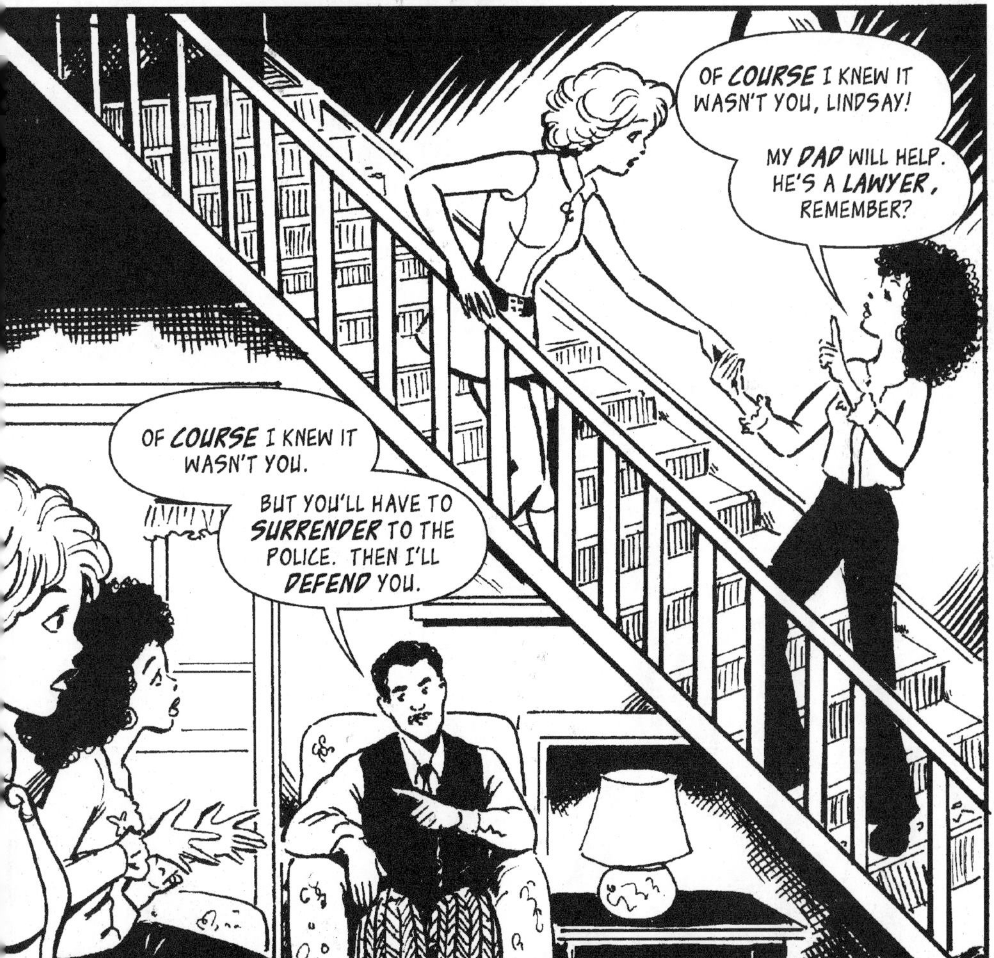
OF COURSE I KNEW IT WASN'T YOU, LINDSAY!
MY DAD WILL HELP. HE'S A LAWYER, REMEMBER?
OF COURSE I KNEW IT WASN'T YOU.
BUT YOU'LL HAVE TO SURRENDER TO THE POLICE. THEN I'LL DEFEND YOU.

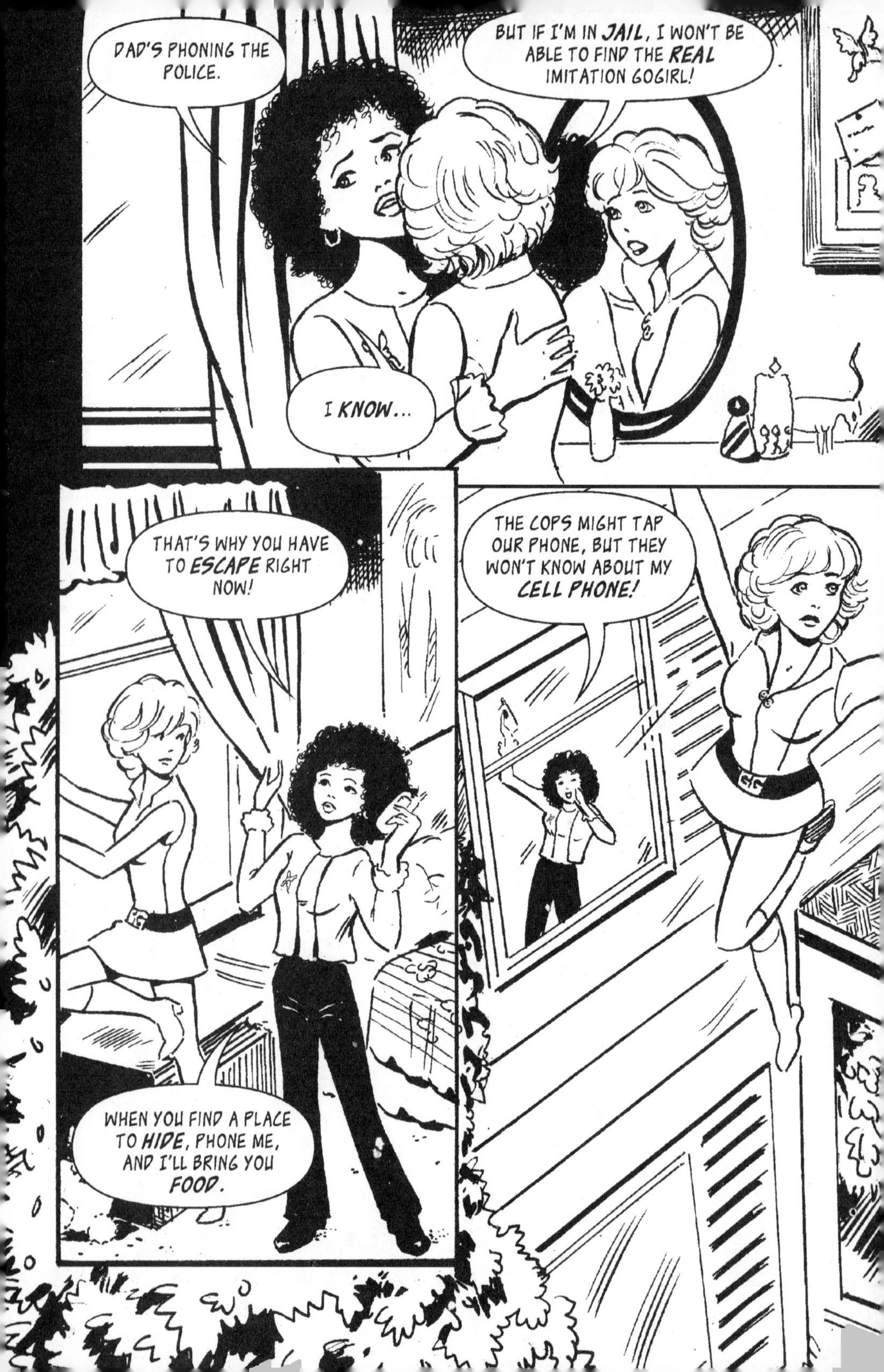
DAD'S PHONING THE POLICE.
BUT IF I'M IN JAIL, I WON'T BE ABLE TO FIND THE REAL IMITATION GOGIRL!
I KNOW...
THAT'S WHY YOU HAVE TO ESCAPE RIGHT NOW!
WHEN YOU FIND A PLACE TO HIDE, PHONE ME, AND I'LL BRING YOU FOOD.
THE COPS MIGHT TAP OUR PHONE, BUT THEY WON'T KNOW ABOUT MY CELL PHONE!

## CHAPTER THREE: FUGITIVE FROM THE LAW

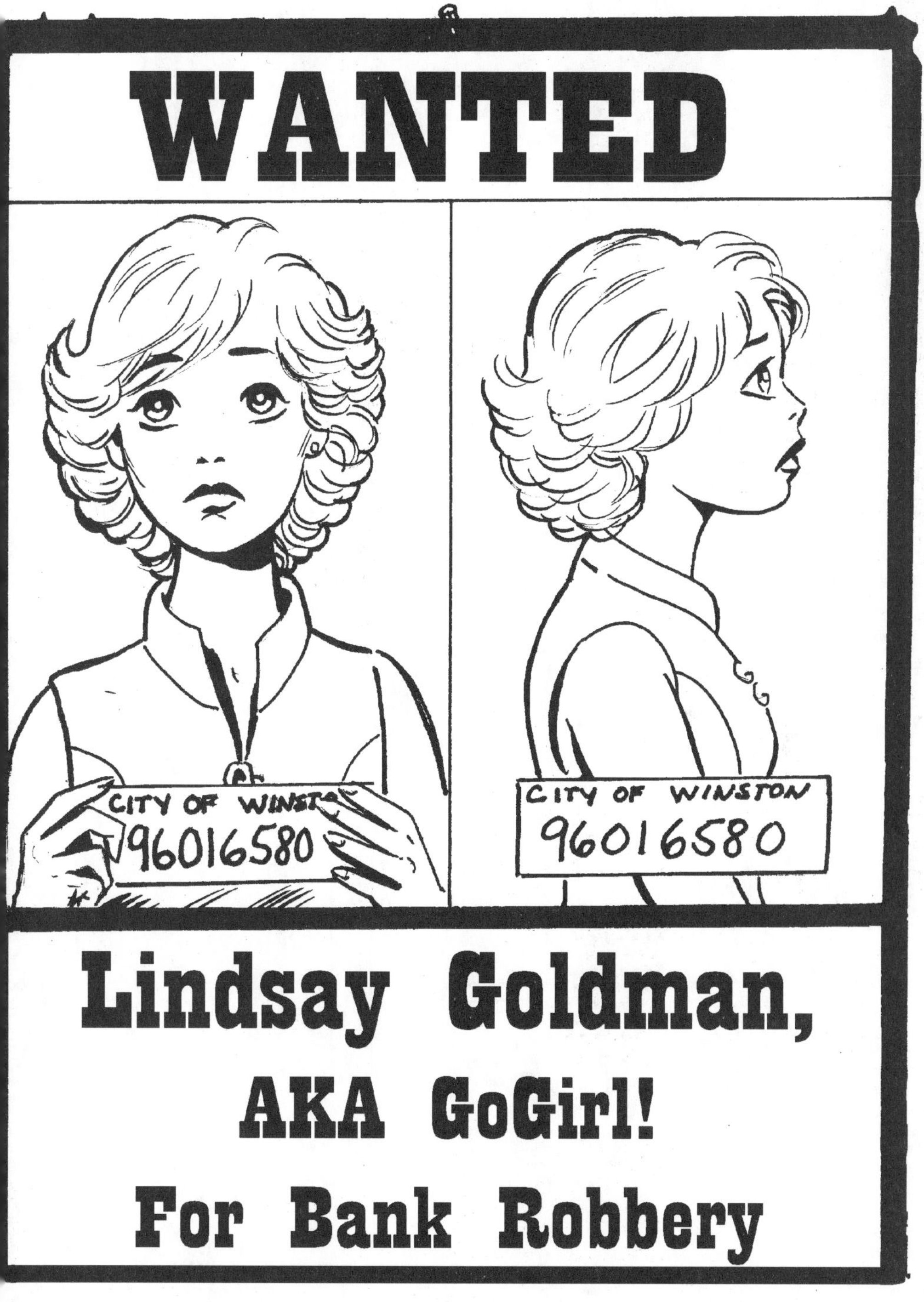
WANTED
CITY OF WINST
96016580
CITY OF WINSTON
96016580
Lindsay Goldman,
AKA GoGirl!
For Bank Robbery

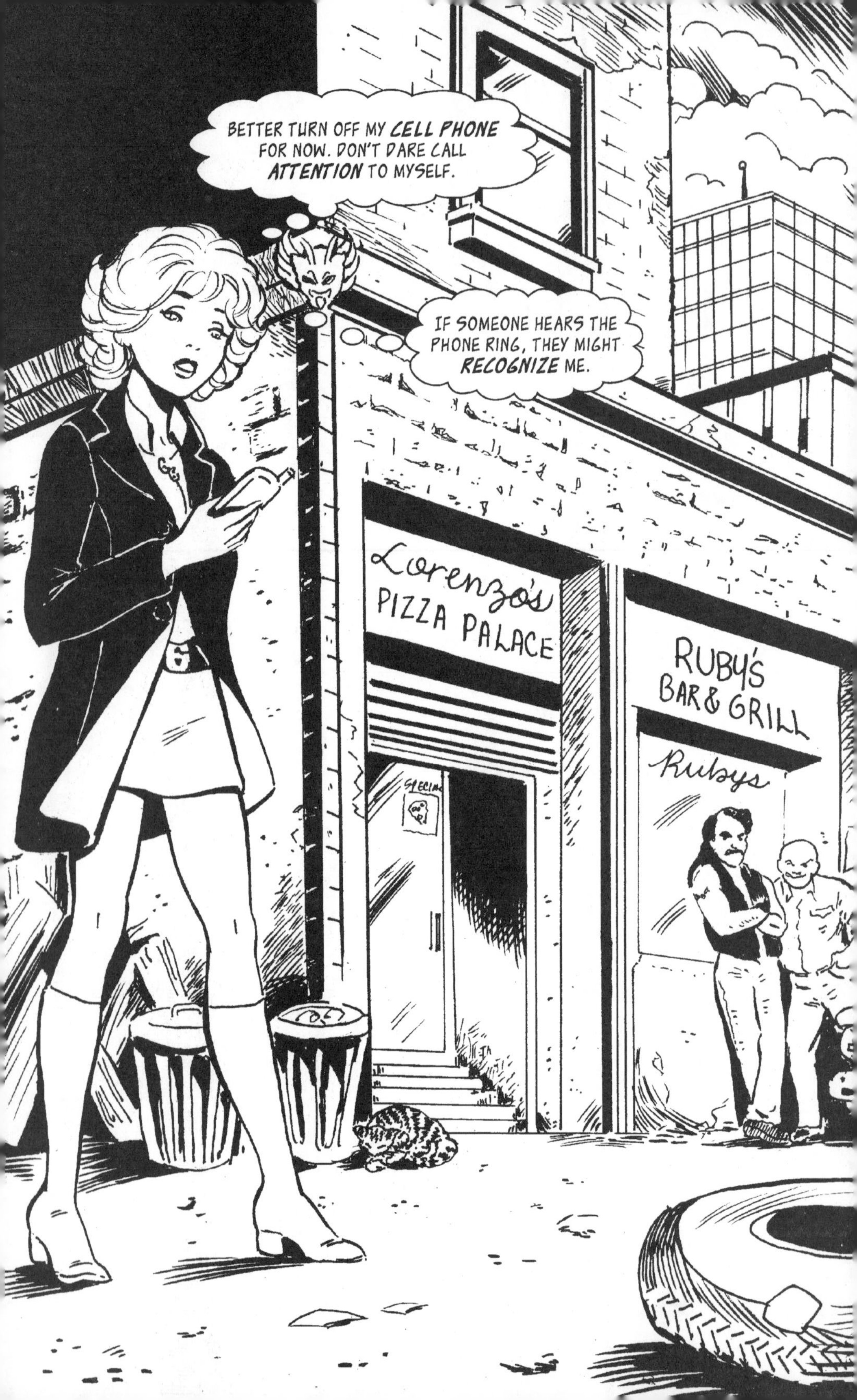
BETTER TURN OFF MY CELL PHONE FOR NOW. DON'T DARE CALL ATTENTION TO MYSELF.
IF SOMEONE HEARS THE PHONE RING, THEY MIGHT RECOGNIZE ME.
Lorenzo's PIZZA PALACE
RUBY'S BAR & GRILL
Rubys

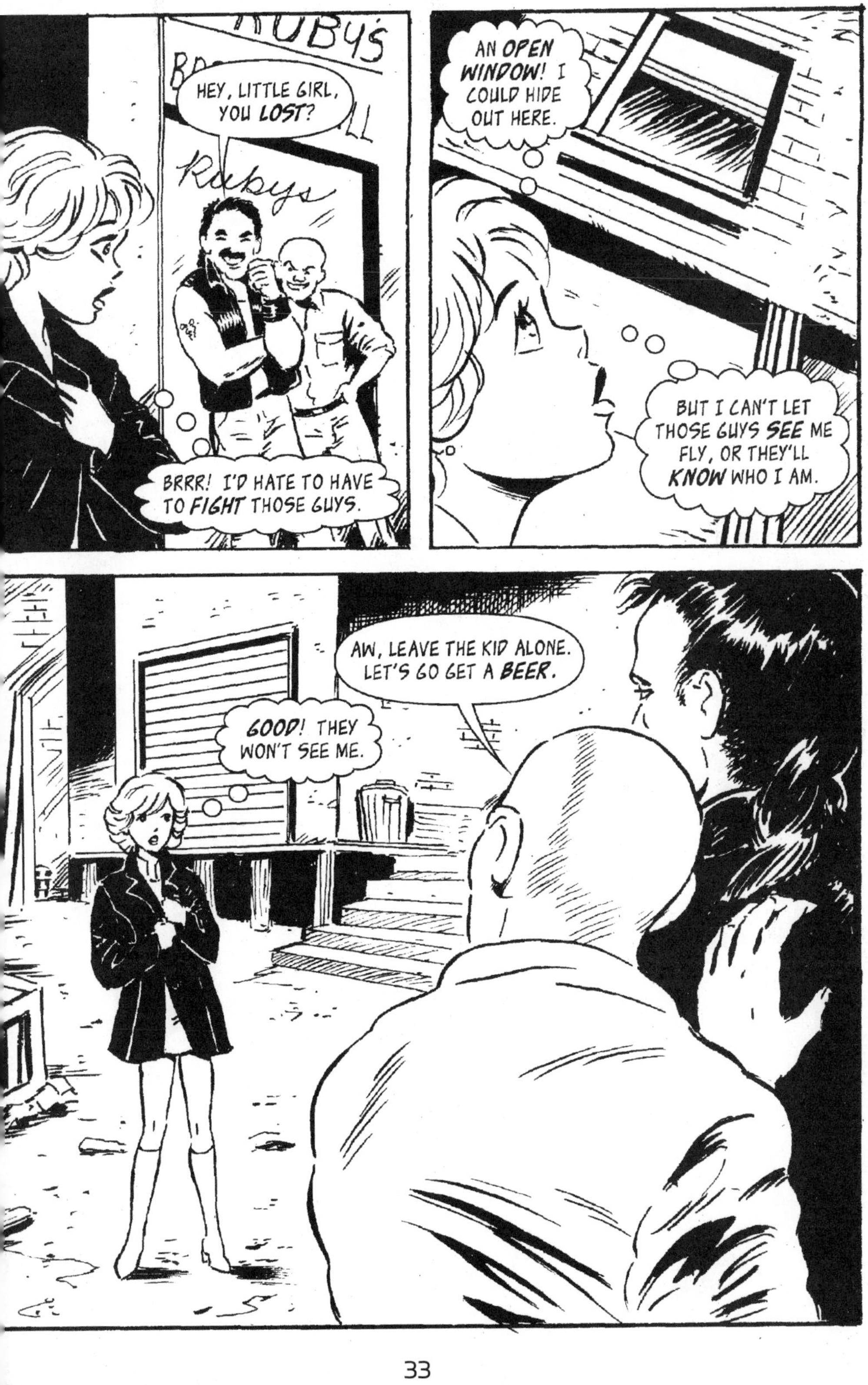
Rubys
HEY, LITTLE GIRL, YOU **LOST**?
BRRR! I'D HATE TO HAVE TO **FIGHT** THOSE GUYS.
AN **OPEN WINDOW**! I COULD HIDE OUT HERE.
BUT I CAN'T LET THOSE GUYS **SEE** ME FLY, OR THEY'LL **KNOW** WHO I AM.
AW, LEAVE THE KID ALONE. LET'S GO GET A **BEER**.
**GOOD**! THEY WON'T SEE ME.

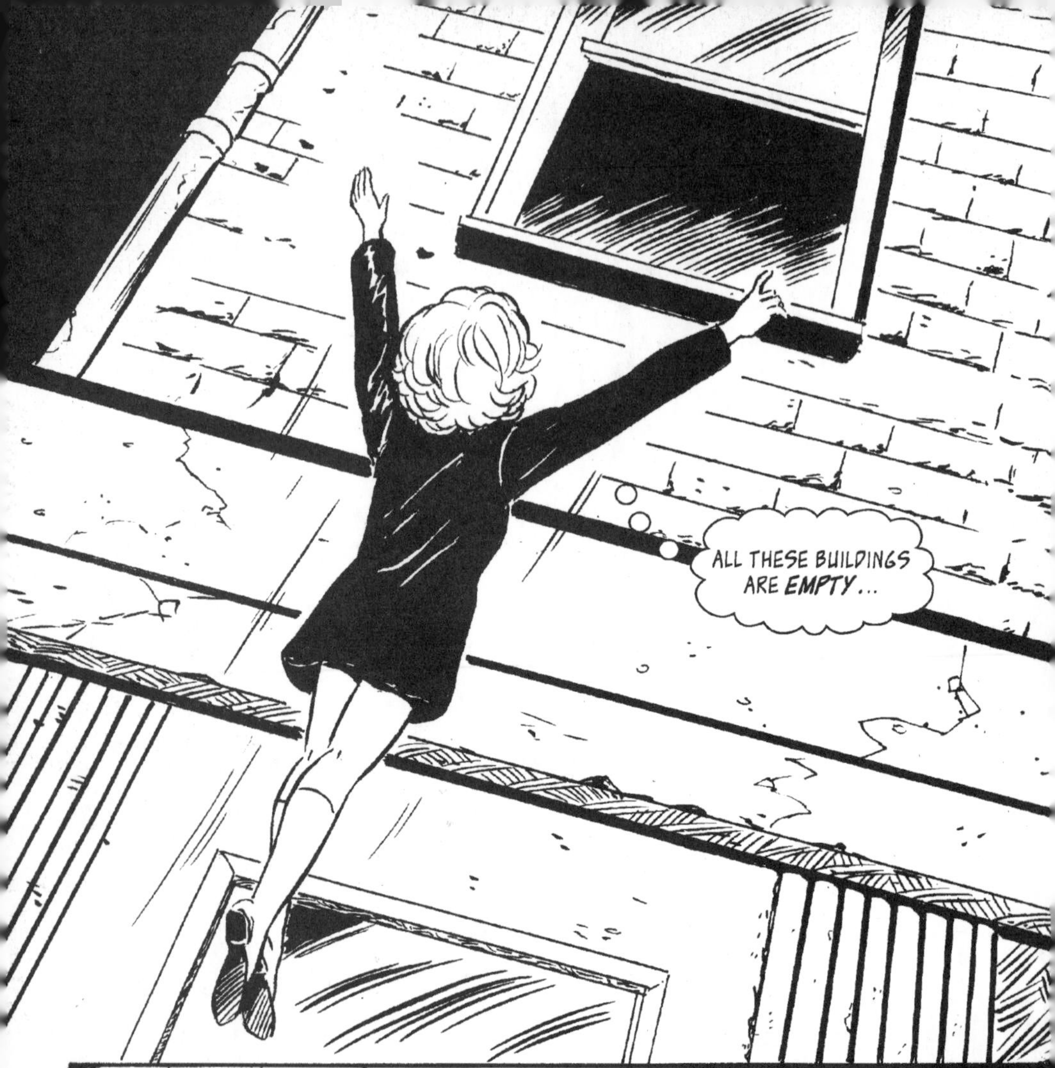
ALL THESE BUILDINGS ARE EMPTY...

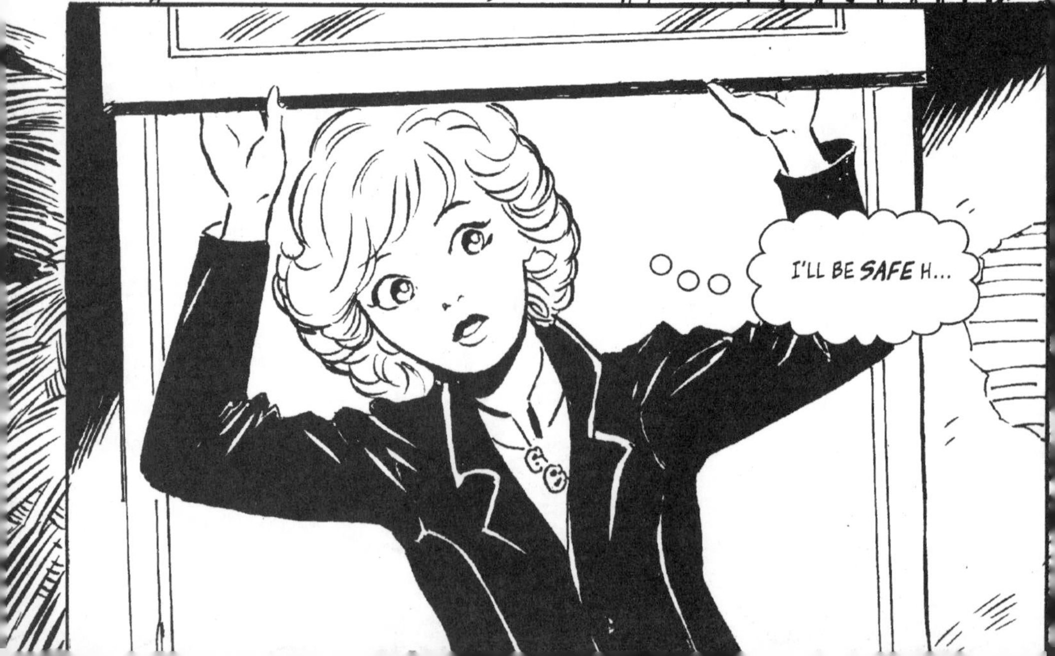
I'LL BE SAFE H...

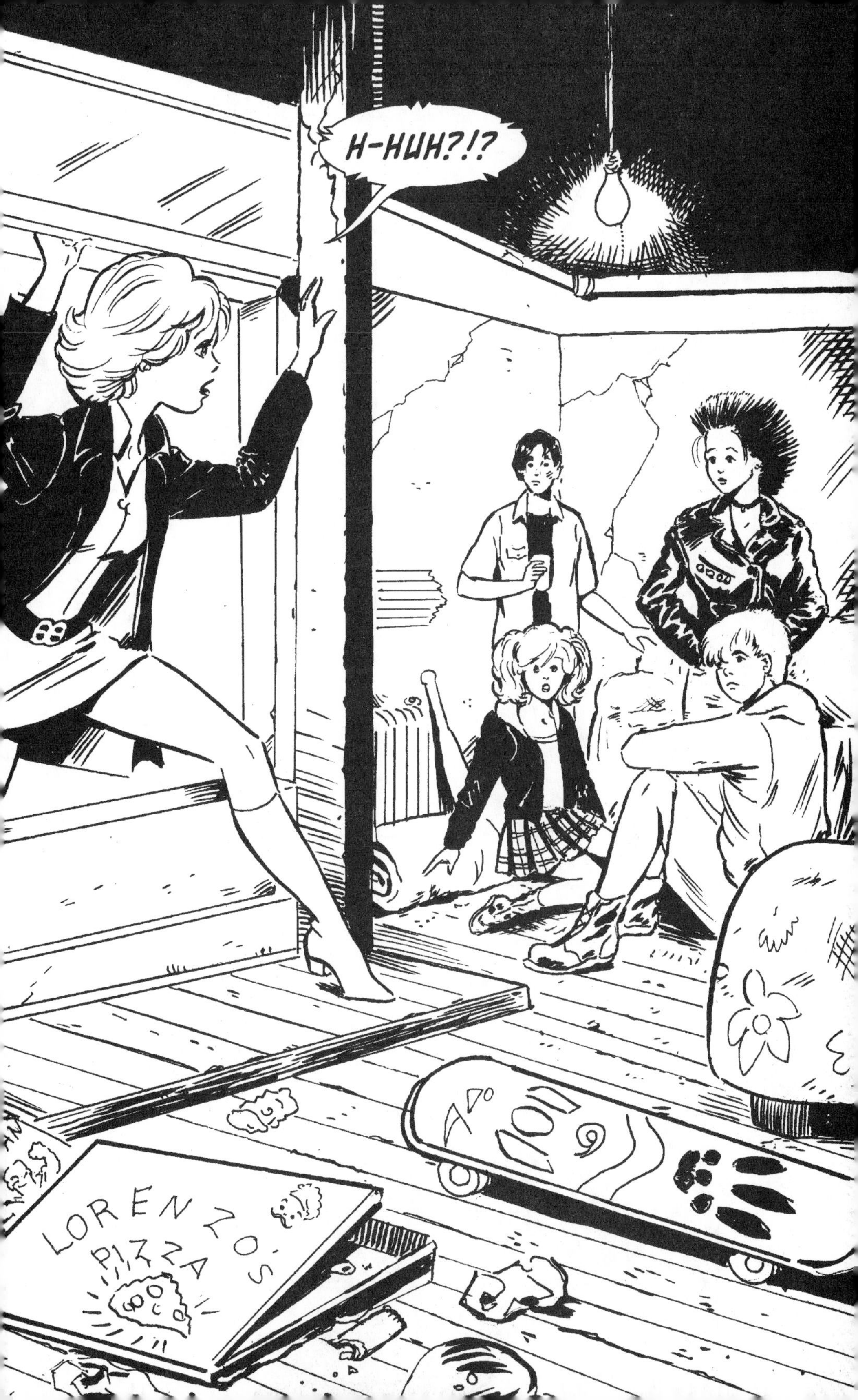
H-HUH?!?
LORENZO'S PIZZA

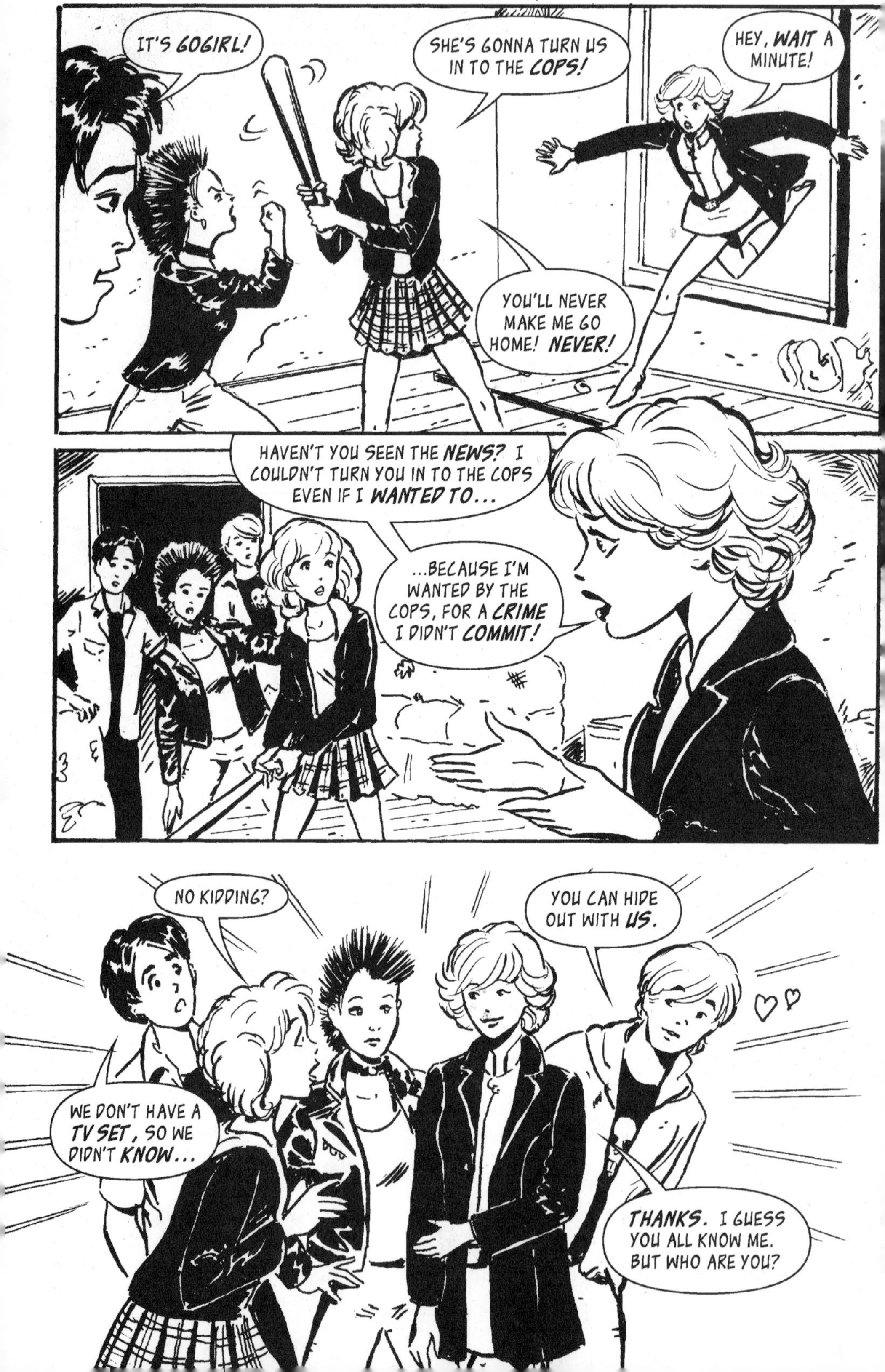
IT'S GOGIRL!
SHE'S GONNA TURN US IN TO THE COPS!
HEY, WAIT A MINUTE!
YOU'LL NEVER MAKE ME GO HOME! NEVER!
HAVEN'T YOU SEEN THE NEWS? I COULDN'T TURN YOU IN TO THE COPS EVEN IF I WANTED TO...
...BECAUSE I'M WANTED BY THE COPS, FOR A CRIME I DIDN'T COMMIT!
NO KIDDING?
YOU CAN HIDE OUT WITH US.
WE DON'T HAVE A TV SET, SO WE DIDN'T KNOW...
THANKS. I GUESS YOU ALL KNOW ME. BUT WHO ARE YOU?

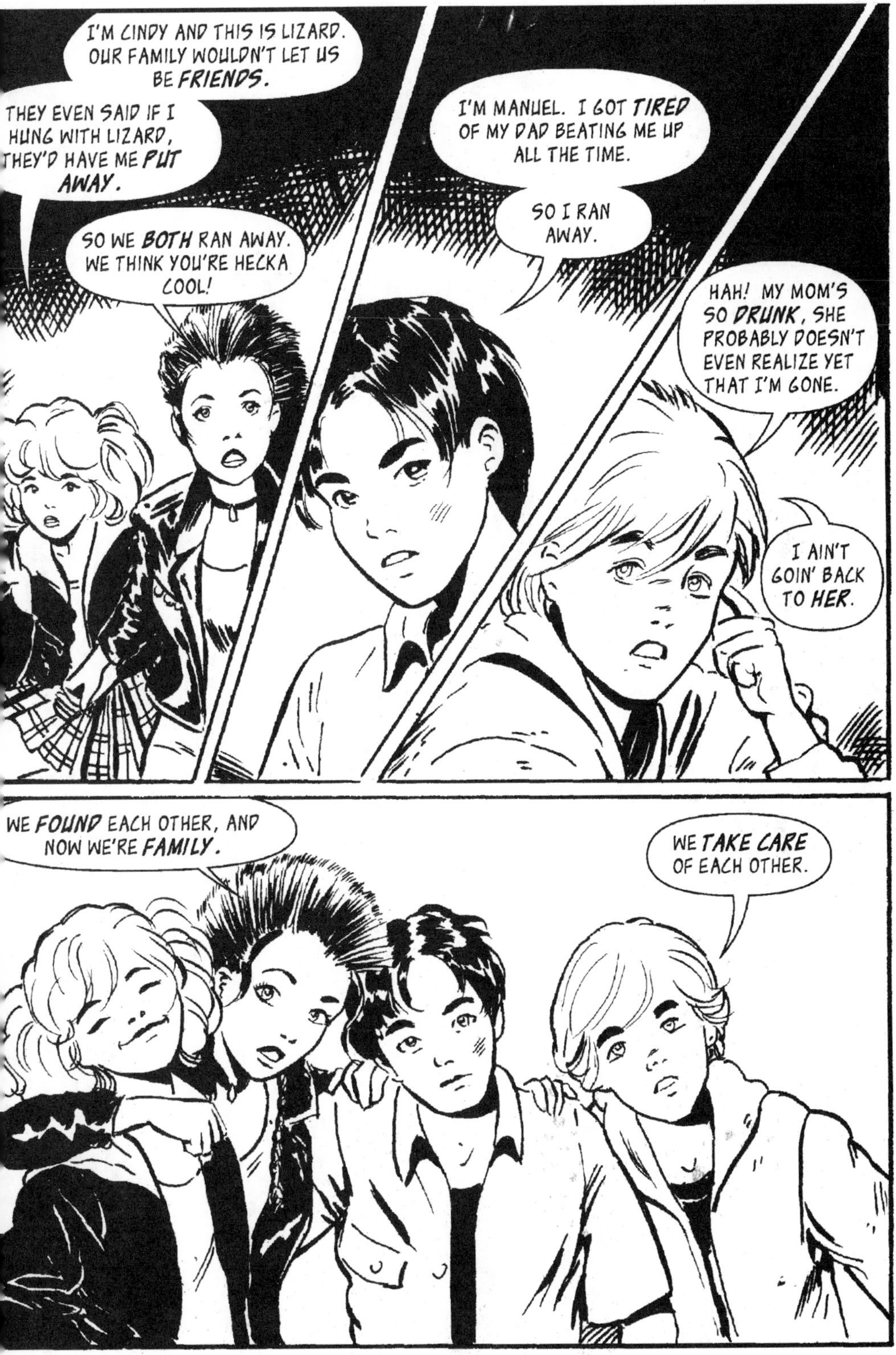
I'M CINDY AND THIS IS LIZARD. OUR FAMILY WOULDN'T LET US BE FRIENDS.
THEY EVEN SAID IF I HUNG WITH LIZARD, THEY'D HAVE ME PUT AWAY.
SO WE BOTH RAN AWAY. WE THINK YOU'RE HECKA COOL!
I'M MANUEL. I GOT TIRED OF MY DAD BEATING ME UP ALL THE TIME.
SO I RAN AWAY.
HAH! MY MOM'S SO DRUNK, SHE PROBABLY DOESN'T EVEN REALIZE YET THAT I'M GONE.
I AIN'T GOIN' BACK TO HER.
WE FOUND EACH OTHER, AND NOW WE'RE FAMILY.
WE TAKE CARE OF EACH OTHER.

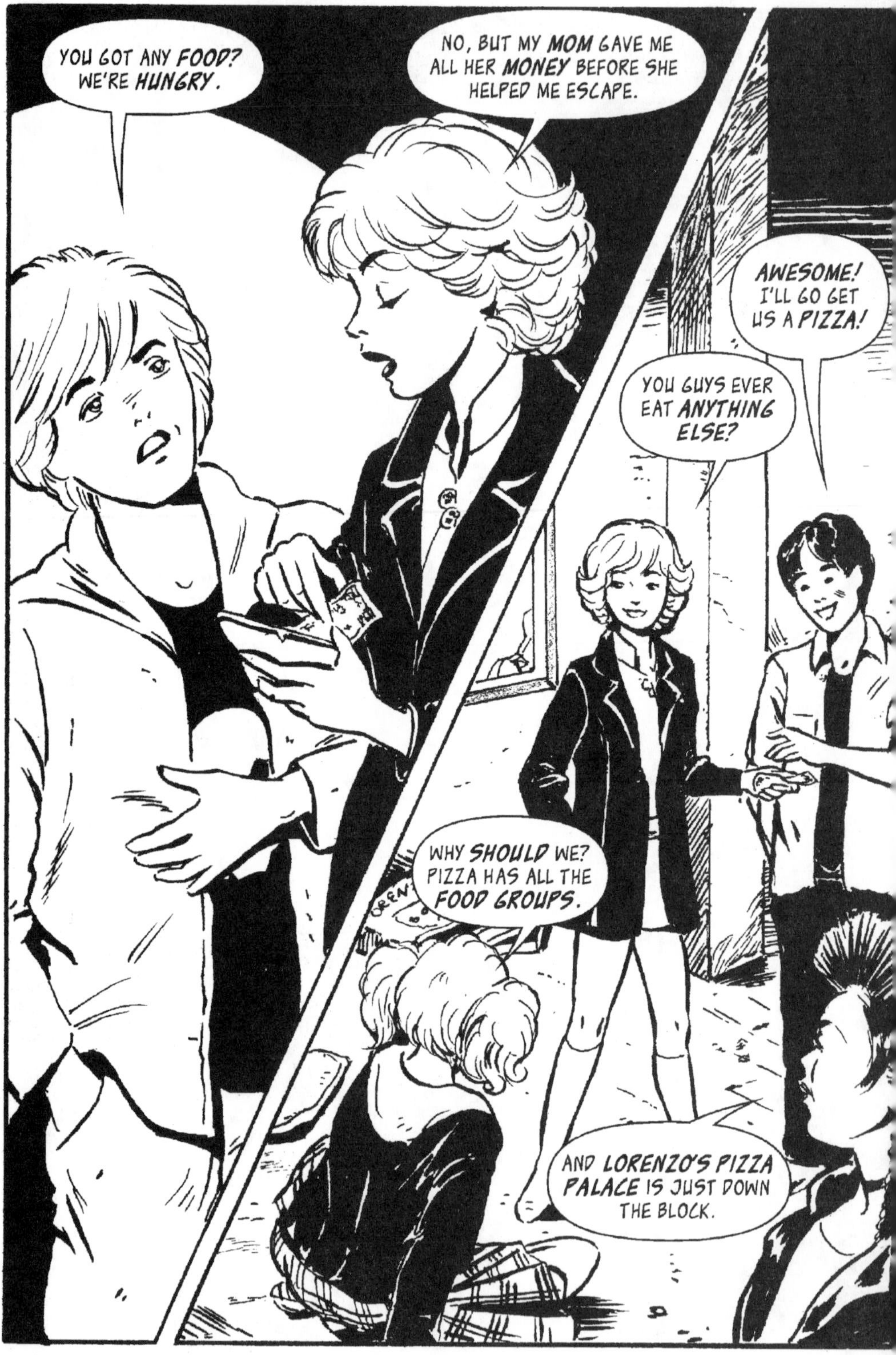
YOU GOT ANY *FOOD?* WE'RE *HUNGRY*.
NO, BUT MY *MOM* GAVE ME ALL HER *MONEY* BEFORE SHE HELPED ME ESCAPE.
*AWESOME!* I'LL GO GET US A *PIZZA!*
YOU GUYS EVER EAT *ANYTHING ELSE?*
WHY *SHOULD* WE? PIZZA HAS ALL THE *FOOD GROUPS*.
AND *LORENZO'S PIZZA PALACE* IS JUST DOWN THE BLOCK.

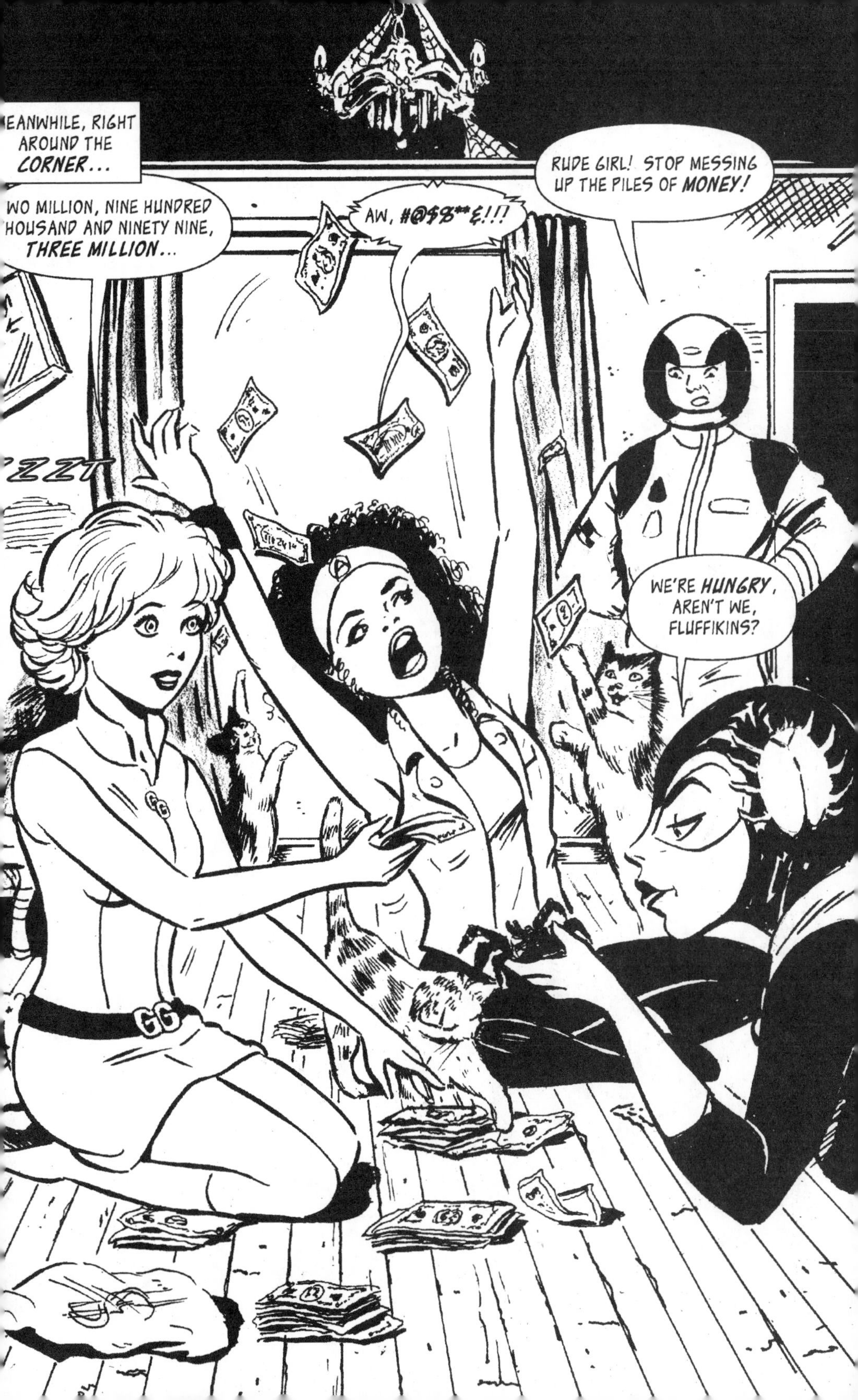
EANWHILE, RIGHT AROUND THE CORNER...
WO MILLION, NINE HUNDRED HOUSAND AND NINETY NINE, THREE MILLION...
AW, #@$8**&!!!
RUDE GIRL! STOP MESSING UP THE PILES OF MONEY!
ZZZT
WE'RE HUNGRY, AREN'T WE, FLUFFIKINS?

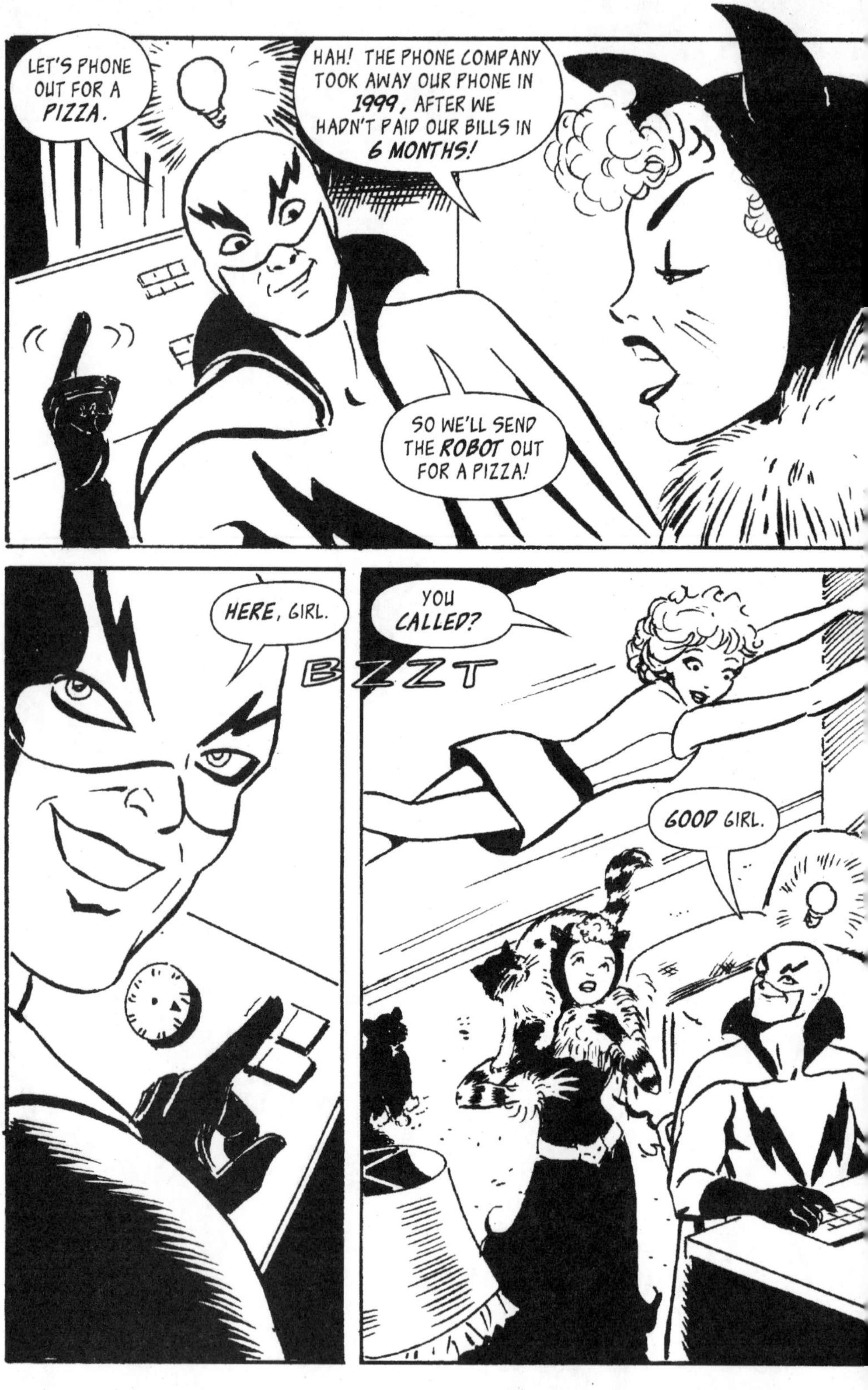
LET'S PHONE OUT FOR A PIZZA.
HAH! THE PHONE COMPANY TOOK AWAY OUR PHONE IN 1999, AFTER WE HADN'T PAID OUR BILLS IN 6 MONTHS!
SO WE'LL SEND THE ROBOT OUT FOR A PIZZA!
HERE, GIRL.
YOU CALLED?
BZZT
GOOD GIRL.

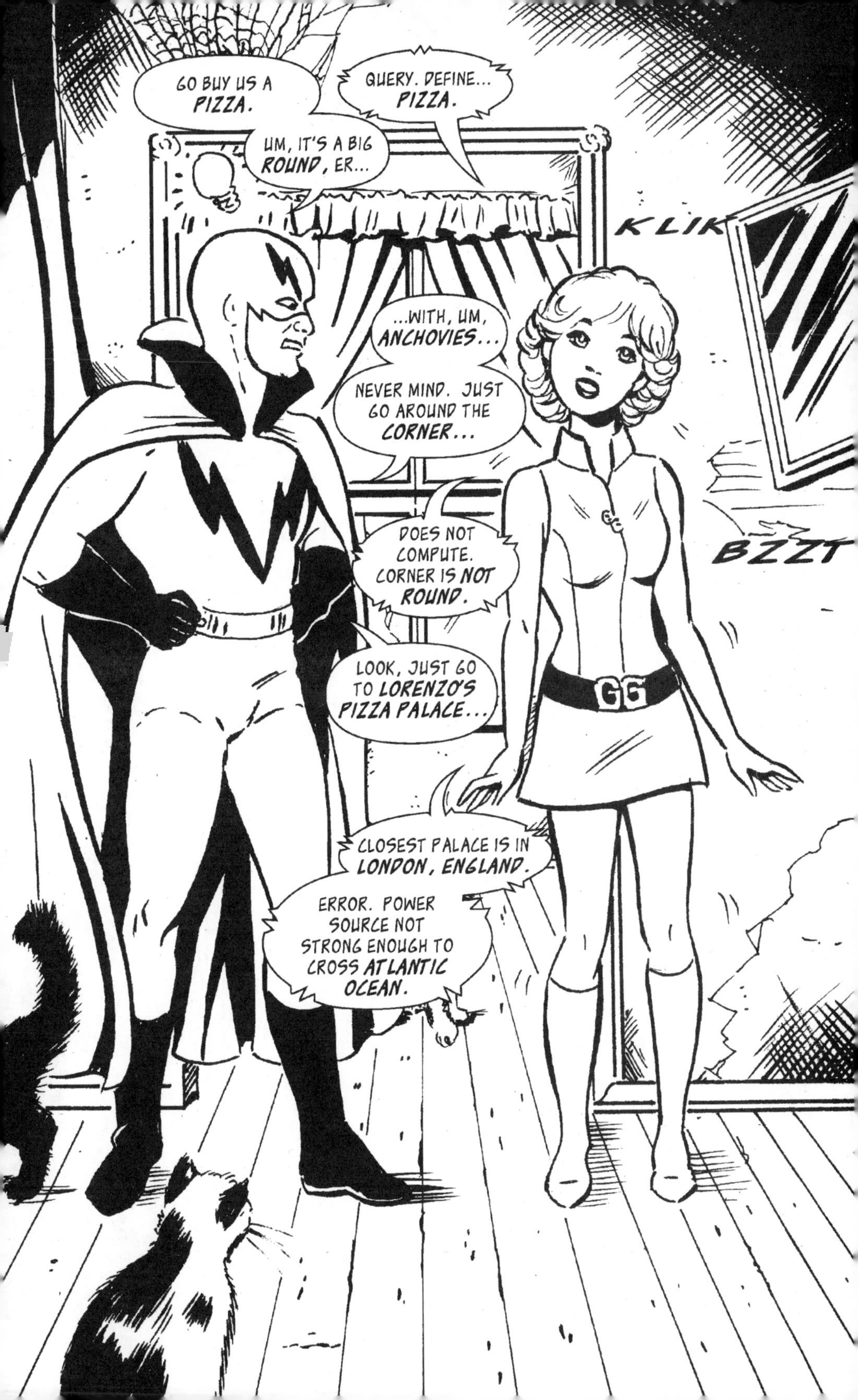
GO BUY US A PIZZA.
QUERY. DEFINE... PIZZA.
UM, IT'S A BIG ROUND, ER...
KLIK
...WITH, UM, ANCHOVIES...
NEVER MIND. JUST GO AROUND THE CORNER...
DOES NOT COMPUTE. CORNER IS NOT ROUND.
BZZT
LOOK, JUST GO TO LORENZO'S PIZZA PALACE...
CLOSEST PALACE IS IN LONDON, ENGLAND.
ERROR. POWER SOURCE NOT STRONG ENOUGH TO CROSS ATLANTIC OCEAN.

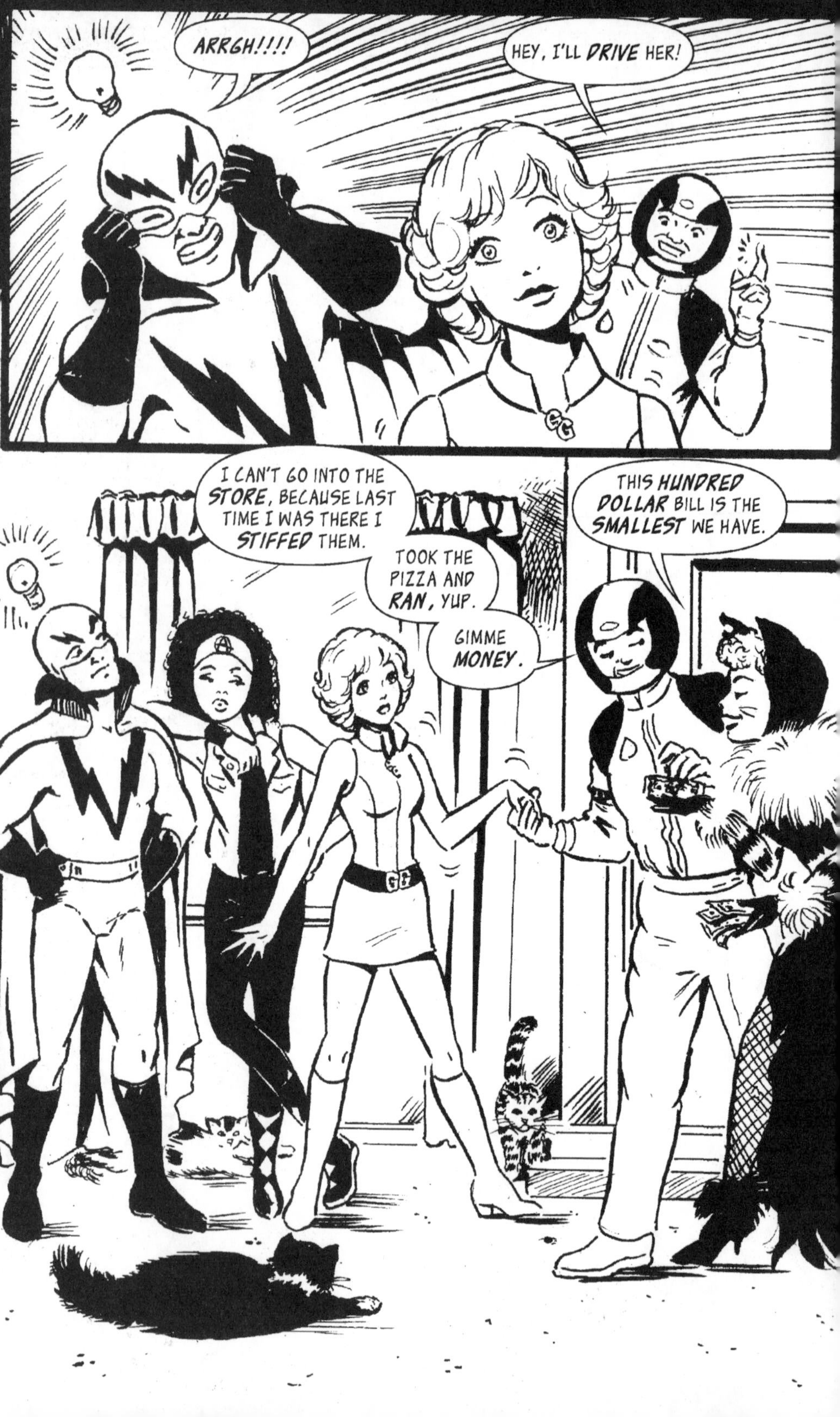
ARRGH!!!!
HEY, I'LL DRIVE HER!
I CAN'T GO INTO THE STORE, BECAUSE LAST TIME I WAS THERE I STIFFED THEM.
TOOK THE PIZZA AND RAN, YUP.
GIMME MONEY.
THIS HUNDRED DOLLAR BILL IS THE SMALLEST WE HAVE.

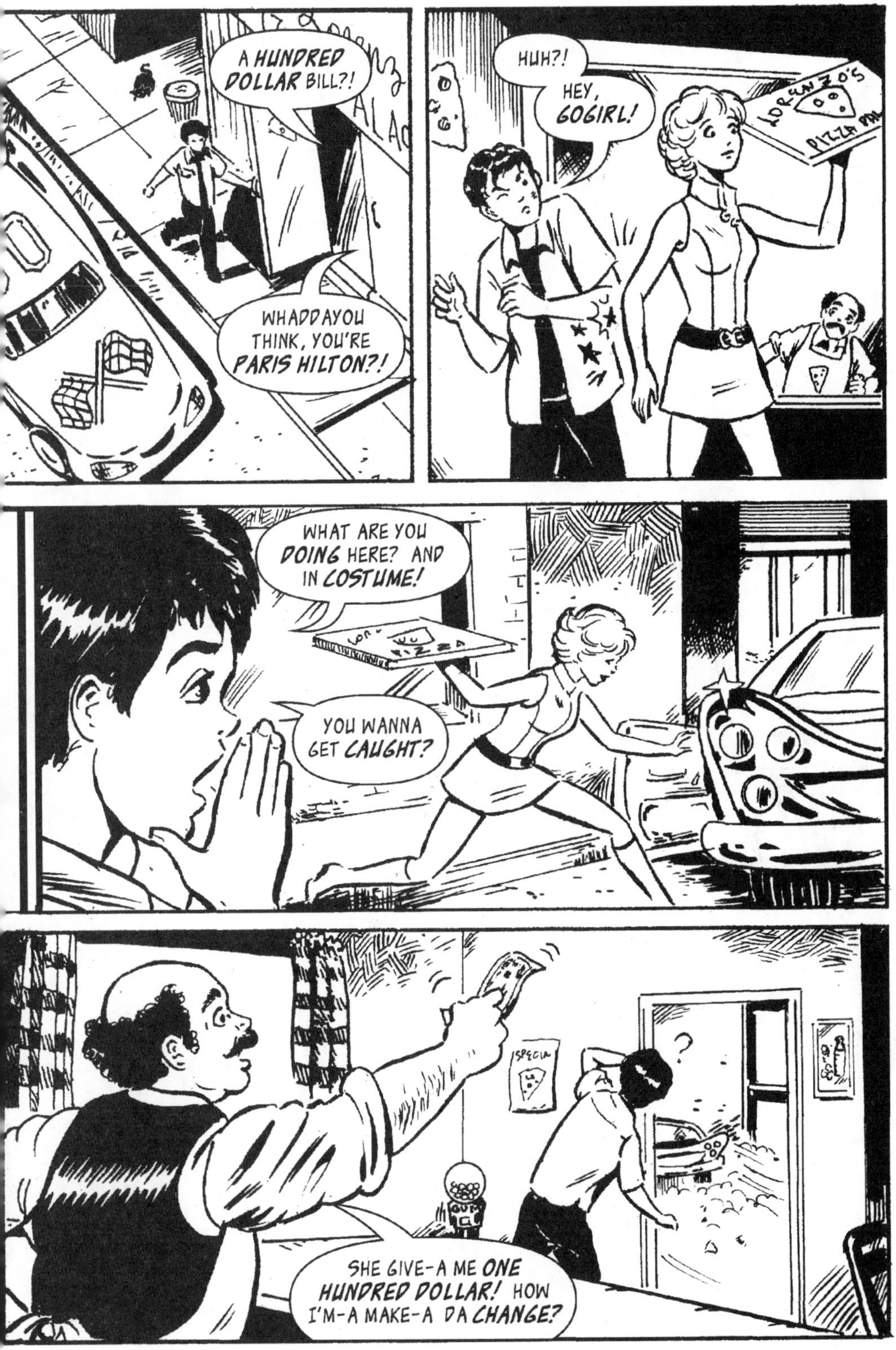
A HUNDRED DOLLAR BILL?!
WHADDAYOU THINK, YOU'RE PARIS HILTON?!
HUH?!
HEY, GOGIRL!
LORENZO'S PIZZA
WHAT ARE YOU DOING HERE? AND IN COSTUME!
YOU WANNA GET CAUGHT?
SHE GIVE-A ME ONE HUNDRED DOLLAR! HOW I'M-A MAKE-A DA CHANGE?

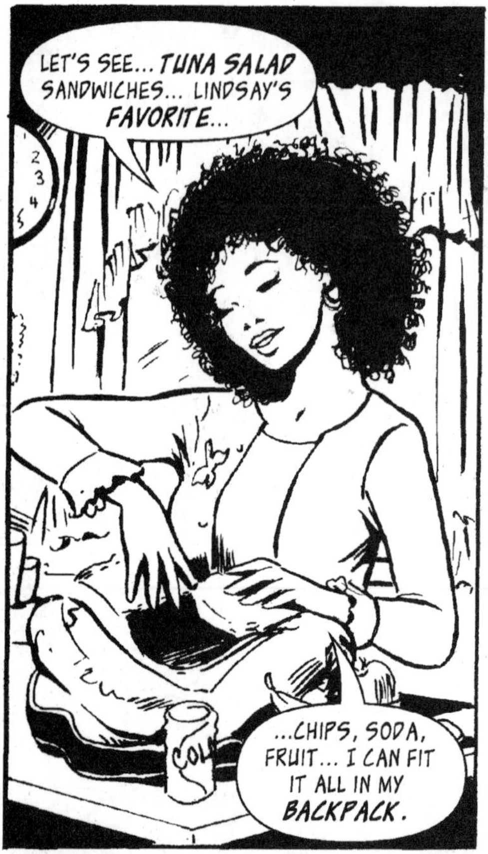
LET'S SEE... TUNA SALAD SANDWICHES... LINDSAY'S FAVORITE...
...CHIPS, SODA, FRUIT... I CAN FIT IT ALL IN MY BACKPACK.
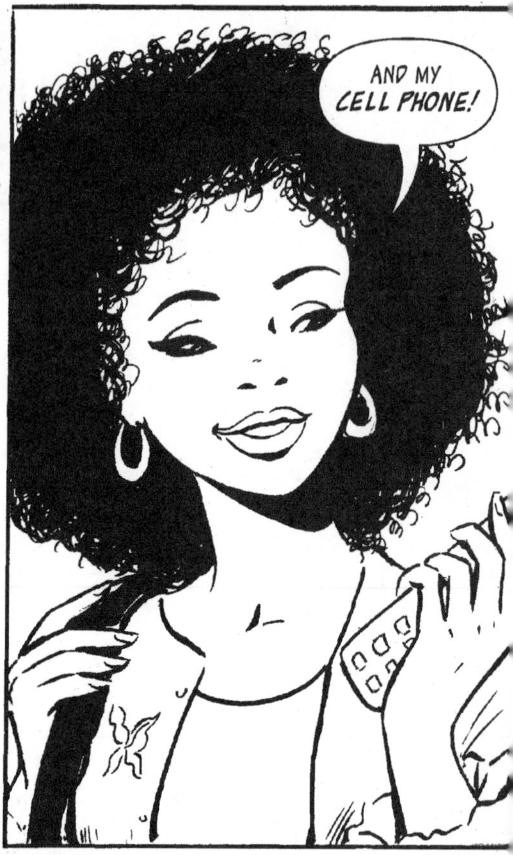
AND MY CELL PHONE!
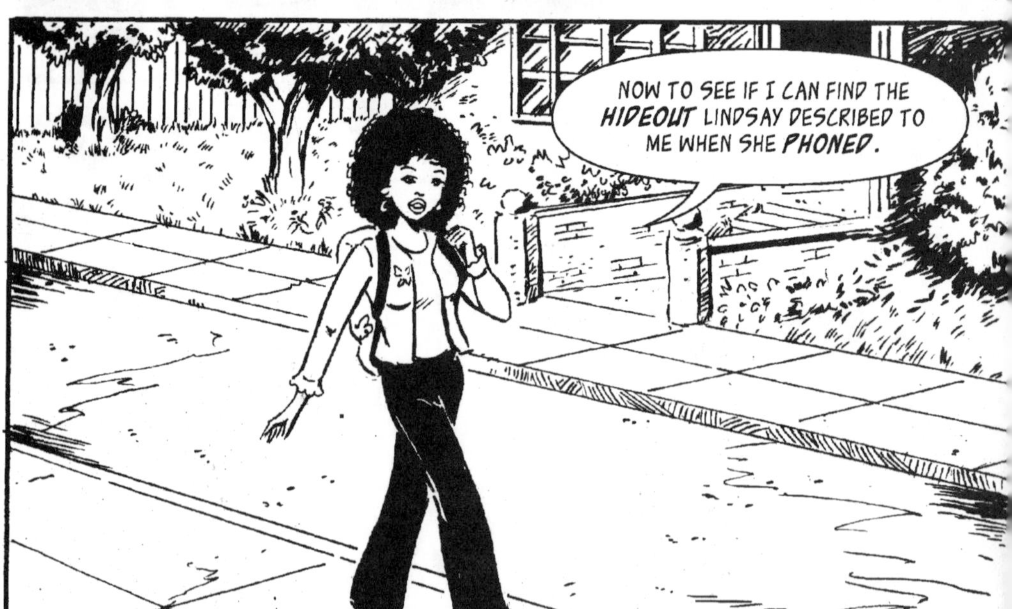
NOW TO SEE IF I CAN FIND THE HIDEOUT LINDSAY DESCRIBED TO ME WHEN SHE PHONED.

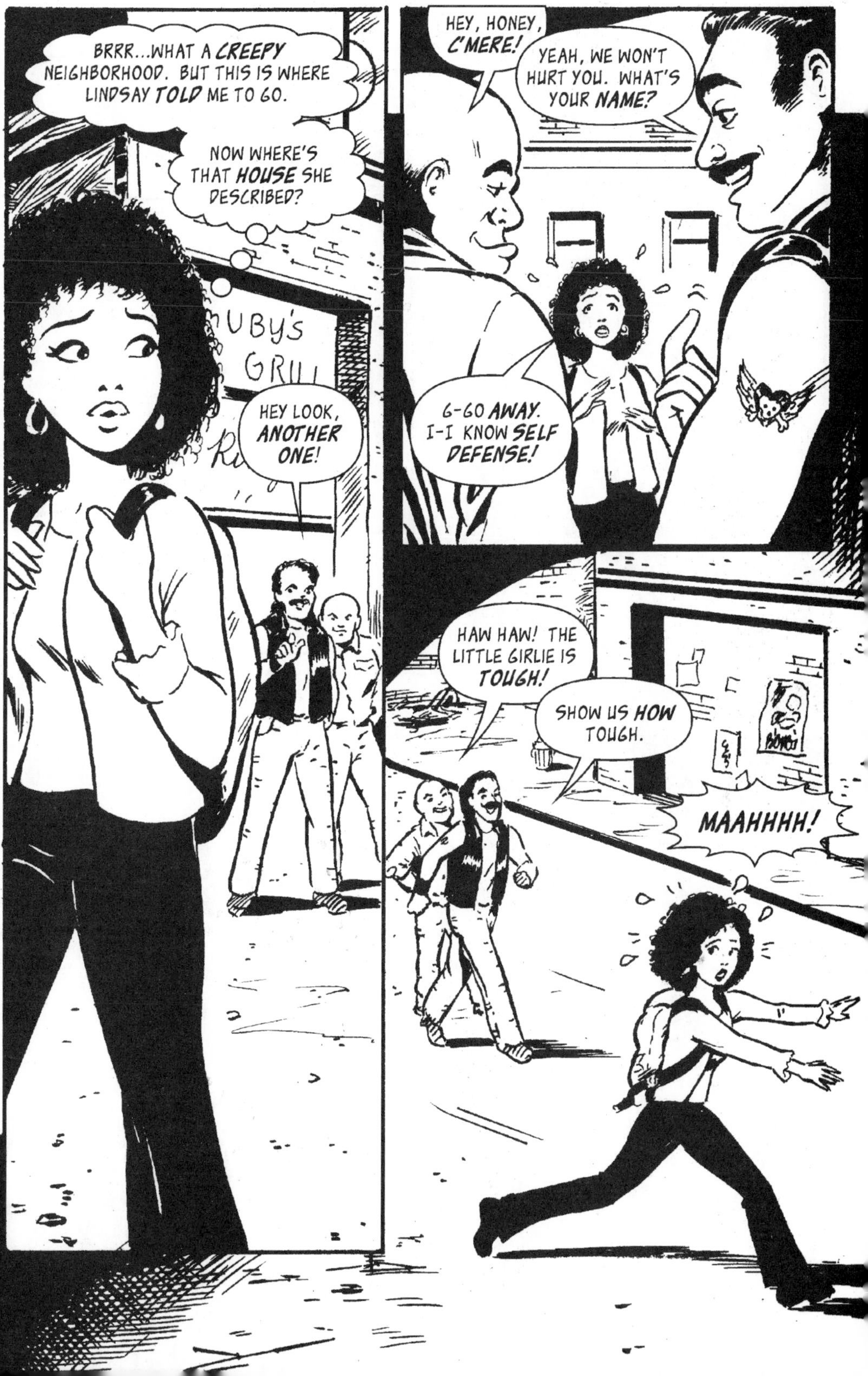
BRRR...WHAT A CREEPY NEIGHBORHOOD. BUT THIS IS WHERE LINDSAY TOLD ME TO GO.
NOW WHERE'S THAT HOUSE SHE DESCRIBED?
HEY LOOK, ANOTHER ONE!
HEY, HONEY, C'MERE!
YEAH, WE WON'T HURT YOU. WHAT'S YOUR NAME?
G-GO AWAY. I-I KNOW SELF DEFENSE!
HAW HAW! THE LITTLE GIRLIE IS TOUGH!
SHOW US HOW TOUGH.
MAAHHHH!

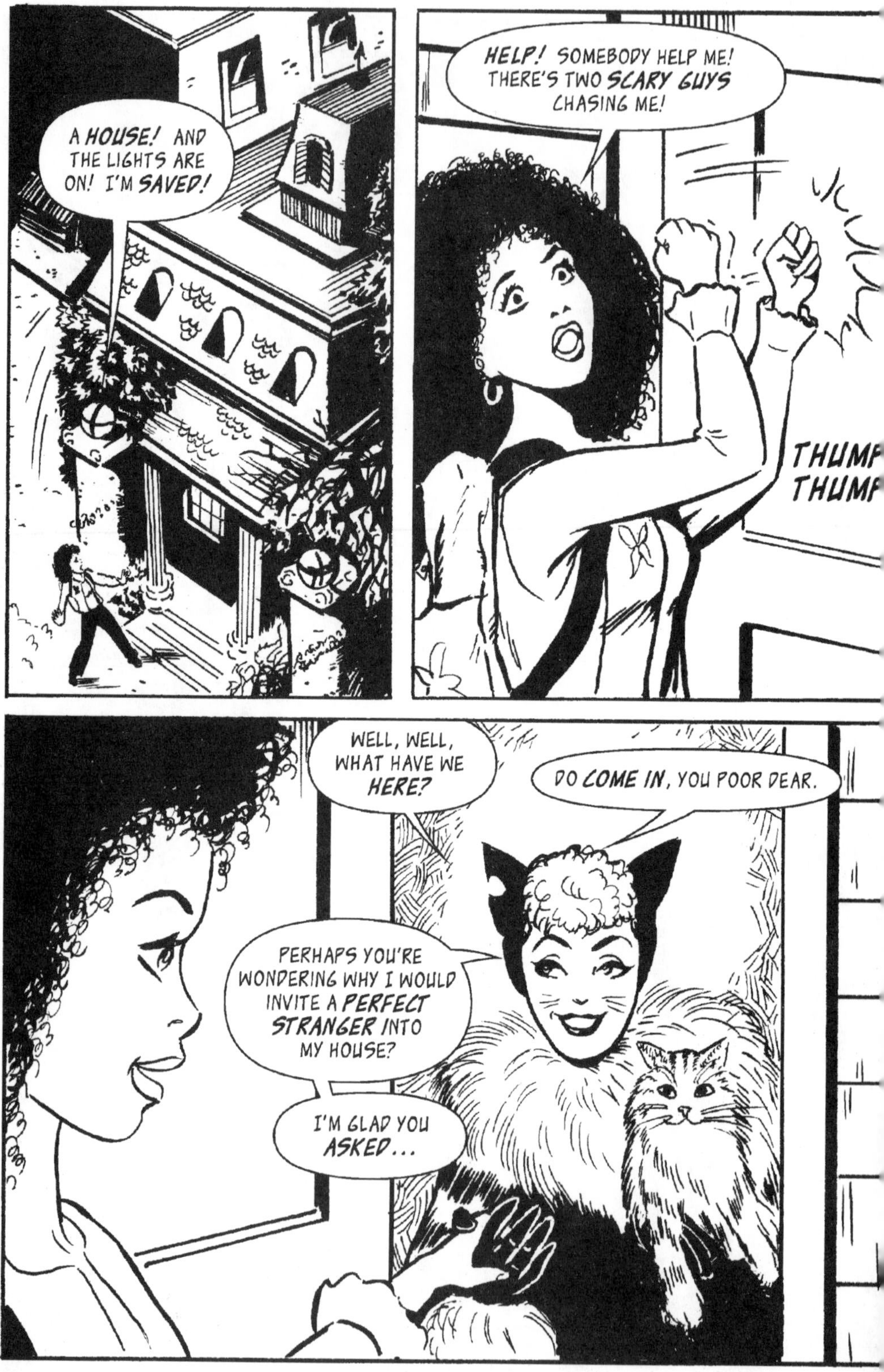
A HOUSE! AND THE LIGHTS ARE ON! I'M SAVED!
HELP! SOMEBODY HELP ME! THERE'S TWO SCARY GUYS CHASING ME!
THUMP
THUMP
WELL, WELL, WHAT HAVE WE HERE?
DO COME IN, YOU POOR DEAR.
PERHAPS YOU'RE WONDERING WHY I WOULD INVITE A PERFECT STRANGER INTO MY HOUSE?
I'M GLAD YOU ASKED...

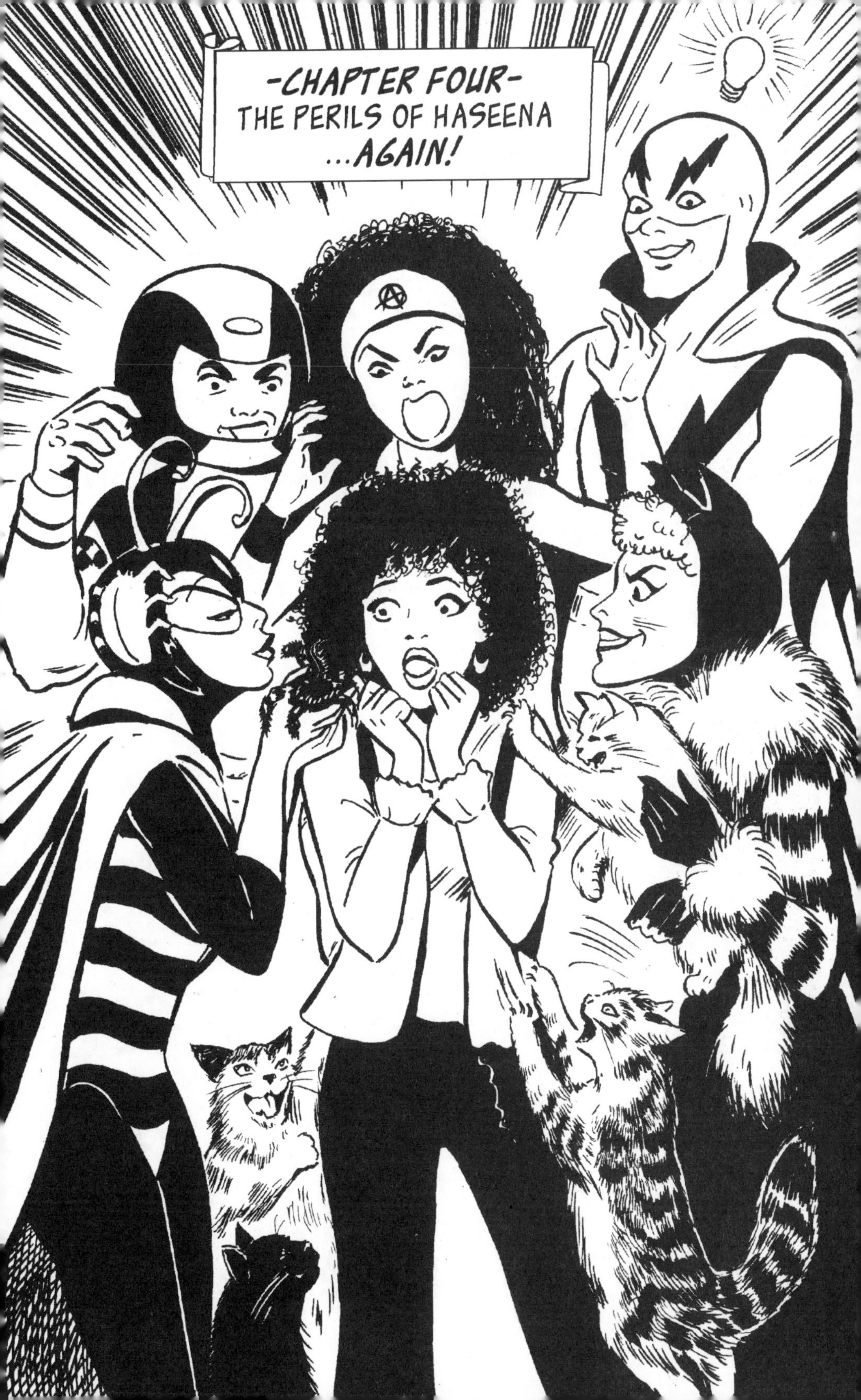
-CHAPTER FOUR-
THE PERILS OF HASEENA
...AGAIN!

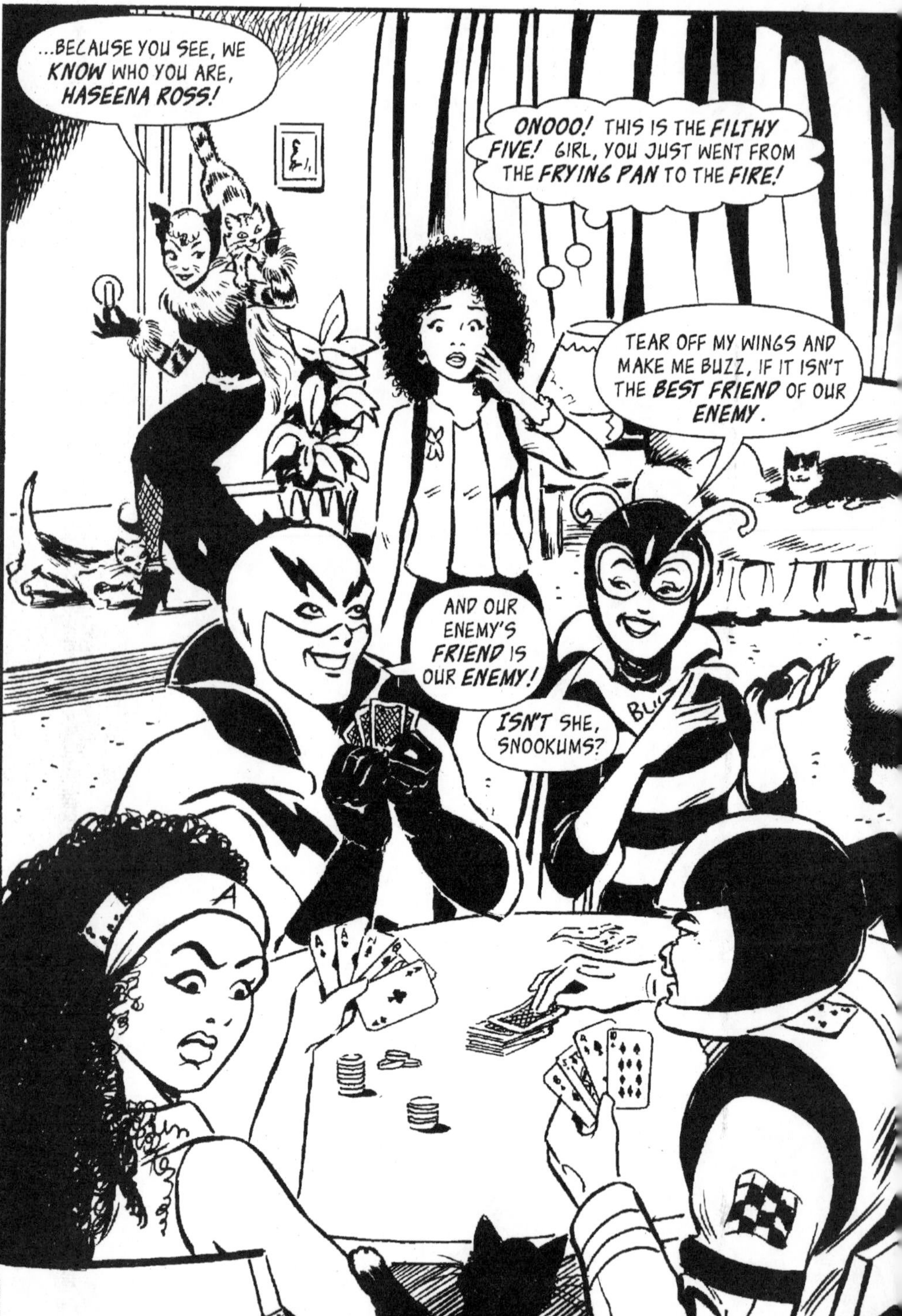
...BECAUSE YOU SEE, WE KNOW WHO YOU ARE, HASEENA ROSS!
ONOOO! THIS IS THE FILTHY FIVE! GIRL, YOU JUST WENT FROM THE FRYING PAN TO THE FIRE!
TEAR OFF MY WINGS AND MAKE ME BUZZ, IF IT ISN'T THE BEST FRIEND OF OUR ENEMY.
AND OUR ENEMY'S FRIEND IS OUR ENEMY!
ISN'T SHE, SNOOKUMS?

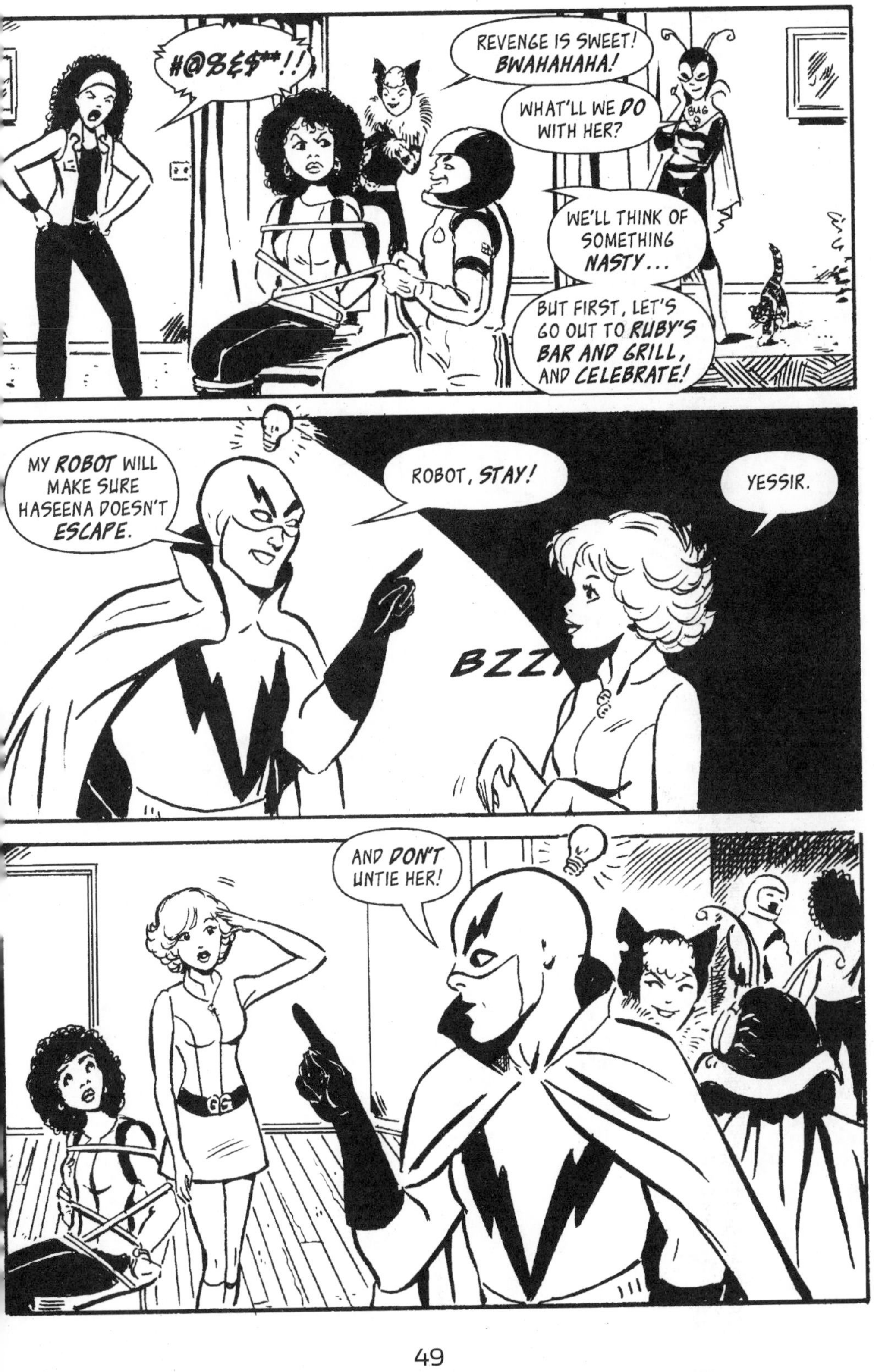
#@%¢$**!!
REVENGE IS SWEET! BWAHAHAHA!
WHAT'LL WE DO WITH HER?
WE'LL THINK OF SOMETHING NASTY...
BUT FIRST, LET'S GO OUT TO RUBY'S BAR AND GRILL, AND CELEBRATE!
MY ROBOT WILL MAKE SURE HASEENA DOESN'T ESCAPE.
ROBOT, STAY!
YESSIR.
BZZT
AND DON'T UNTIE HER!

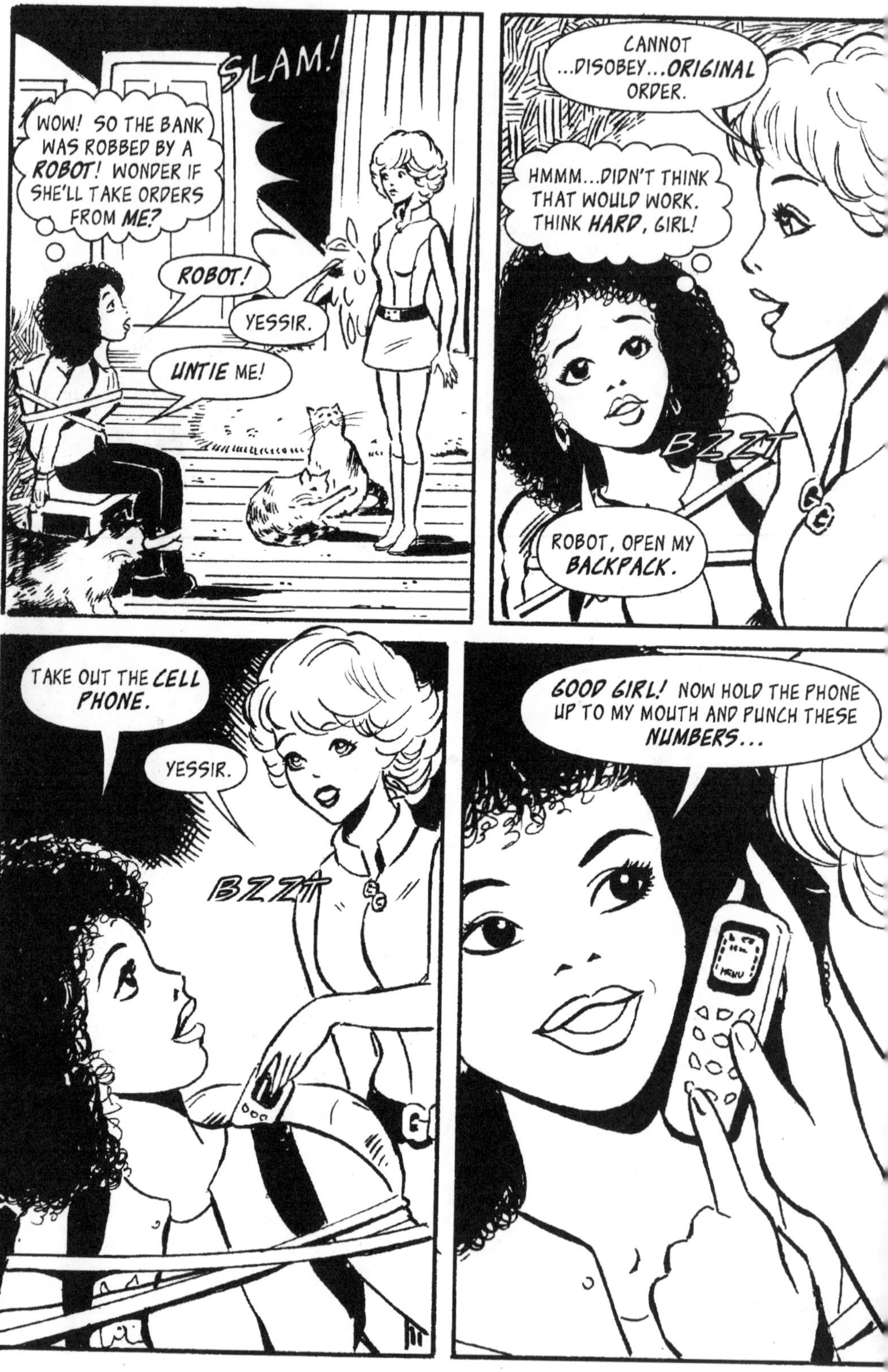
SLAM!
WOW! SO THE BANK WAS ROBBED BY A ROBOT! WONDER IF SHE'LL TAKE ORDERS FROM ME?
ROBOT!
YESSIR.
UNTIE ME!
CANNOT ...DISOBEY...ORIGINAL ORDER.
HMMM...DIDN'T THINK THAT WOULD WORK. THINK HARD, GIRL!
BZZT
ROBOT, OPEN MY BACKPACK.
TAKE OUT THE CELL PHONE.
YESSIR.
BZZT
GOOD GIRL! NOW HOLD THE PHONE UP TO MY MOUTH AND PUNCH THESE NUMBERS...

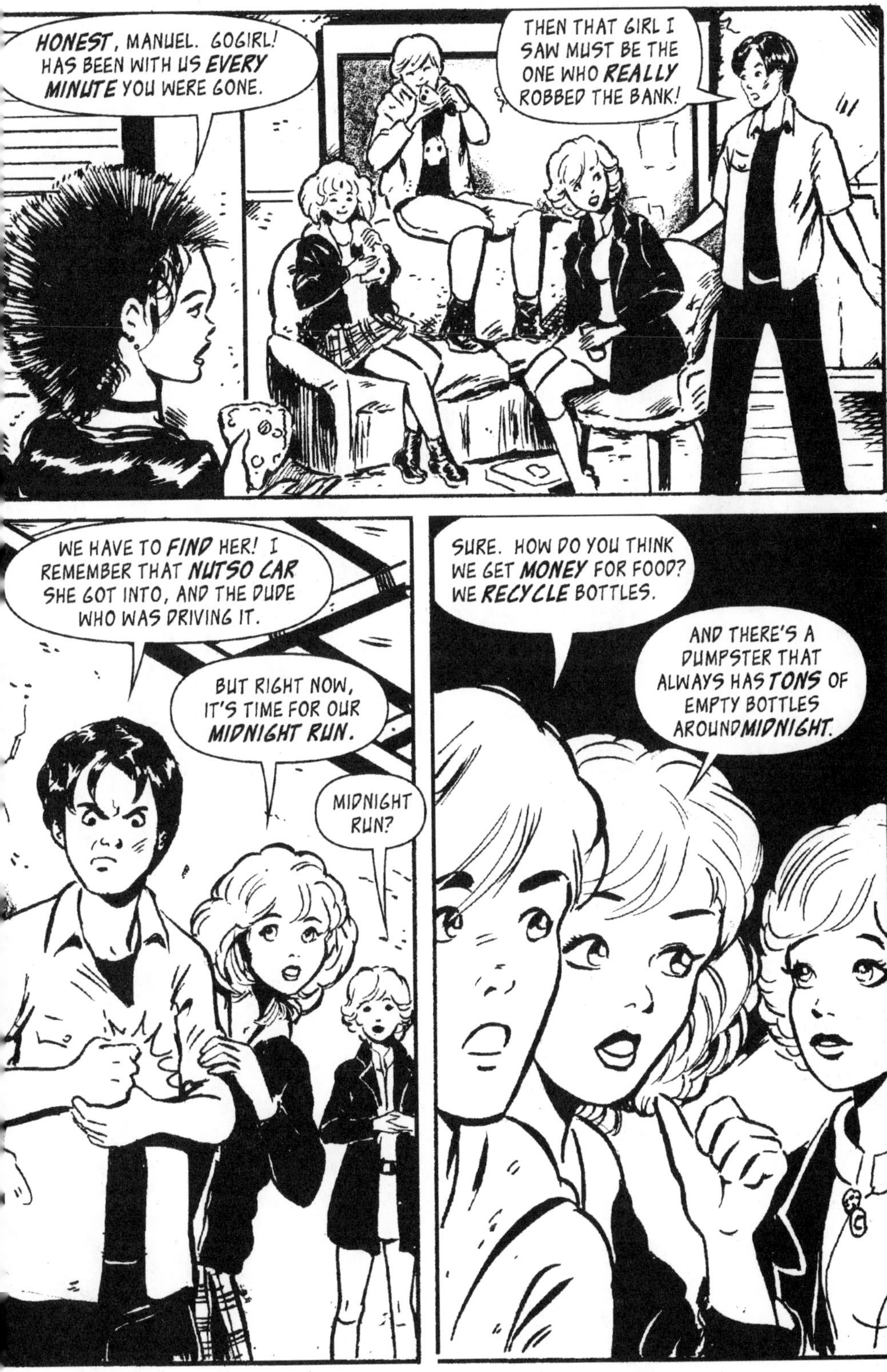
HONEST, MANUEL. GOGIRL! HAS BEEN WITH US EVERY MINUTE YOU WERE GONE.
THEN THAT GIRL I SAW MUST BE THE ONE WHO REALLY ROBBED THE BANK!
WE HAVE TO FIND HER! I REMEMBER THAT NUTSO CAR SHE GOT INTO, AND THE DUDE WHO WAS DRIVING IT.
BUT RIGHT NOW, IT'S TIME FOR OUR MIDNIGHT RUN.
MIDNIGHT RUN?
SURE. HOW DO YOU THINK WE GET MONEY FOR FOOD? WE RECYCLE BOTTLES.
AND THERE'S A DUMPSTER THAT ALWAYS HAS TONS OF EMPTY BOTTLES AROUND MIDNIGHT.

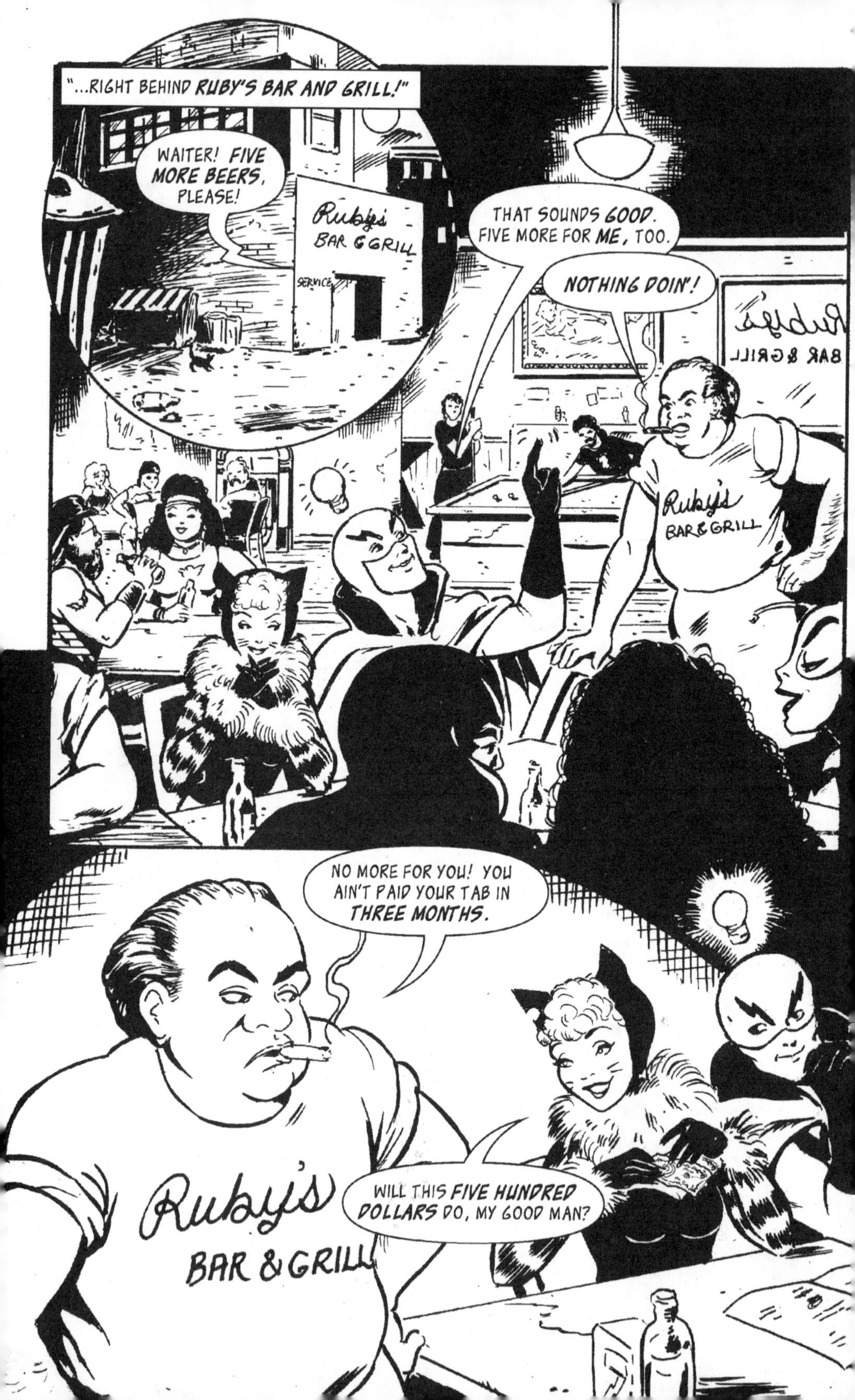
"...RIGHT BEHIND RUBY'S BAR AND GRILL!"
WAITER! FIVE MORE BEERS, PLEASE!
Ruby's BAR & GRILL
SERVICE
THAT SOUNDS GOOD. FIVE MORE FOR ME, TOO.
NOTHING DOIN'!
Ruby's BAR & GRILL
NO MORE FOR YOU! YOU AIN'T PAID YOUR TAB IN THREE MONTHS.
Ruby's BAR & GRILL
WILL THIS FIVE HUNDRED DOLLARS DO, MY GOOD MAN?

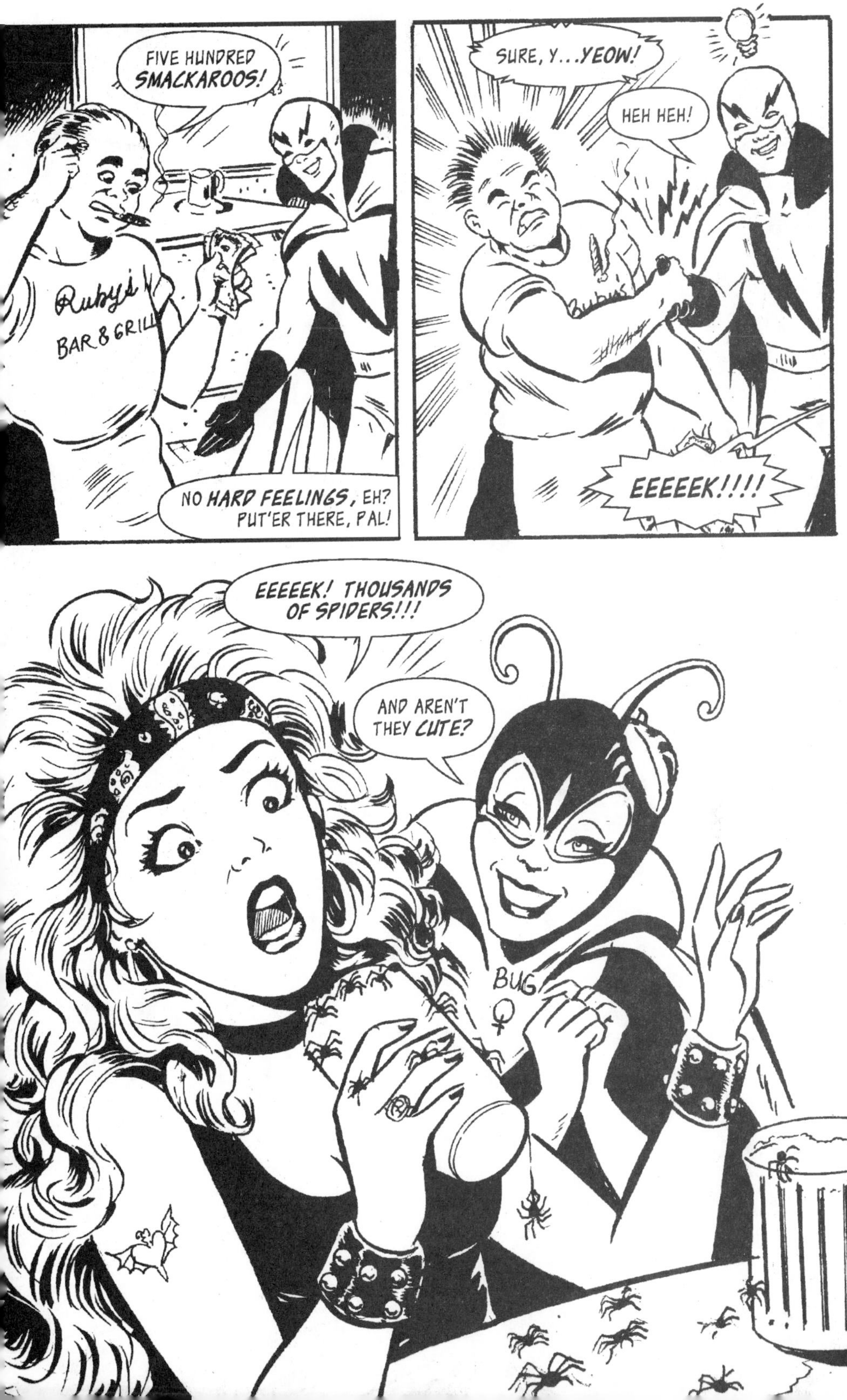
FIVE HUNDRED SMACKAROOS!
Ruby's BAR & GRILL
NO HARD FEELINGS, EH? PUT'ER THERE, PAL!
SURE, Y...YEOW!
HEH HEH!
EEEEEK!!!!
EEEEEK! THOUSANDS OF SPIDERS!!!
AND AREN'T THEY CUTE?
BUG

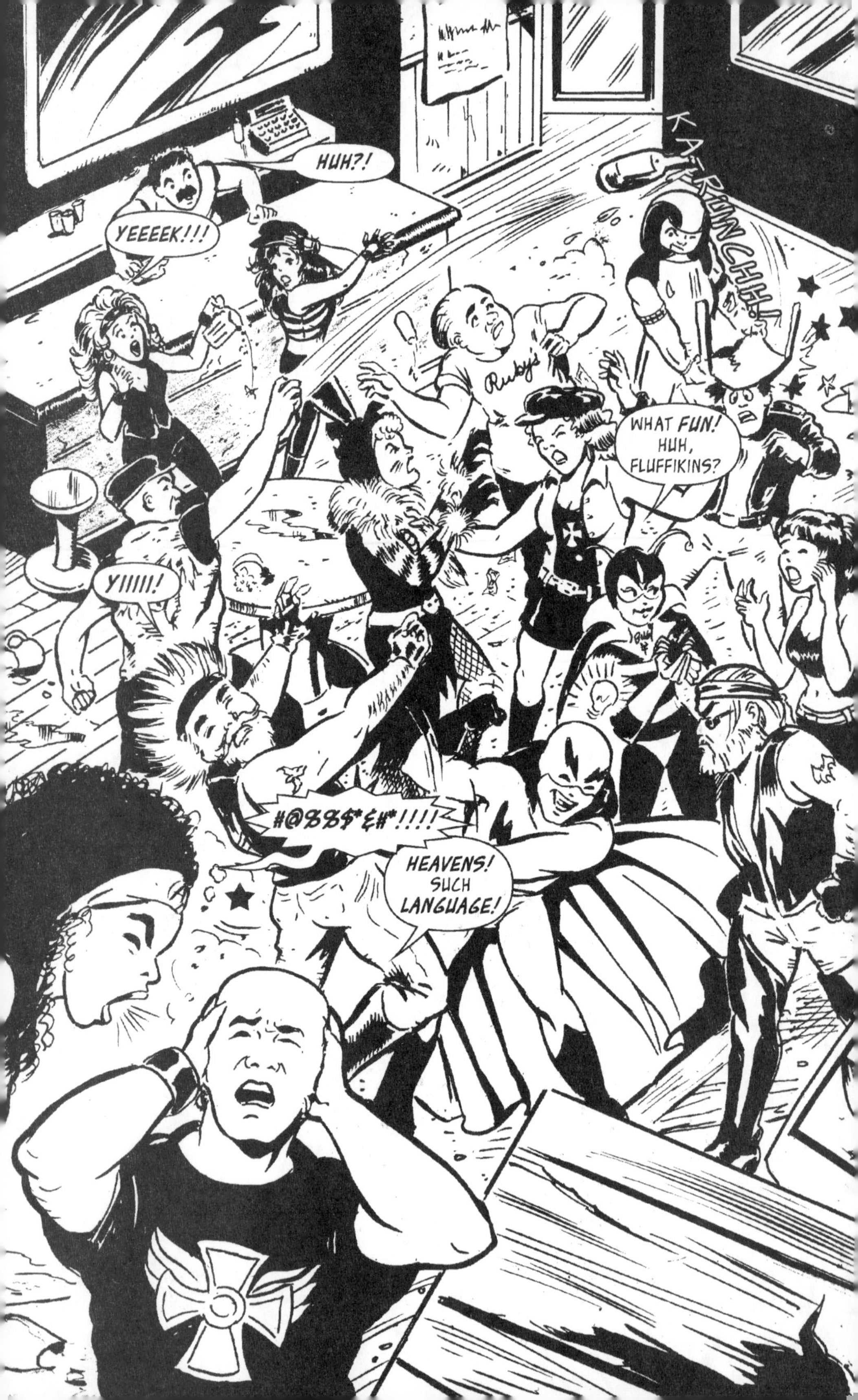
HUH?!
YEEEEK!!!
KA-RUNCHHH!
WHAT FUN! HUH, FLUFFIKINS?
YIIIII!
#@%%$*&#*!!!!
HEAVENS! SUCH LANGUAGE!

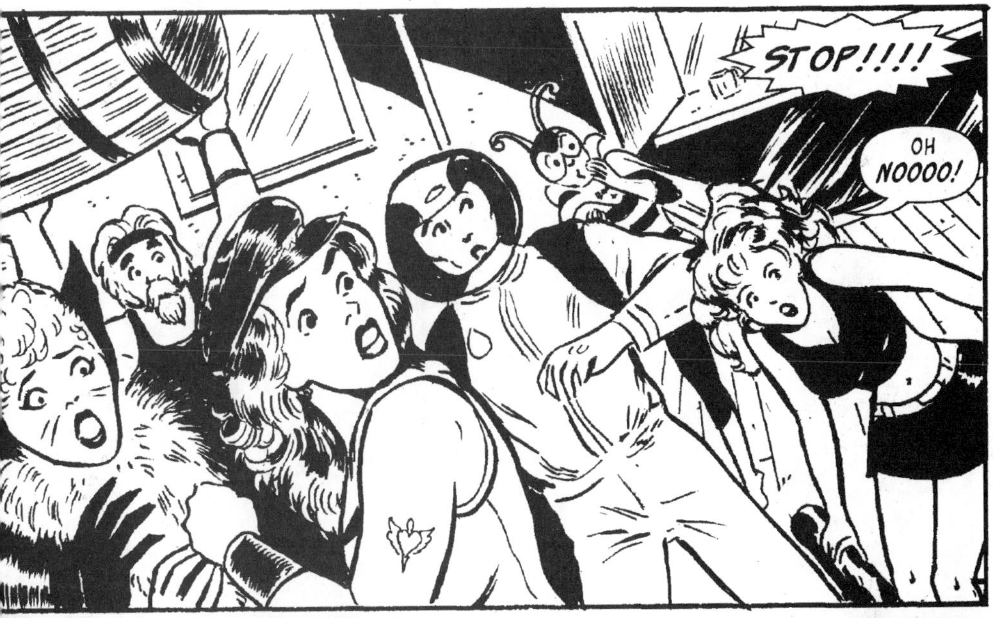
STOP!!!!!
OH NOOOO!

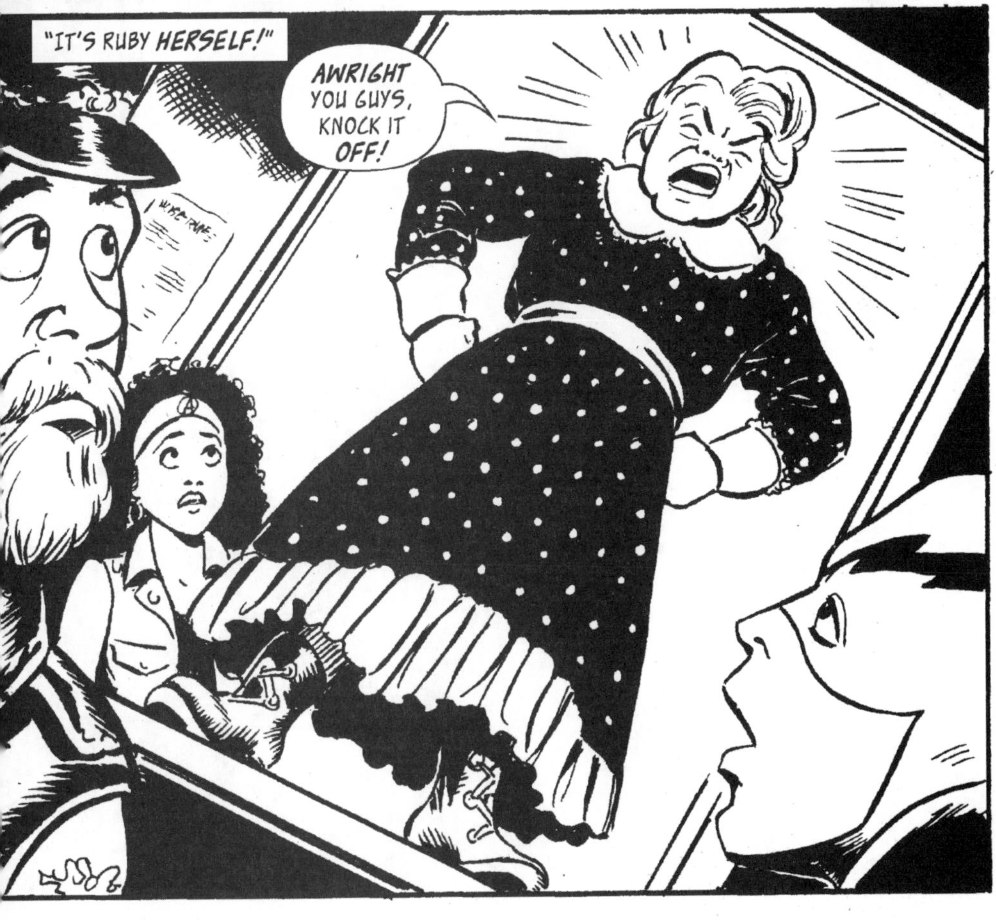
"IT'S RUBY HERSELF!"
AWRIGHT YOU GUYS, KNOCK IT OFF!

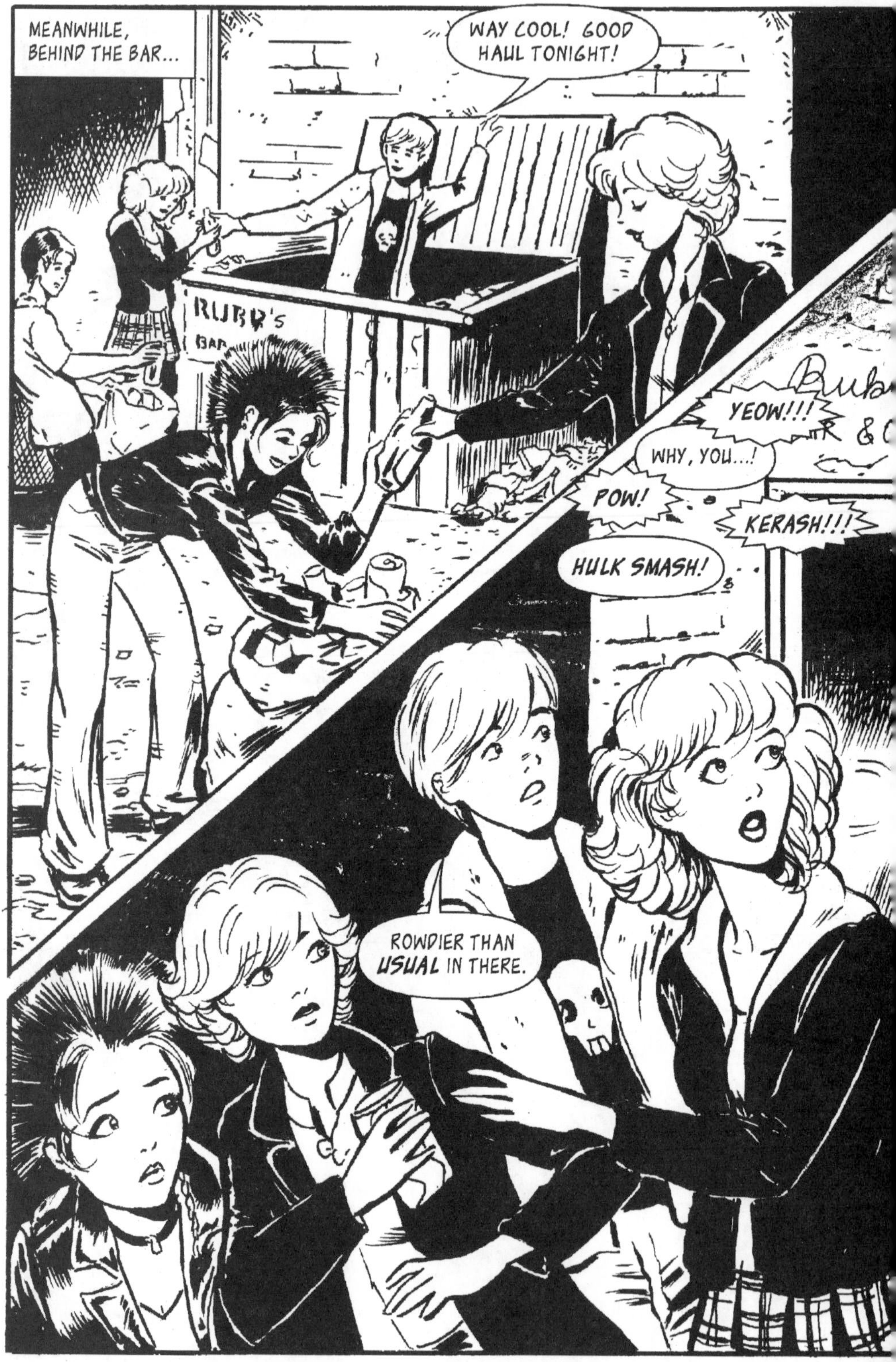
MEANWHILE, BEHIND THE BAR...
WAY COOL! GOOD HAUL TONIGHT!
RUBB's
YEOW!!!
WHY, YOU...!
POW!
KERASH!!!
HULK SMASH!
ROWDIER THAN *USUAL* IN THERE.

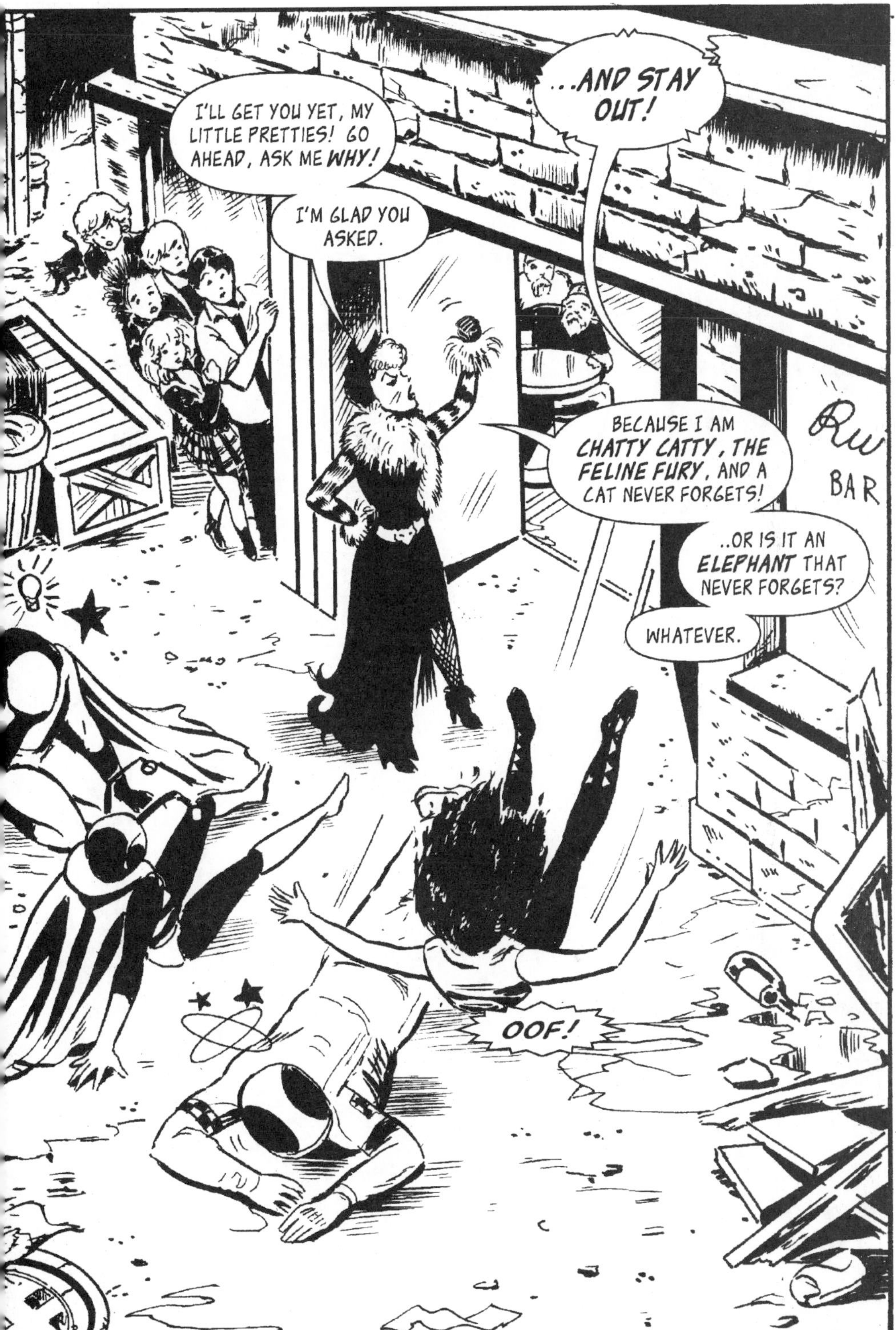
I'LL GET YOU YET, MY LITTLE PRETTIES! GO AHEAD, ASK ME WHY!
...AND STAY OUT!
I'M GLAD YOU ASKED.
BECAUSE I AM CHATTY CATTY, THE FELINE FURY, AND A CAT NEVER FORGETS!
BAR
..OR IS IT AN ELEPHANT THAT NEVER FORGETS?
WHATEVER.
OOF!

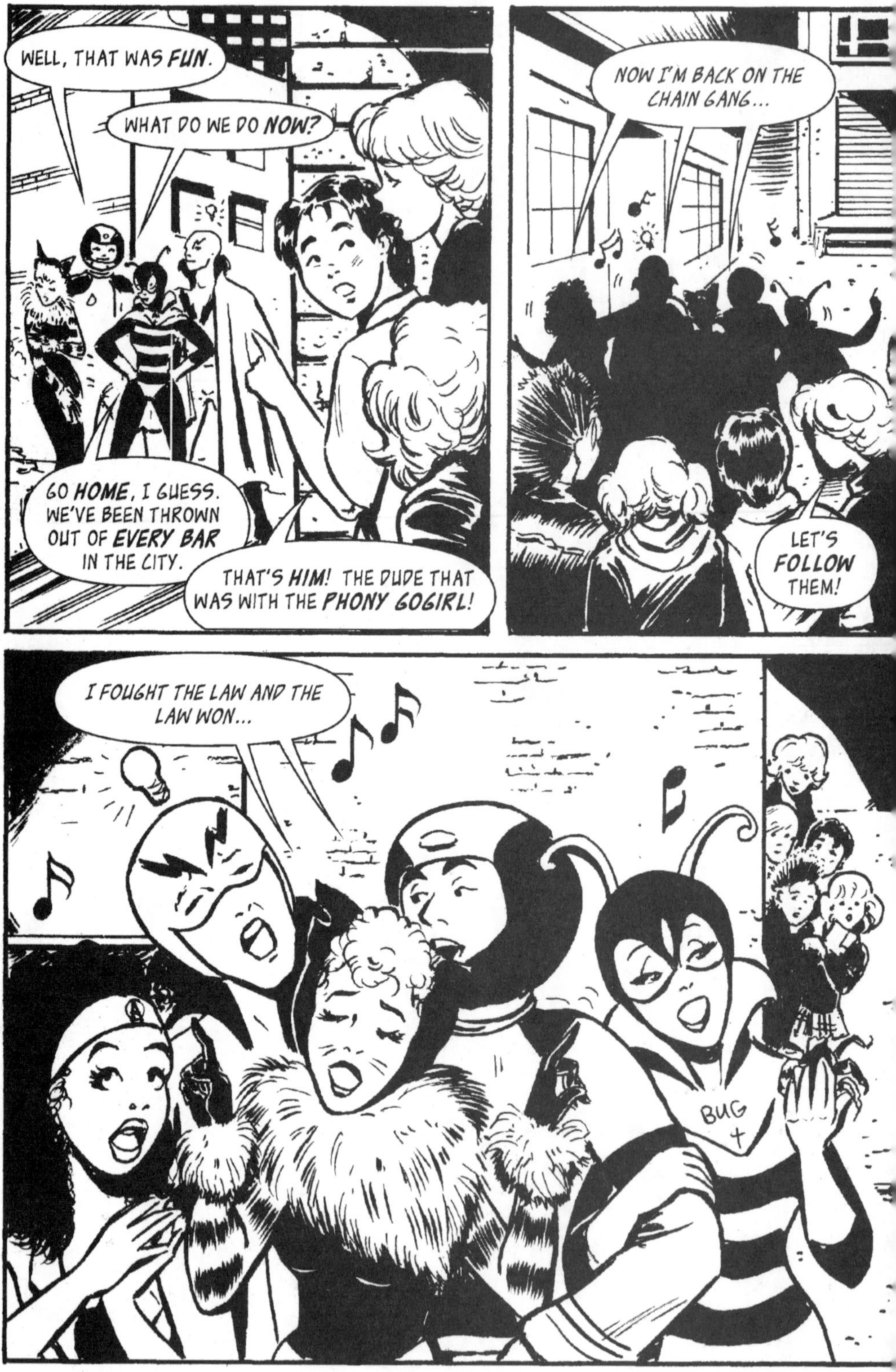
WELL, THAT WAS FUN.
WHAT DO WE DO NOW?
GO HOME, I GUESS. WE'VE BEEN THROWN OUT OF EVERY BAR IN THE CITY.
THAT'S HIM! THE DUDE THAT WAS WITH THE PHONY GOGIRL!
NOW I'M BACK ON THE CHAIN GANG...
LET'S FOLLOW THEM!
I FOUGHT THE LAW AND THE LAW WON...
BUG

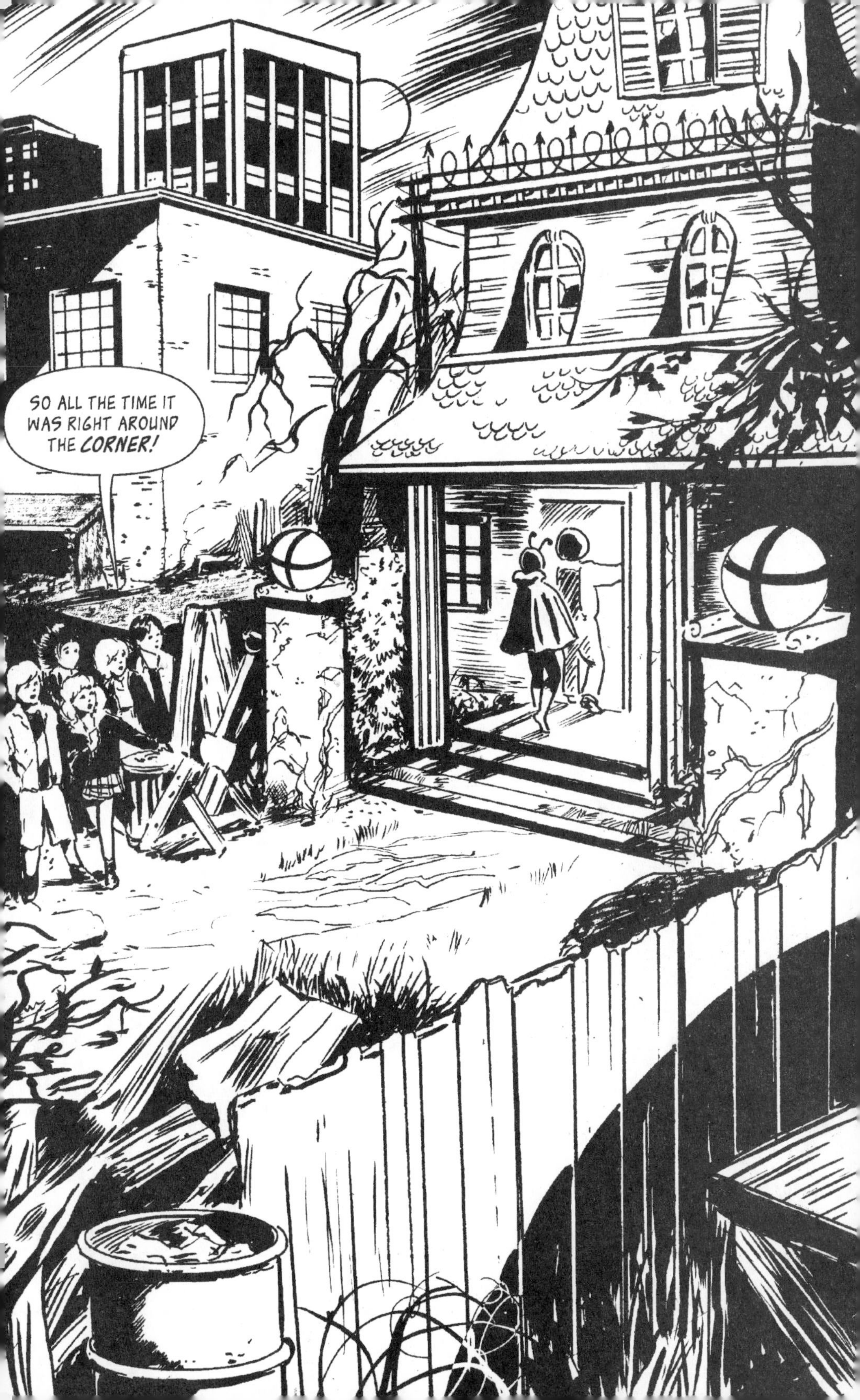
SO ALL THE TIME IT WAS RIGHT AROUND THE *CORNER!*

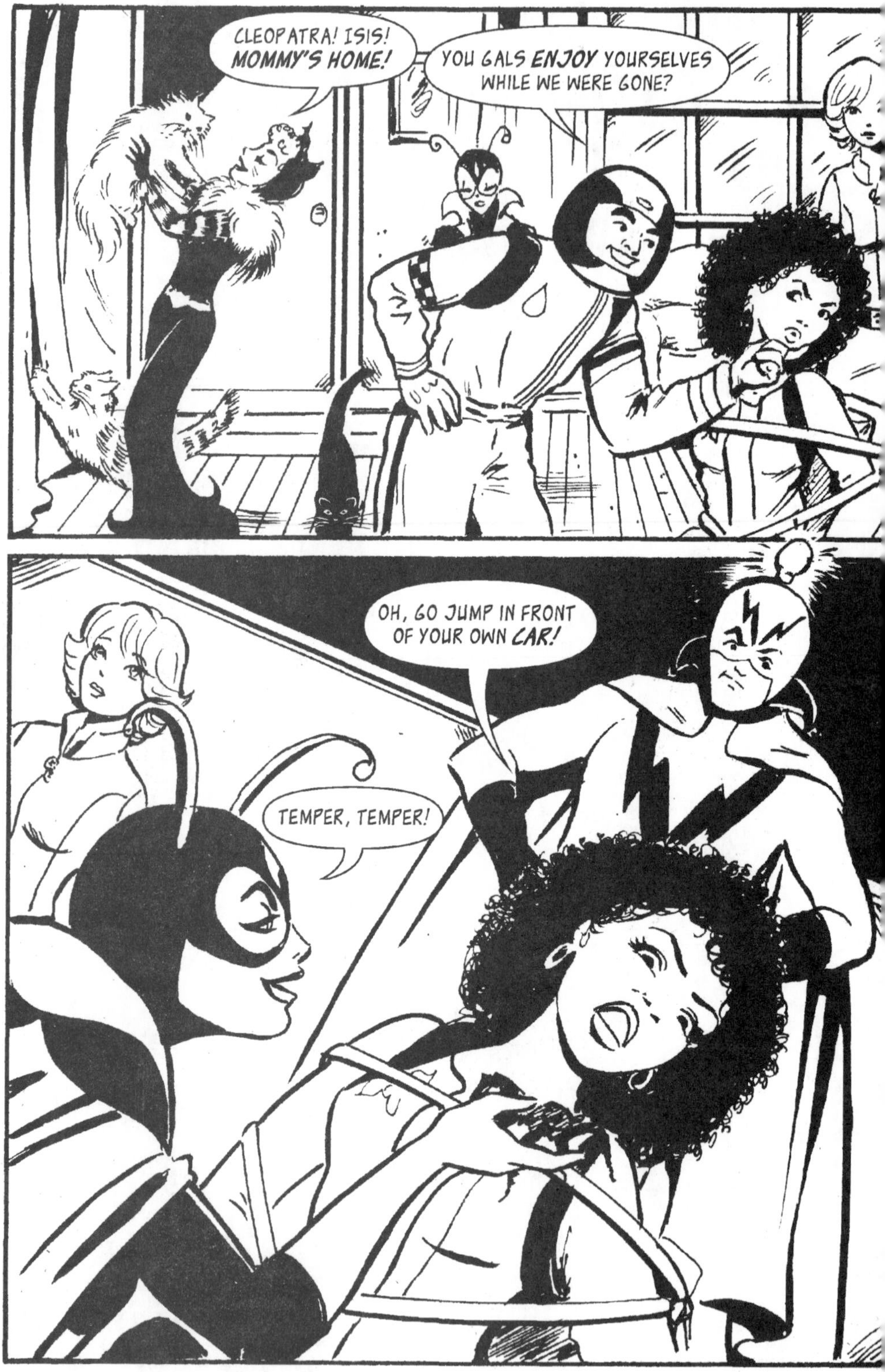
CLEOPATRA! ISIS! MOMMY'S HOME!
YOU GALS ENJOY YOURSELVES WHILE WE WERE GONE?
OH, GO JUMP IN FRONT OF YOUR OWN CAR!
TEMPER, TEMPER!

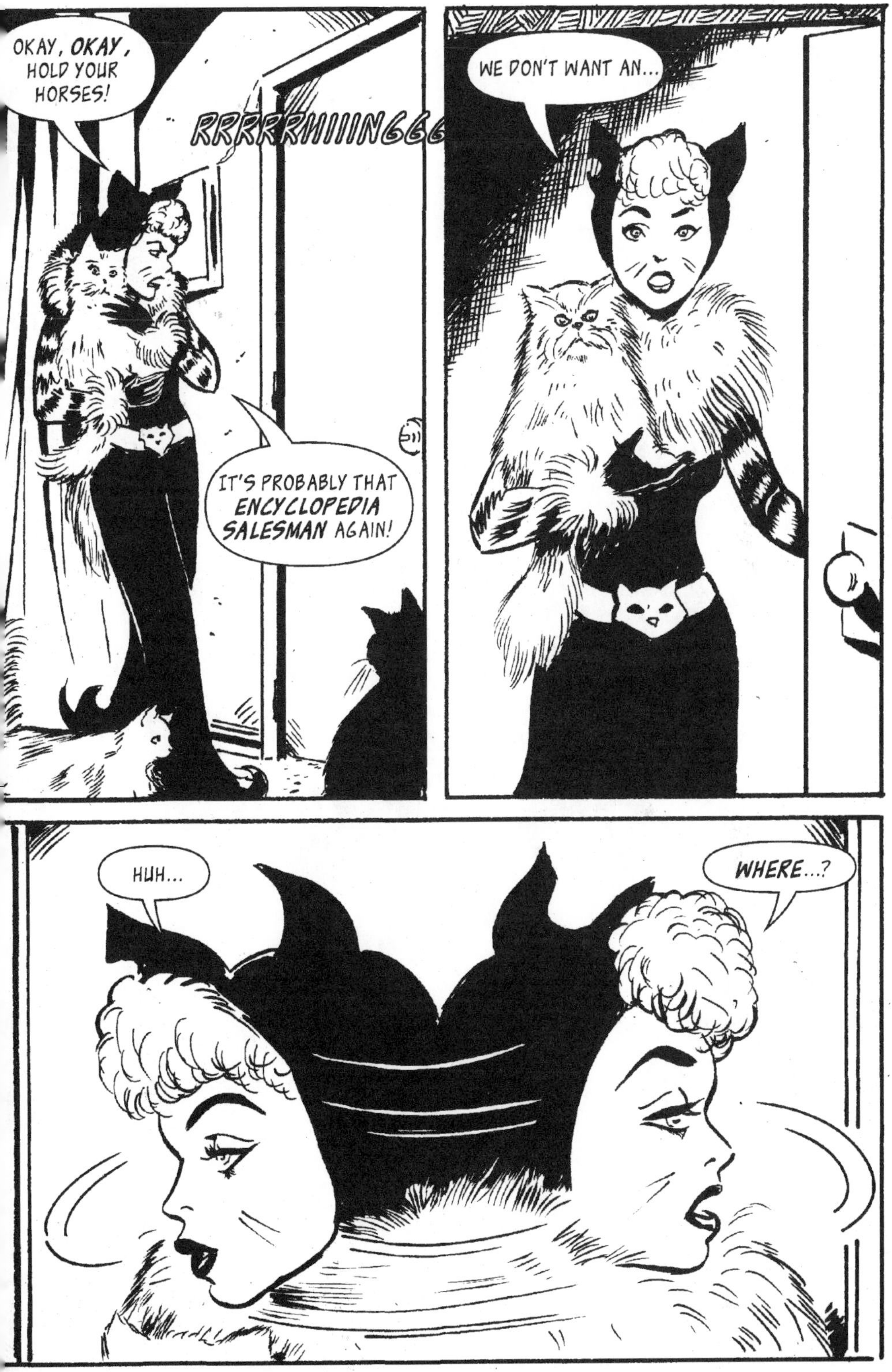
OKAY, OKAY, HOLD YOUR HORSES!
RRRRRHIIIING666
IT'S PROBABLY THAT ENCYCLOPEDIA SALESMAN AGAIN!
WE DON'T WANT AN...
HUH...
WHERE...?

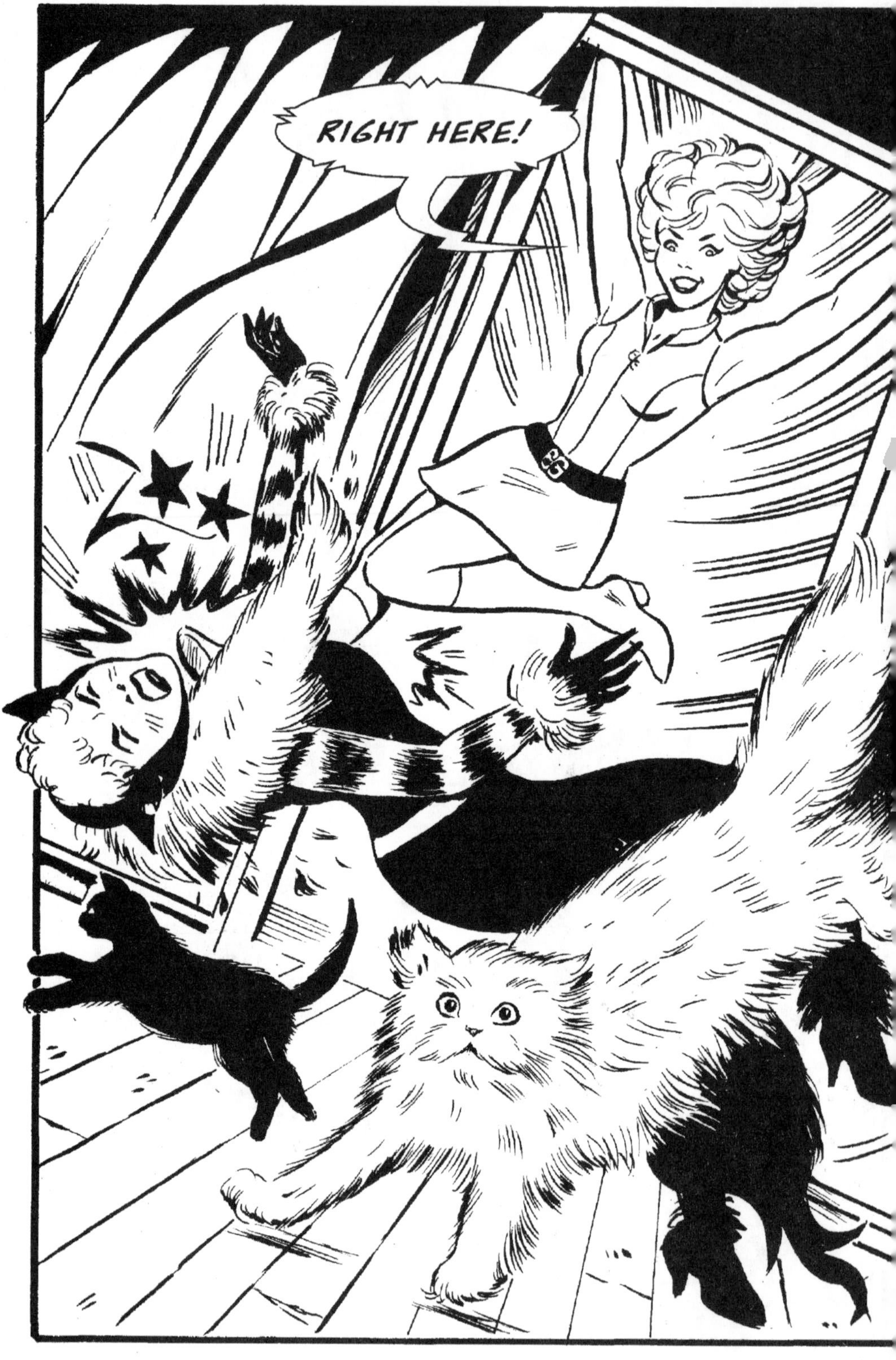
RIGHT HERE!

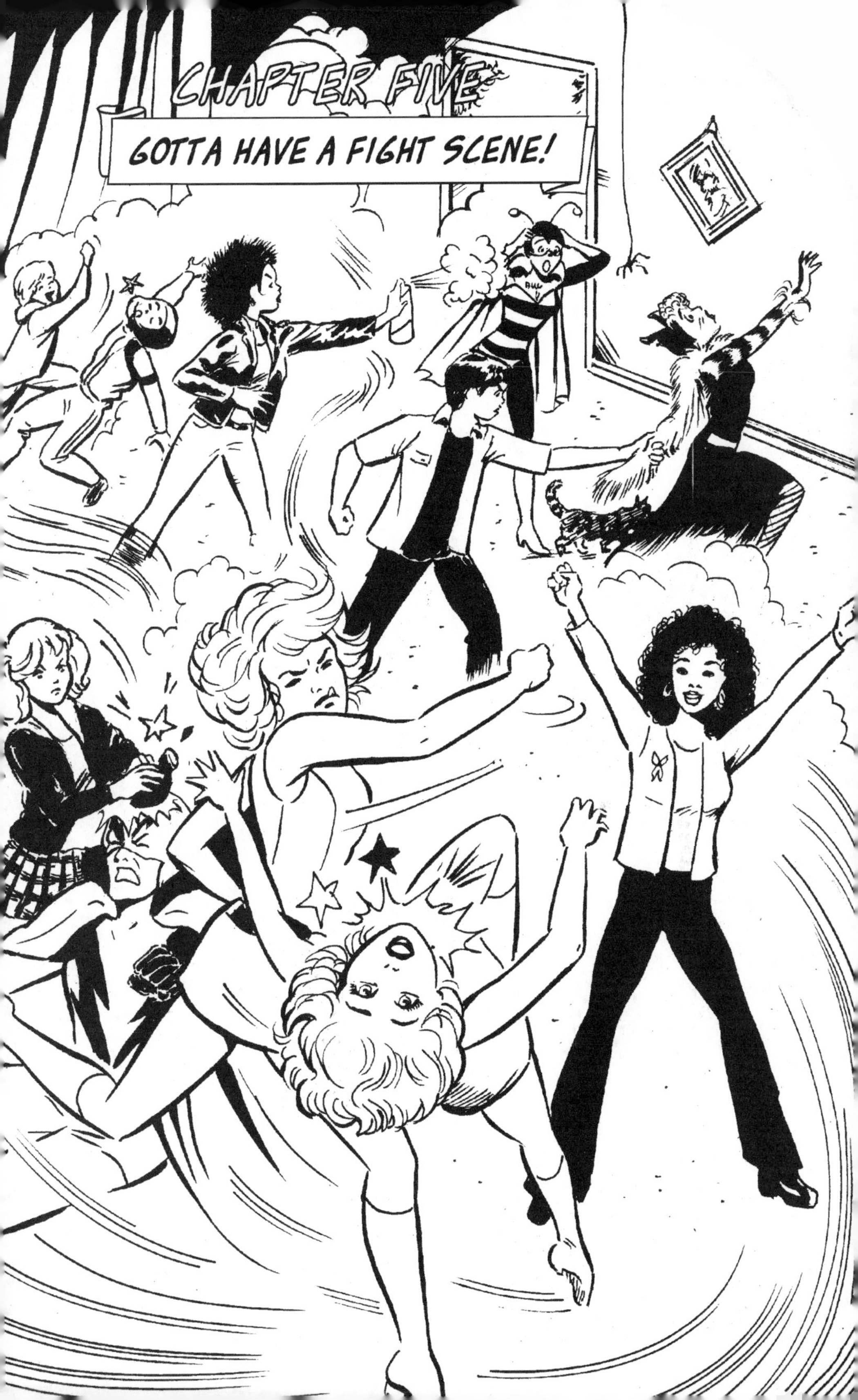
CHAPTER FIVE
GOTTA HAVE A FIGHT SCENE!

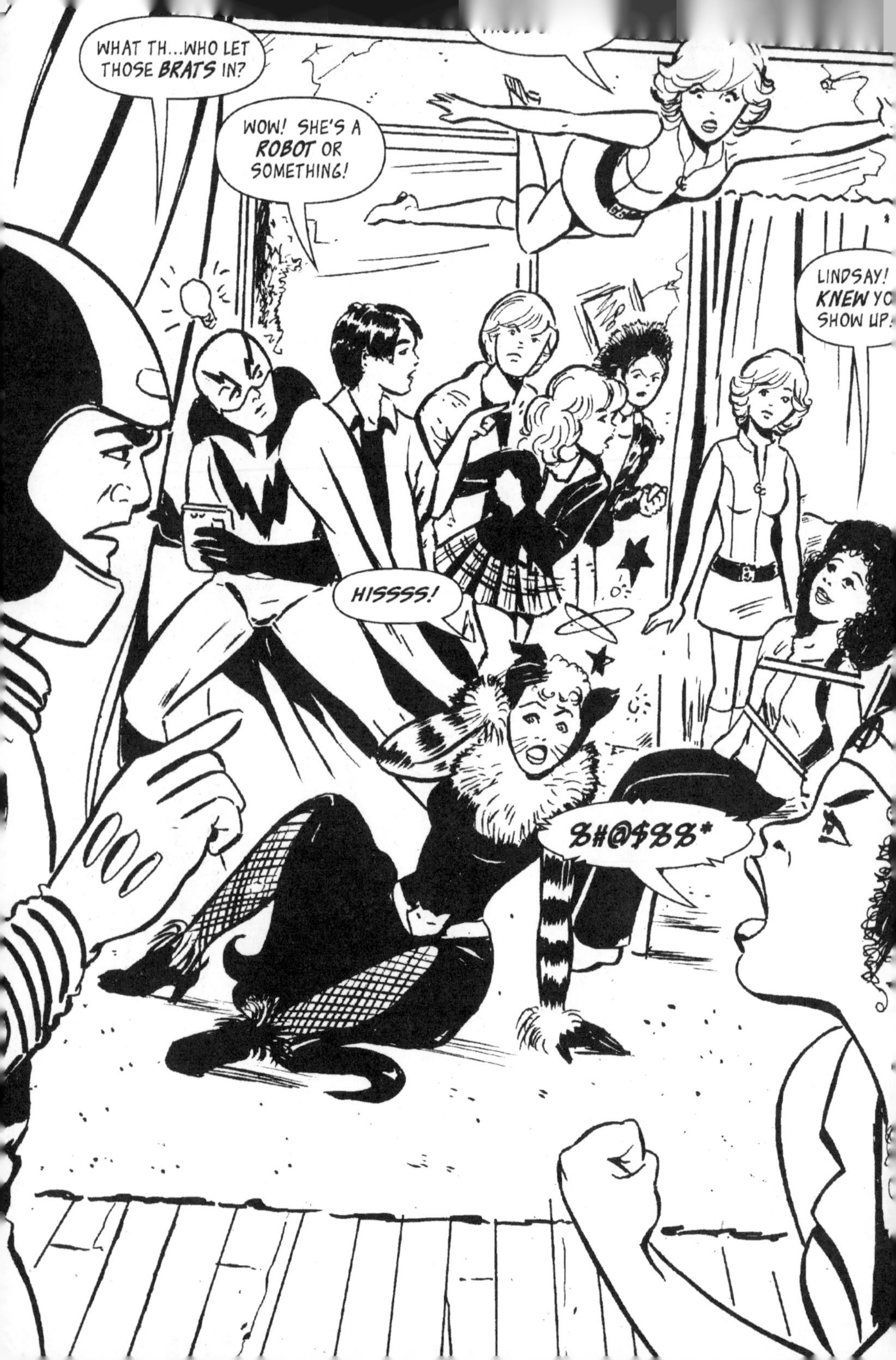
WHAT TH...WHO LET THOSE BRATS IN?
WOW! SHE'S A ROBOT OR SOMETHING!
LINDSAY! KNEW YO SHOW UP.
HISSSS!
%#@$%%*

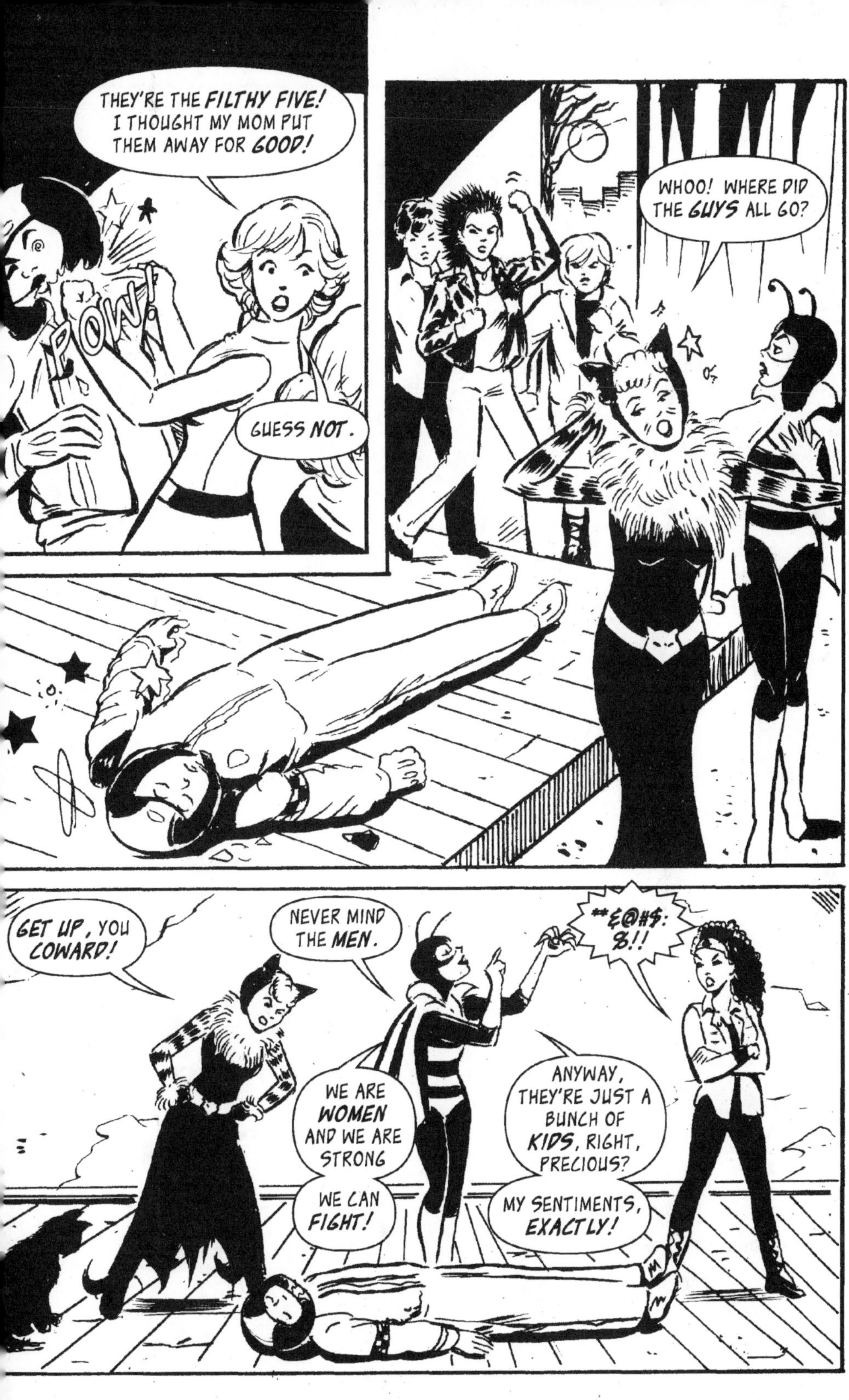
THEY'RE THE FILTHY FIVE! I THOUGHT MY MOM PUT THEM AWAY FOR GOOD!
POW!
GUESS NOT.
WHOO! WHERE DID THE GUYS ALL GO?
GET UP, YOU COWARD!
NEVER MIND THE MEN.
**&@#$: %!!
WE ARE WOMEN AND WE ARE STRONG
WE CAN FIGHT!
ANYWAY, THEY'RE JUST A BUNCH OF KIDS, RIGHT, PRECIOUS?
MY SENTIMENTS, EXACTLY!

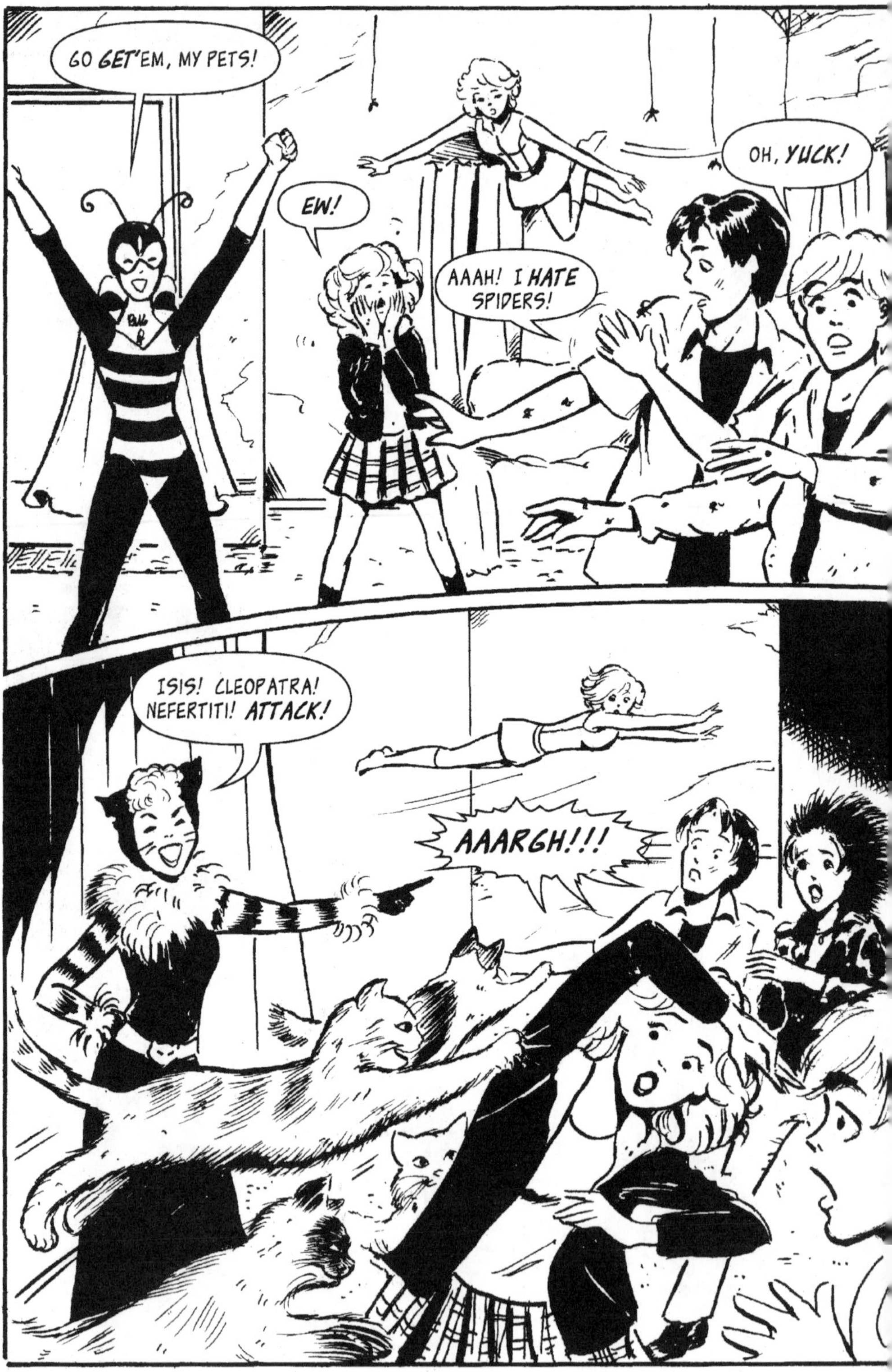
GO GET'EM, MY PETS!
EW!
AAAH! I HATE SPIDERS!
OH, YUCK!
ISIS! CLEOPATRA! NEFERTITI! ATTACK!
AAARGH!!!

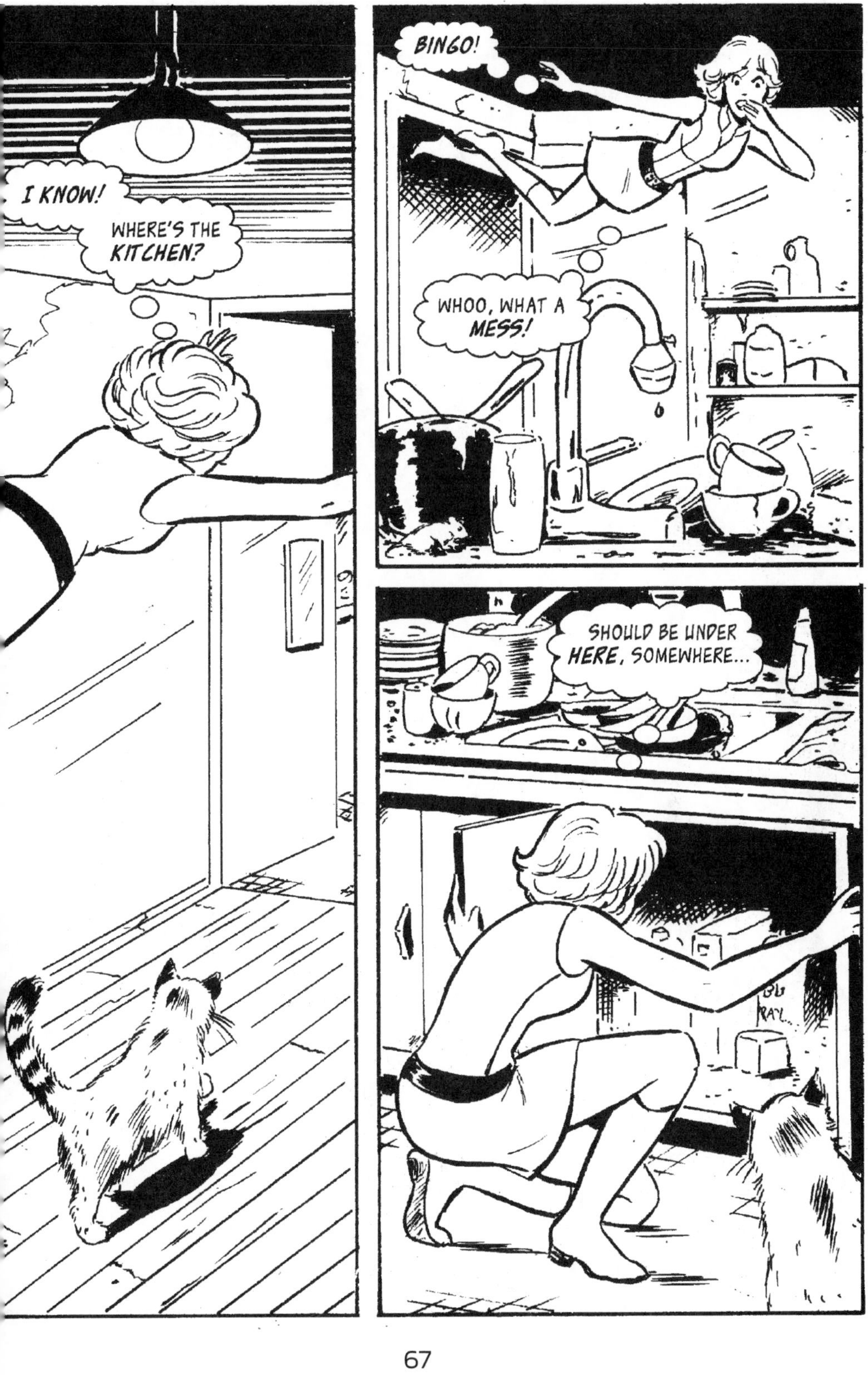
I KNOW!
WHERE'S THE *KITCHEN?*
*BINGO!*
WHOO, WHAT A *MESS!*
SHOULD BE UNDER *HERE*, SOMEWHERE...

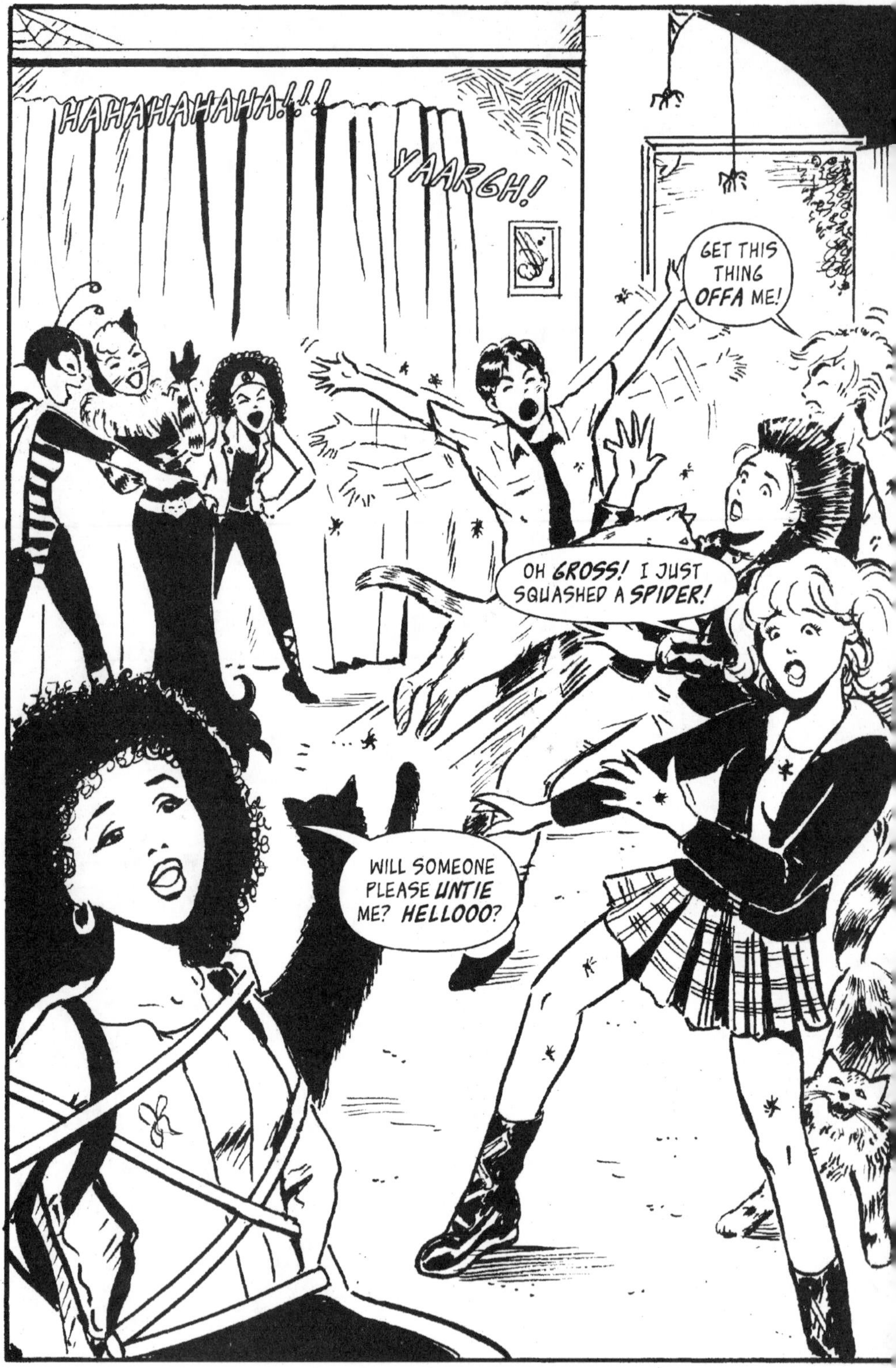
HAHAHAHAHAHA!!!!
YAARGH!
GET THIS THING OFFA ME!
OH GROSS! I JUST SQUASHED A SPIDER!
WILL SOMEONE PLEASE UNTIE ME? HELLOOO?

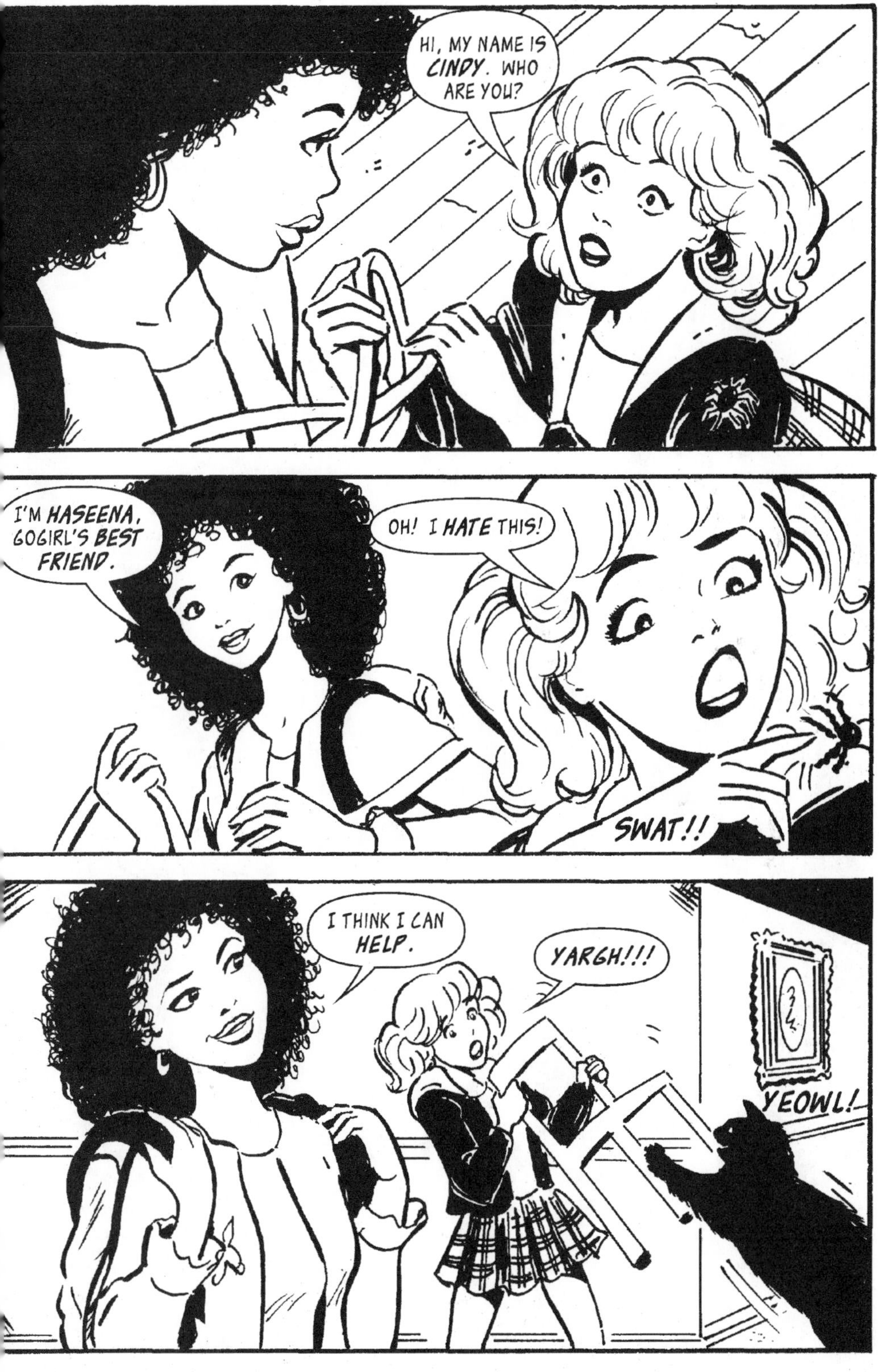
HI, MY NAME IS CINDY. WHO ARE YOU?
I'M HASEENA, GOGIRL'S BEST FRIEND.
OH! I HATE THIS!
SWAT!!
I THINK I CAN HELP.
YARGH!!!
YEOWL!

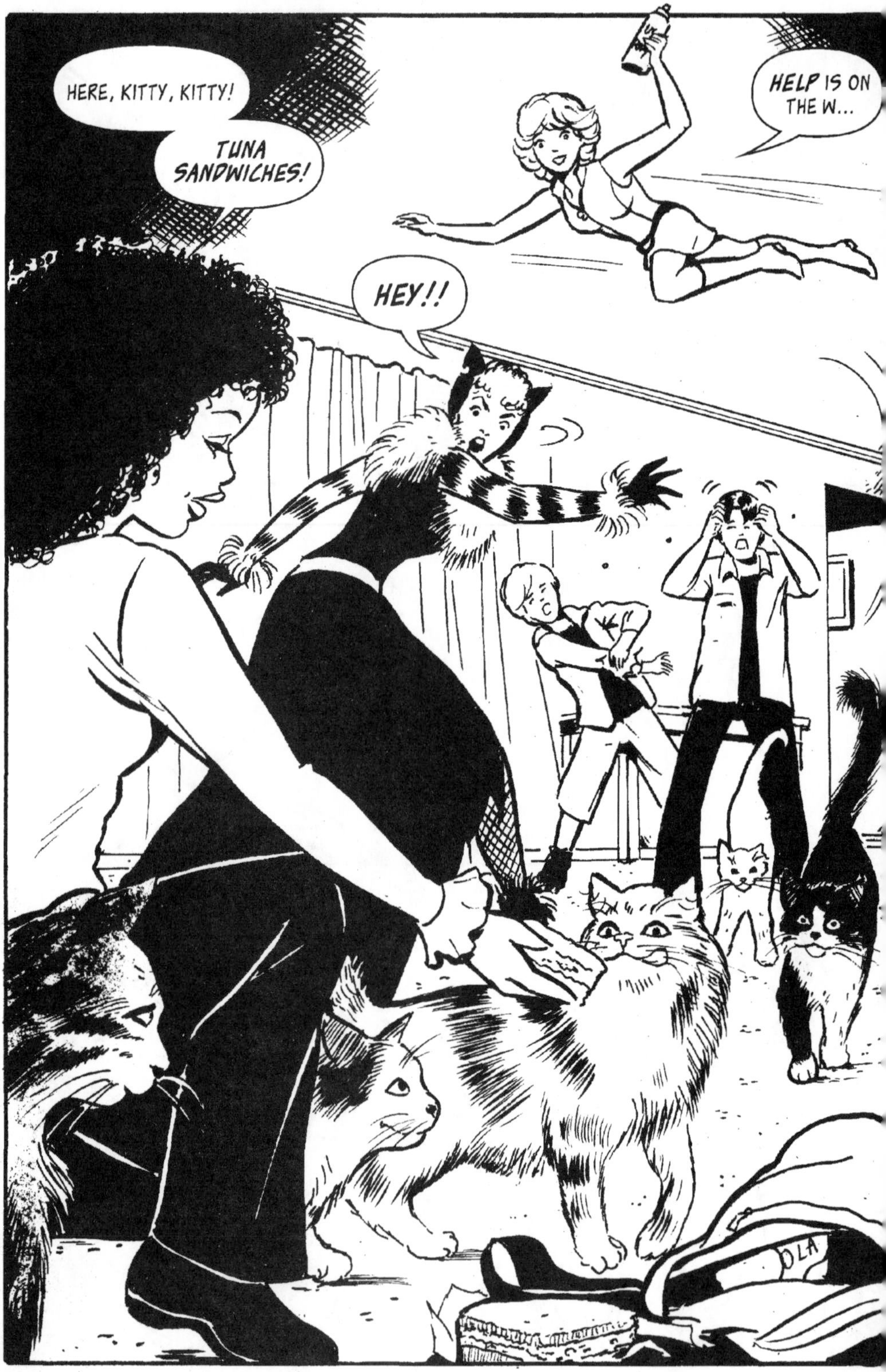
HERE, KITTY, KITTY!
TUNA SANDWICHES!
HELP IS ON THE W...
HEY!!
OLA

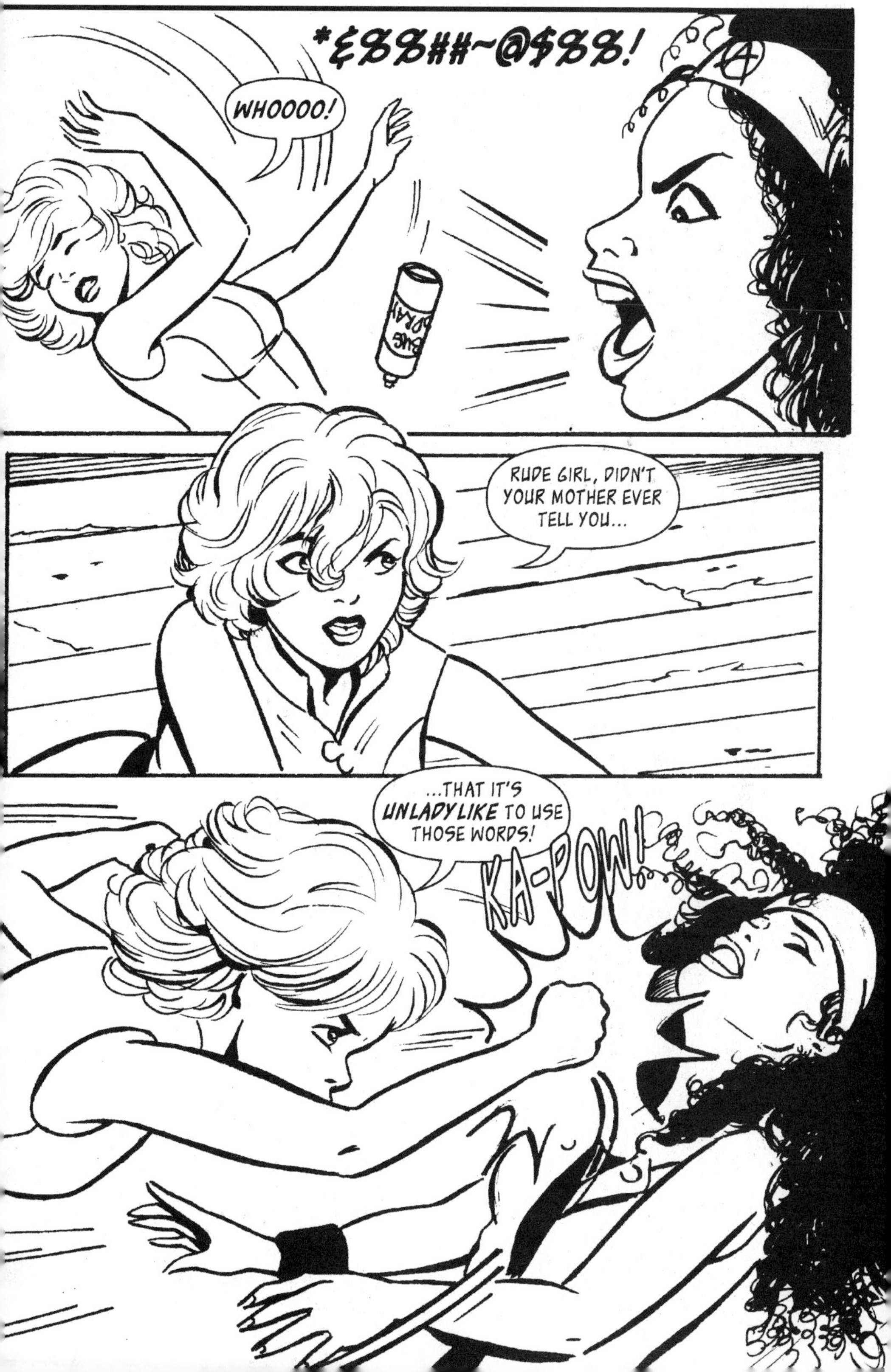
*&%%##~@$%%!
WHOOOO!
RUDE GIRL, DIDN'T YOUR MOTHER EVER TELL YOU...
...THAT IT'S UNLADYLIKE TO USE THOSE WORDS!
KA-POW!

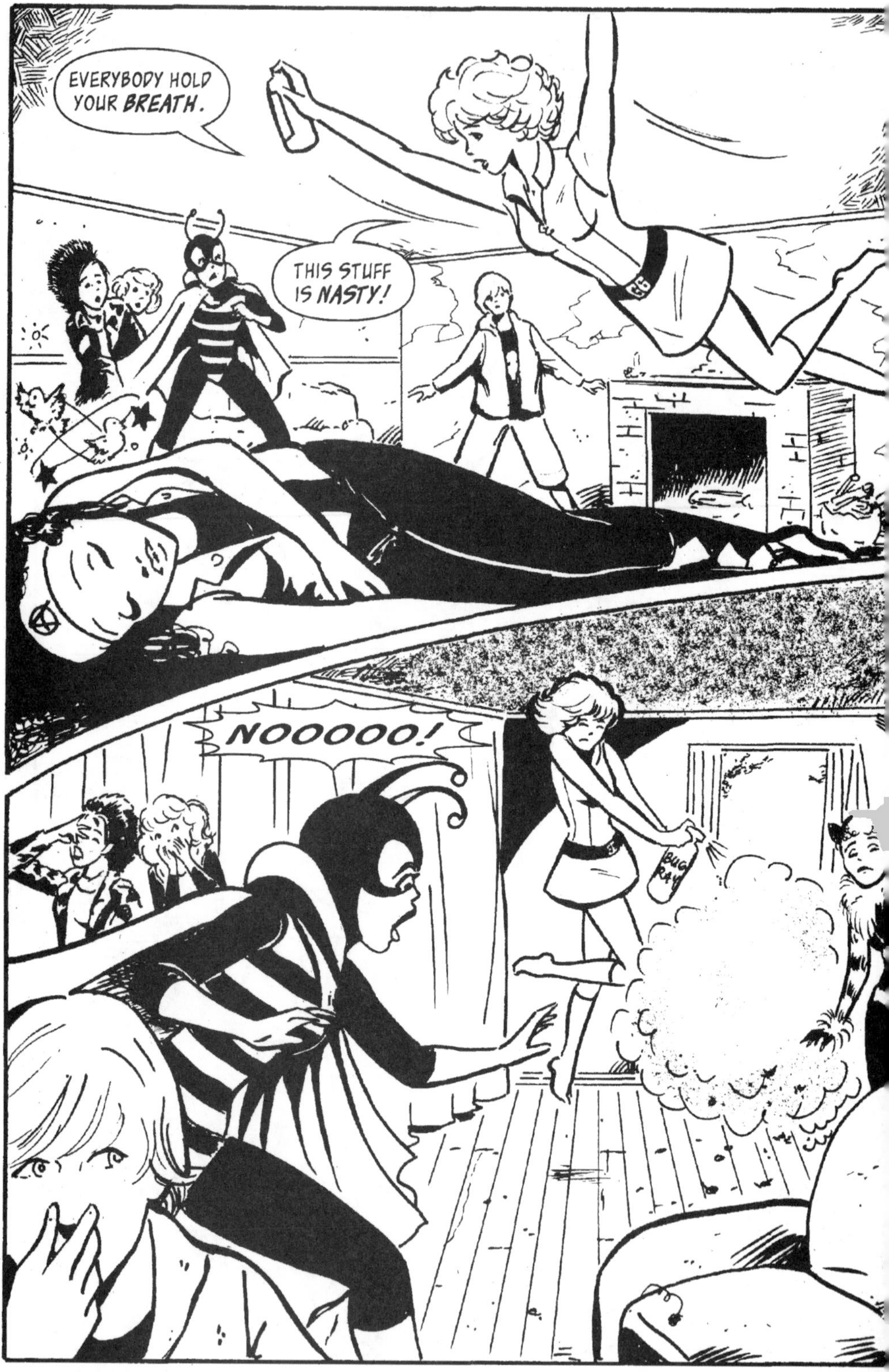
EVERYBODY HOLD YOUR BREATH.
THIS STUFF IS NASTY!
NOOOOO!
BUG RAY

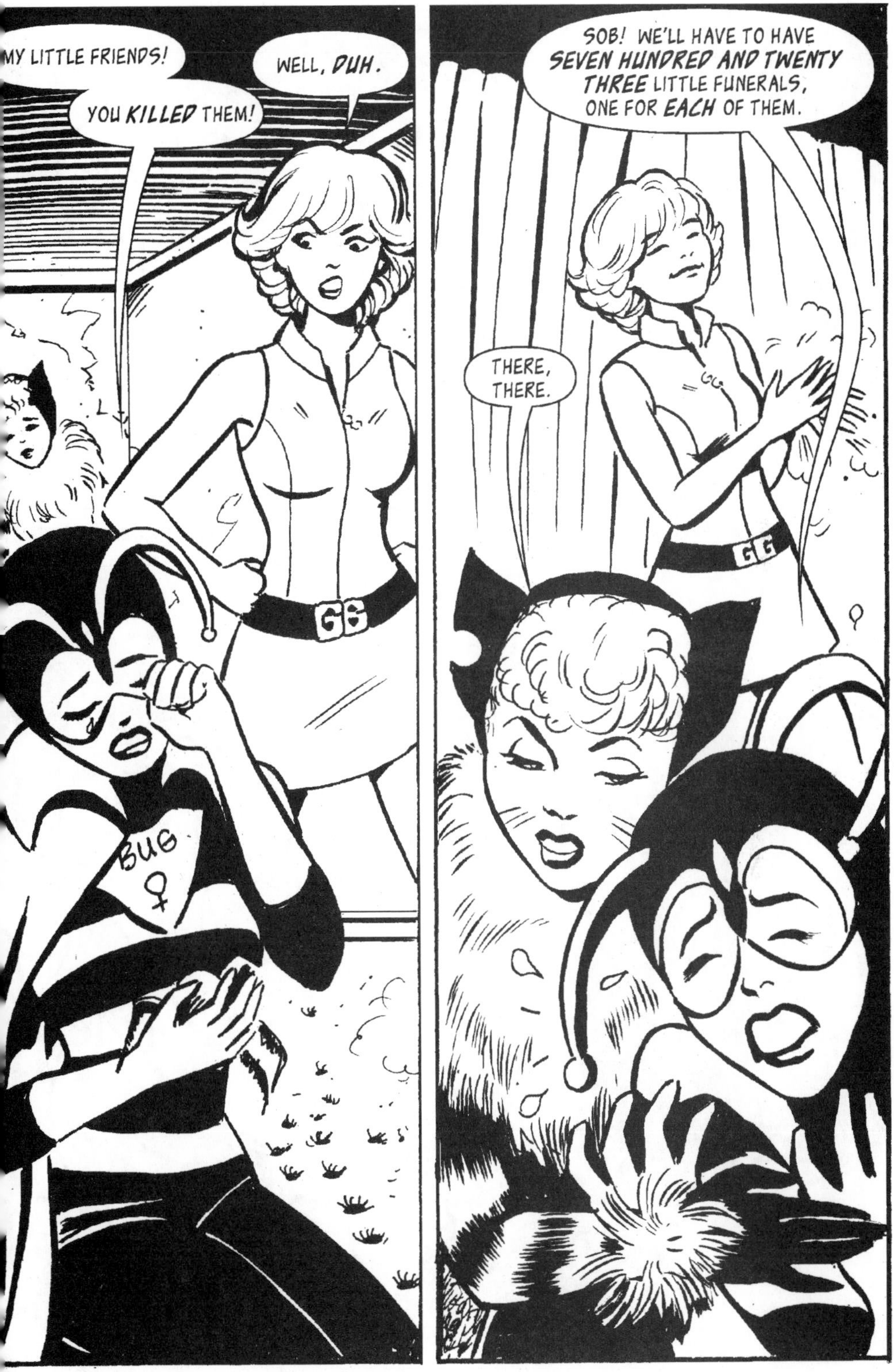
MY LITTLE FRIENDS!
YOU KILLED THEM!
WELL, DUH.
SOB! WE'LL HAVE TO HAVE SEVEN HUNDRED AND TWENTY THREE LITTLE FUNERALS, ONE FOR EACH OF THEM.
THERE, THERE.

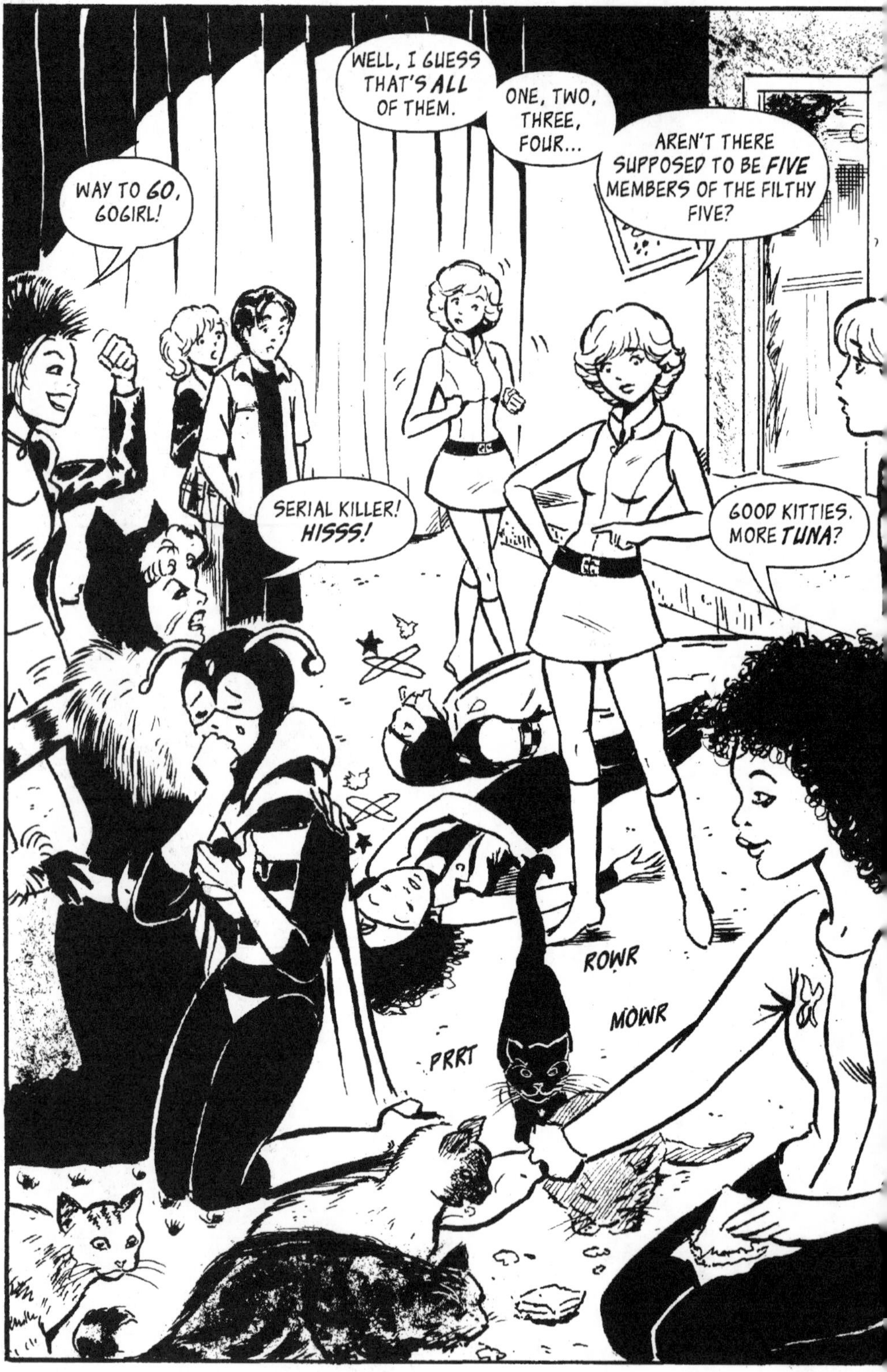
WAY TO GO, GOGIRL!
WELL, I GUESS THAT'S ALL OF THEM.
ONE, TWO, THREE, FOUR...
AREN'T THERE SUPPOSED TO BE FIVE MEMBERS OF THE FILTHY FIVE?
SERIAL KILLER! HISSS!
GOOD KITTIES. MORE TUNA?
ROWR
MOWR
PRRT

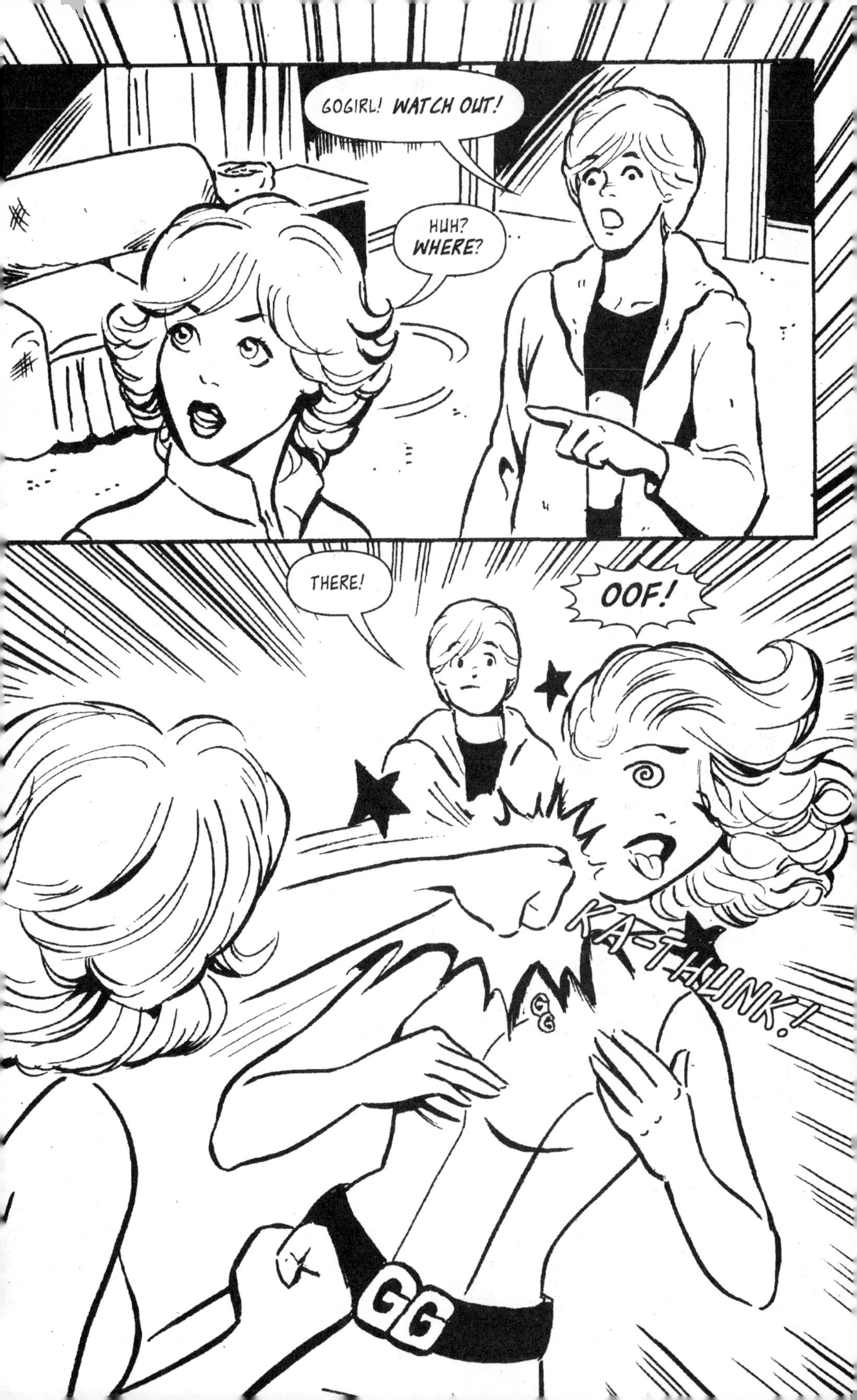
GOGIRL! WATCH OUT!
HUH? WHERE?
THERE!
OOF!
KA-THUNK!
GG
GG

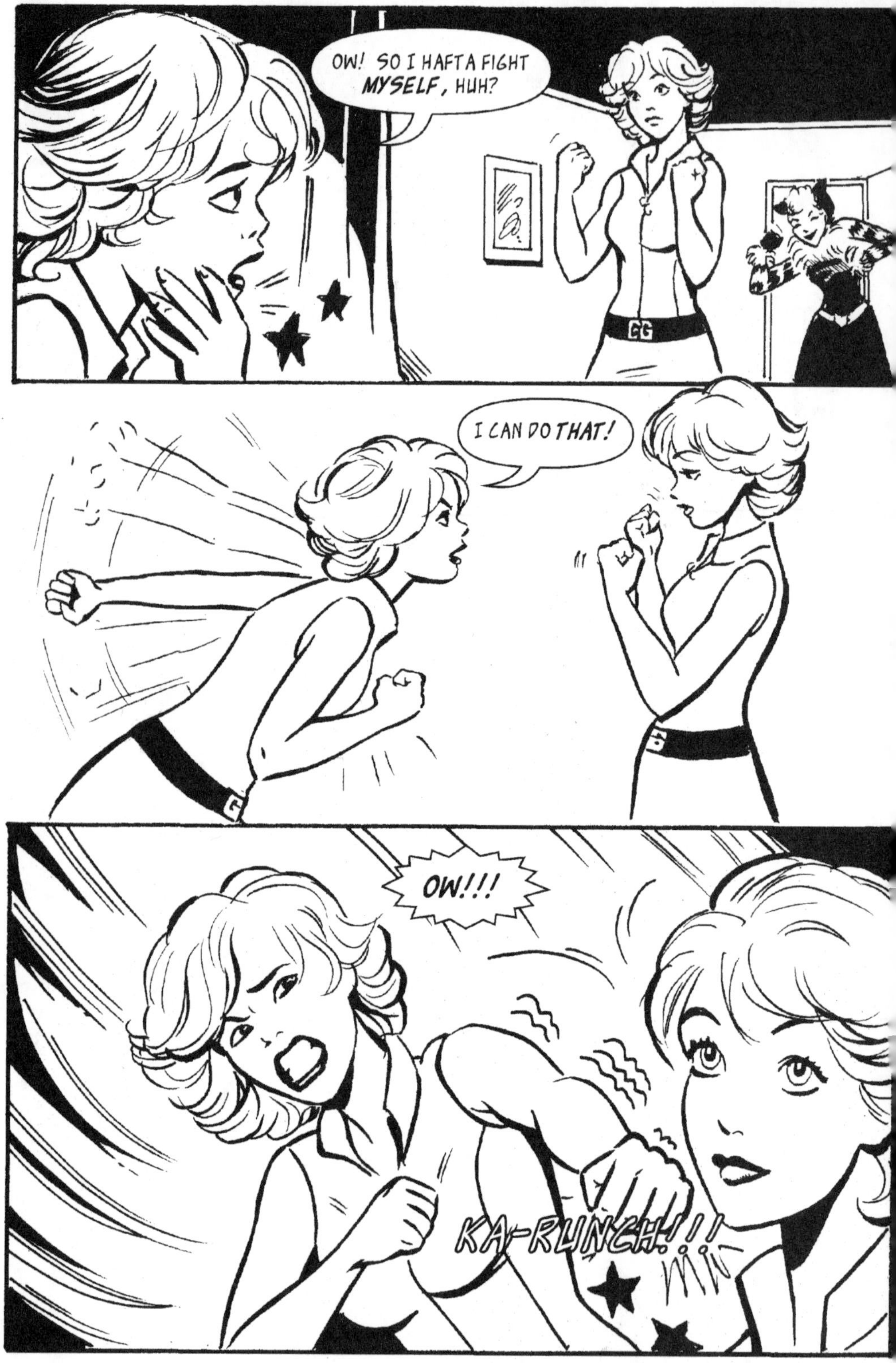

OW! SO I HAFTA FIGHT MYSELF, HUH?
I CAN DO THAT!
OW!!!
KA-RUNCH!!!

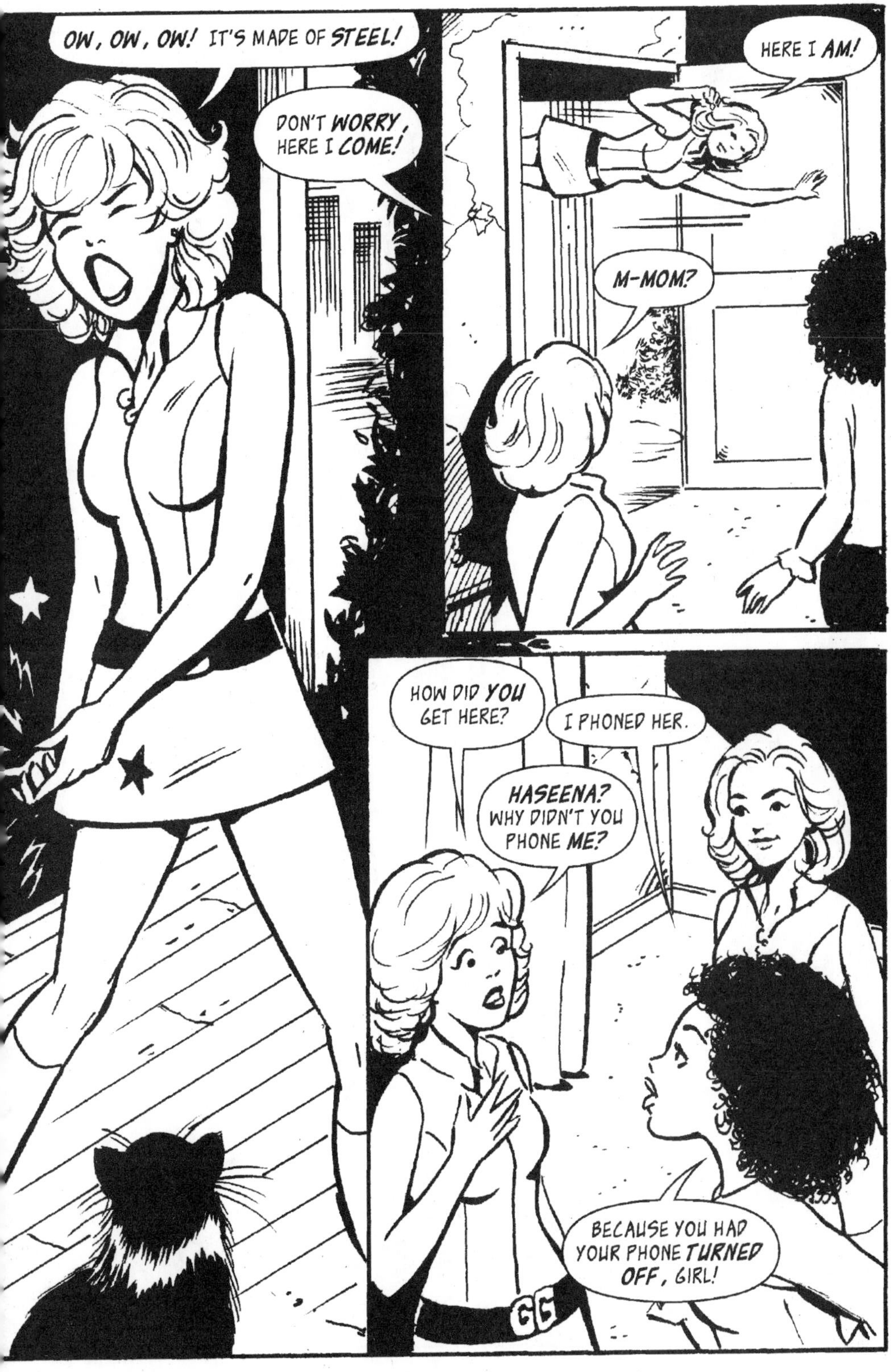

OW, OW, OW! IT'S MADE OF STEEL!
DON'T WORRY, HERE I COME!
...
HERE I AM!
M-MOM?
HOW DID YOU GET HERE?
I PHONED HER.
HASEENA? WHY DIDN'T YOU PHONE ME?
BECAUSE YOU HAD YOUR PHONE TURNED OFF, GIRL!

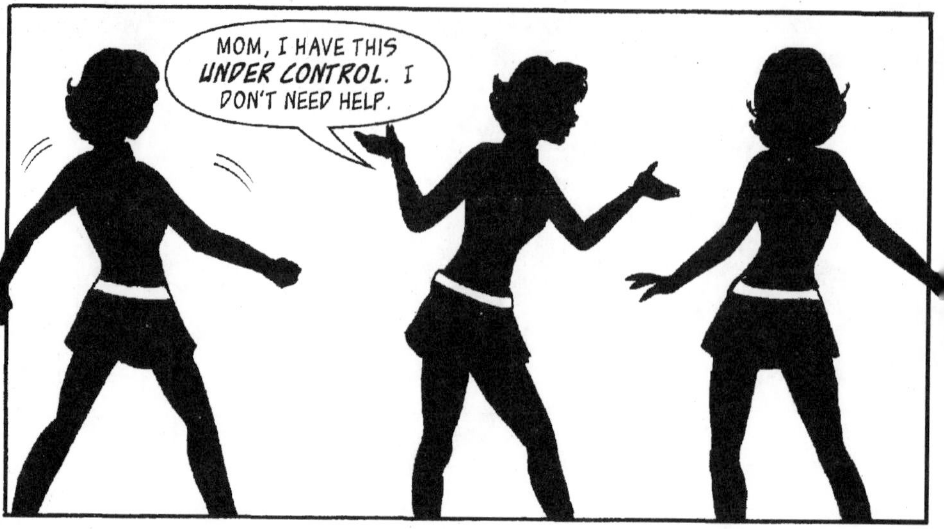
MOM, I HAVE THIS *UNDER CONTROL*. I DON'T NEED HELP.
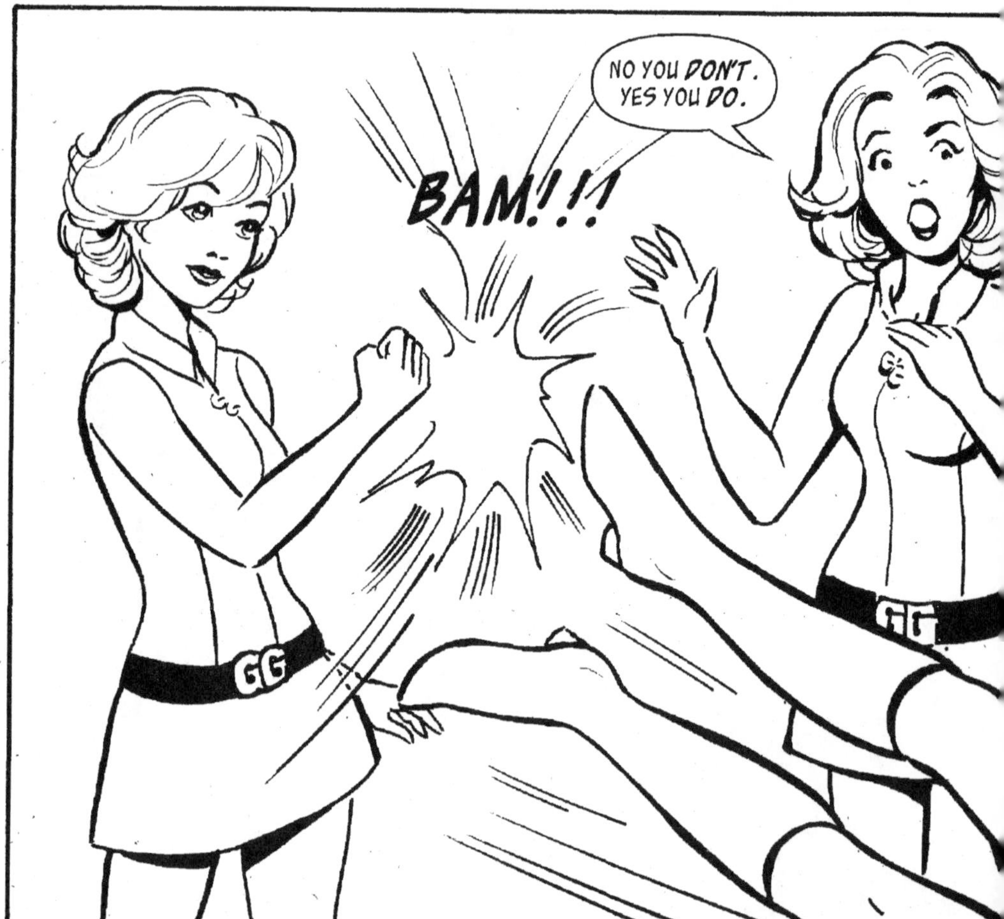
NO YOU *DON'T*. YES YOU *DO*.
BAM!!!
GG
GG

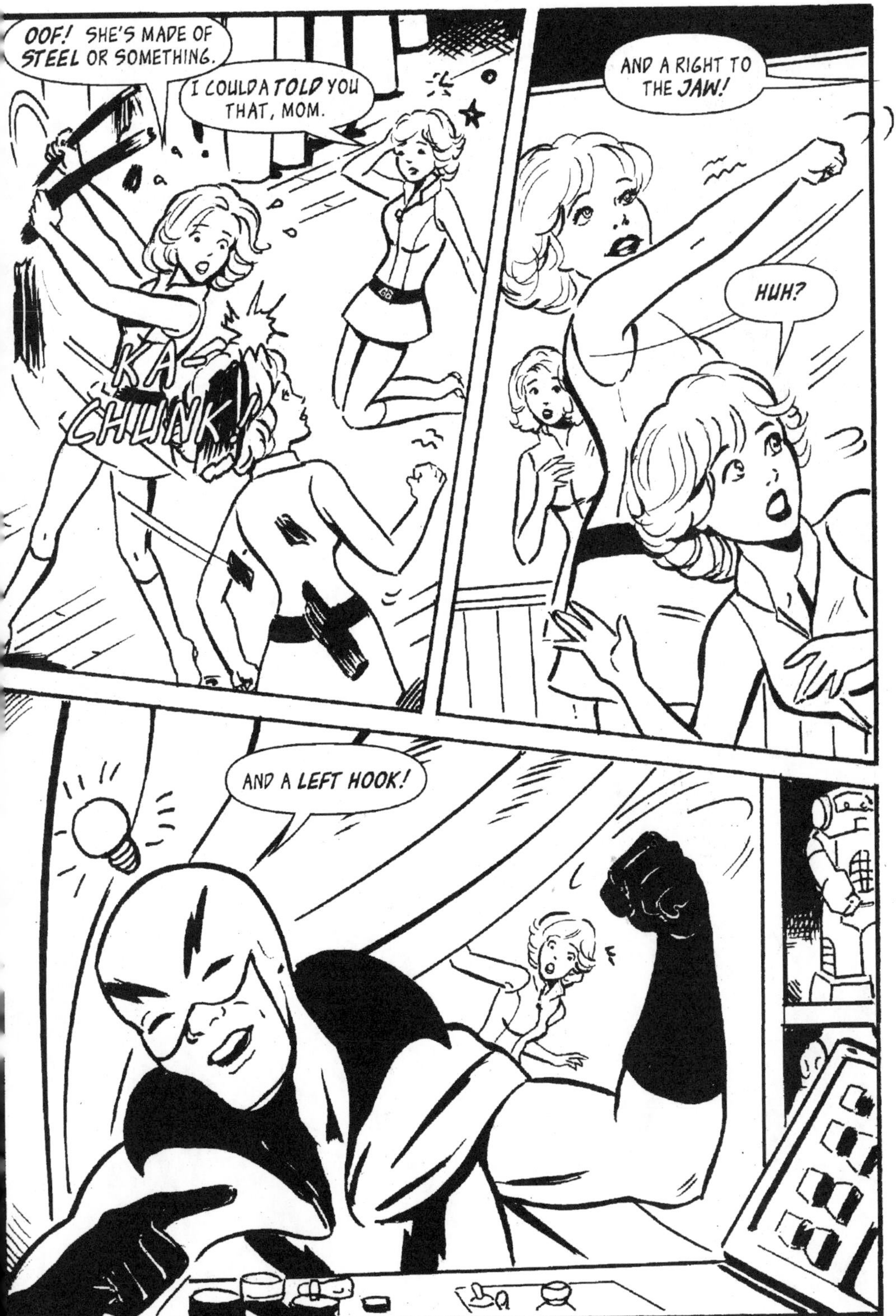
OOF! SHE'S MADE OF STEEL OR SOMETHING.
I COULDA TOLD YOU THAT, MOM.
KA-CHUNK!
AND A RIGHT TO THE JAW!
HUH?
AND A LEFT HOOK!

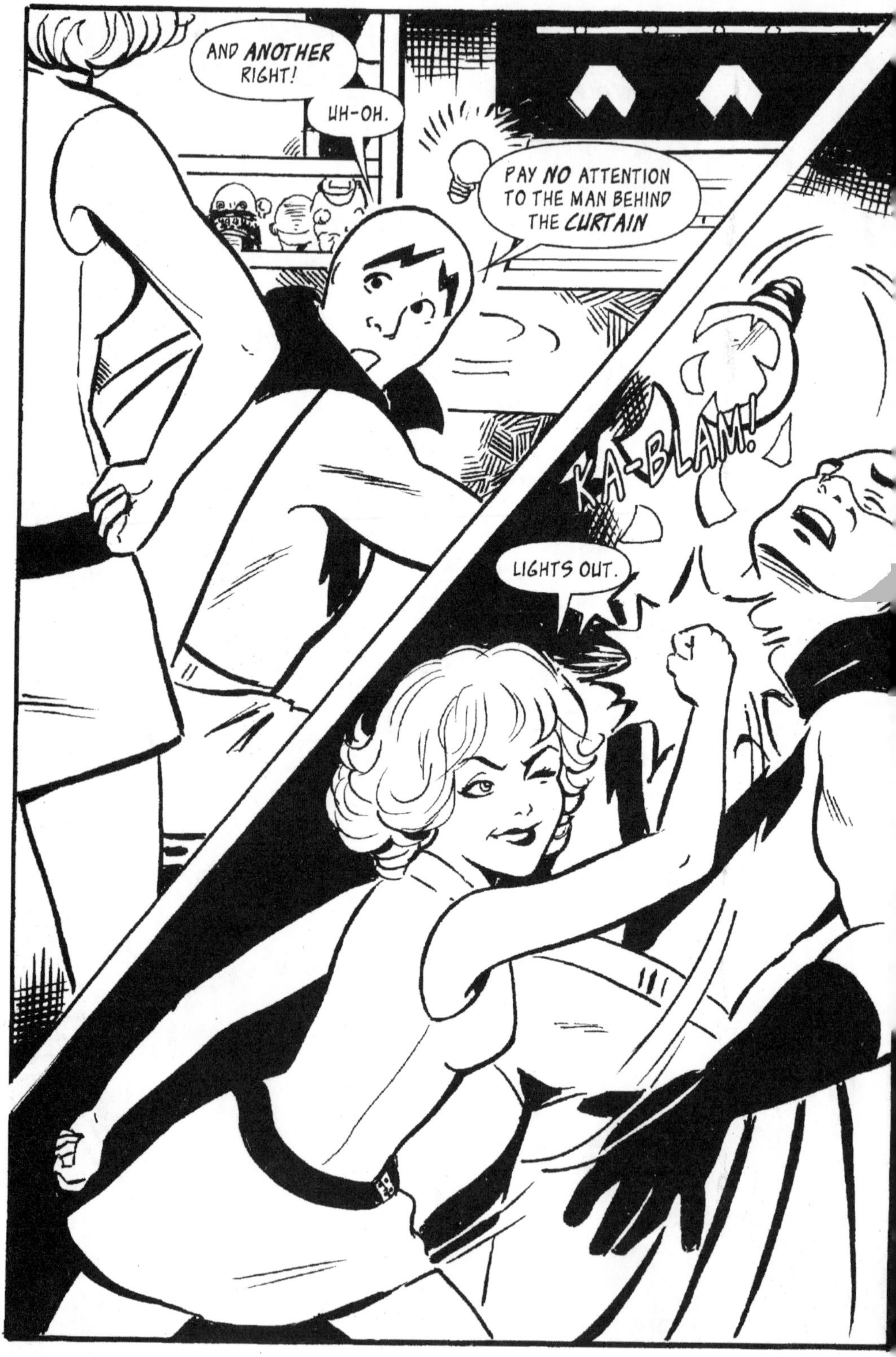
AND ANOTHER RIGHT!
UH-OH.
PAY NO ATTENTION TO THE MAN BEHIND THE CURTAIN
KA-BLAM!
LIGHTS OUT.

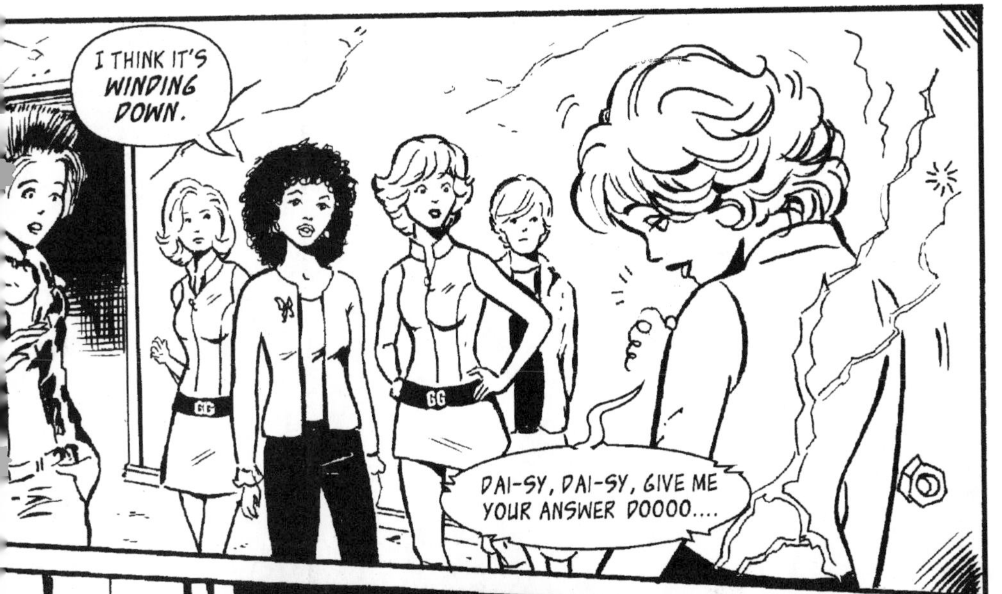
I THINK IT'S WINDING DOWN.
DAI-SY, DAI-SY, GIVE ME YOUR ANSWER DOOOO....

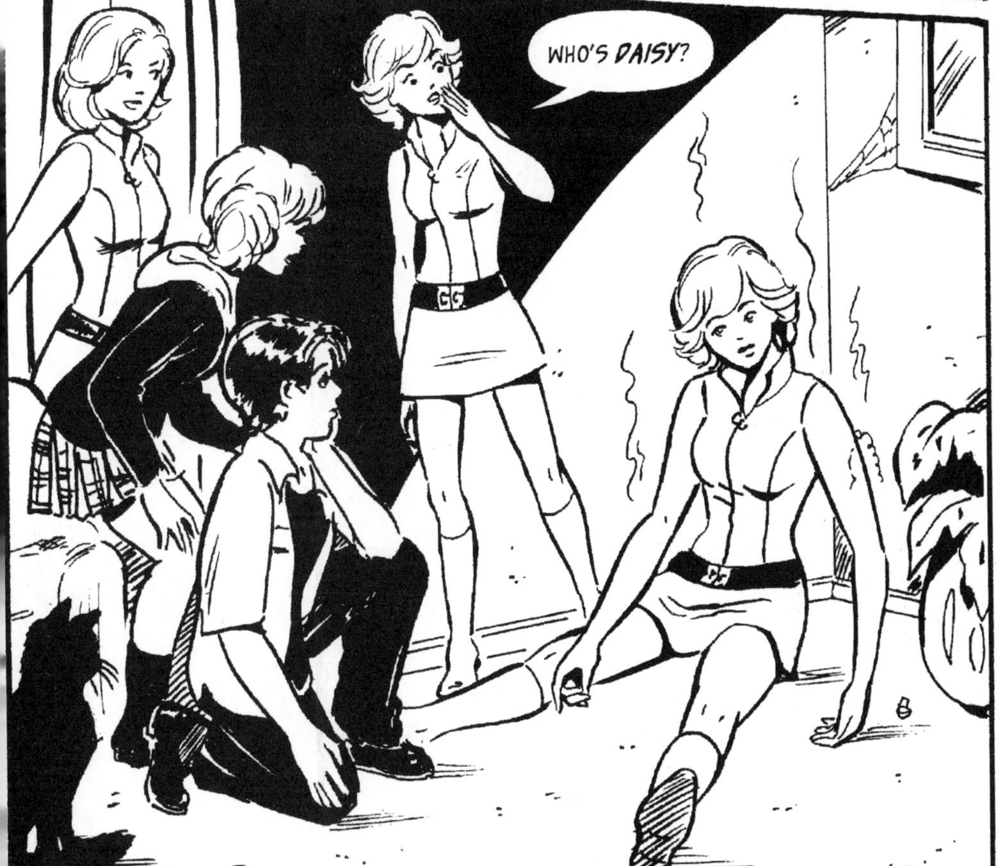
WHO'S DAISY?

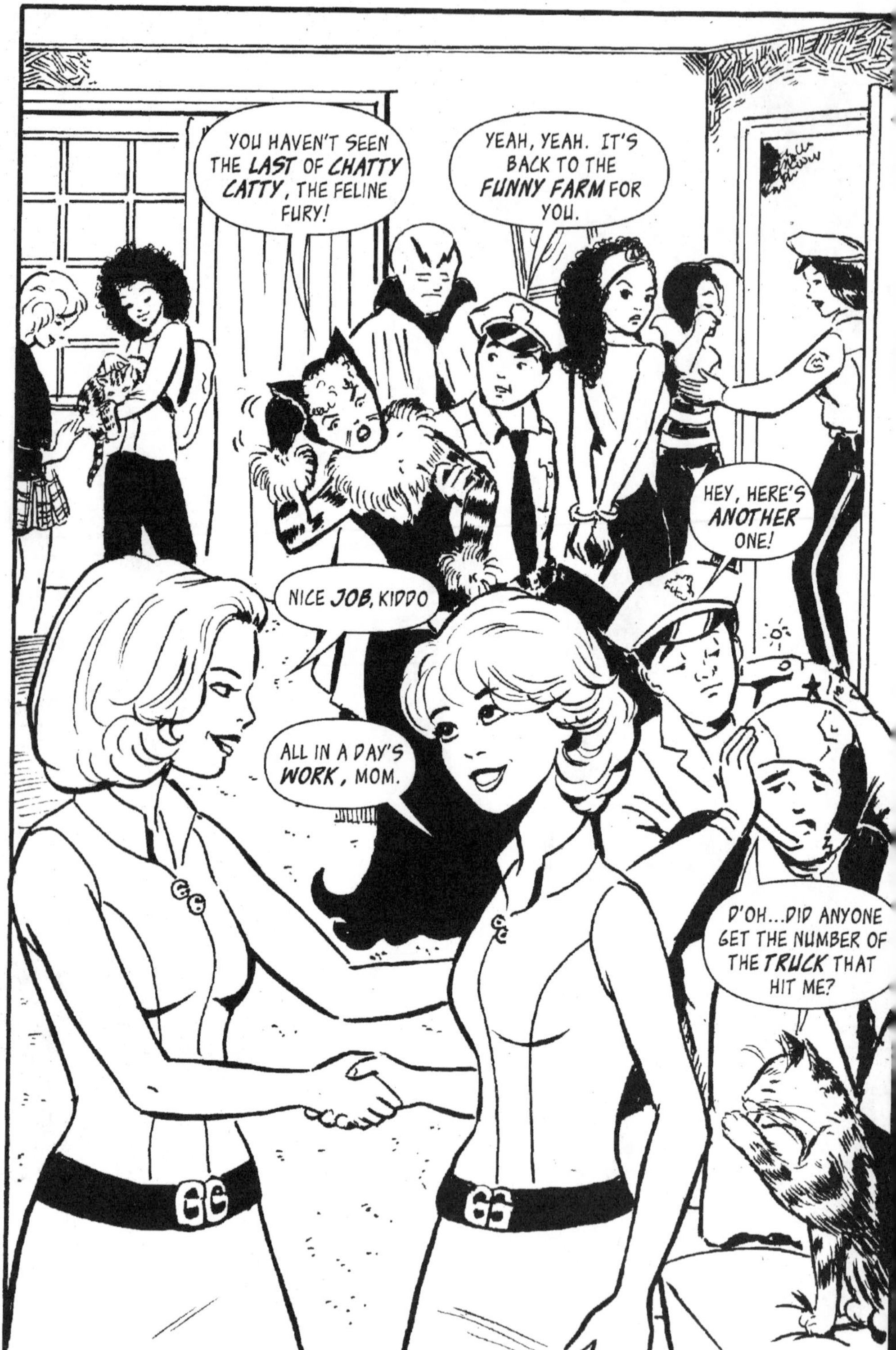

YOU HAVEN'T SEEN THE LAST OF CHATTY CATTY, THE FELINE FURY!
YEAH, YEAH. IT'S BACK TO THE FUNNY FARM FOR YOU.
HEY, HERE'S ANOTHER ONE!
NICE JOB, KIDDO
ALL IN A DAY'S WORK, MOM.
D'OH...DID ANYONE GET THE NUMBER OF THE TRUCK THAT HIT ME?

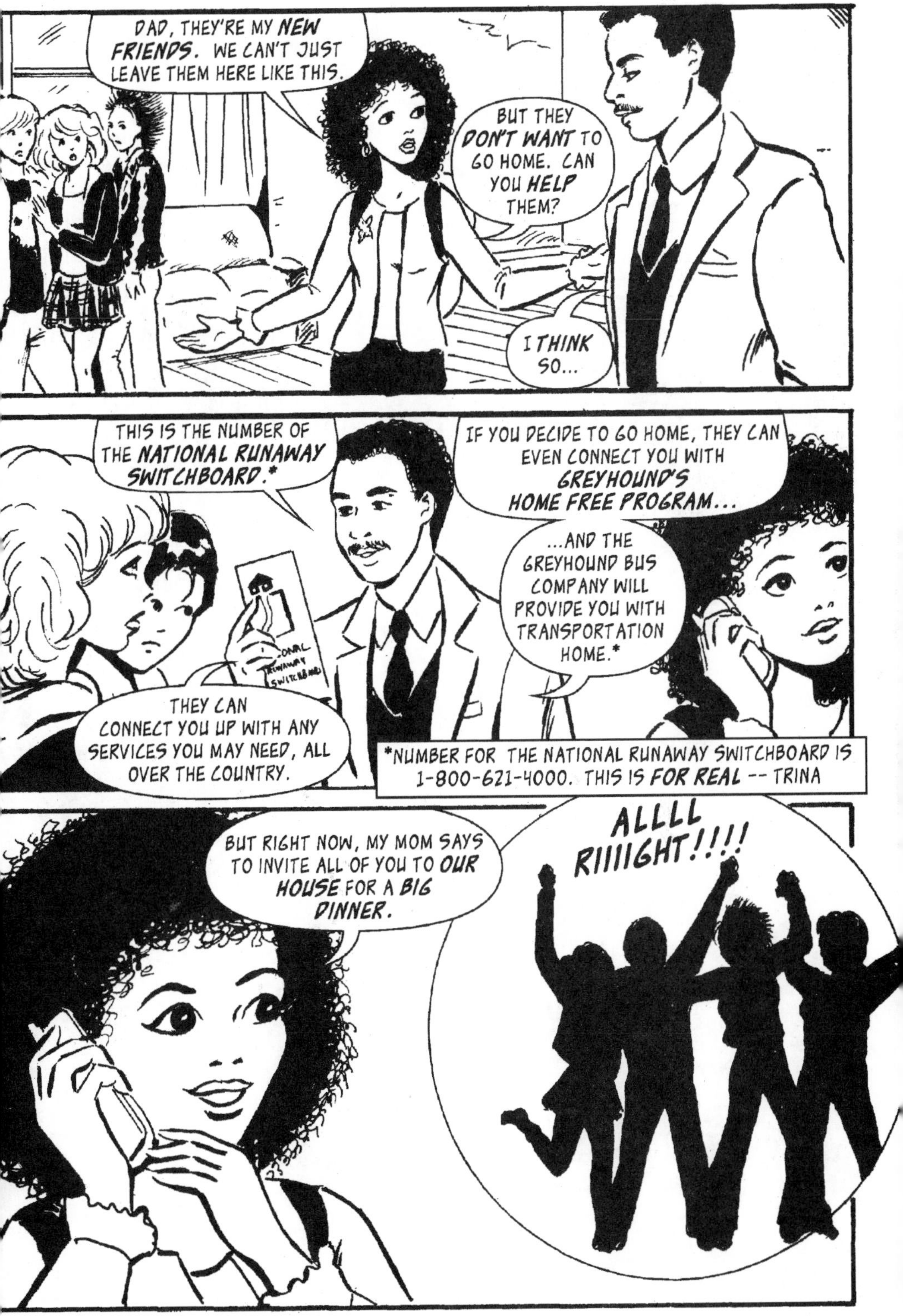
DAD, THEY'RE MY NEW FRIENDS. WE CAN'T JUST LEAVE THEM HERE LIKE THIS.
BUT THEY DON'T WANT TO GO HOME. CAN YOU HELP THEM?
I THINK SO...
THIS IS THE NUMBER OF THE NATIONAL RUNAWAY SWITCHBOARD.*
IF YOU DECIDE TO GO HOME, THEY CAN EVEN CONNECT YOU WITH GREYHOUND'S HOME FREE PROGRAM...
...AND THE GREYHOUND BUS COMPANY WILL PROVIDE YOU WITH TRANSPORTATION HOME.*
THEY CAN CONNECT YOU UP WITH ANY SERVICES YOU MAY NEED, ALL OVER THE COUNTRY.
*NUMBER FOR THE NATIONAL RUNAWAY SWITCHBOARD IS 1-800-621-4000. THIS IS FOR REAL -- TRINA
BUT RIGHT NOW, MY MOM SAYS TO INVITE ALL OF YOU TO OUR HOUSE FOR A BIG DINNER.
ALLLL RIIIIGHT!!!!

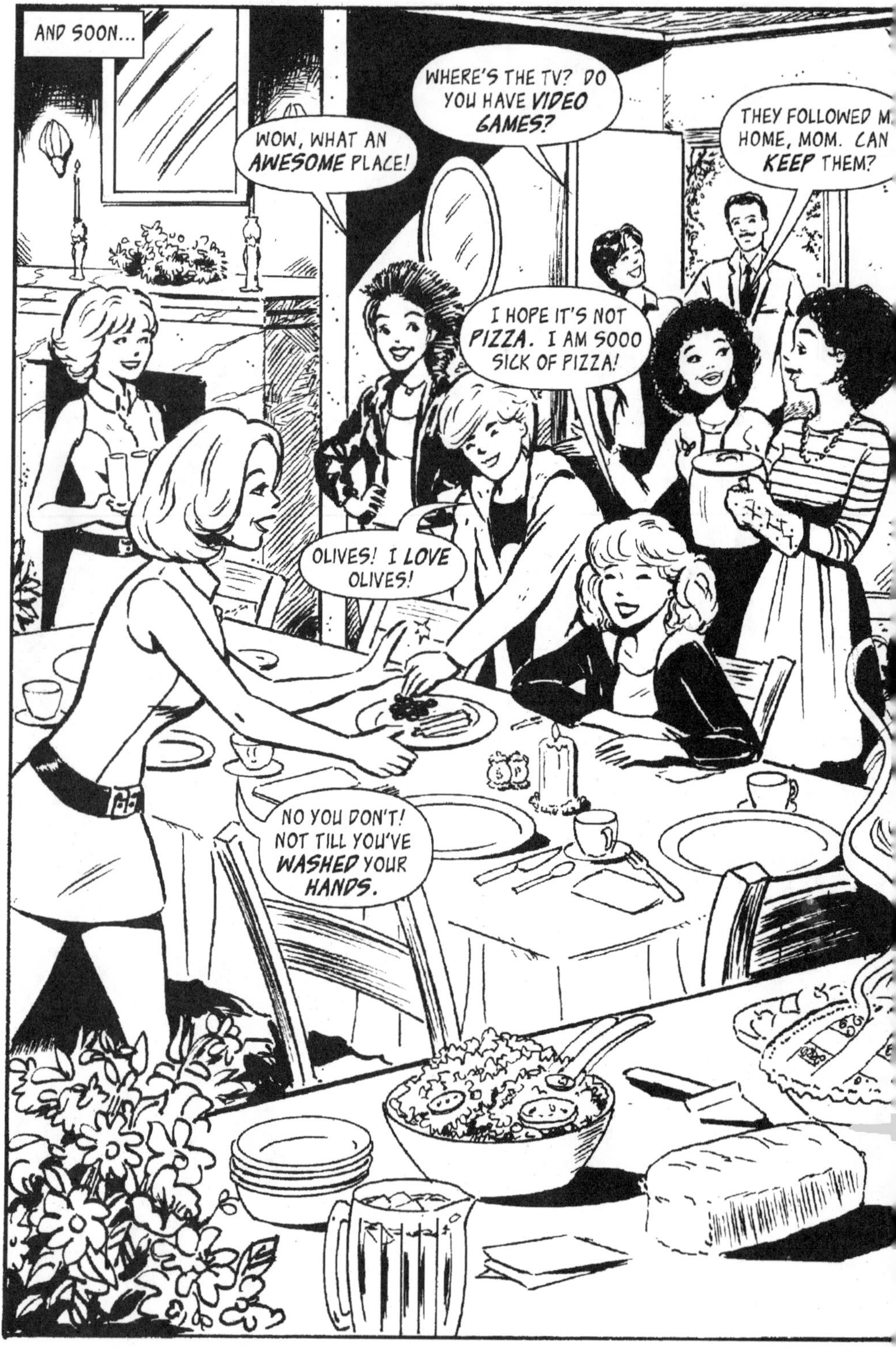
AND SOON...
WOW, WHAT AN AWESOME PLACE!
WHERE'S THE TV? DO YOU HAVE VIDEO GAMES?
THEY FOLLOWED M HOME, MOM. CAN KEEP THEM?
I HOPE IT'S NOT PIZZA. I AM SOOO SICK OF PIZZA!
OLIVES! I LOVE OLIVES!
NO YOU DON'T! NOT TILL YOU'VE WASHED YOUR HANDS.

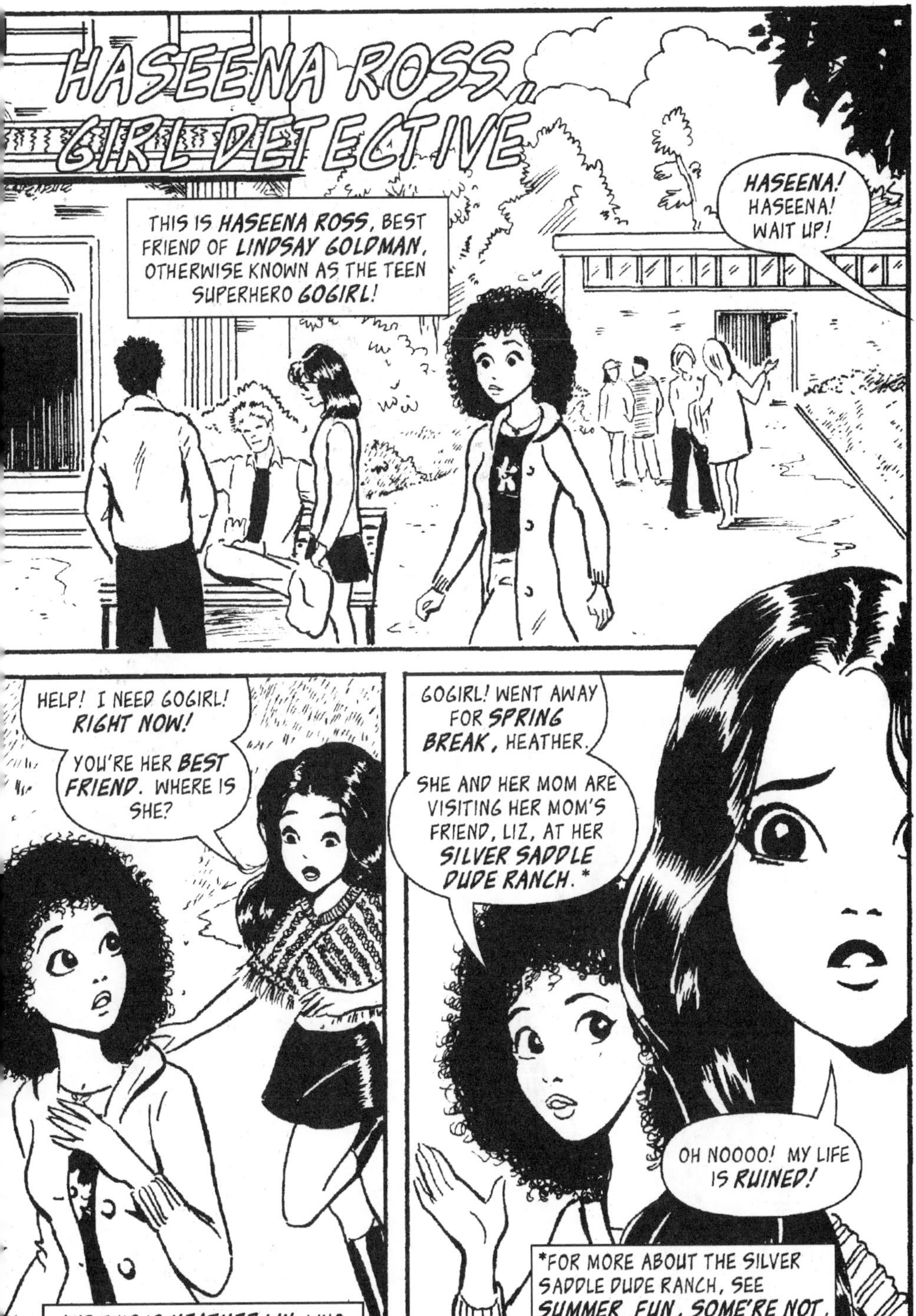
HASEENA ROSS, GIRL DETECTIVE
THIS IS HASEENA ROSS, BEST FRIEND OF LINDSAY GOLDMAN, OTHERWISE KNOWN AS THE TEEN SUPERHERO GOGIRL!
HASEENA! HASEENA! WAIT UP!
HELP! I NEED GOGIRL! RIGHT NOW!
YOU'RE HER BEST FRIEND. WHERE IS SHE?
AND THIS IS HEATHER WU, WHO HAD AN ADVENTURE WITH LINDSAY IN GOGIRL! #1, THE TIME TEAM.
GOGIRL! WENT AWAY FOR SPRING BREAK, HEATHER.
SHE AND HER MOM ARE VISITING HER MOM'S FRIEND, LIZ, AT HER SILVER SADDLE DUDE RANCH.*
OH NOOOO! MY LIFE IS RUINED!
*FOR MORE ABOUT THE SILVER SADDLE DUDE RANCH, SEE SUMMER FUN, SOME'RE NOT, IN THE COLLECTED GOGIRL!

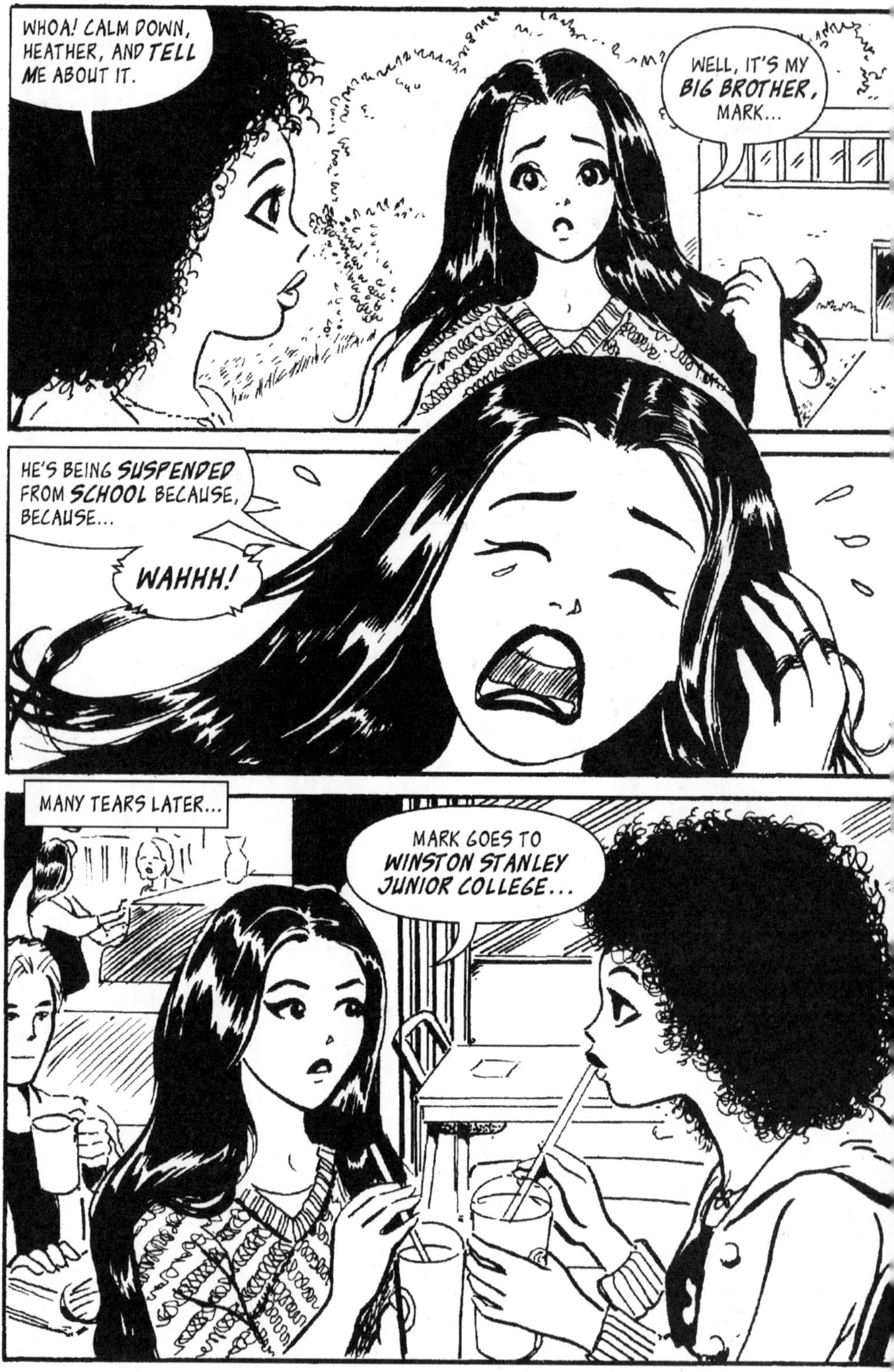
WHOA! CALM DOWN, HEATHER, AND TELL ME ABOUT IT.
WELL, IT'S MY BIG BROTHER, MARK...
HE'S BEING SUSPENDED FROM SCHOOL BECAUSE, BECAUSE...
WAHHH!
MANY TEARS LATER...
MARK GOES TO WINSTON STANLEY JUNIOR COLLEGE...

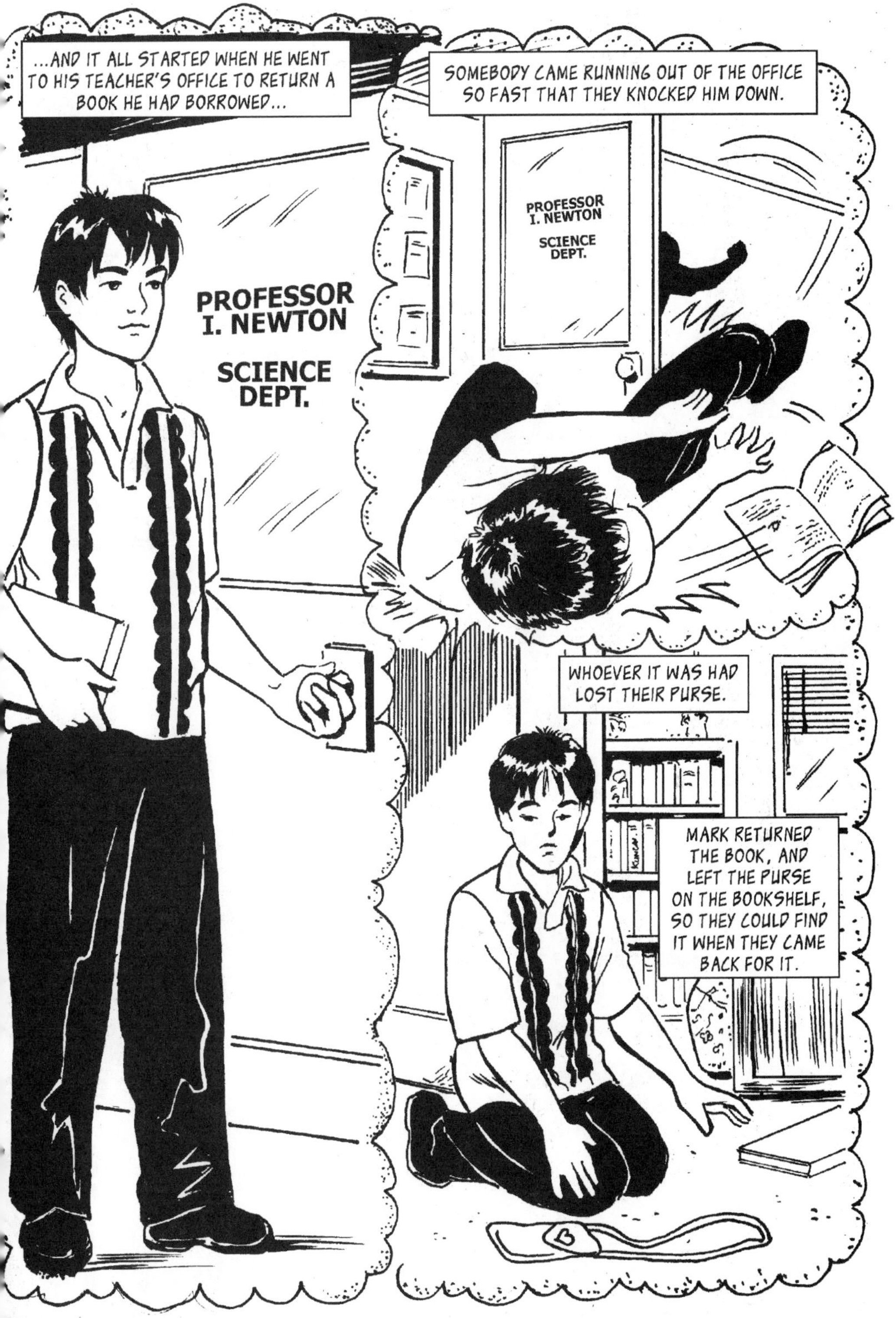
...AND IT ALL STARTED WHEN HE WENT TO HIS TEACHER'S OFFICE TO RETURN A BOOK HE HAD BORROWED...
PROFESSOR I. NEWTON
SCIENCE DEPT.
SOMEBODY CAME RUNNING OUT OF THE OFFICE SO FAST THAT THEY KNOCKED HIM DOWN.
PROFESSOR I. NEWTON
SCIENCE DEPT.
WHOEVER IT WAS HAD LOST THEIR PURSE.
MARK RETURNED THE BOOK, AND LEFT THE PURSE ON THE BOOKSHELF, SO THEY COULD FIND IT WHEN THEY CAME BACK FOR IT.

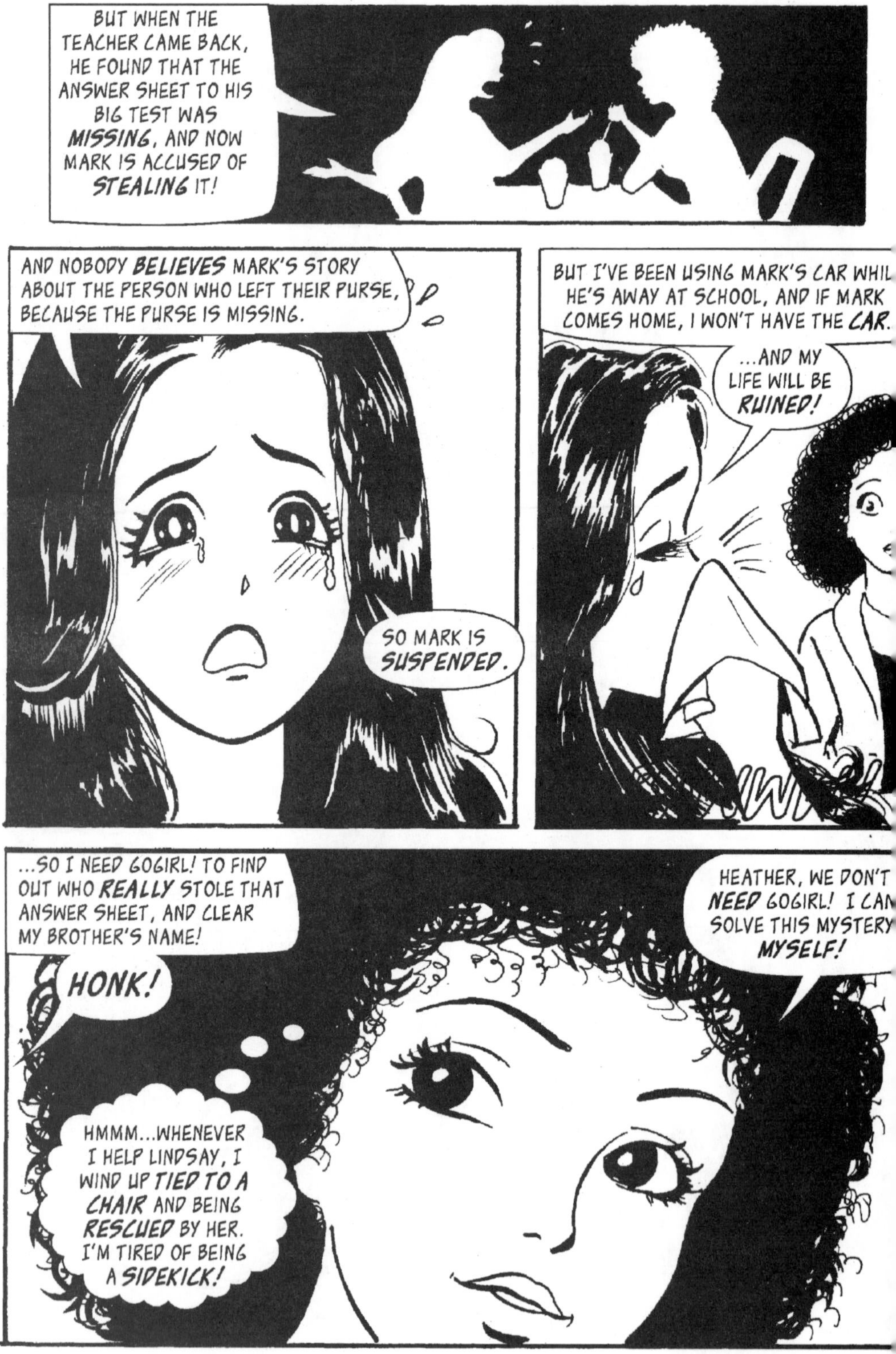
BUT WHEN THE TEACHER CAME BACK, HE FOUND THAT THE ANSWER SHEET TO HIS BIG TEST WAS MISSING, AND NOW MARK IS ACCUSED OF STEALING IT!
AND NOBODY BELIEVES MARK'S STORY ABOUT THE PERSON WHO LEFT THEIR PURSE, BECAUSE THE PURSE IS MISSING.
SO MARK IS SUSPENDED.
BUT I'VE BEEN USING MARK'S CAR WHIL HE'S AWAY AT SCHOOL, AND IF MARK COMES HOME, I WON'T HAVE THE CAR.
...AND MY LIFE WILL BE RUINED!
...SO I NEED GOGIRL! TO FIND OUT WHO REALLY STOLE THAT ANSWER SHEET, AND CLEAR MY BROTHER'S NAME!
HONK!
HEATHER, WE DON'T NEED GOGIRL! I CAN SOLVE THIS MYSTERY MYSELF!
HMMM...WHENEVER I HELP LINDSAY, I WIND UP TIED TO A CHAIR AND BEING RESCUED BY HER. I'M TIRED OF BEING A SIDEKICK!

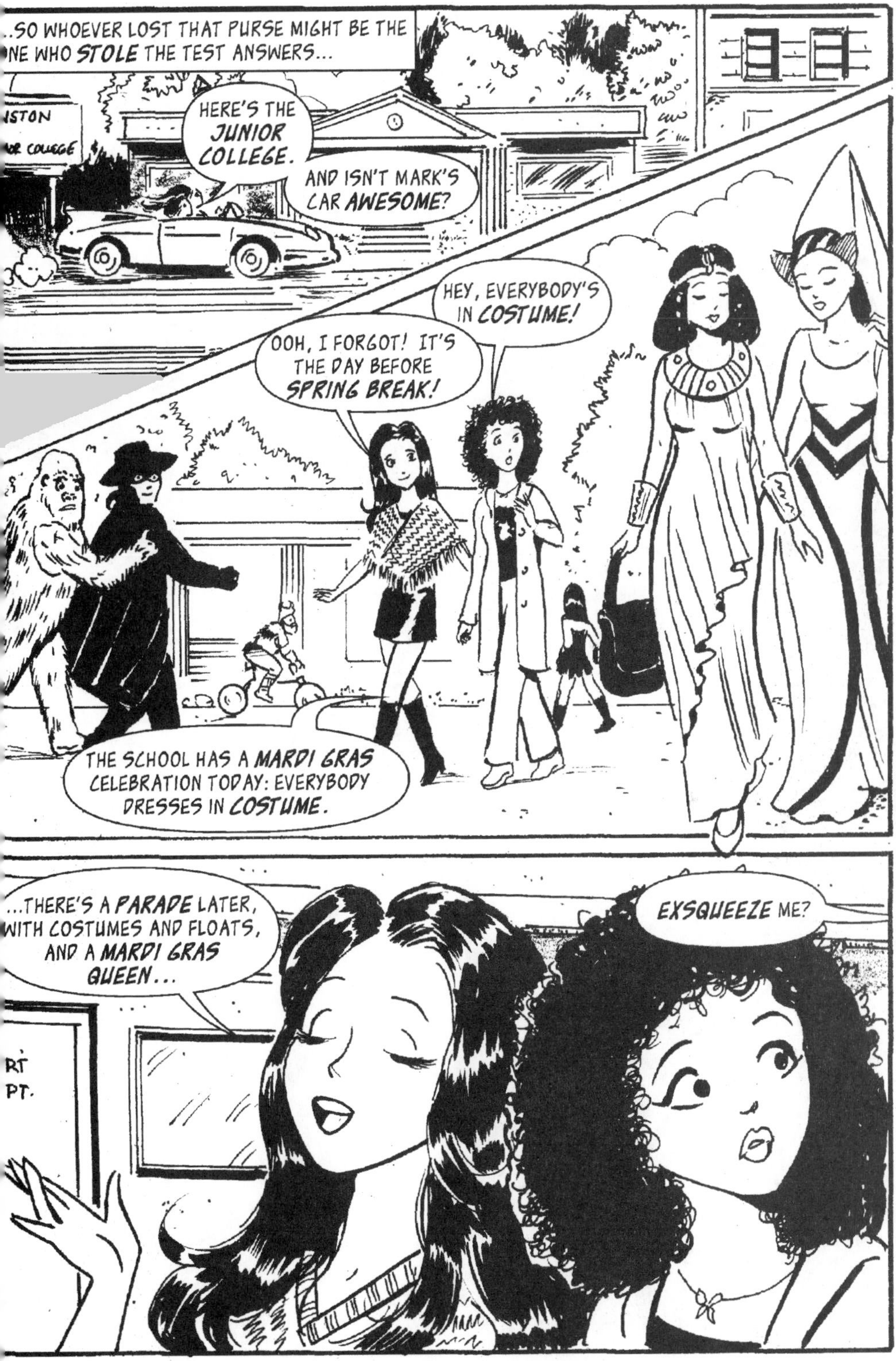
..SO WHOEVER LOST THAT PURSE MIGHT BE THE
NE WHO STOLE THE TEST ANSWERS...
ISTON
OR COLLEGE
HERE'S THE JUNIOR COLLEGE.
AND ISN'T MARK'S CAR AWESOME?
HEY, EVERYBODY'S IN COSTUME!
OOH, I FORGOT! IT'S THE DAY BEFORE SPRING BREAK!
THE SCHOOL HAS A MARDI GRAS CELEBRATION TODAY: EVERYBODY DRESSES IN COSTUME.
...THERE'S A PARADE LATER, WITH COSTUMES AND FLOATS, AND A MARDI GRAS QUEEN...
EXSQUEEZE ME?
RT
PT.

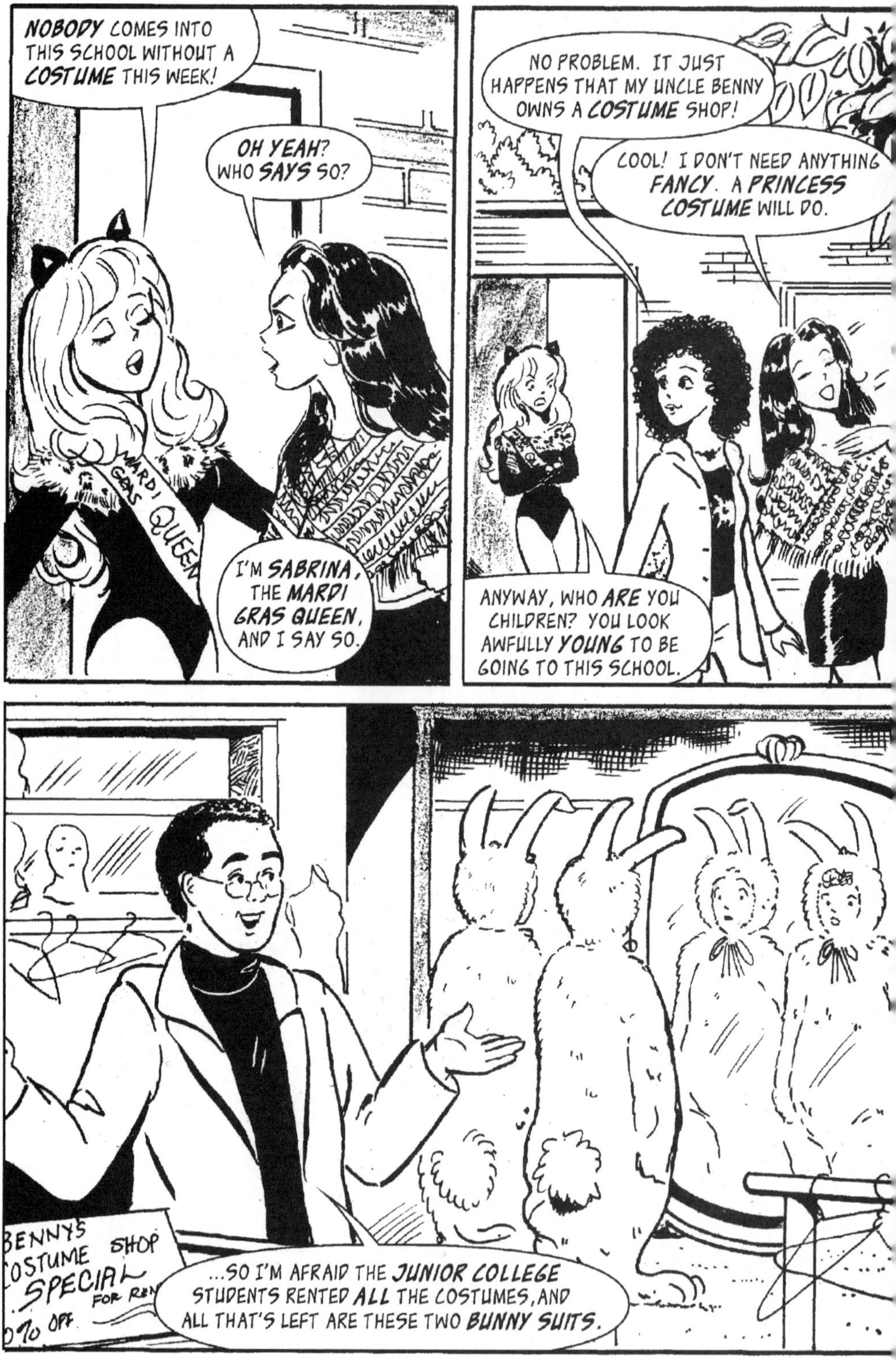
NOBODY COMES INTO THIS SCHOOL WITHOUT A COSTUME THIS WEEK!
OH YEAH? WHO SAYS SO?
I'M SABRINA, THE MARDI GRAS QUEEN, AND I SAY SO.
MARDI GRAS QUEEN
NO PROBLEM. IT JUST HAPPENS THAT MY UNCLE BENNY OWNS A COSTUME SHOP!
COOL! I DON'T NEED ANYTHING FANCY. A PRINCESS COSTUME WILL DO.
ANYWAY, WHO ARE YOU CHILDREN? YOU LOOK AWFULLY YOUNG TO BE GOING TO THIS SCHOOL.
...SO I'M AFRAID THE JUNIOR COLLEGE STUDENTS RENTED ALL THE COSTUMES, AND ALL THAT'S LEFT ARE THESE TWO BUNNY SUITS.

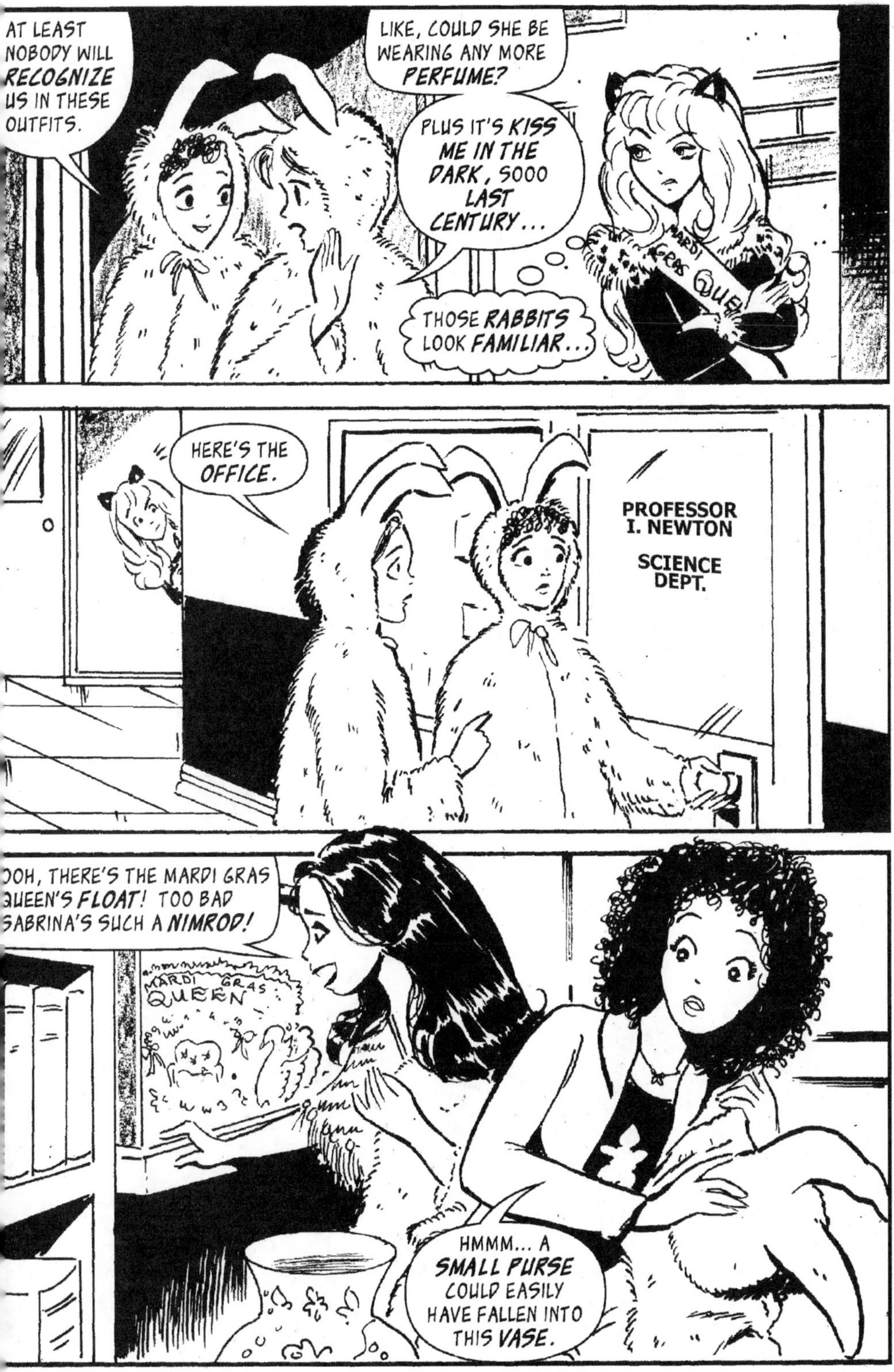
AT LEAST NOBODY WILL RECOGNIZE US IN THESE OUTFITS.
LIKE, COULD SHE BE WEARING ANY MORE PERFUME?
PLUS IT'S KISS ME IN THE DARK, SOOO LAST CENTURY...
THOSE RABBITS LOOK FAMILIAR...
MARDI GRAS QUE
HERE'S THE OFFICE.
PROFESSOR I. NEWTON
SCIENCE DEPT.
OOH, THERE'S THE MARDI GRAS QUEEN'S FLOAT! TOO BAD SABRINA'S SUCH A NIMROD!
MARDI GRAS QUEEN
HMMM... A SMALL PURSE COULD EASILY HAVE FALLEN INTO THIS VASE.

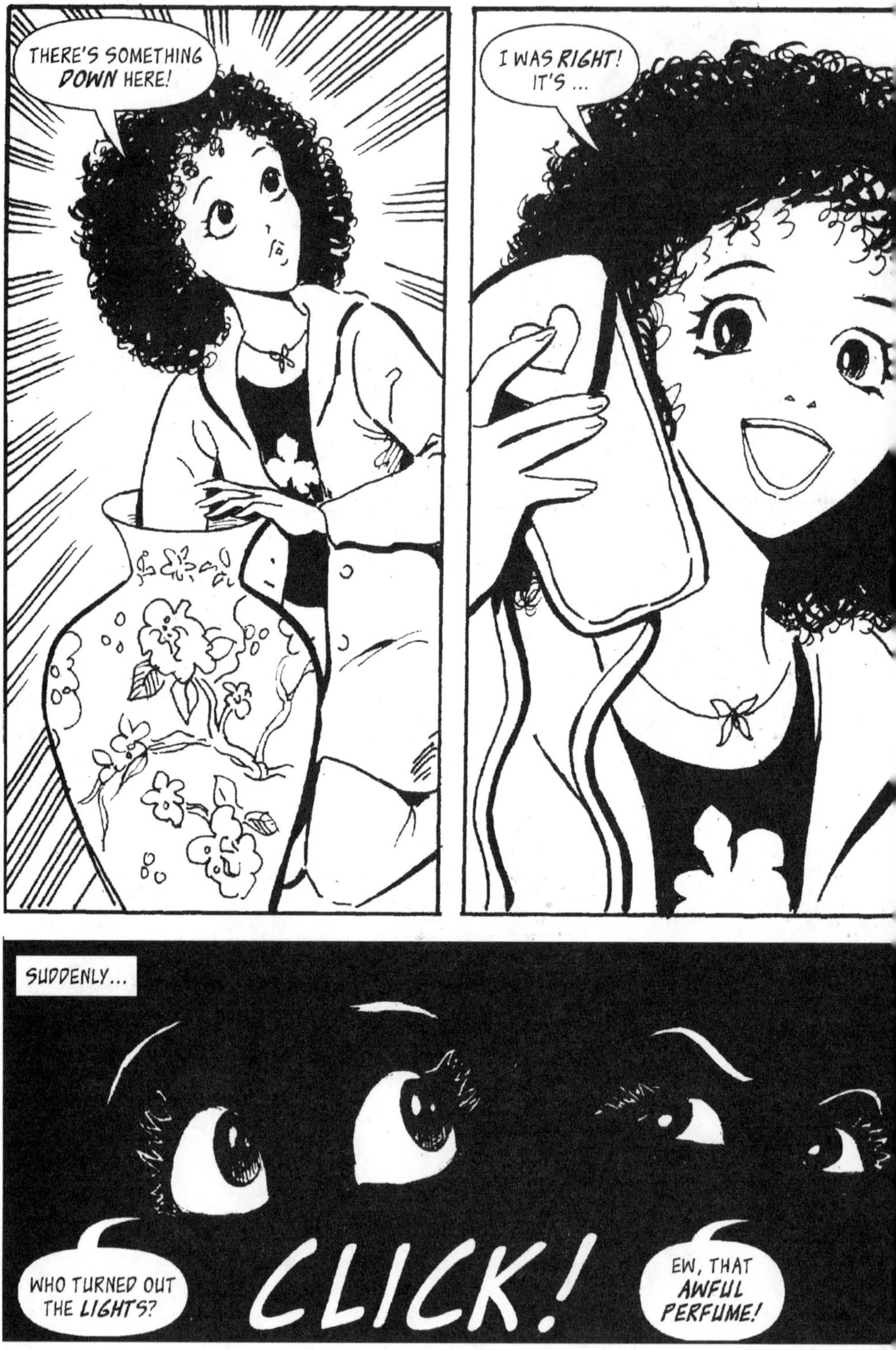
THERE'S SOMETHING DOWN HERE!
I WAS RIGHT! IT'S ...
SUDDENLY...
WHO TURNED OUT THE LIGHTS?
CLICK!
EW, THAT AWFUL PERFUME!

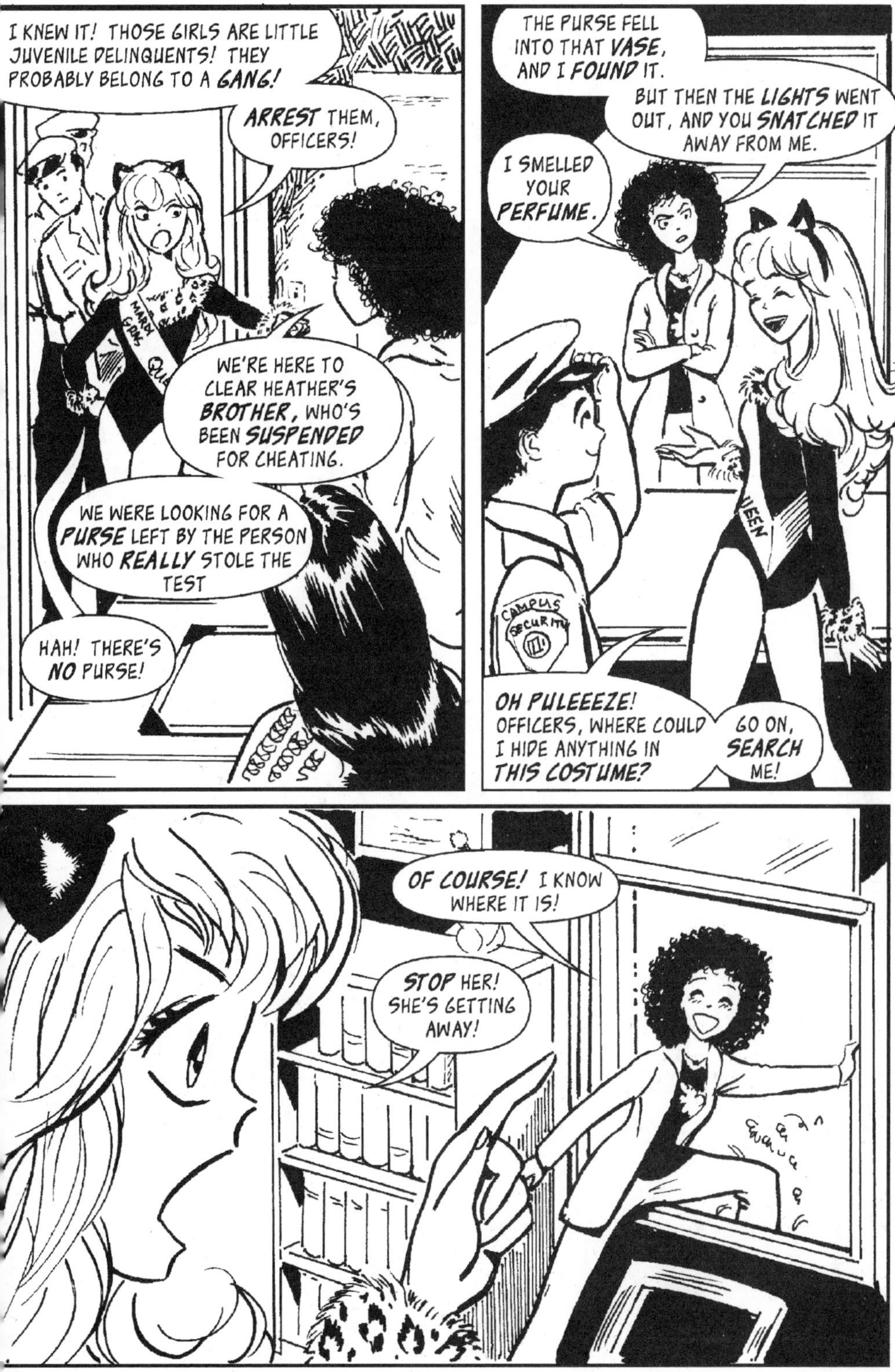
I KNEW IT! THOSE GIRLS ARE LITTLE JUVENILE DELINQUENTS! THEY PROBABLY BELONG TO A GANG!
ARREST THEM, OFFICERS!
WE'RE HERE TO CLEAR HEATHER'S BROTHER, WHO'S BEEN SUSPENDED FOR CHEATING.
WE WERE LOOKING FOR A PURSE LEFT BY THE PERSON WHO REALLY STOLE THE TEST
HAH! THERE'S NO PURSE!
THE PURSE FELL INTO THAT VASE, AND I FOUND IT.
BUT THEN THE LIGHTS WENT OUT, AND YOU SNATCHED IT AWAY FROM ME.
I SMELLED YOUR PERFUME.
CAMPUS SECURITY
OH PULEEEZE! OFFICERS, WHERE COULD I HIDE ANYTHING IN THIS COSTUME?
GO ON, SEARCH ME!
OF COURSE! I KNOW WHERE IT IS!
STOP HER! SHE'S GETTING AWAY!

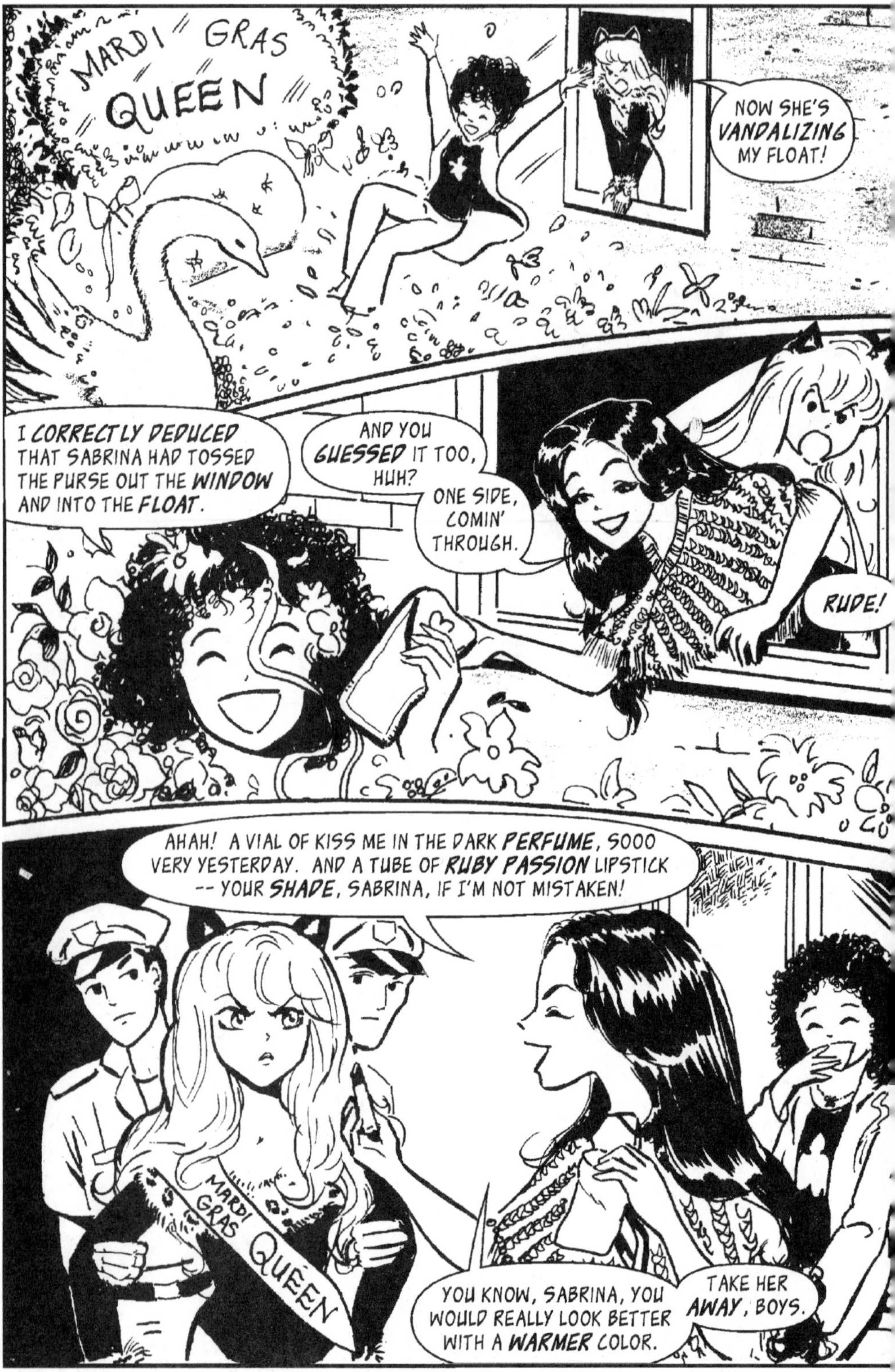
MARDI GRAS QUEEN
NOW SHE'S VANDALIZING MY FLOAT!
I CORRECTLY DEDUCED THAT SABRINA HAD TOSSED THE PURSE OUT THE WINDOW AND INTO THE FLOAT.
AND YOU GUESSED IT TOO, HUH?
ONE SIDE, COMIN' THROUGH.
RUDE!
AHAH! A VIAL OF KISS ME IN THE DARK PERFUME, SOOO VERY YESTERDAY. AND A TUBE OF RUBY PASSION LIPSTICK -- YOUR SHADE, SABRINA, IF I'M NOT MISTAKEN!
MARDI GRAS QUEEN
YOU KNOW, SABRINA, YOU WOULD REALLY LOOK BETTER WITH A WARMER COLOR.
TAKE HER AWAY, BOYS.

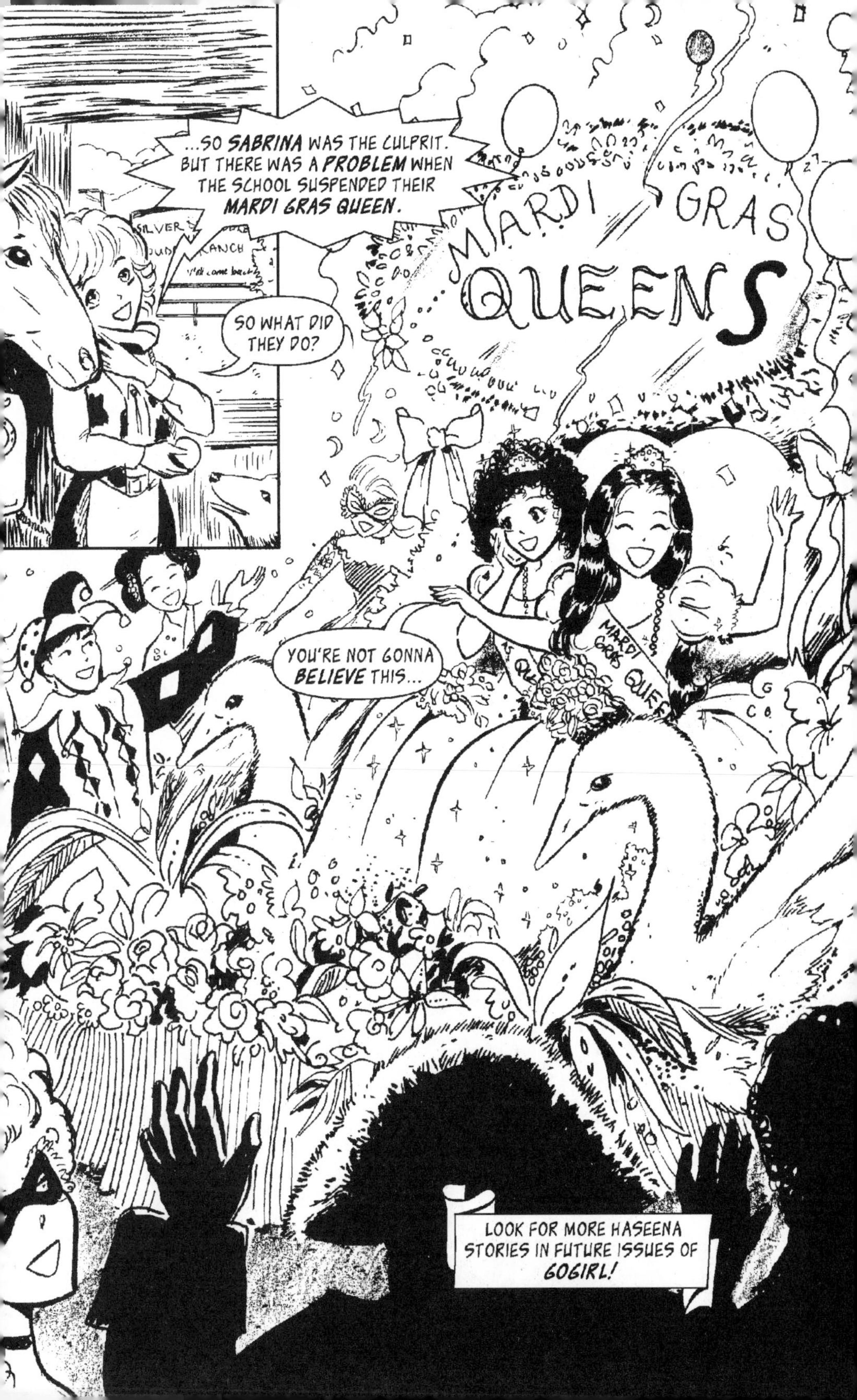
...SO *SABRINA* WAS THE CULPRIT. BUT THERE WAS A *PROBLEM* WHEN THE SCHOOL SUSPENDED THEIR *MARDI GRAS QUEEN*.
SO WHAT DID THEY DO?
MARDI GRAS QUEENS
YOU'RE NOT GONNA *BELIEVE* THIS...
LOOK FOR MORE HASEENA STORIES IN FUTURE ISSUES OF *GOGIRL!*

***GO GIRL!*** IS READY FOR SUMMER, BUT SHE ALWAYS NEEDS MORE CLOTHES!

SEND US DESIGNS FOR HER WARDROBE!

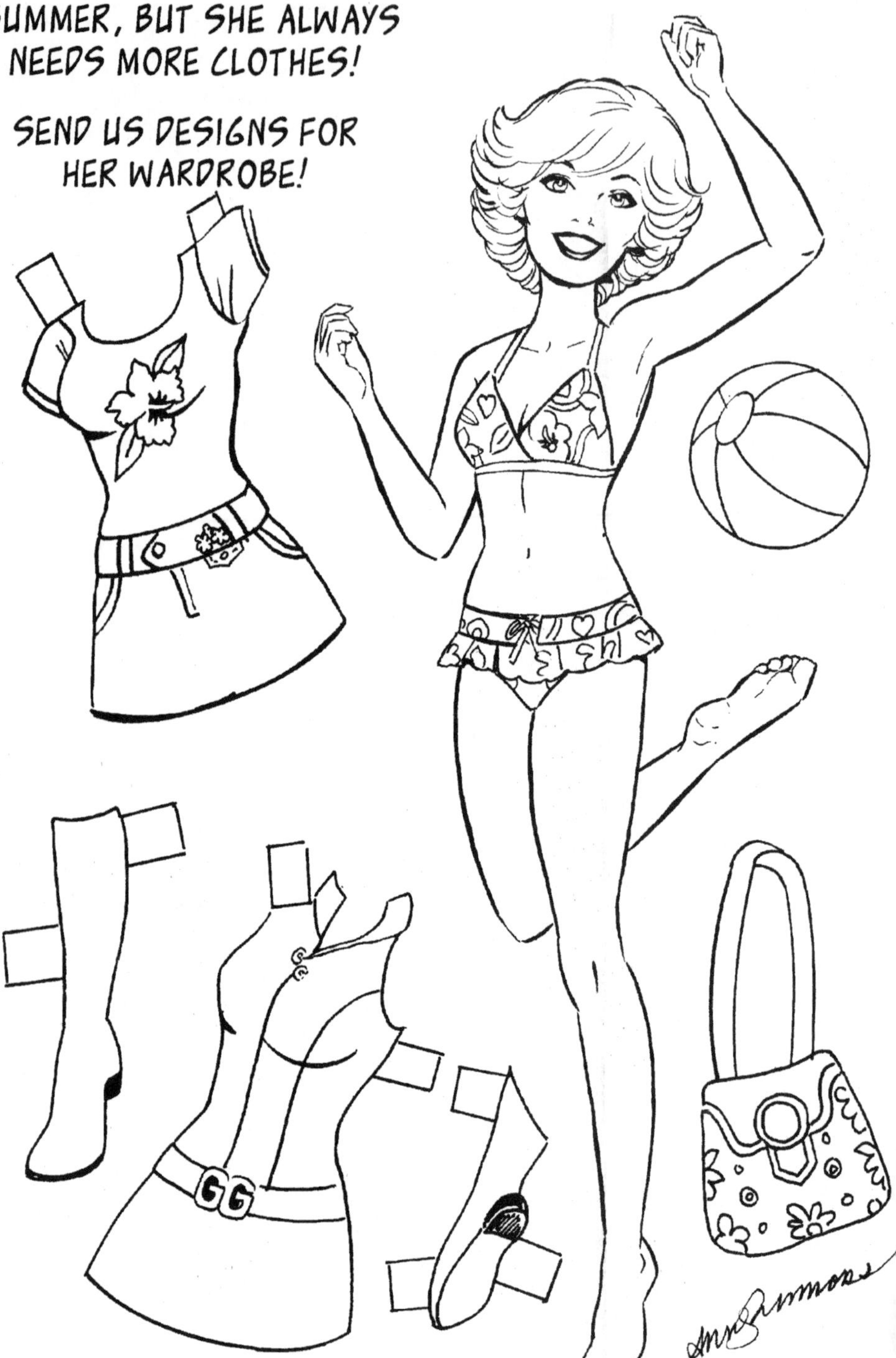

GG

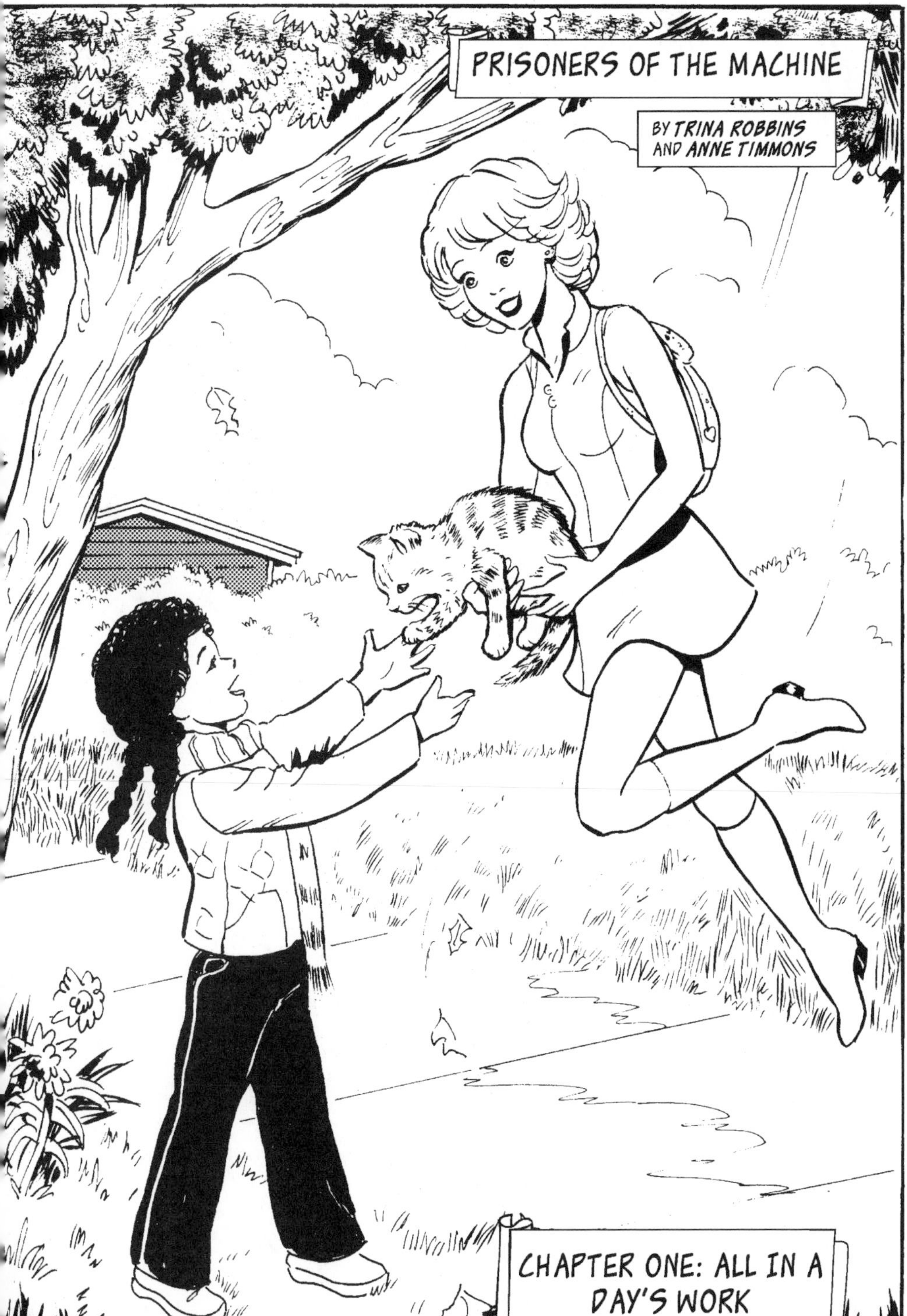
PRISONERS OF THE MACHINE
BY TRINA ROBBINS AND ANNE TIMMONS
CHAPTER ONE: ALL IN A DAY'S WORK

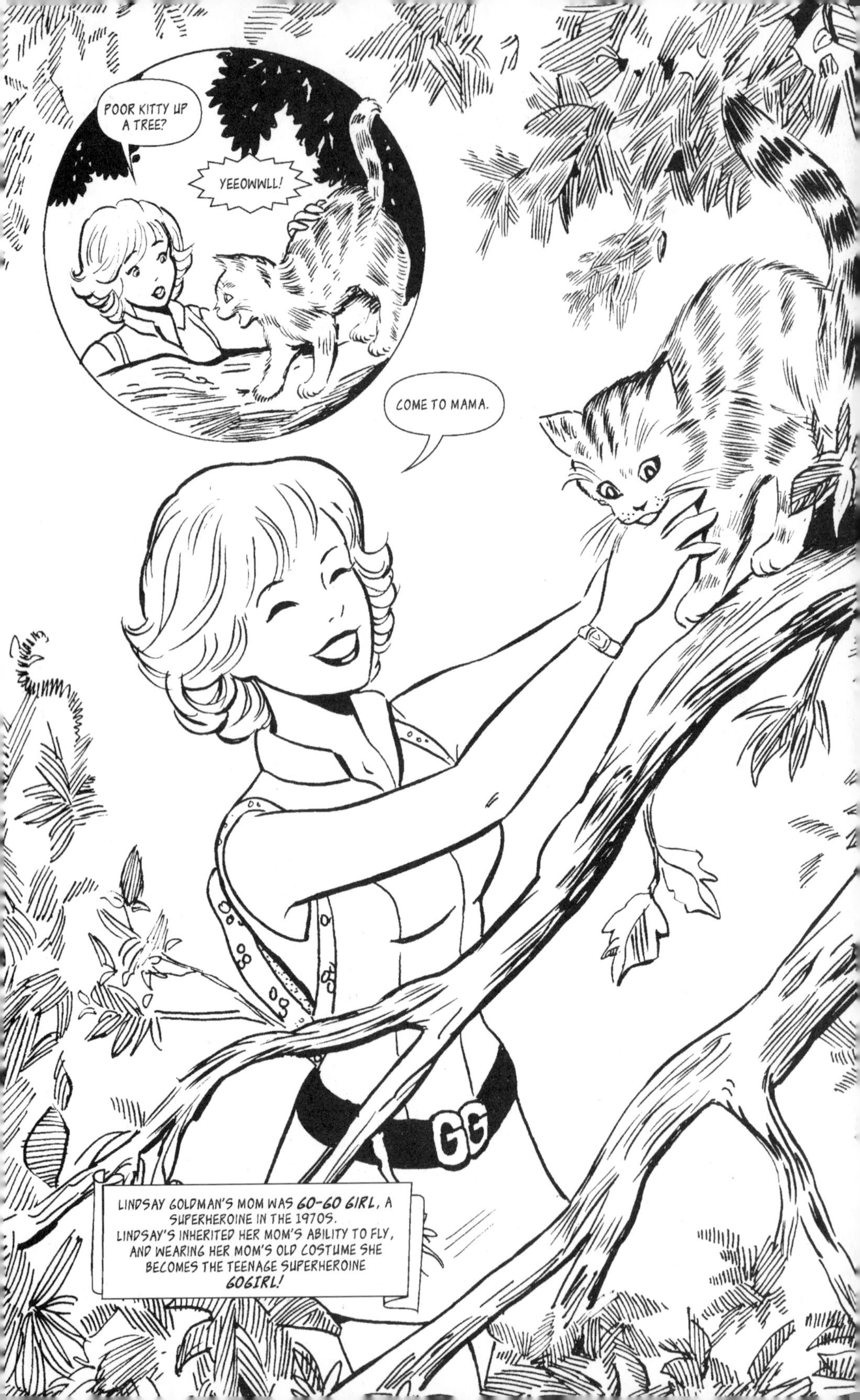

POOR KITTY UP A TREE?
YEEOWWLL!
COME TO MAMA.
LINDSAY GOLDMAN'S MOM WAS GO-GO GIRL, A SUPERHEROINE IN THE 1970S.
LINDSAY'S INHERITED HER MOM'S ABILITY TO FLY, AND WEARING HER MOM'S OLD COSTUME SHE BECOMES THE TEENAGE SUPERHEROINE GOGIRL!

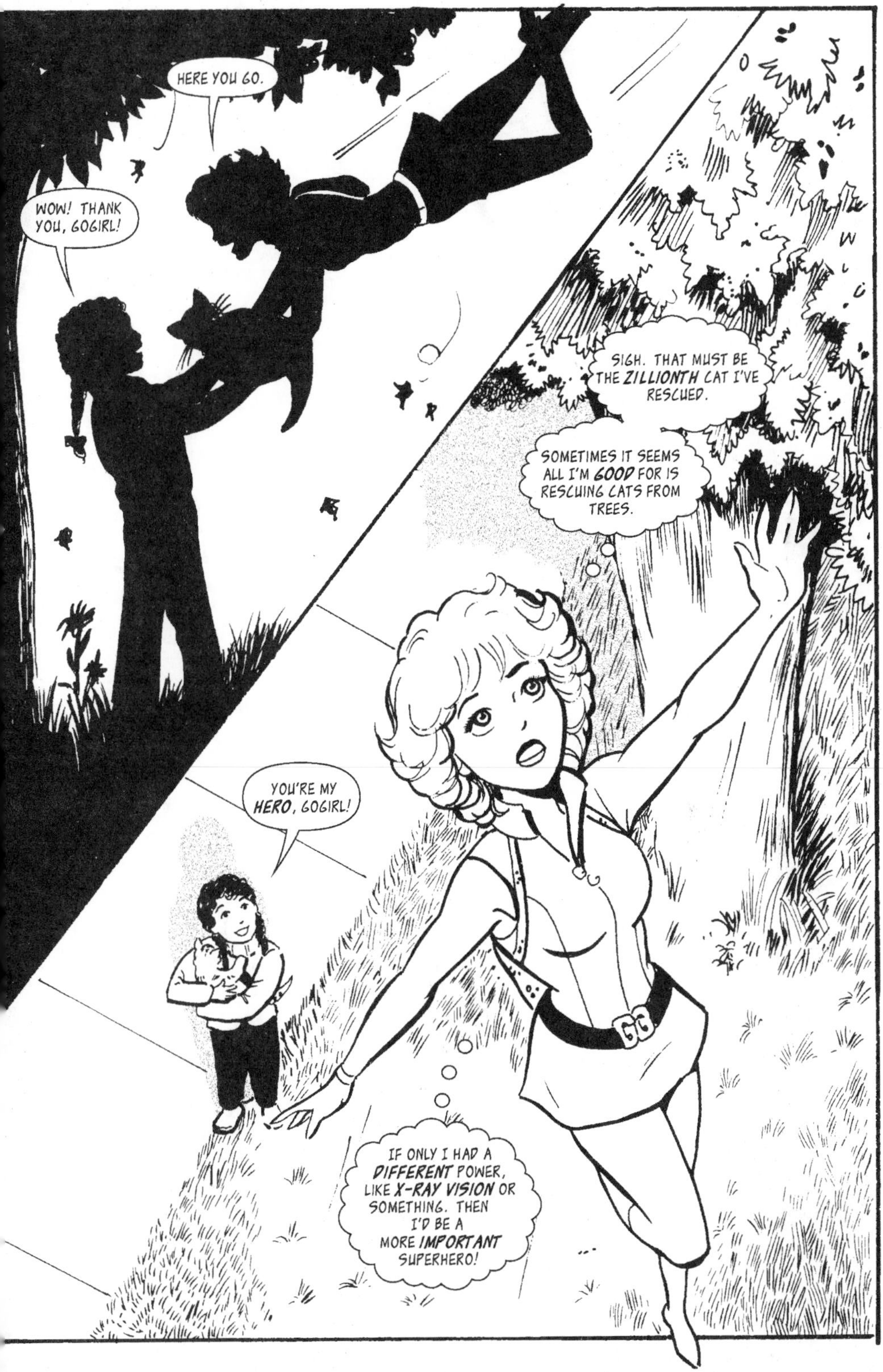
HERE YOU GO.
WOW! THANK YOU, GOGIRL!
SIGH. THAT MUST BE THE ZILLIONTH CAT I'VE RESCUED.
SOMETIMES IT SEEMS ALL I'M GOOD FOR IS RESCUING CATS FROM TREES.
YOU'RE MY HERO, GOGIRL!
IF ONLY I HAD A DIFFERENT POWER, LIKE X-RAY VISION OR SOMETHING. THEN I'D BE A MORE IMPORTANT SUPERHERO!

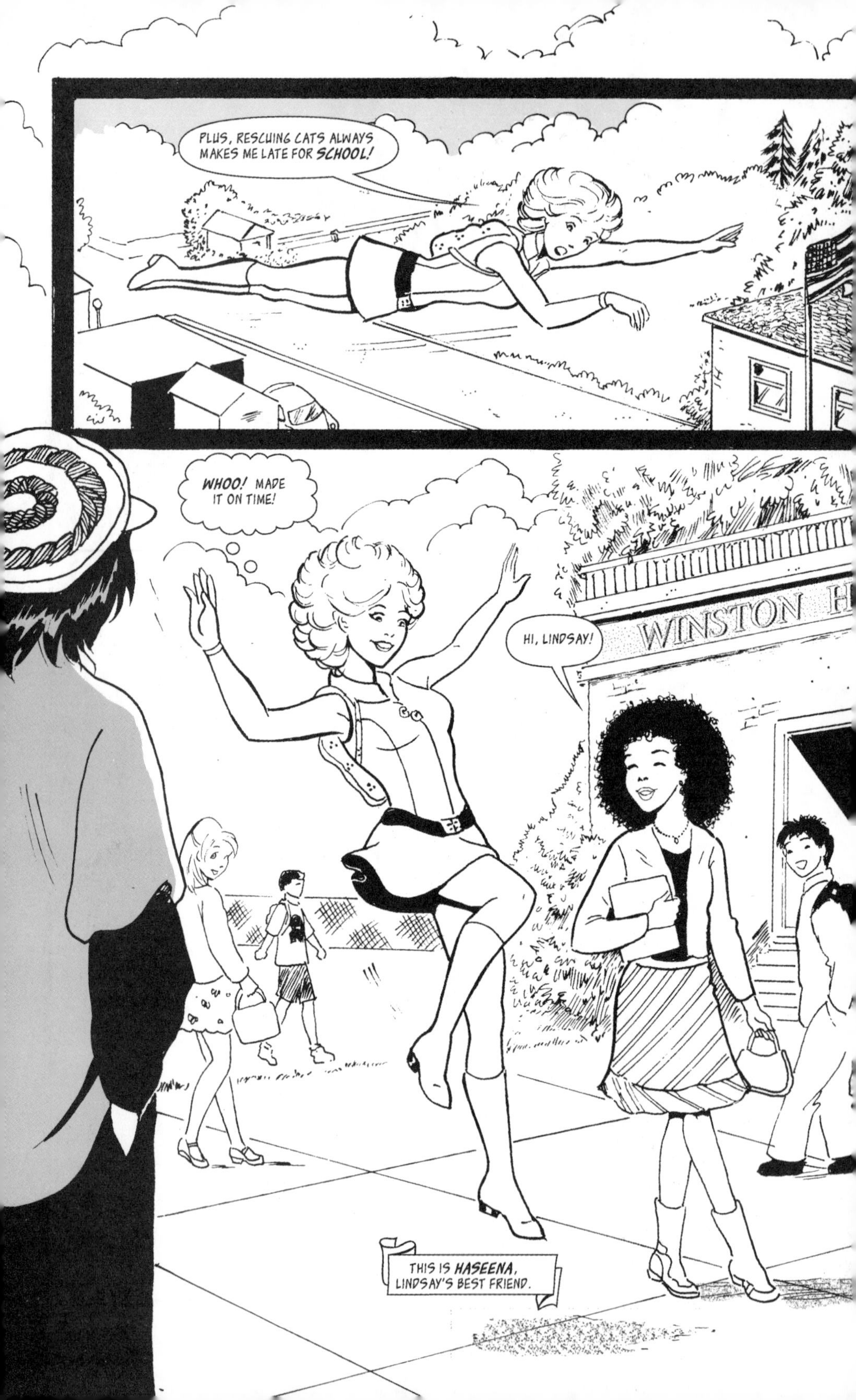
PLUS, RESCUING CATS ALWAYS MAKES ME LATE FOR SCHOOL!
WHOO! MADE IT ON TIME!
WINSTON H
HI, LINDSAY!
THIS IS HASEENA, LINDSAY'S BEST FRIEND.

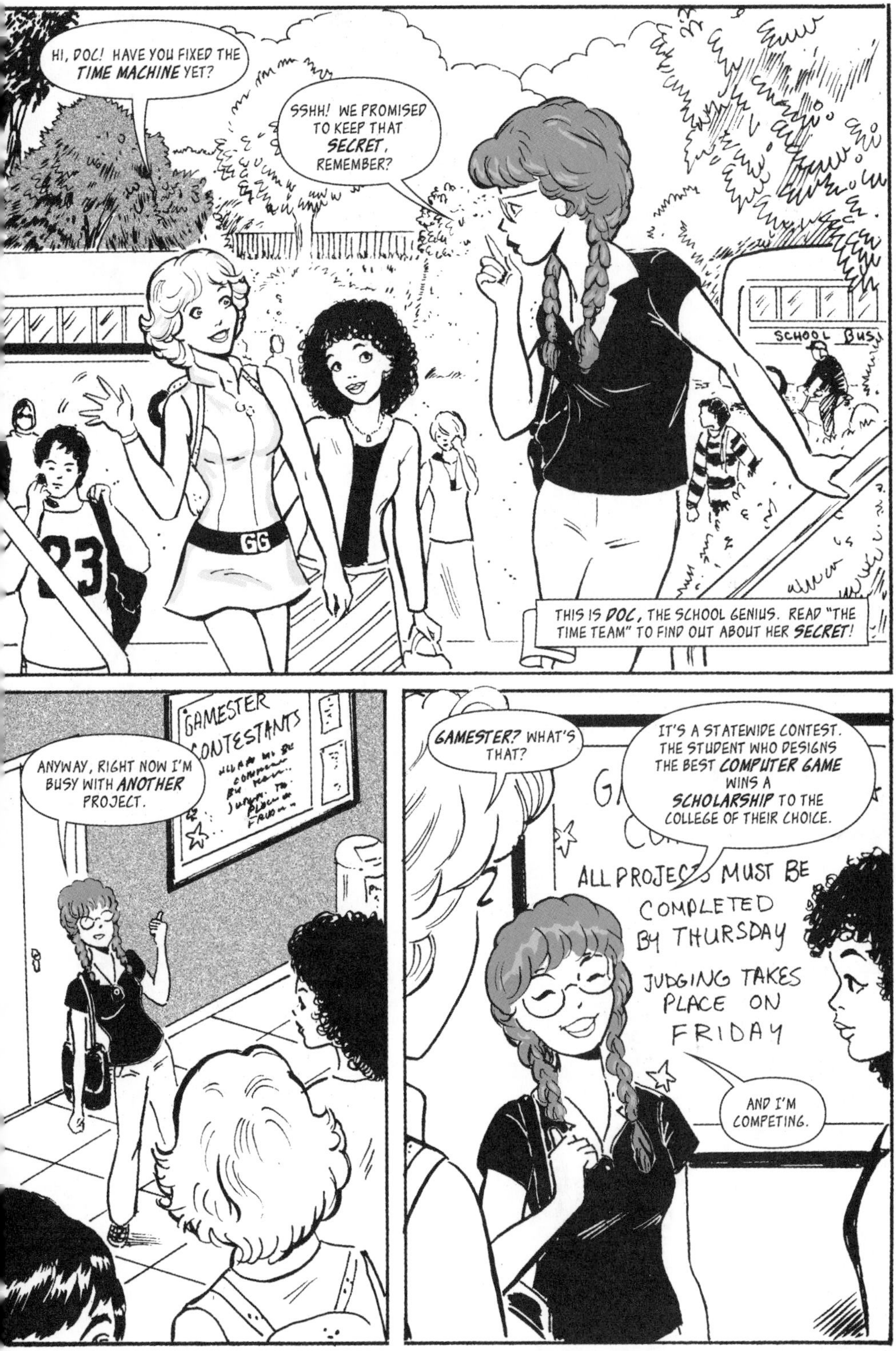
HI, DOC! HAVE YOU FIXED THE TIME MACHINE YET?
SSHH! WE PROMISED TO KEEP THAT SECRET, REMEMBER?
SCHOOL BUS
GG
23
THIS IS DOC, THE SCHOOL GENIUS. READ "THE TIME TEAM" TO FIND OUT ABOUT HER SECRET!
GAMESTER CONTESTANTS
ANYWAY, RIGHT NOW I'M BUSY WITH ANOTHER PROJECT.
GAMESTER? WHAT'S THAT?
IT'S A STATEWIDE CONTEST. THE STUDENT WHO DESIGNS THE BEST COMPUTER GAME WINS A SCHOLARSHIP TO THE COLLEGE OF THEIR CHOICE.
ALL PROJECTS MUST BE COMPLETED BY THURSDAY
JUDGING TAKES PLACE ON FRIDAY
AND I'M COMPETING.

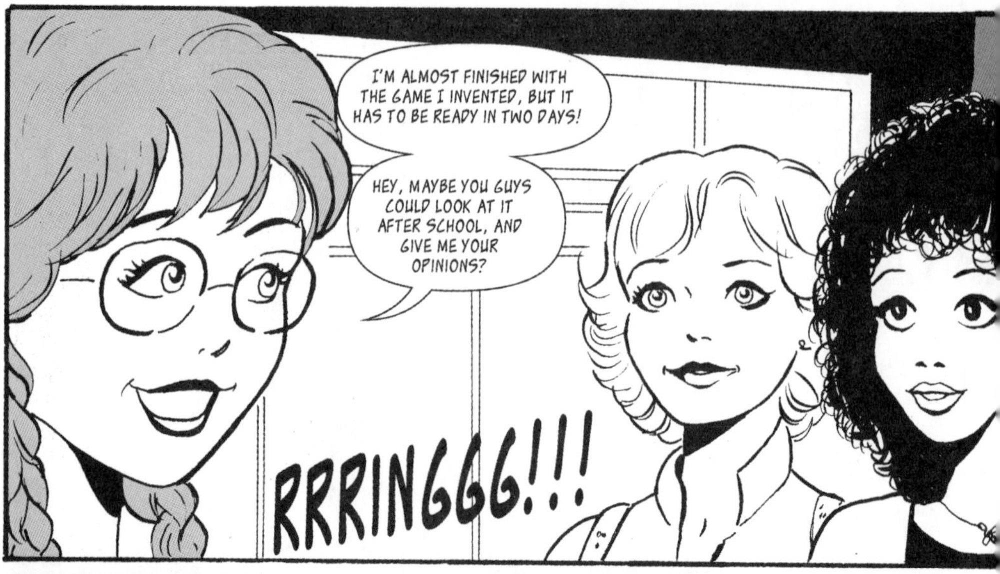
I'M ALMOST FINISHED WITH THE GAME I INVENTED, BUT IT HAS TO BE READY IN TWO DAYS!
HEY, MAYBE YOU GUYS COULD LOOK AT IT AFTER SCHOOL, AND GIVE ME YOUR OPINIONS?
RRRINGGG!!!

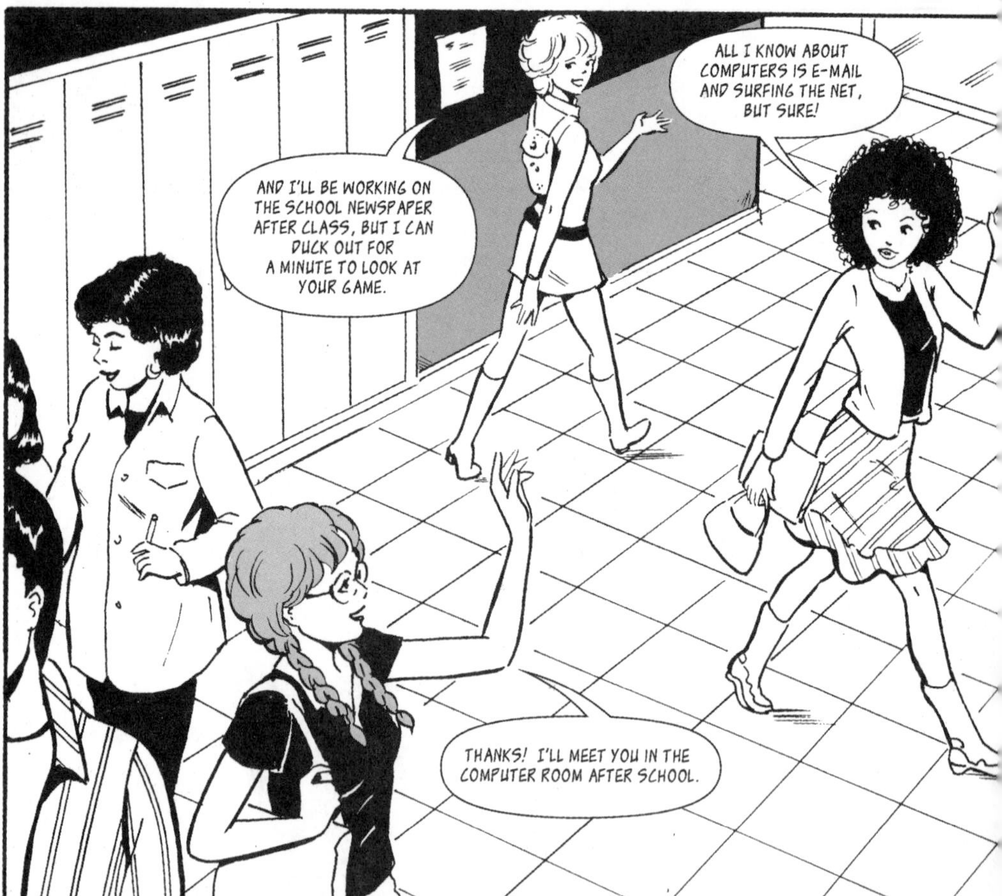
AND I'LL BE WORKING ON THE SCHOOL NEWSPAPER AFTER CLASS, BUT I CAN DUCK OUT FOR A MINUTE TO LOOK AT YOUR GAME.
ALL I KNOW ABOUT COMPUTERS IS E-MAIL AND SURFING THE NET, BUT SURE!
THANKS! I'LL MEET YOU IN THE COMPUTER ROOM AFTER SCHOOL.

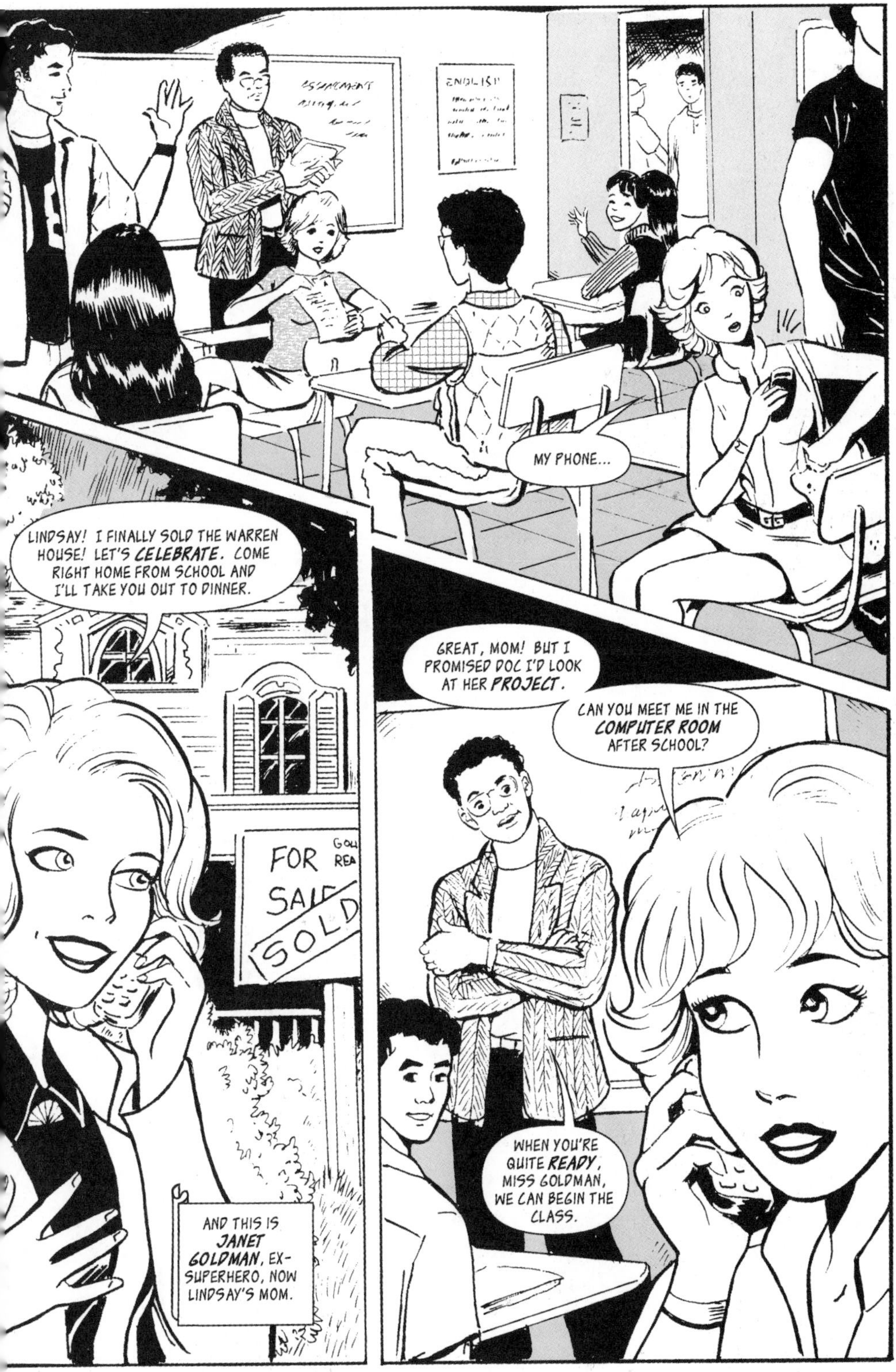

MY PHONE...
LINDSAY! I FINALLY SOLD THE WARREN HOUSE! LET'S CELEBRATE. COME RIGHT HOME FROM SCHOOL AND I'LL TAKE YOU OUT TO DINNER.
FOR SALE
SOLD
AND THIS IS JANET GOLDMAN, EX-SUPERHERO, NOW LINDSAY'S MOM.
GREAT, MOM! BUT I PROMISED DOC I'D LOOK AT HER PROJECT.
CAN YOU MEET ME IN THE COMPUTER ROOM AFTER SCHOOL?
WHEN YOU'RE QUITE READY, MISS GOLDMAN, WE CAN BEGIN THE CLASS.

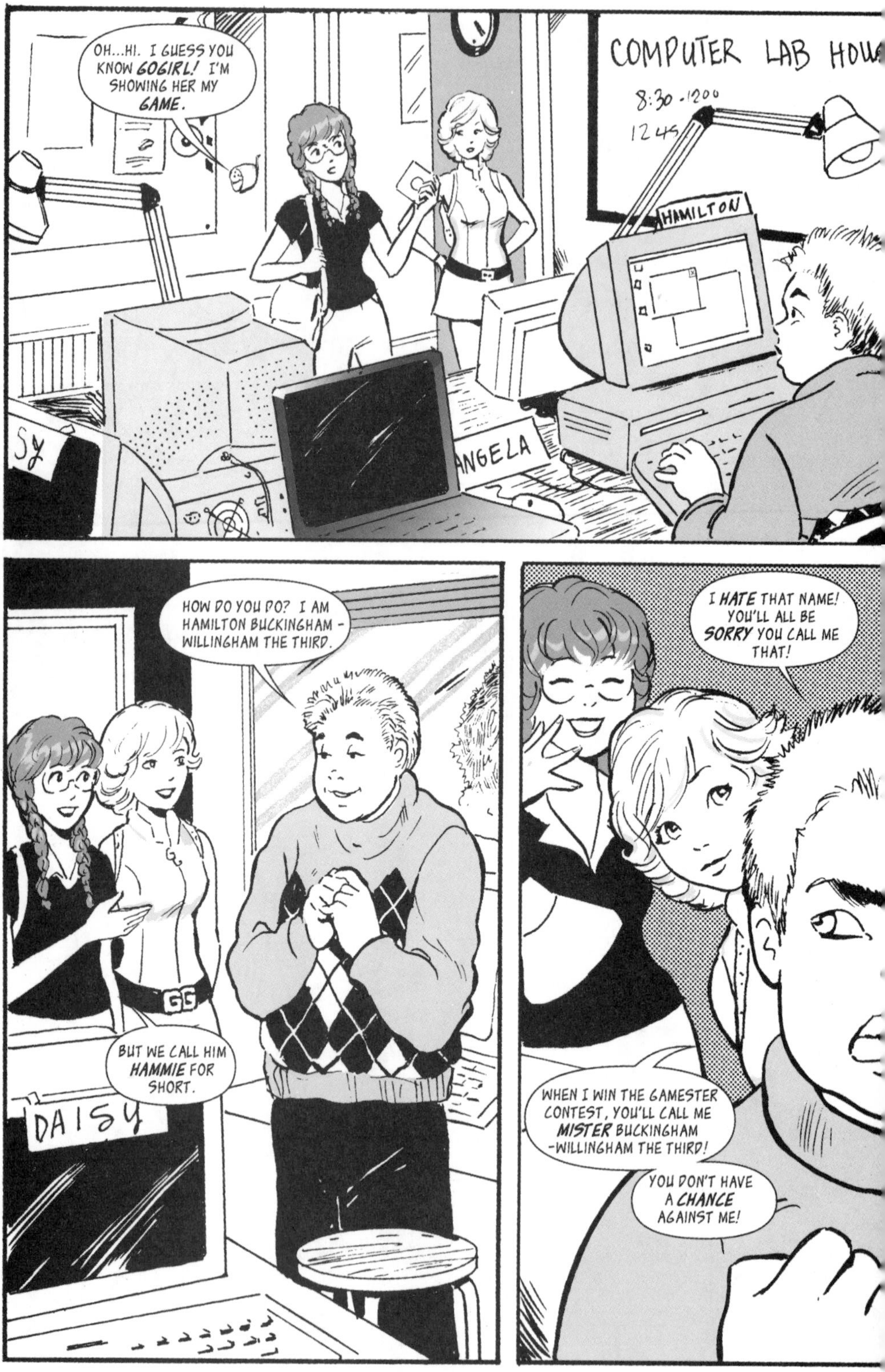
OH...HI. I GUESS YOU KNOW GOGIRL! I'M SHOWING HER MY GAME.
COMPUTER LAB
8:30 - 1200
1245
HAMILTON
ANGELA
HOW DO YOU DO? I AM HAMILTON BUCKINGHAM-WILLINGHAM THE THIRD.
BUT WE CALL HIM HAMMIE FOR SHORT.
DAISY
I HATE THAT NAME! YOU'LL ALL BE SORRY YOU CALL ME THAT!
WHEN I WIN THE GAMESTER CONTEST, YOU'LL CALL ME MISTER BUCKINGHAM-WILLINGHAM THE THIRD!
YOU DON'T HAVE A CHANCE AGAINST ME!

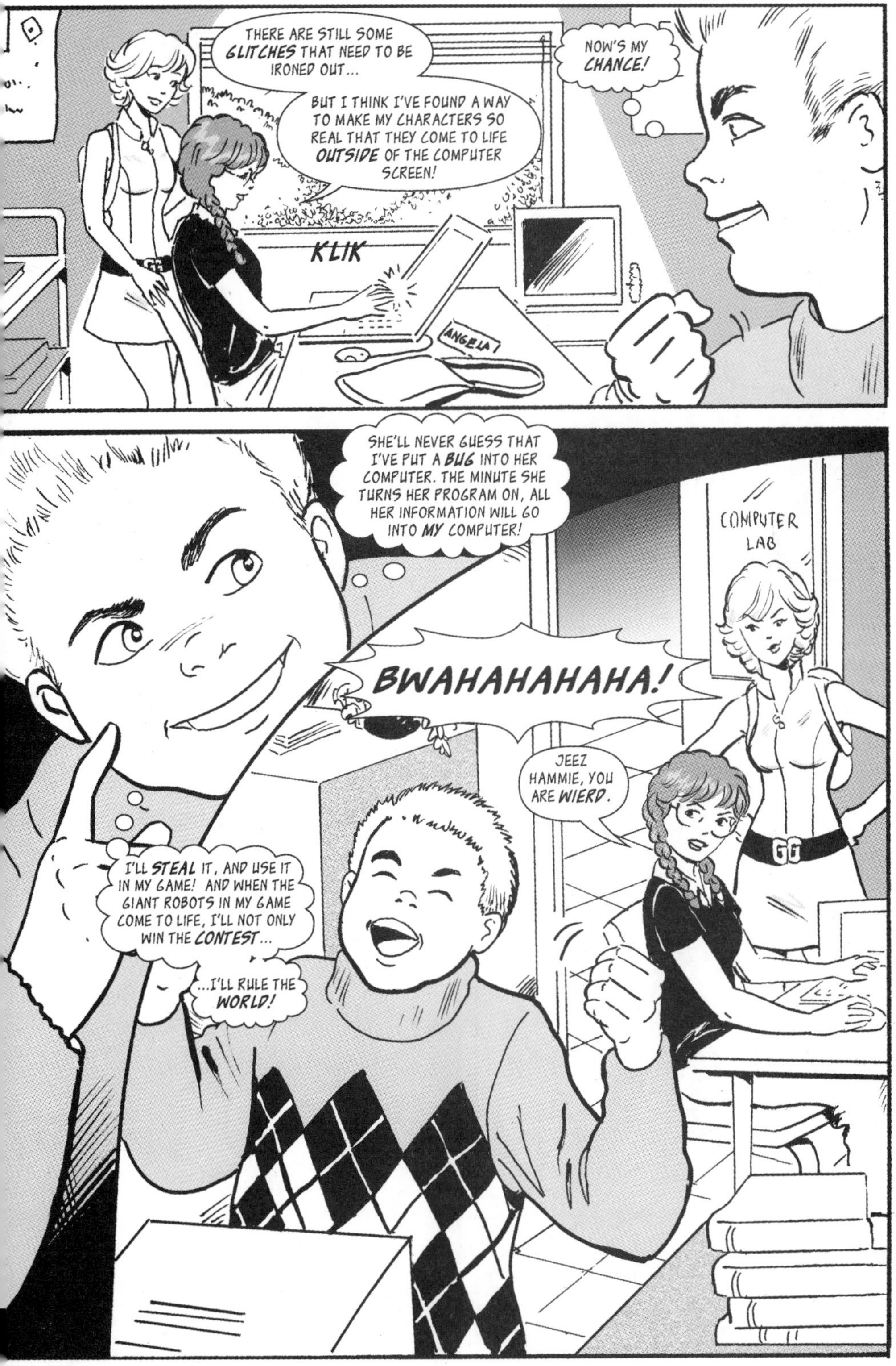
THERE ARE STILL SOME GLITCHES THAT NEED TO BE IRONED OUT...
BUT I THINK I'VE FOUND A WAY TO MAKE MY CHARACTERS SO REAL THAT THEY COME TO LIFE OUTSIDE OF THE COMPUTER SCREEN!
KLIK
ANGELA
NOW'S MY CHANCE!
SHE'LL NEVER GUESS THAT I'VE PUT A BUG INTO HER COMPUTER. THE MINUTE SHE TURNS HER PROGRAM ON, ALL HER INFORMATION WILL GO INTO MY COMPUTER!
COMPUTER LAB
BWAHAHAHAHA!
I'LL STEAL IT, AND USE IT IN MY GAME! AND WHEN THE GIANT ROBOTS IN MY GAME COME TO LIFE, I'LL NOT ONLY WIN THE CONTEST...
...I'LL RULE THE WORLD!
JEEZ HAMMIE, YOU ARE WIERD.

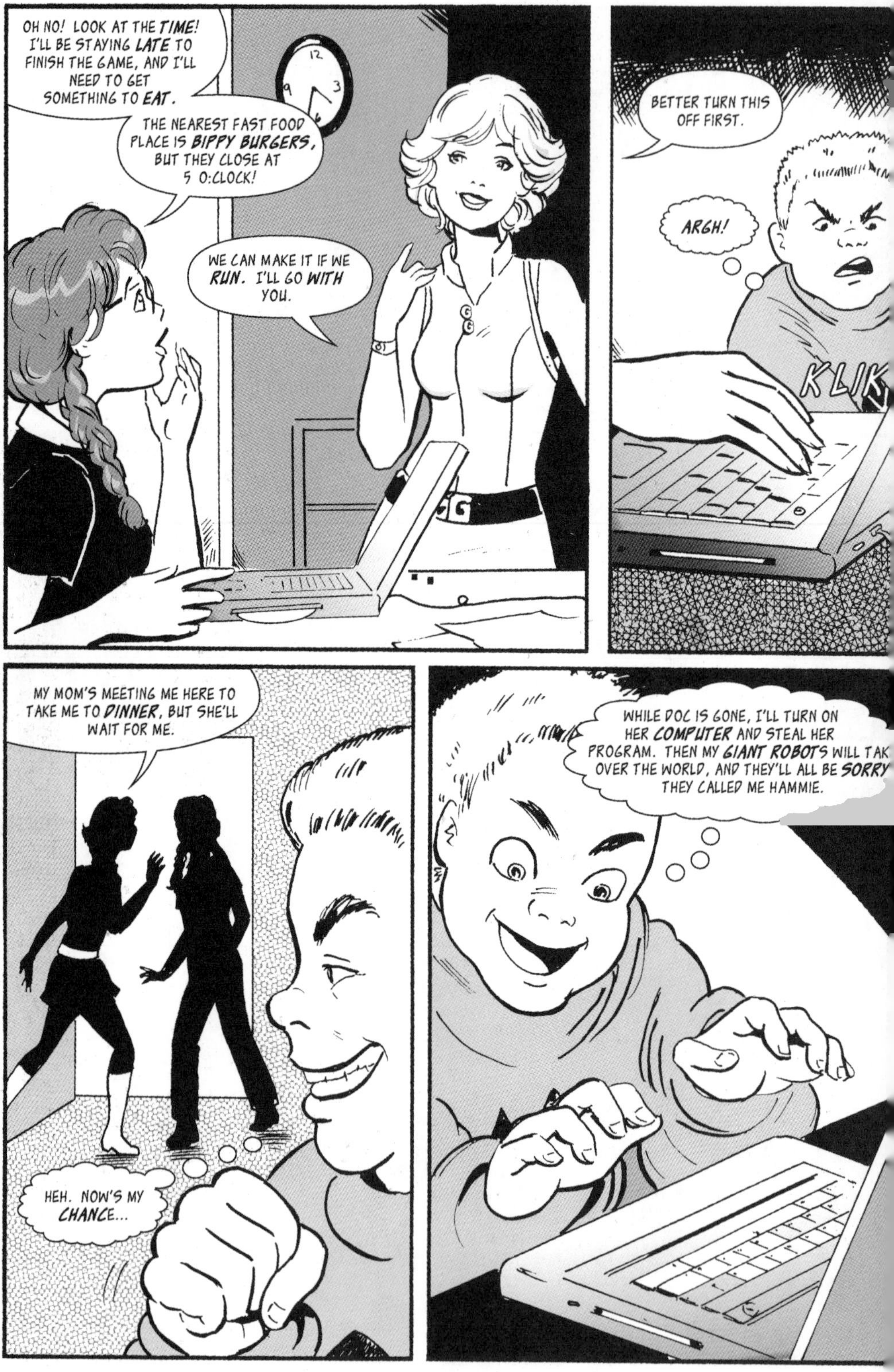
OH NO! LOOK AT THE TIME! I'LL BE STAYING LATE TO FINISH THE GAME, AND I'LL NEED TO GET SOMETHING TO EAT.
THE NEAREST FAST FOOD PLACE IS BIPPY BURGERS, BUT THEY CLOSE AT 5 O:CLOCK!
WE CAN MAKE IT IF WE RUN. I'LL GO WITH YOU.
BETTER TURN THIS OFF FIRST.
ARGH!
KLIK
MY MOM'S MEETING ME HERE TO TAKE ME TO DINNER, BUT SHE'LL WAIT FOR ME.
HEH. NOW'S MY CHANCE...
WHILE DOC IS GONE, I'LL TURN ON HER COMPUTER AND STEAL HER PROGRAM. THEN MY GIANT ROBOTS WILL TAK OVER THE WORLD, AND THEY'LL ALL BE SORRY THEY CALLED ME HAMMIE.

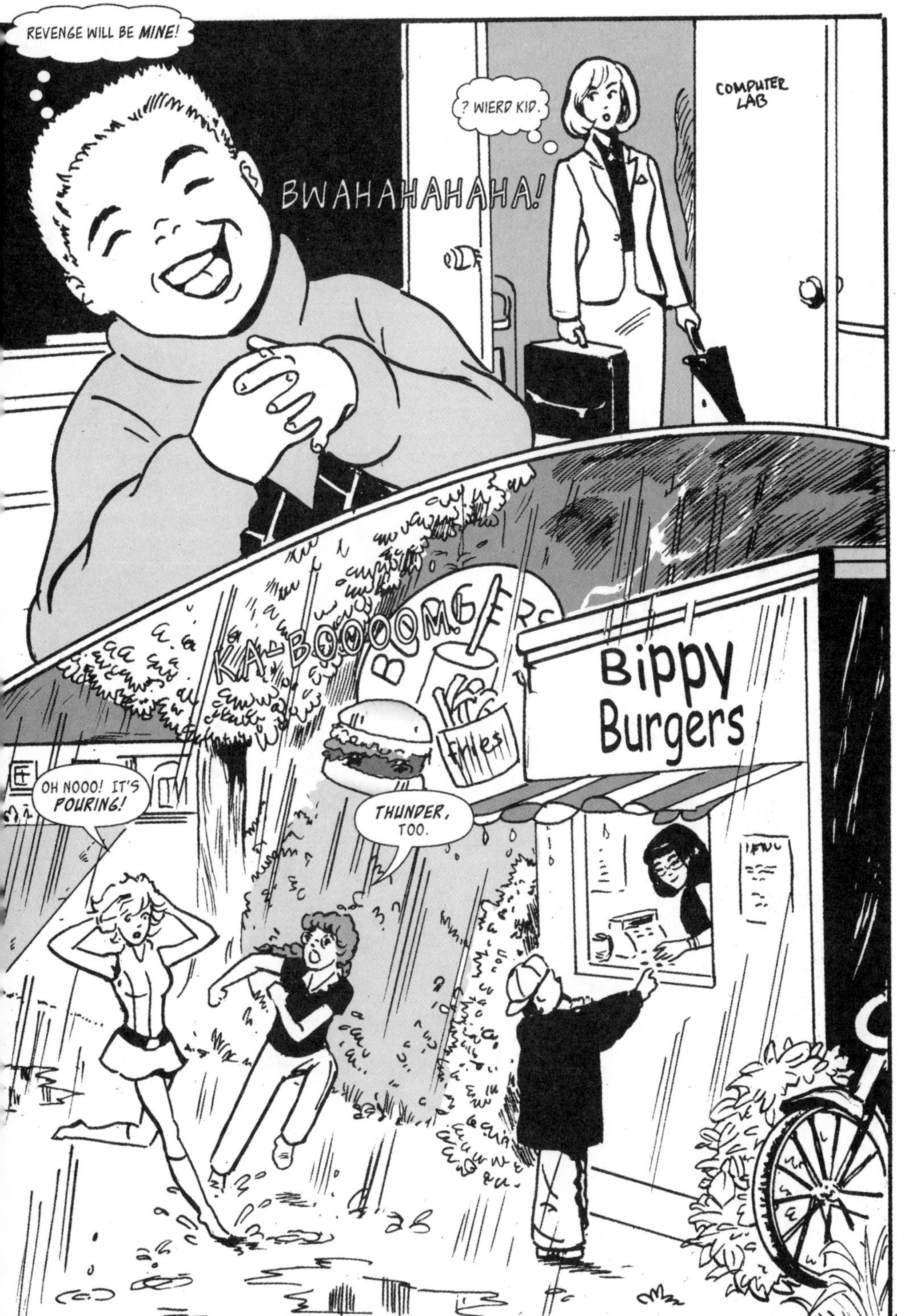
REVENGE WILL BE *MINE!*
? WIERD KID.
COMPUTER LAB
BWAHAHAHAHA!
KA-BOOOOOM!
Bippy Burgers
fries
OH NOOO! IT'S *POURING!*
*THUNDER,* TOO.

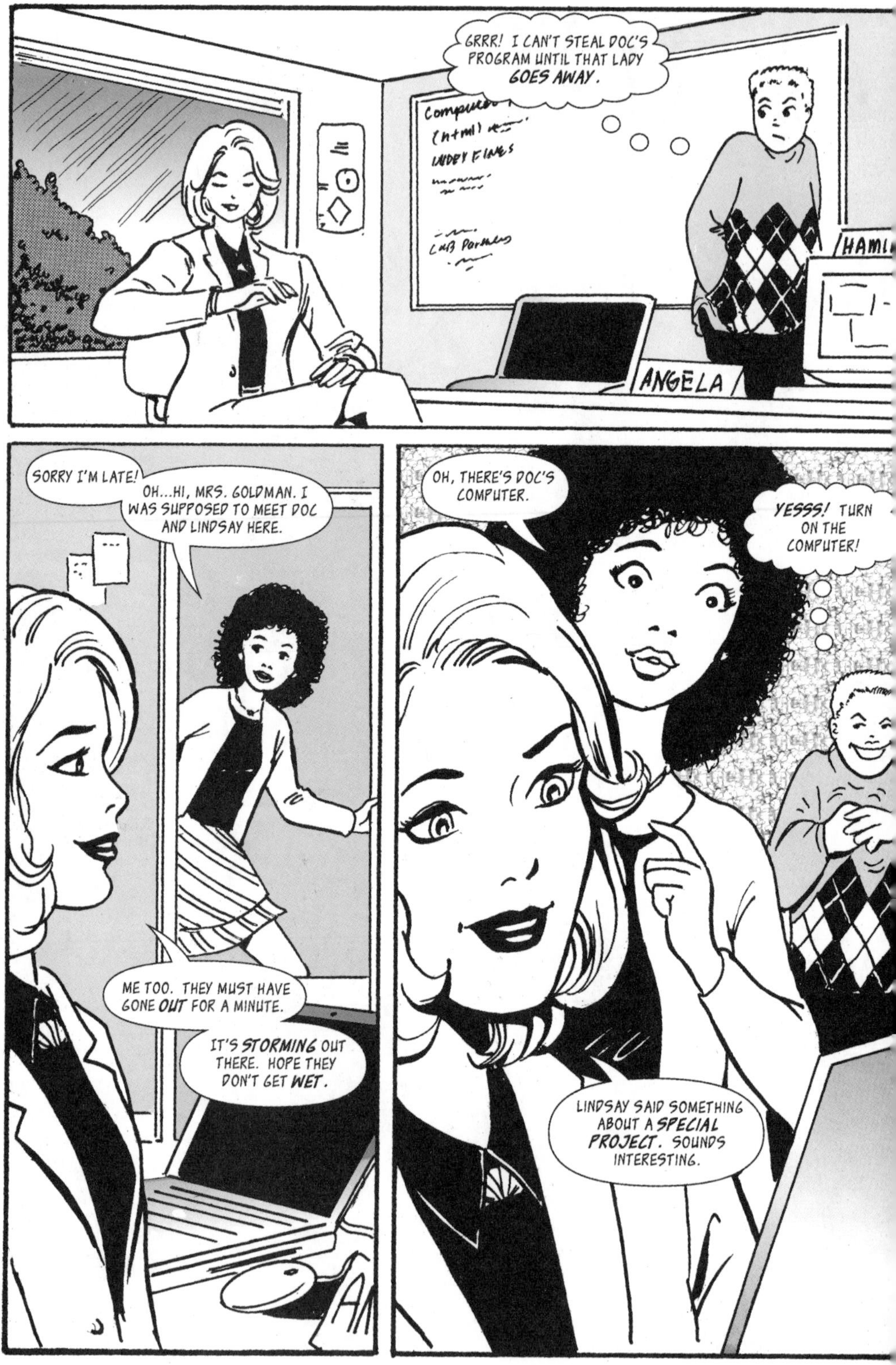
GRRR! I CAN'T STEAL DOC'S PROGRAM UNTIL THAT LADY GOES AWAY.
ANGELA
SORRY I'M LATE!
OH...HI, MRS. GOLDMAN. I WAS SUPPOSED TO MEET DOC AND LINDSAY HERE.
ME TOO. THEY MUST HAVE GONE OUT FOR A MINUTE.
IT'S STORMING OUT THERE. HOPE THEY DON'T GET WET.
OH, THERE'S DOC'S COMPUTER.
YESSS! TURN ON THE COMPUTER!
LINDSAY SAID SOMETHING ABOUT A SPECIAL PROJECT. SOUNDS INTERESTING.

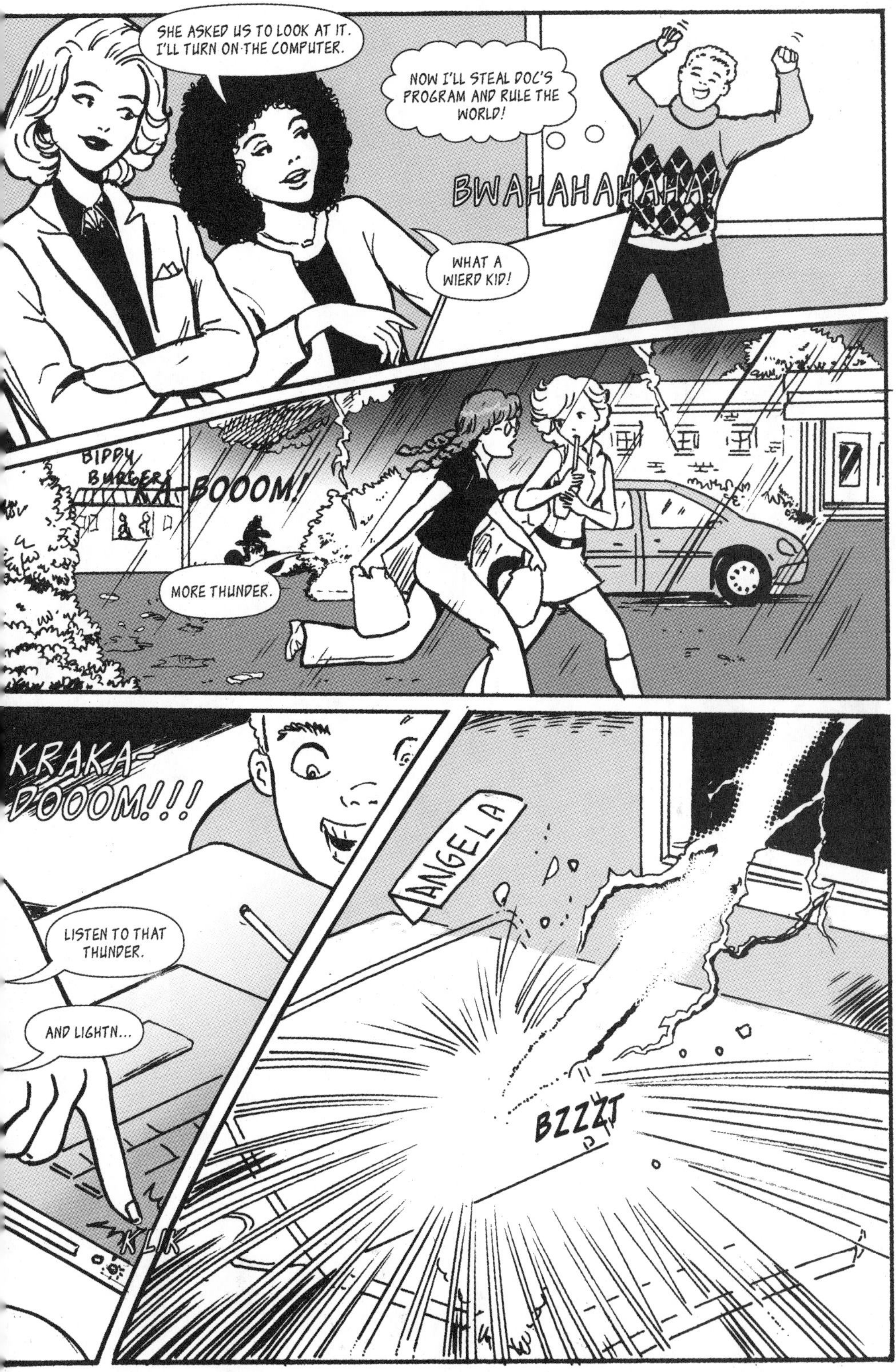
SHE ASKED US TO LOOK AT IT. I'LL TURN ON THE COMPUTER.
NOW I'LL STEAL DOC'S PROGRAM AND RULE THE WORLD!
BWAHAHAHAHAHA!
WHAT A WIERD KID!
BIPPY BURGERS
KA-BOOOM!
MORE THUNDER.
KRAKA-DOOOM!!!
LISTEN TO THAT THUNDER.
AND LIGHTN...
KLIK
ANGELA
BZZZT

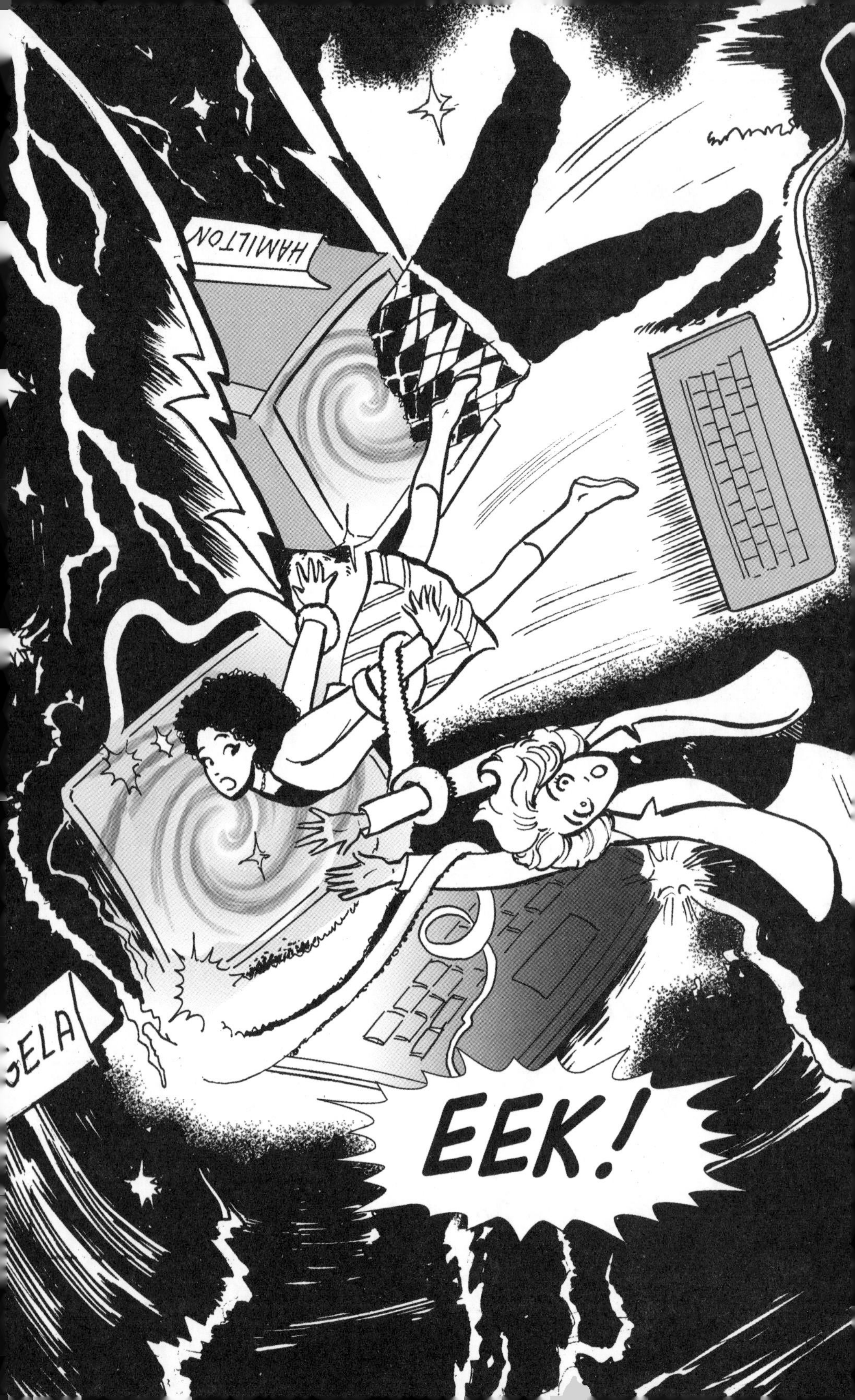
HAMILTON
GELA
EEK!

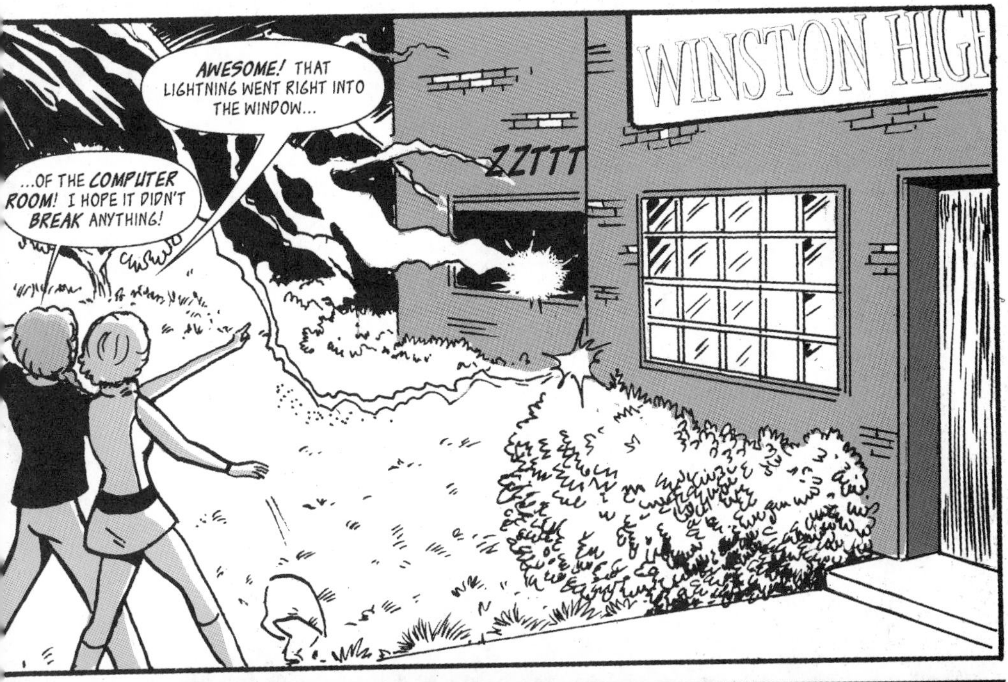
WINSTON HIGH
AWESOME! THAT LIGHTNING WENT RIGHT INTO THE WINDOW...
...OF THE COMPUTER ROOM! I HOPE IT DIDN'T BREAK ANYTHING!
ZZTTT

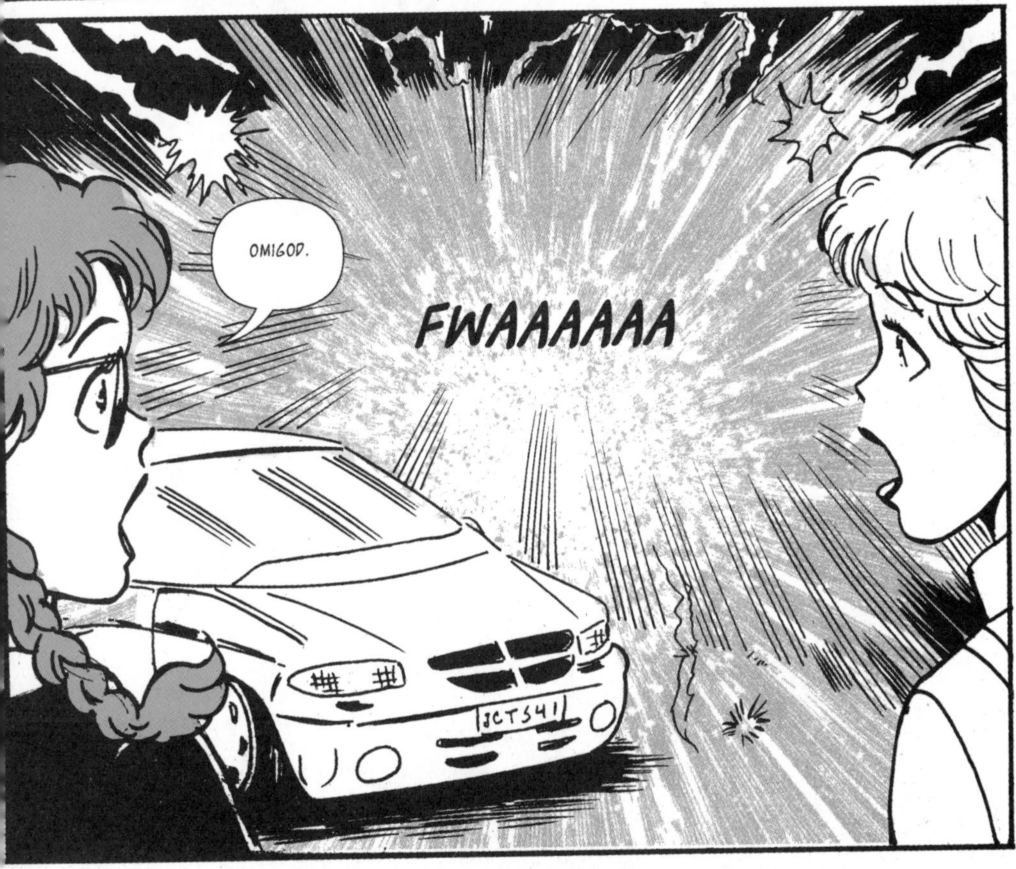
OMIGOD.
FWAAAAAA
JCT541

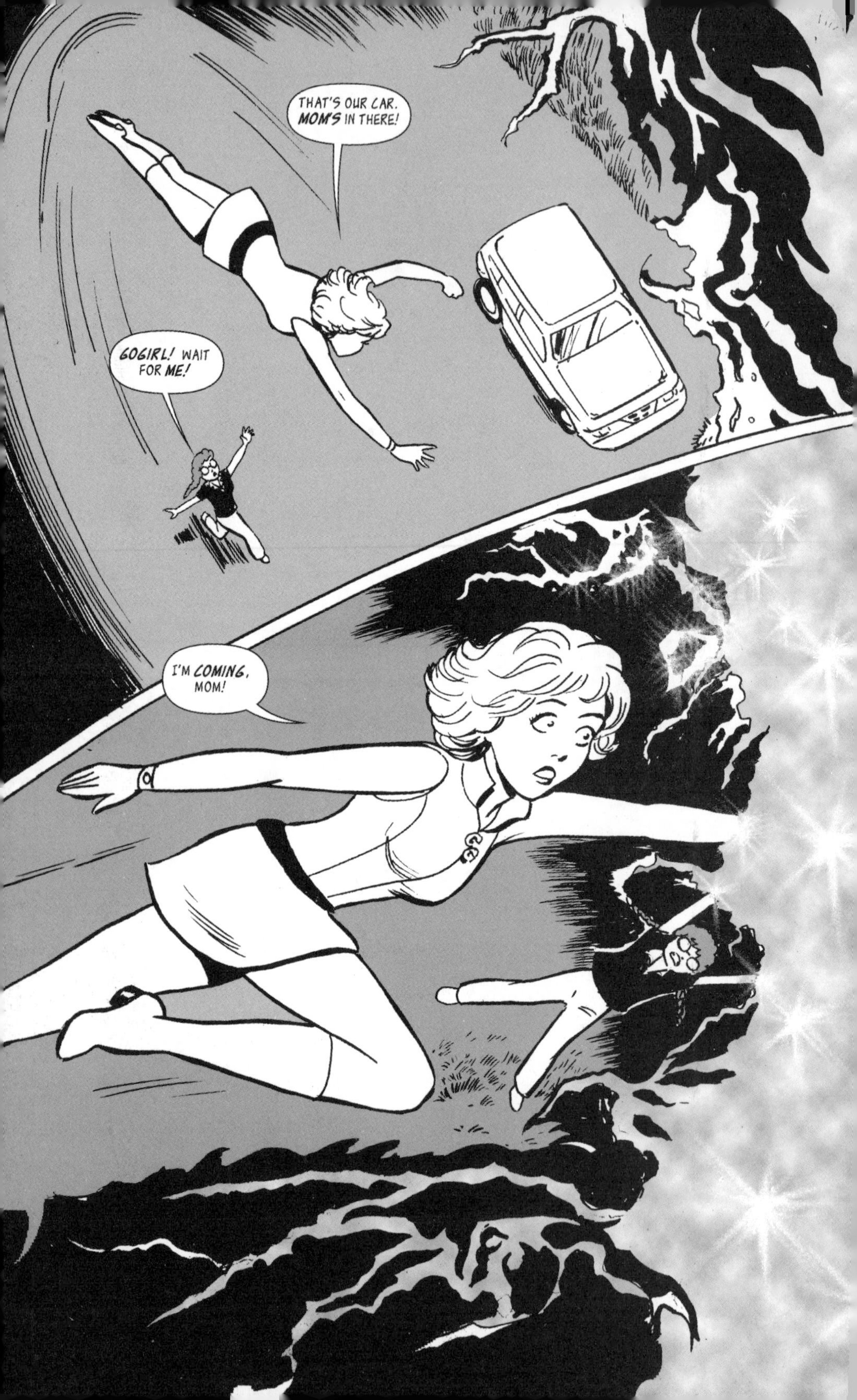

THAT'S OUR CAR. MOM'S IN THERE!
GOGIRL! WAIT FOR ME!
I'M COMING, MOM!

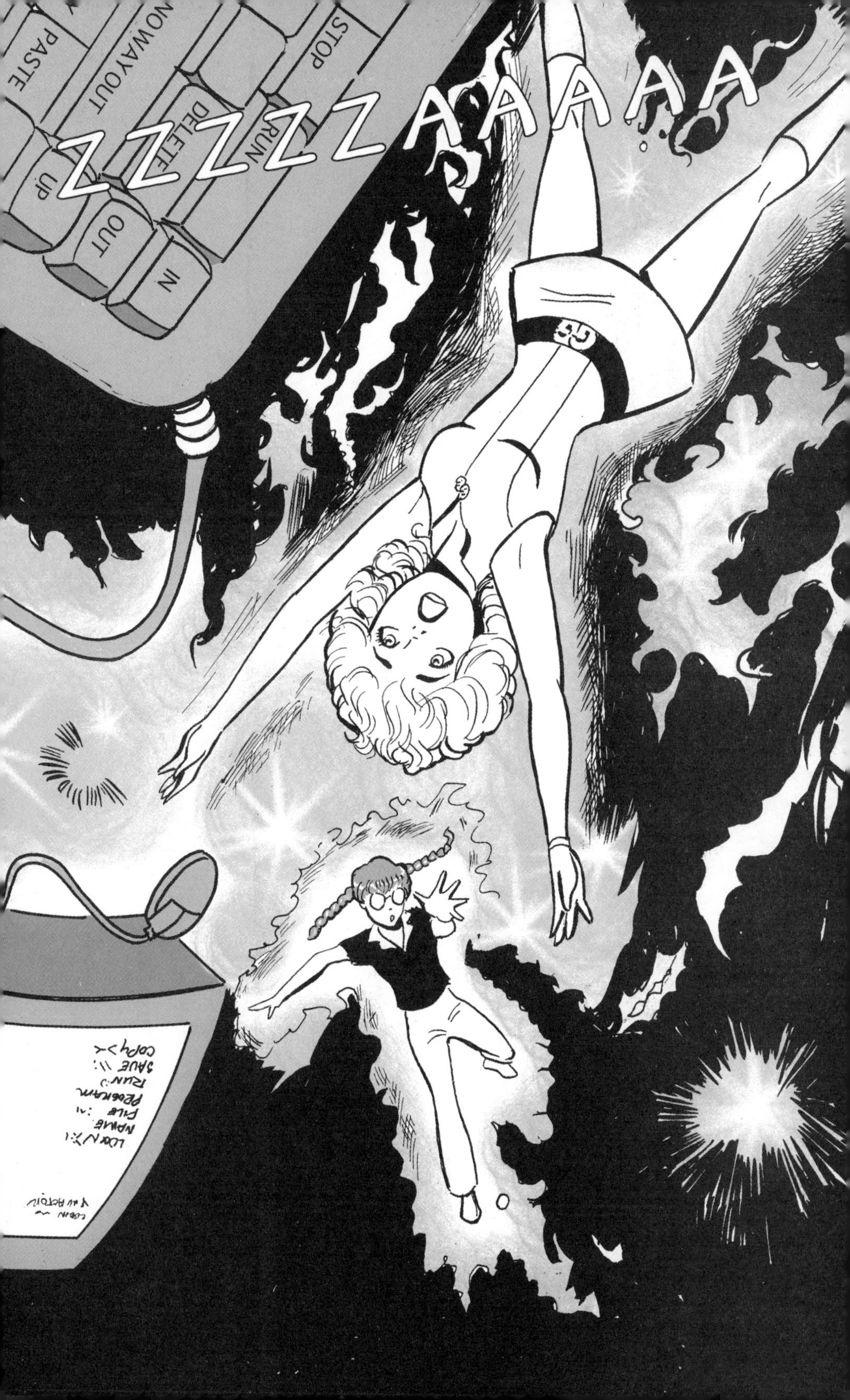
ZZZZZAAAAA
STOP
NOWAYOUT
PASTE
RUN
DELETE
UP
OUT
IN

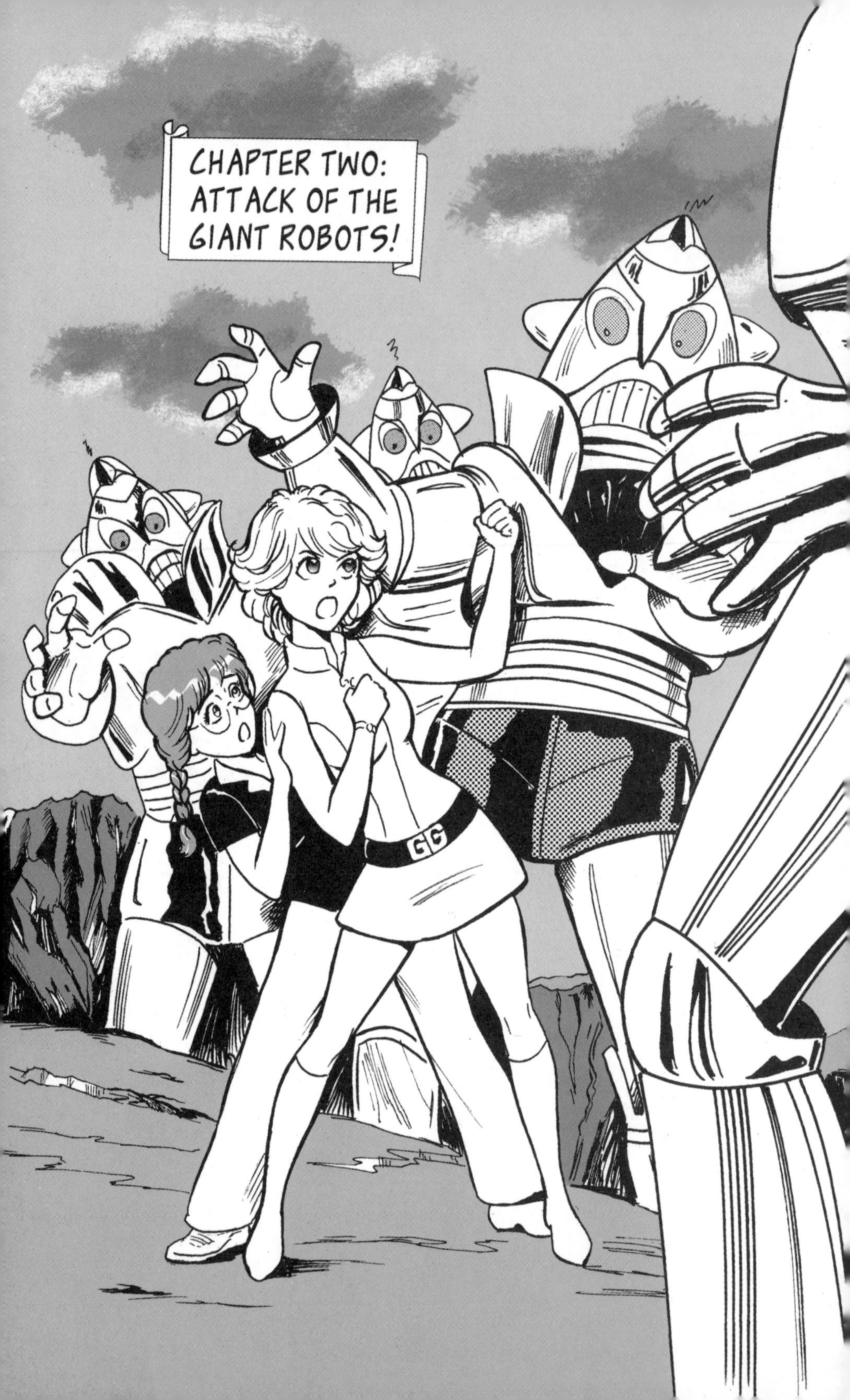
CHAPTER TWO: ATTACK OF THE GIANT ROBOTS!

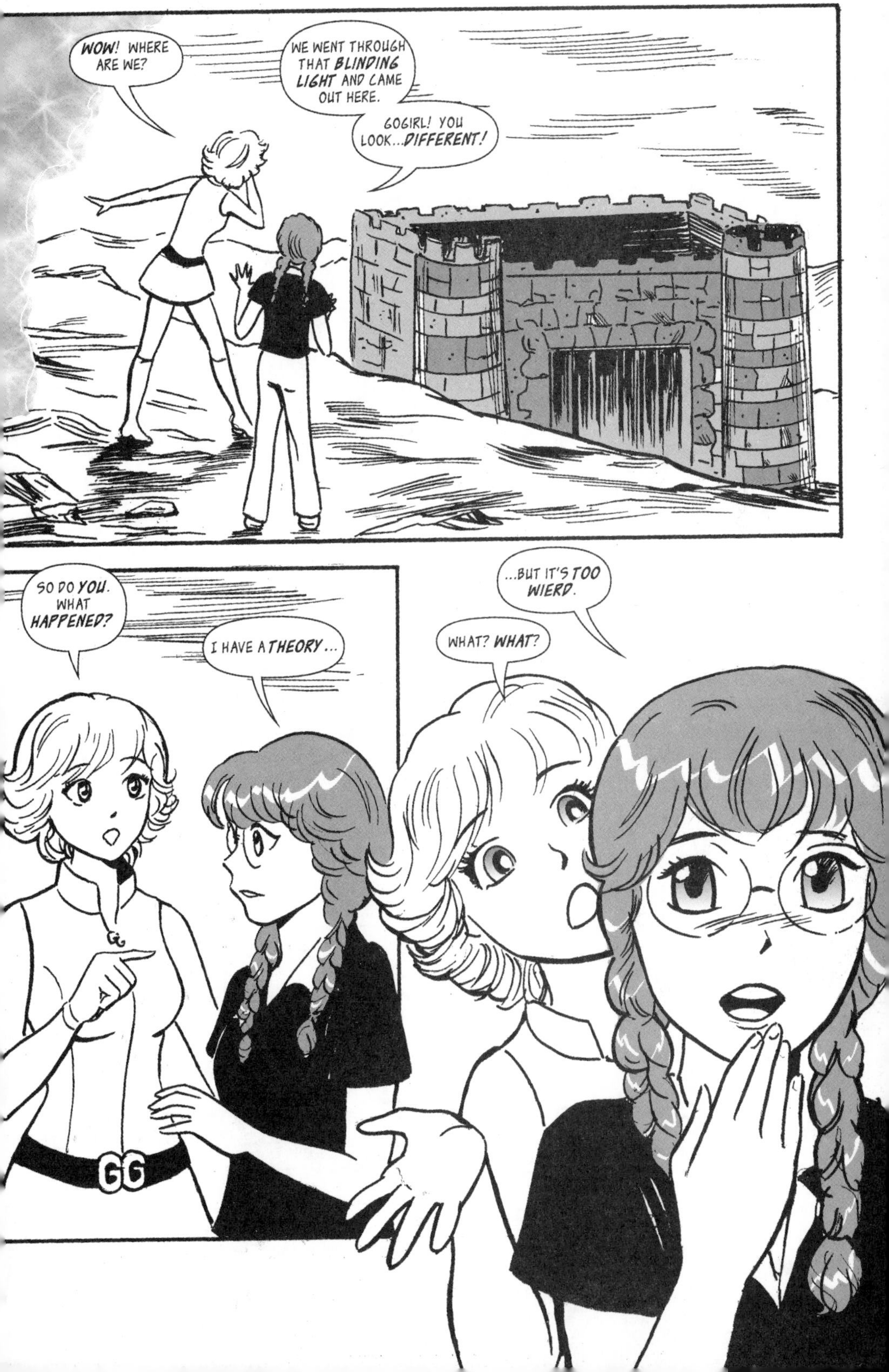
WOW! WHERE ARE WE?
WE WENT THROUGH THAT BLINDING LIGHT AND CAME OUT HERE.
GOGIRL! YOU LOOK...DIFFERENT!
SO DO YOU. WHAT HAPPENED?
I HAVE A THEORY...
WHAT? WHAT?
...BUT IT'S TOO WIERD.

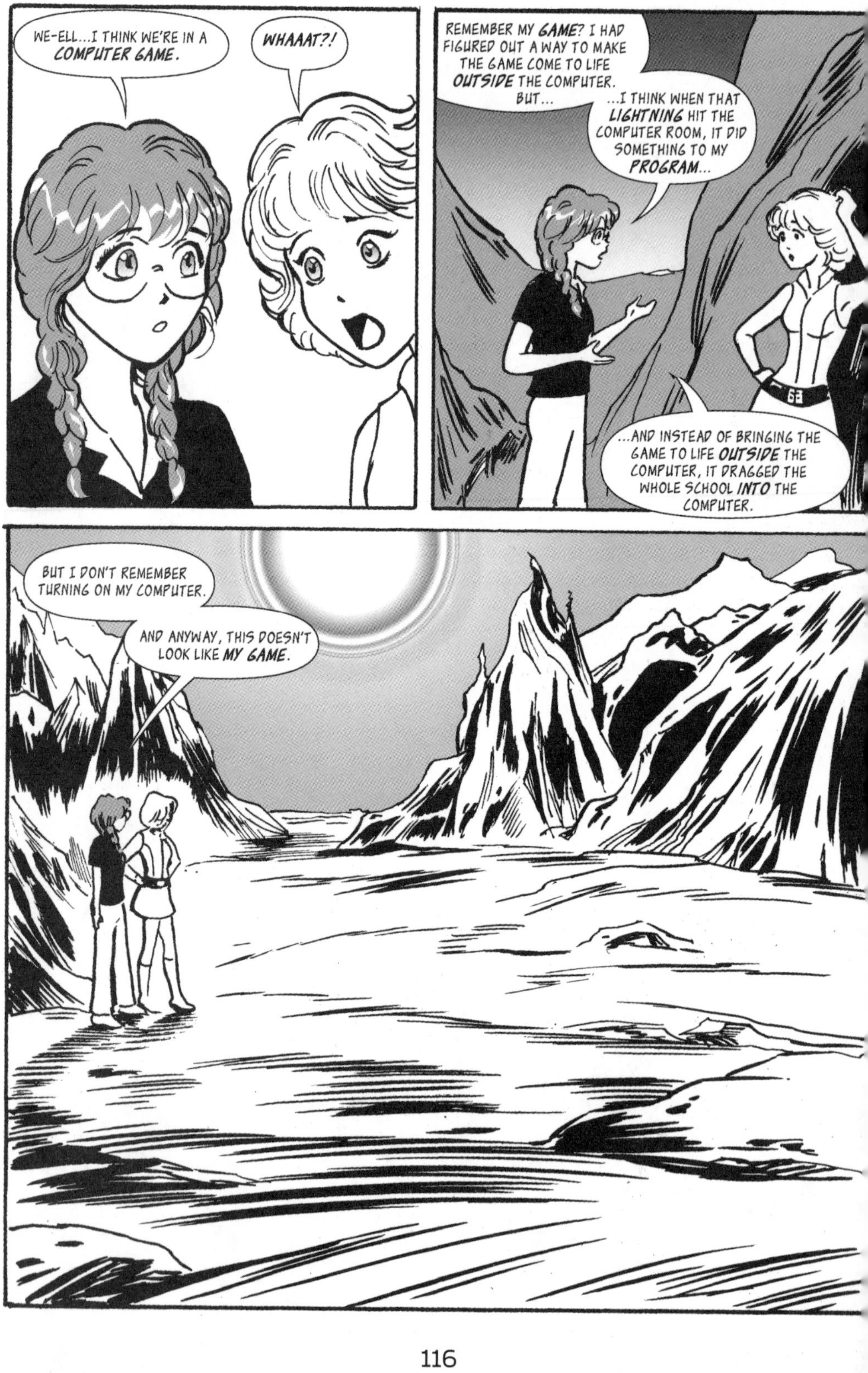
WE-ELL...I THINK WE'RE IN A COMPUTER GAME.
WHAAAT?!
REMEMBER MY GAME? I HAD FIGURED OUT A WAY TO MAKE THE GAME COME TO LIFE OUTSIDE THE COMPUTER. BUT...
...I THINK WHEN THAT LIGHTNING HIT THE COMPUTER ROOM, IT DID SOMETHING TO MY PROGRAM...
...AND INSTEAD OF BRINGING THE GAME TO LIFE OUTSIDE THE COMPUTER, IT DRAGGED THE WHOLE SCHOOL INTO THE COMPUTER.
BUT I DON'T REMEMBER TURNING ON MY COMPUTER.
AND ANYWAY, THIS DOESN'T LOOK LIKE MY GAME.

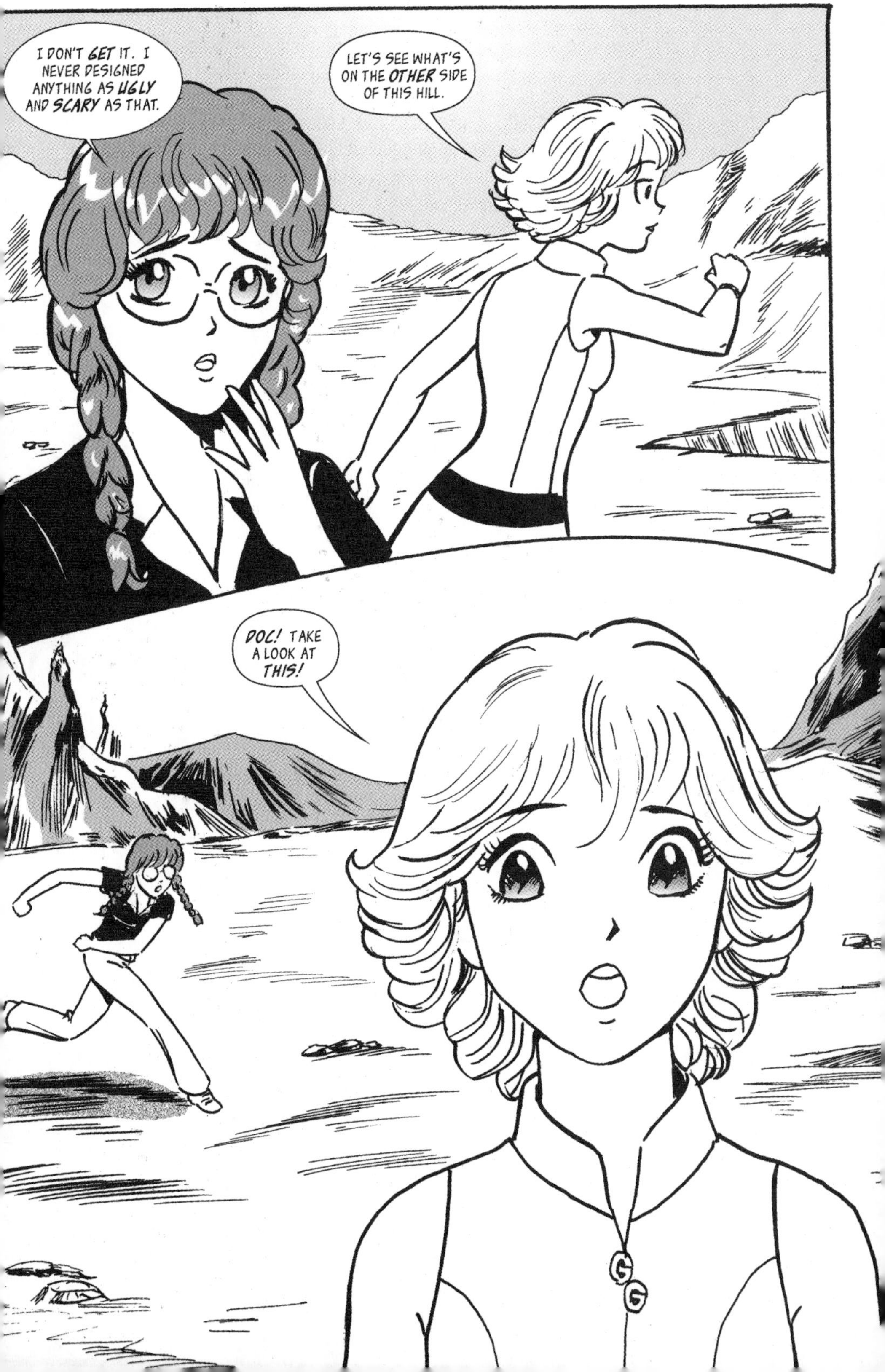
I DON'T GET IT. I NEVER DESIGNED ANYTHING AS UGLY AND SCARY AS THAT.
LET'S SEE WHAT'S ON THE OTHER SIDE OF THIS HILL.
DOC! TAKE A LOOK AT THIS!

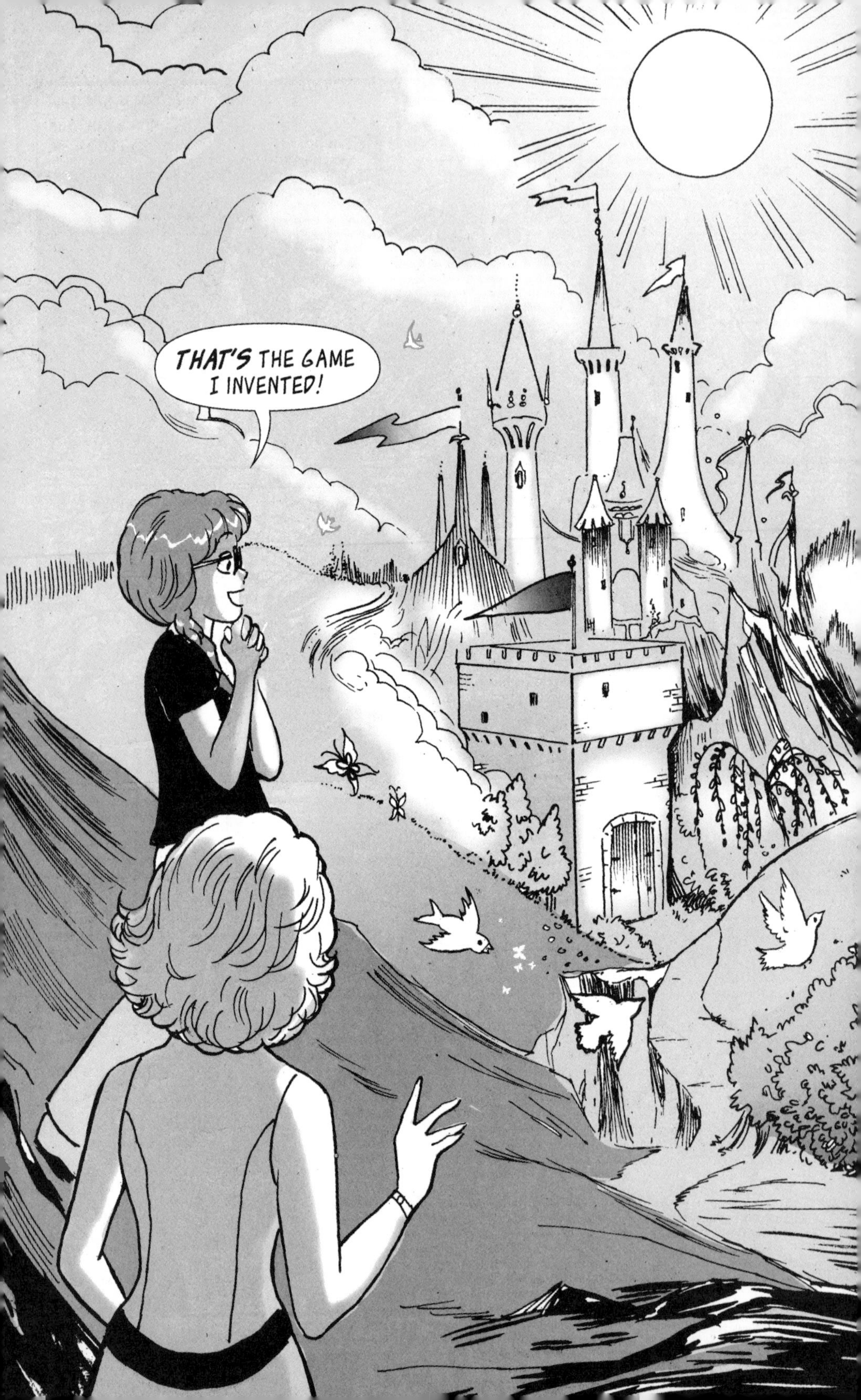
THAT'S THE GAME I INVENTED!

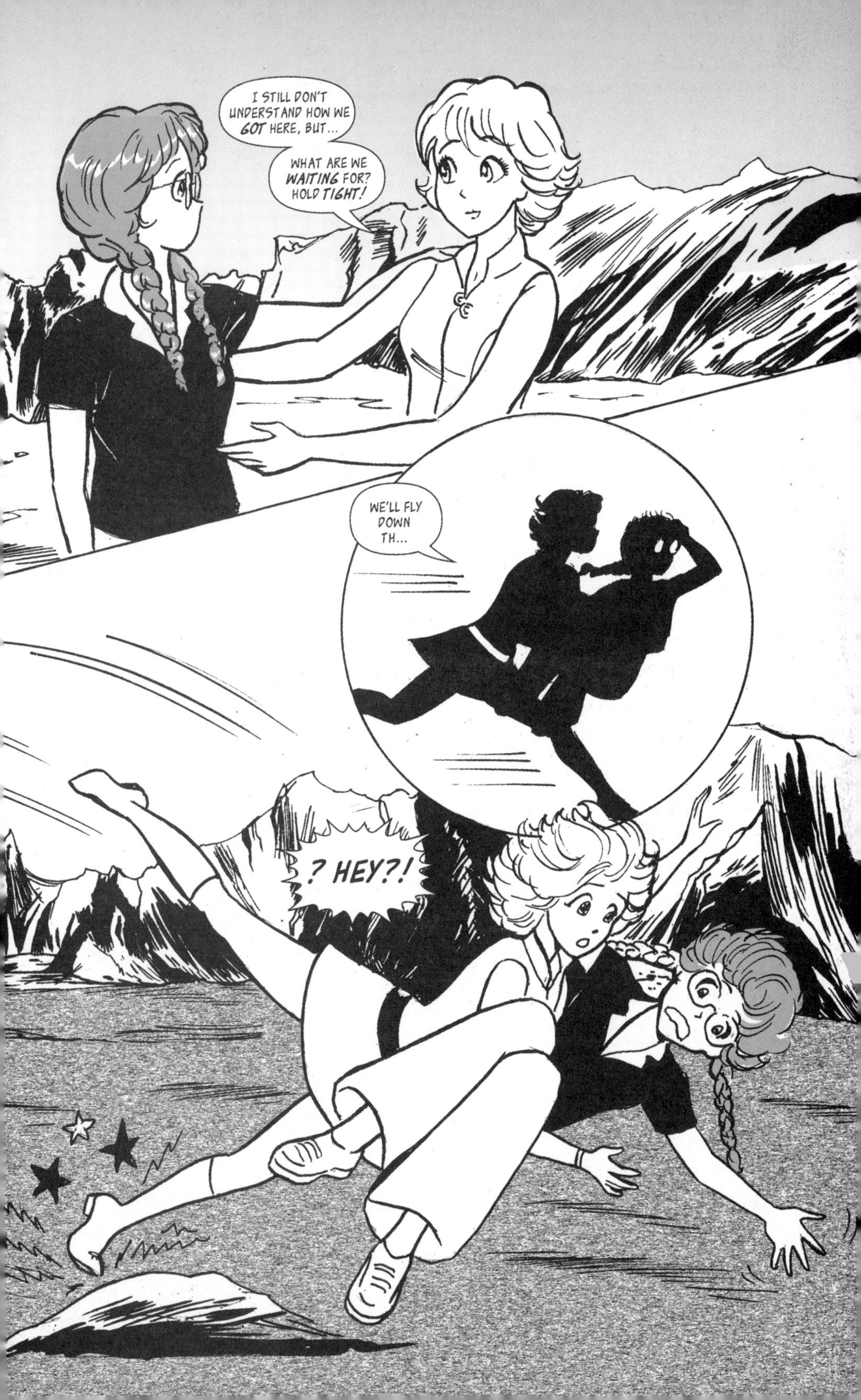
I STILL DON'T UNDERSTAND HOW WE *GOT* HERE, BUT...
WHAT ARE WE *WAITING* FOR? HOLD *TIGHT!*
WE'LL FLY DOWN TH...
? HEY?!

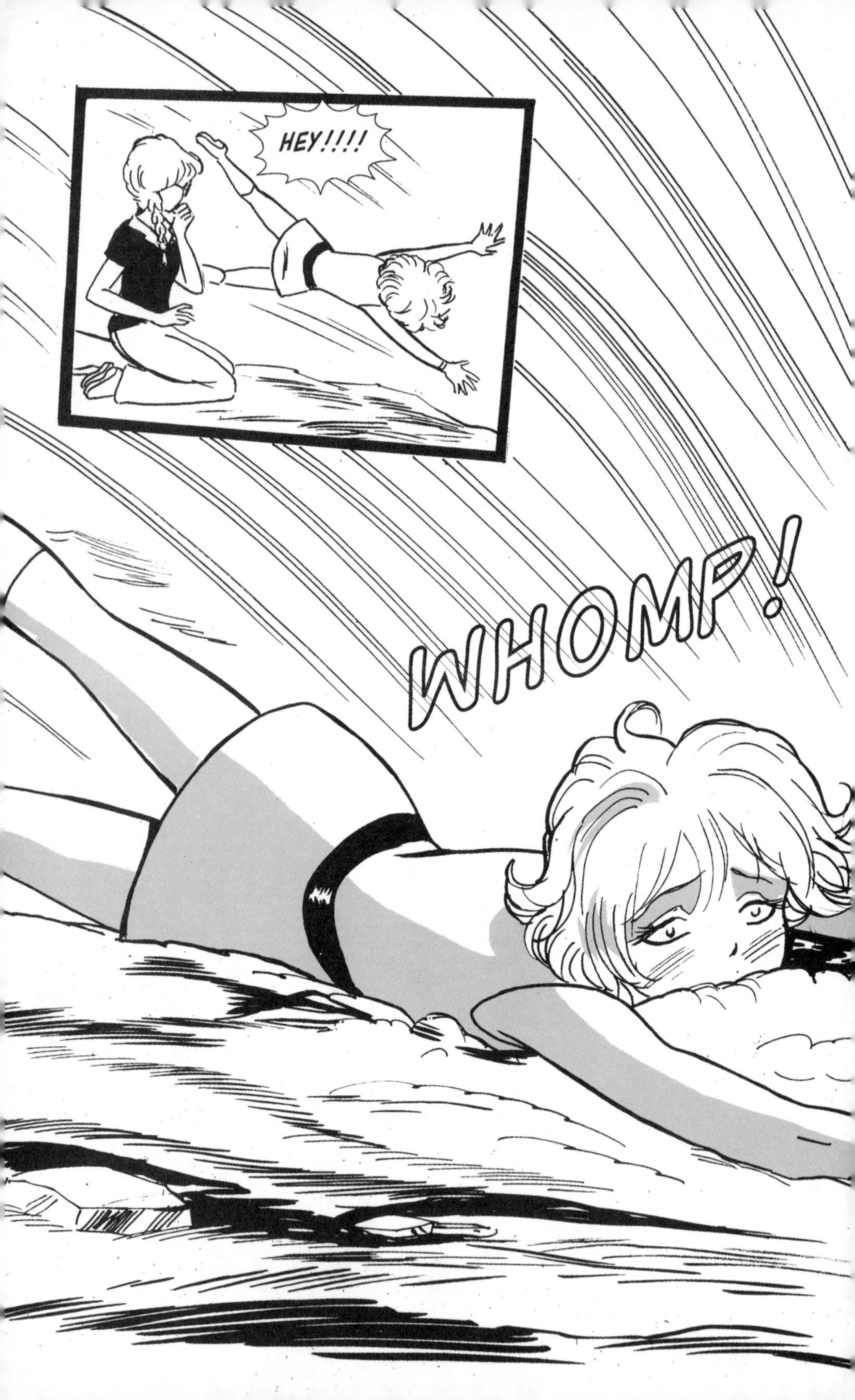
HEY!!!!
WHOMP!

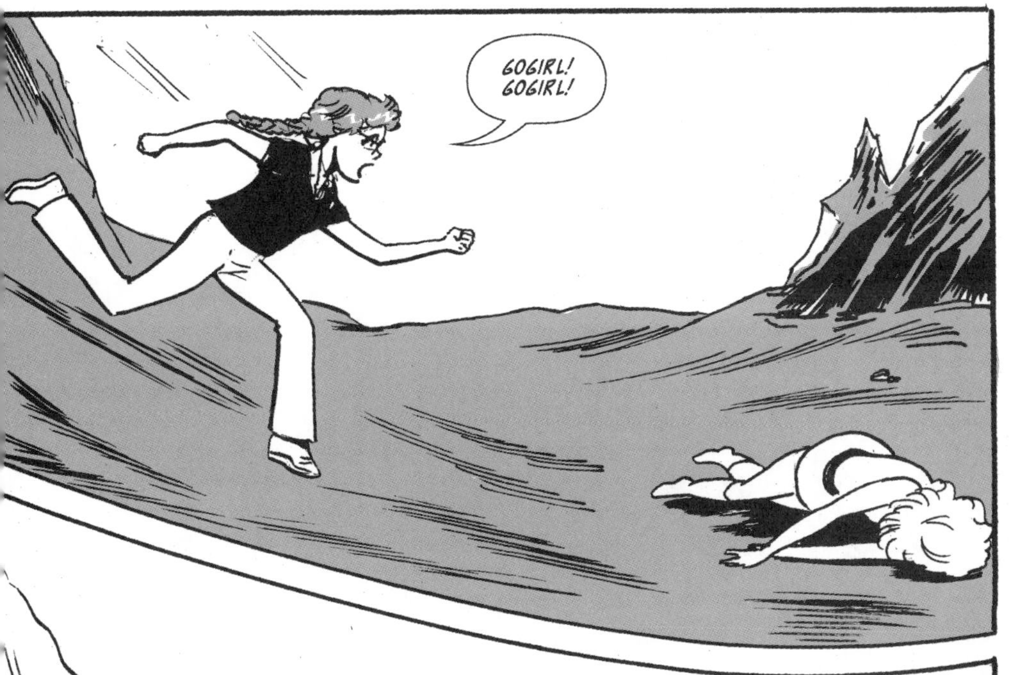
GOGIRL!
GOGIRL!

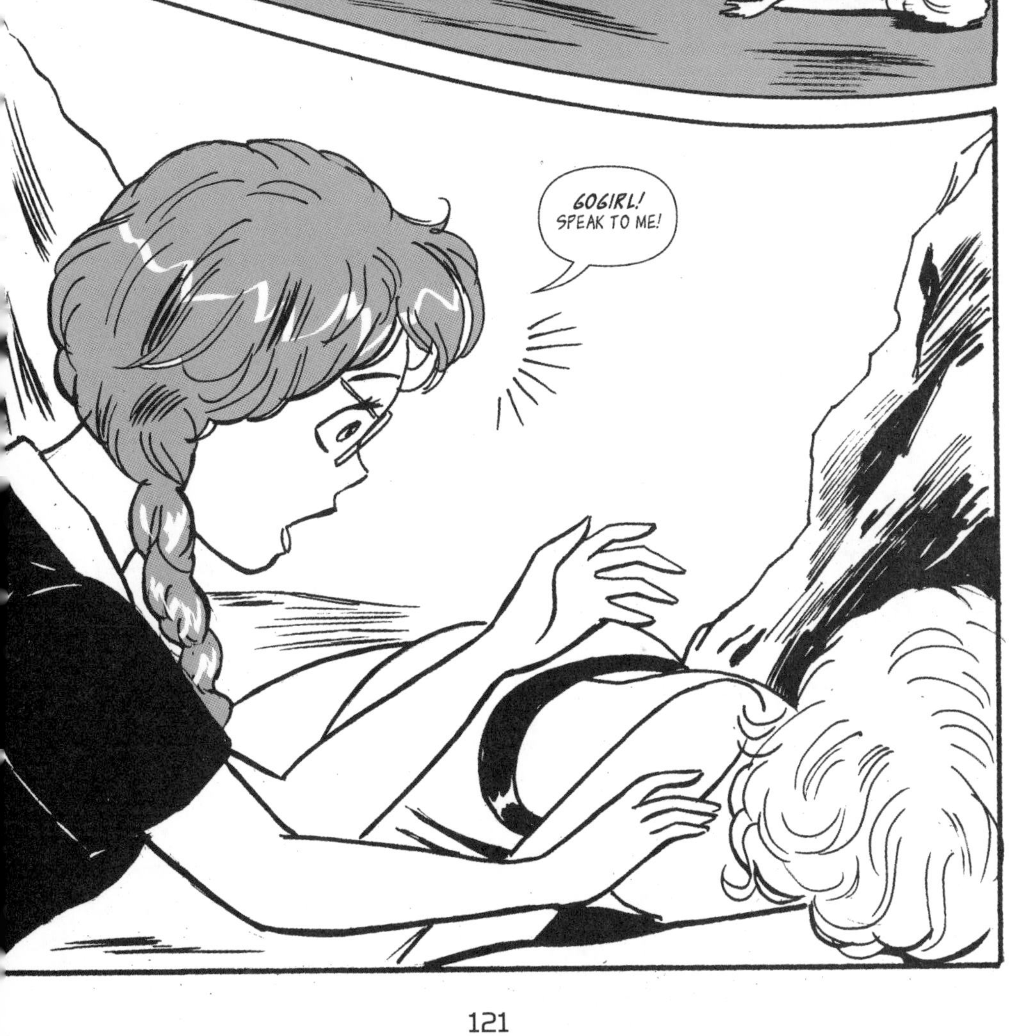
GOGIRL!
SPEAK TO ME!

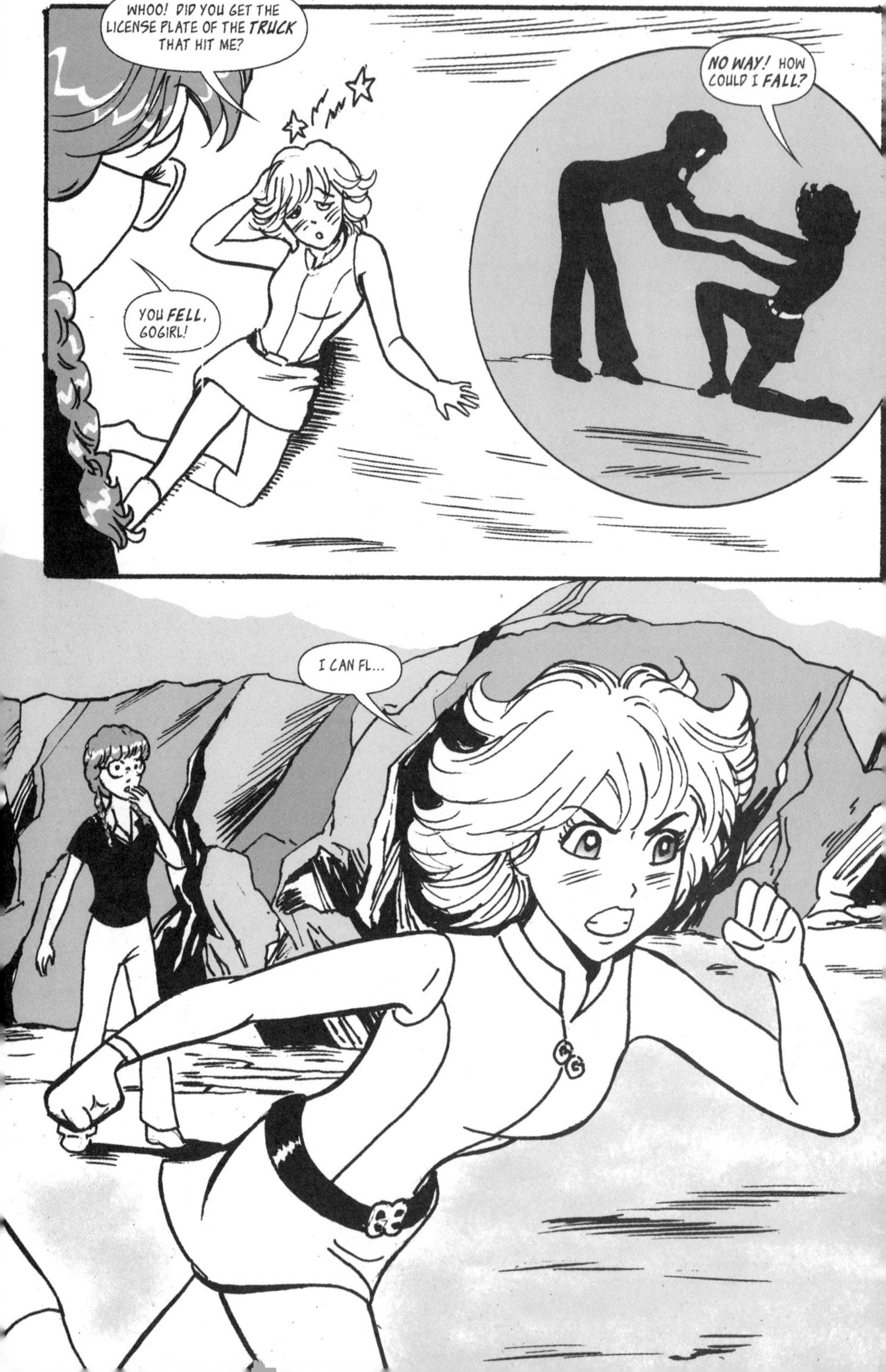
WHOO! DID YOU GET THE LICENSE PLATE OF THE **TRUCK** THAT HIT ME?
YOU **FELL**, GOGIRL!
**NO WAY!** HOW COULD I **FALL?**
I CAN FL...

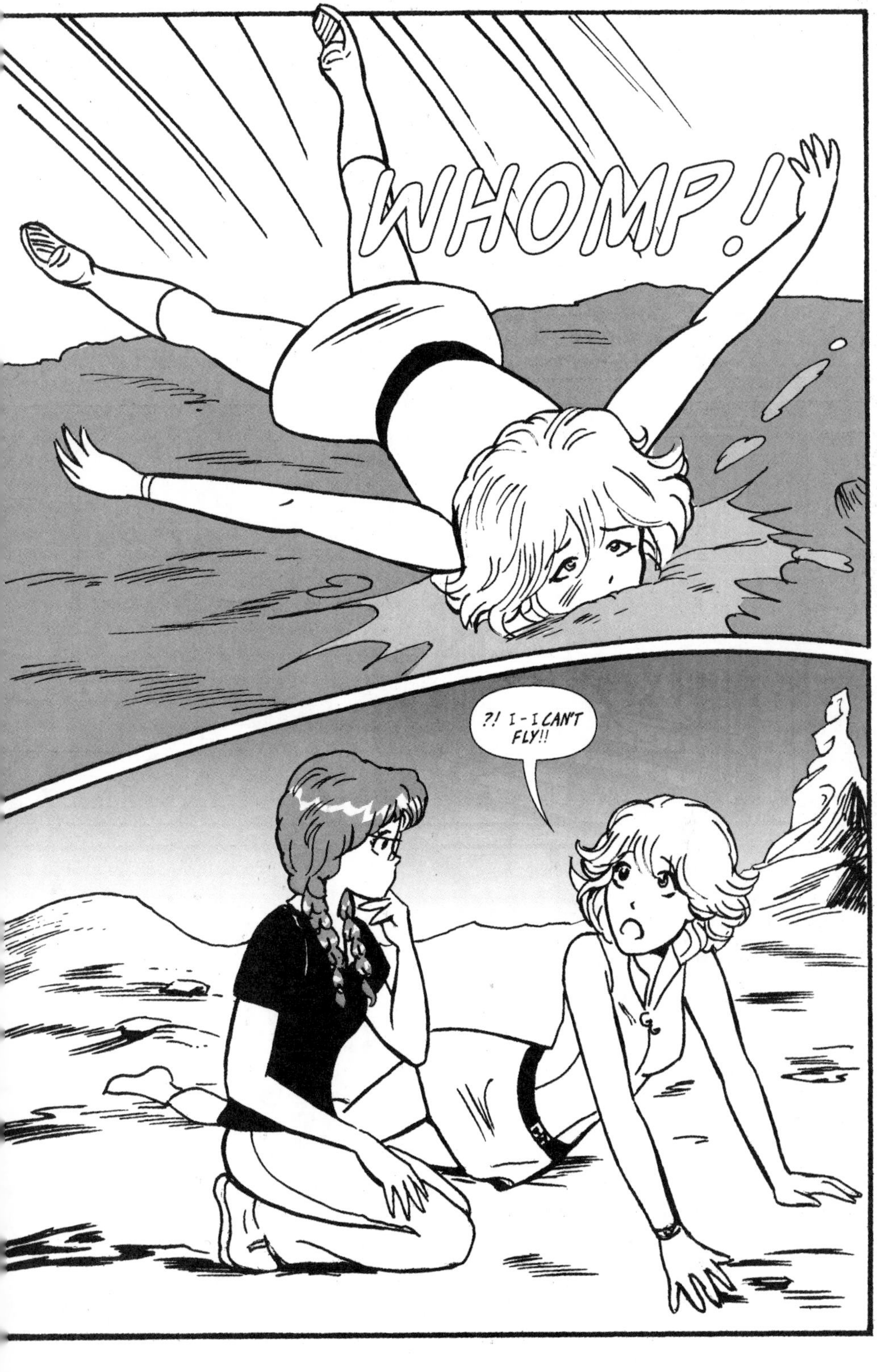
WHOMP!
?! I-I CAN'T FLY!!

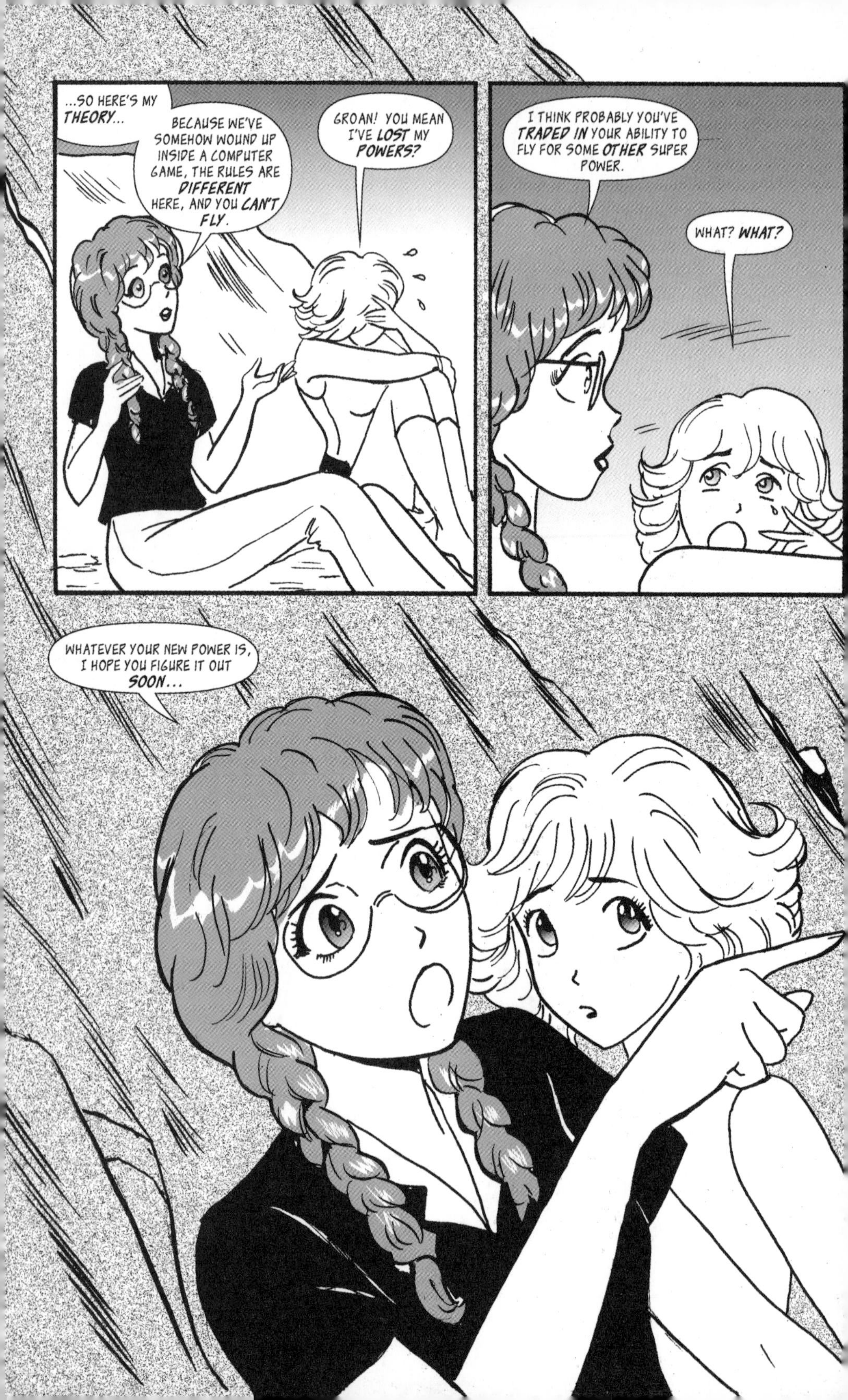
...SO HERE'S MY THEORY...
BECAUSE WE'VE SOMEHOW WOUND UP INSIDE A COMPUTER GAME, THE RULES ARE DIFFERENT HERE, AND YOU CAN'T FLY.
GROAN! YOU MEAN I'VE LOST MY POWERS?
I THINK PROBABLY YOU'VE TRADED IN YOUR ABILITY TO FLY FOR SOME OTHER SUPER POWER.
WHAT? WHAT?
WHATEVER YOUR NEW POWER IS, I HOPE YOU FIGURE IT OUT SOON...

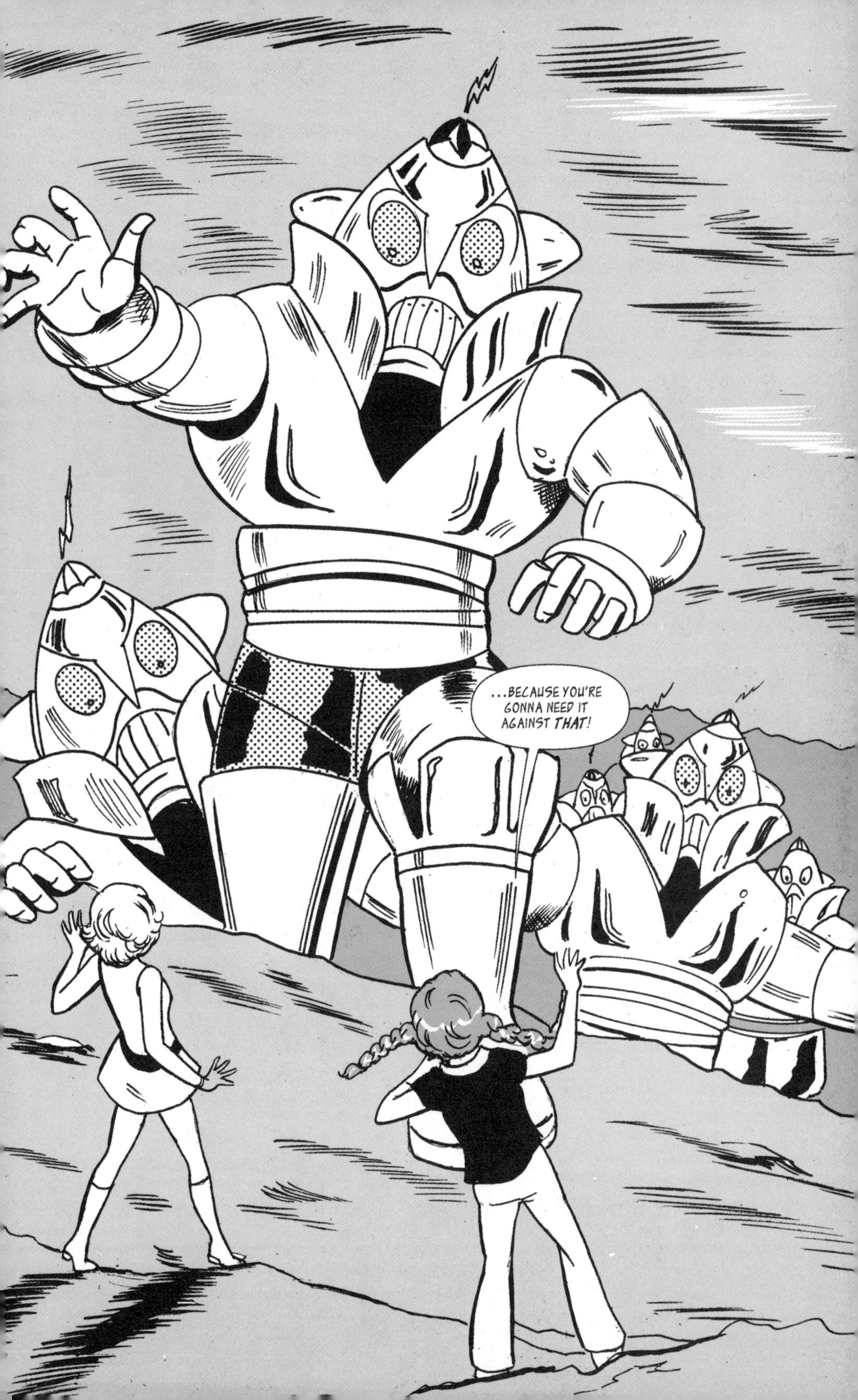
...BECAUSE YOU'RE GONNA NEED IT AGAINST *THAT*!

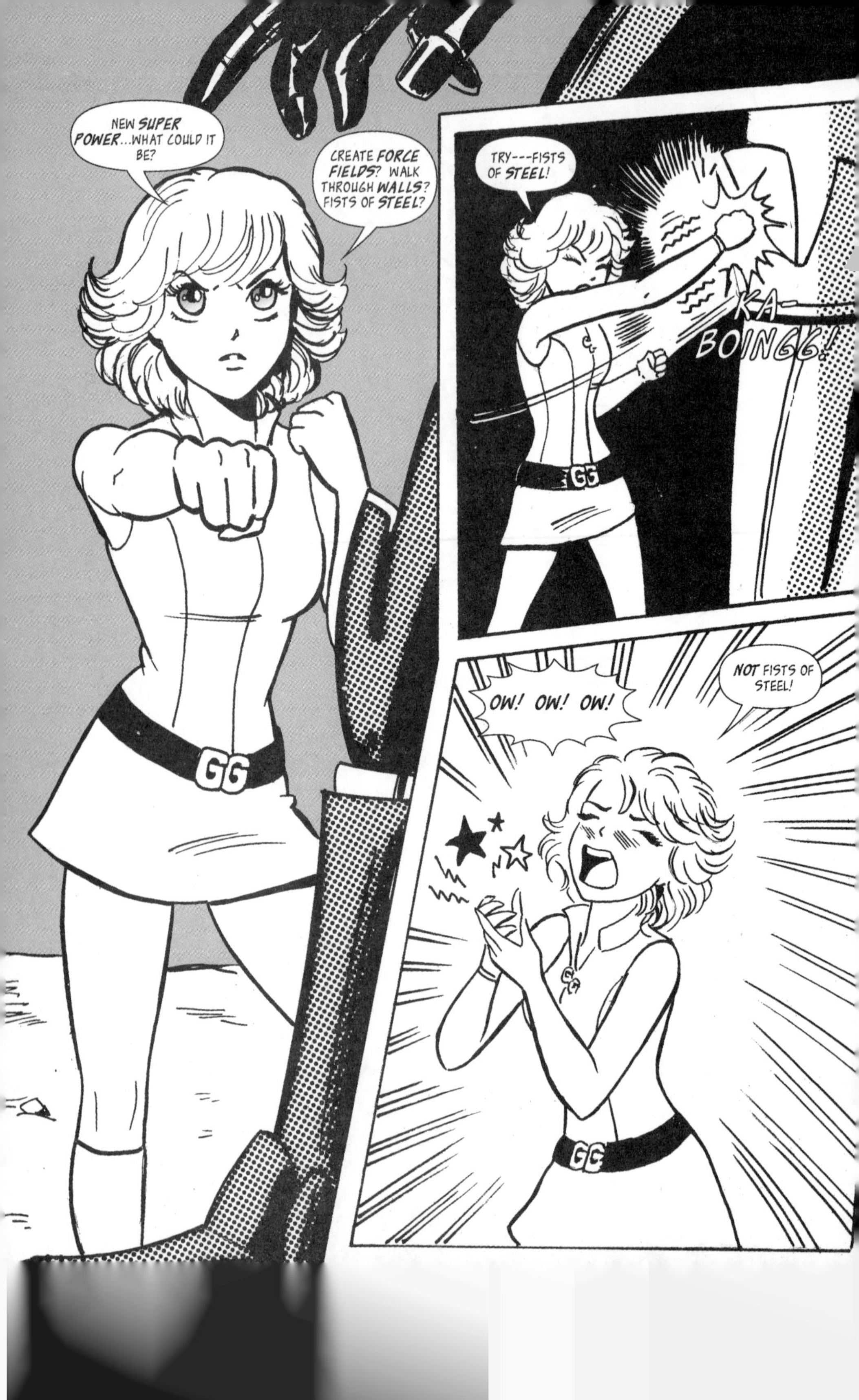
NEW SUPER POWER...WHAT COULD IT BE?
CREATE FORCE FIELDS? WALK THROUGH WALLS? FISTS OF STEEL?
TRY---FISTS OF STEEL!
KA-BOINGG!
OW! OW! OW!
NOT FISTS OF STEEL!

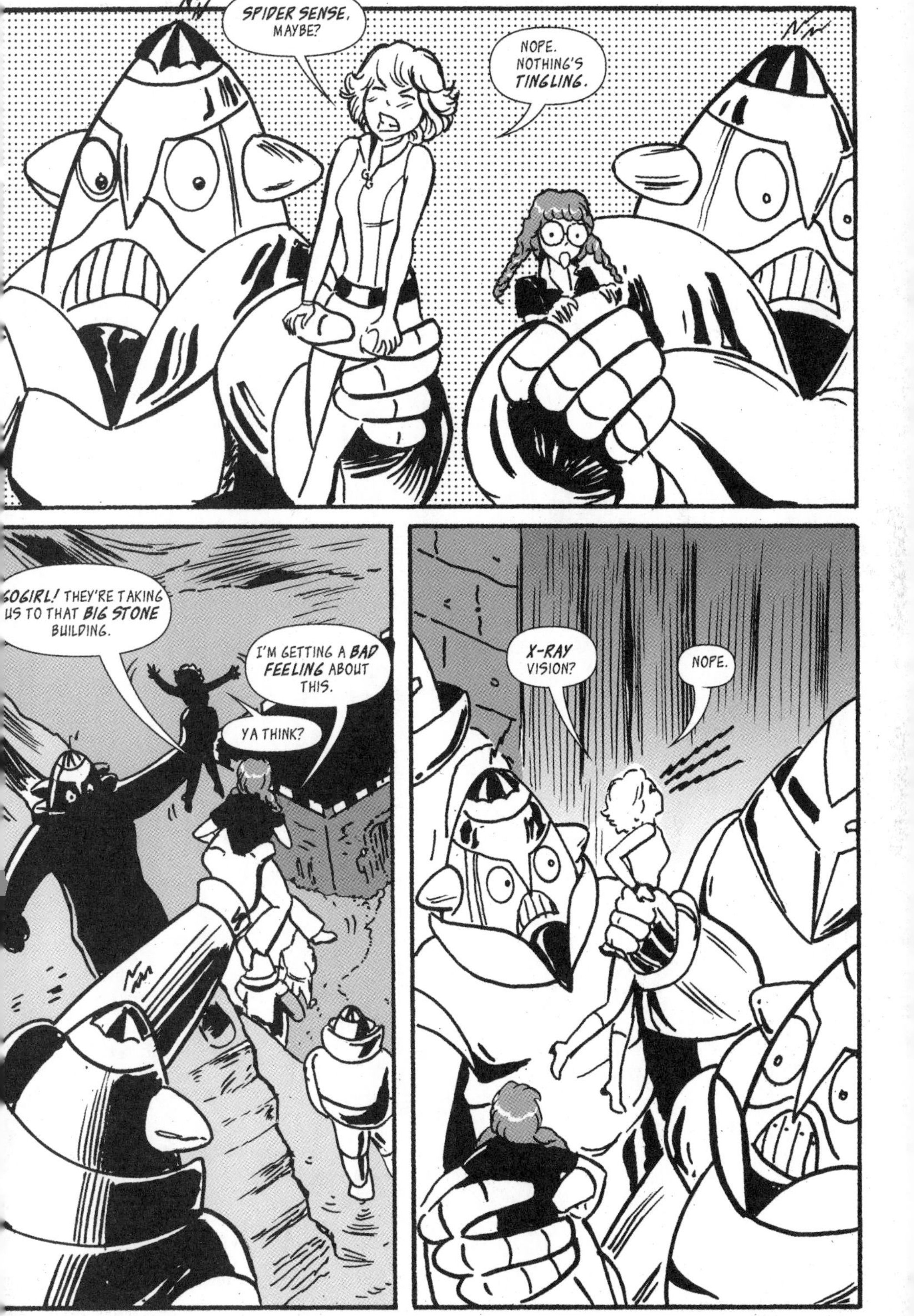
SPIDER SENSE, MAYBE?
NOPE. NOTHING'S TINGLING.
GOGIRL! THEY'RE TAKING US TO THAT BIG STONE BUILDING.
I'M GETTING A BAD FEELING ABOUT THIS.
YA THINK?
X-RAY VISION?
NOPE.

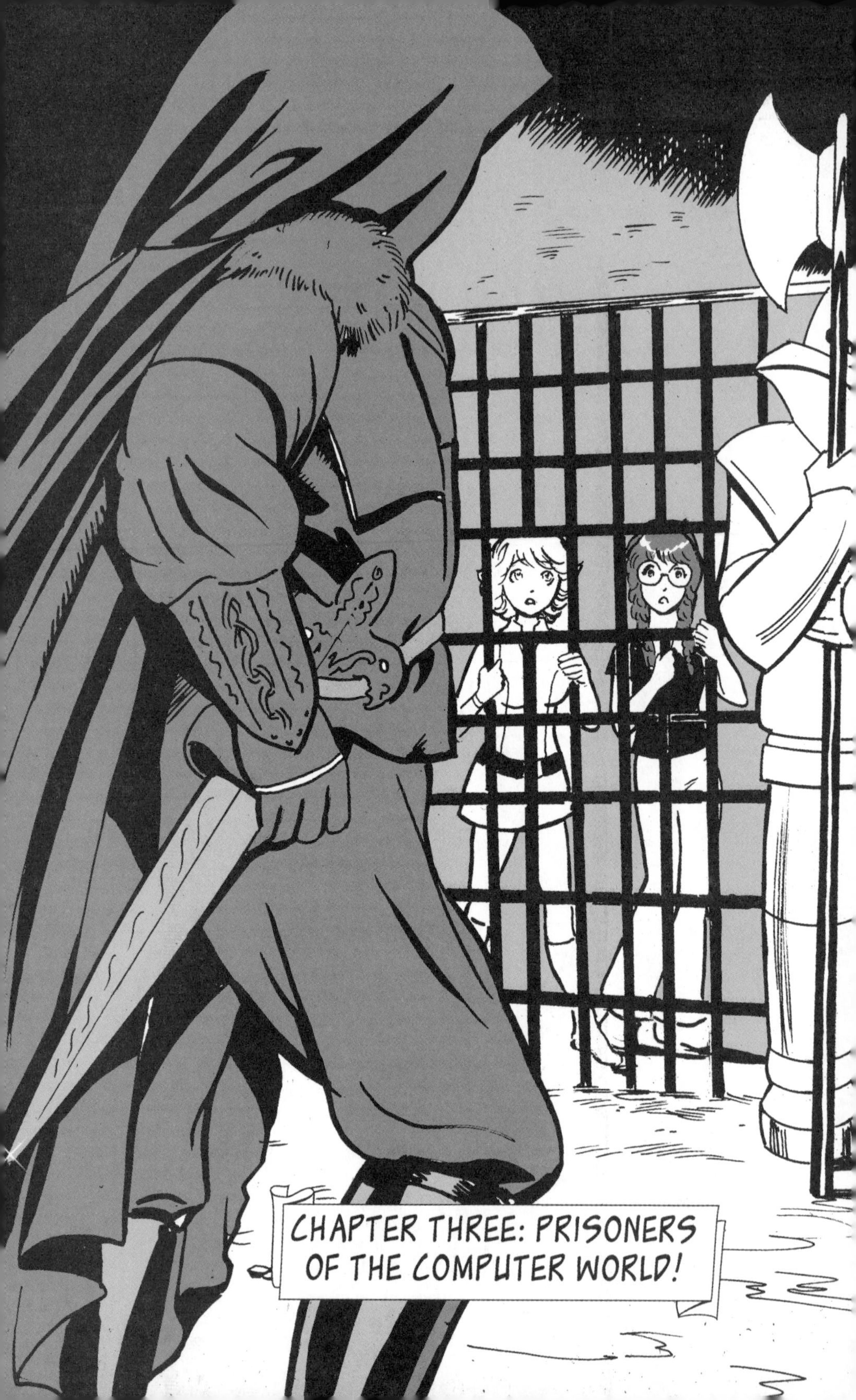
CHAPTER THREE: PRISONERS OF THE COMPUTER WORLD!

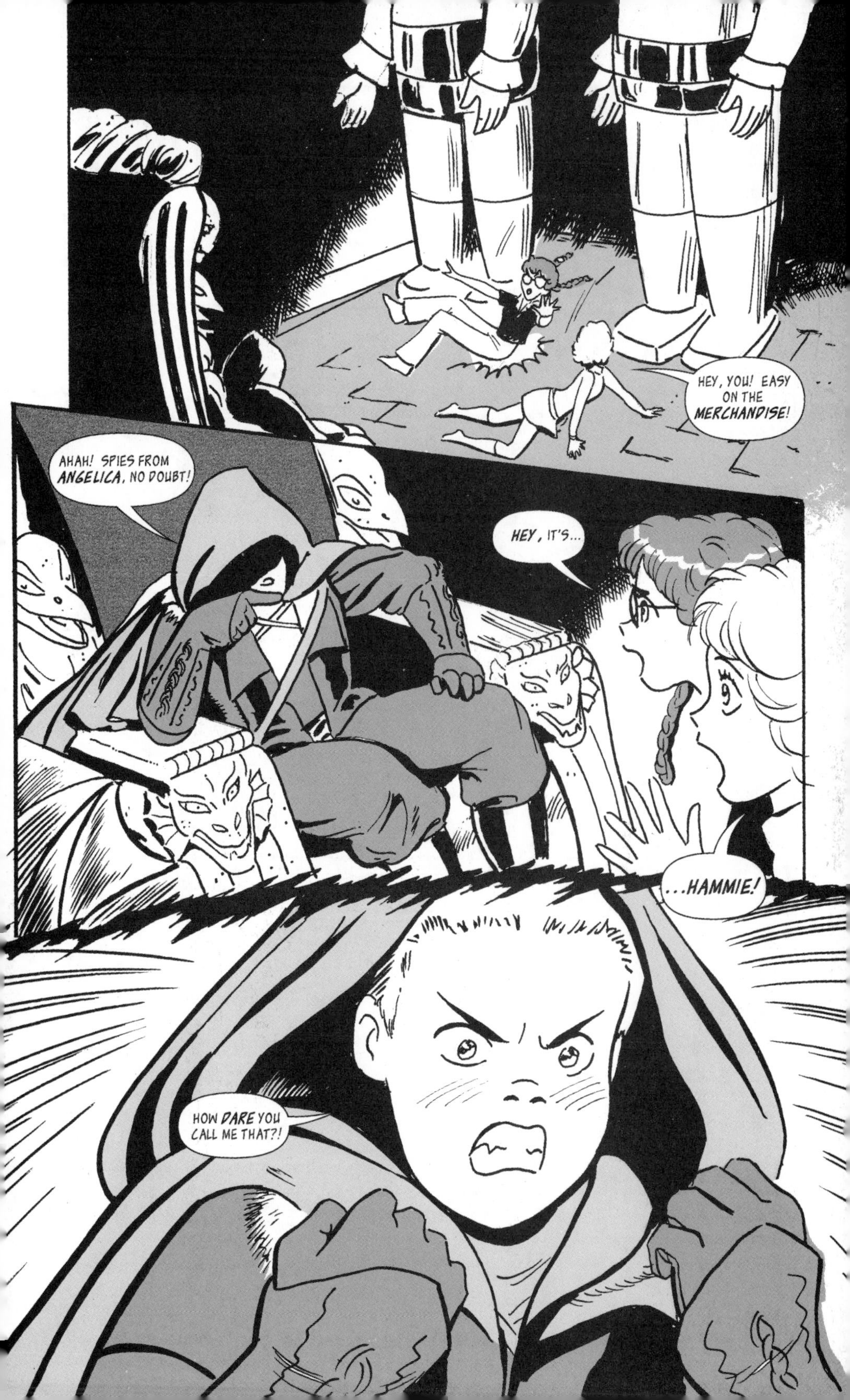
HEY, YOU! EASY ON THE *MERCHANDISE!*
AHAH! SPIES FROM *ANGELICA*, NO DOUBT!
*HEY*, IT'S...
...*HAMMIE!*
HOW *DARE* YOU CALL ME THAT?!

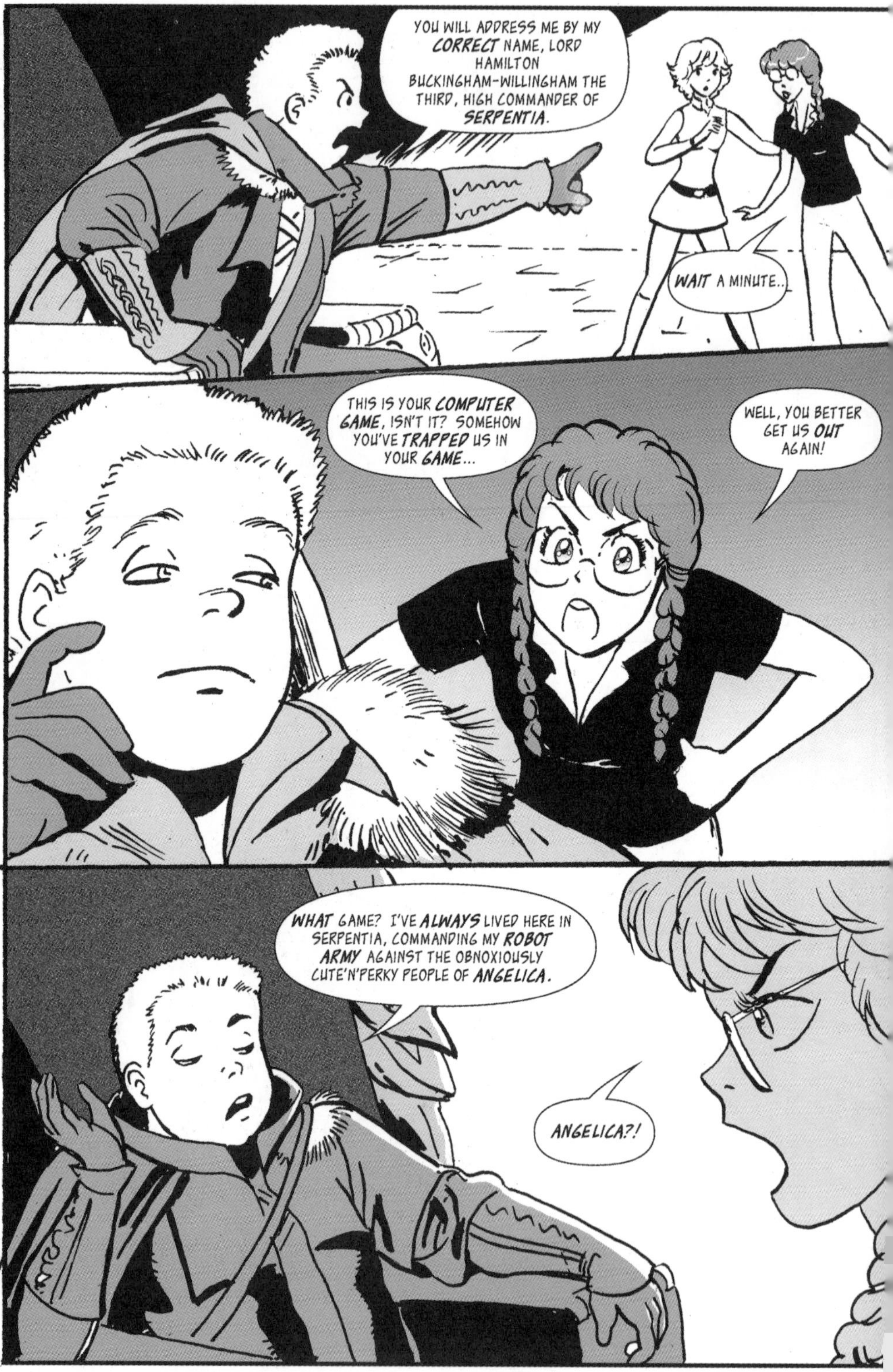
YOU WILL ADDRESS ME BY MY CORRECT NAME, LORD HAMILTON BUCKINGHAM-WILLINGHAM THE THIRD, HIGH COMMANDER OF SERPENTIA.
WAIT A MINUTE...
THIS IS YOUR COMPUTER GAME, ISN'T IT? SOMEHOW YOU'VE TRAPPED US IN YOUR GAME...
WELL, YOU BETTER GET US OUT AGAIN!
WHAT GAME? I'VE ALWAYS LIVED HERE IN SERPENTIA, COMMANDING MY ROBOT ARMY AGAINST THE OBNOXIOUSLY CUTE'N'PERKY PEOPLE OF ANGELICA.
ANGELICA?!

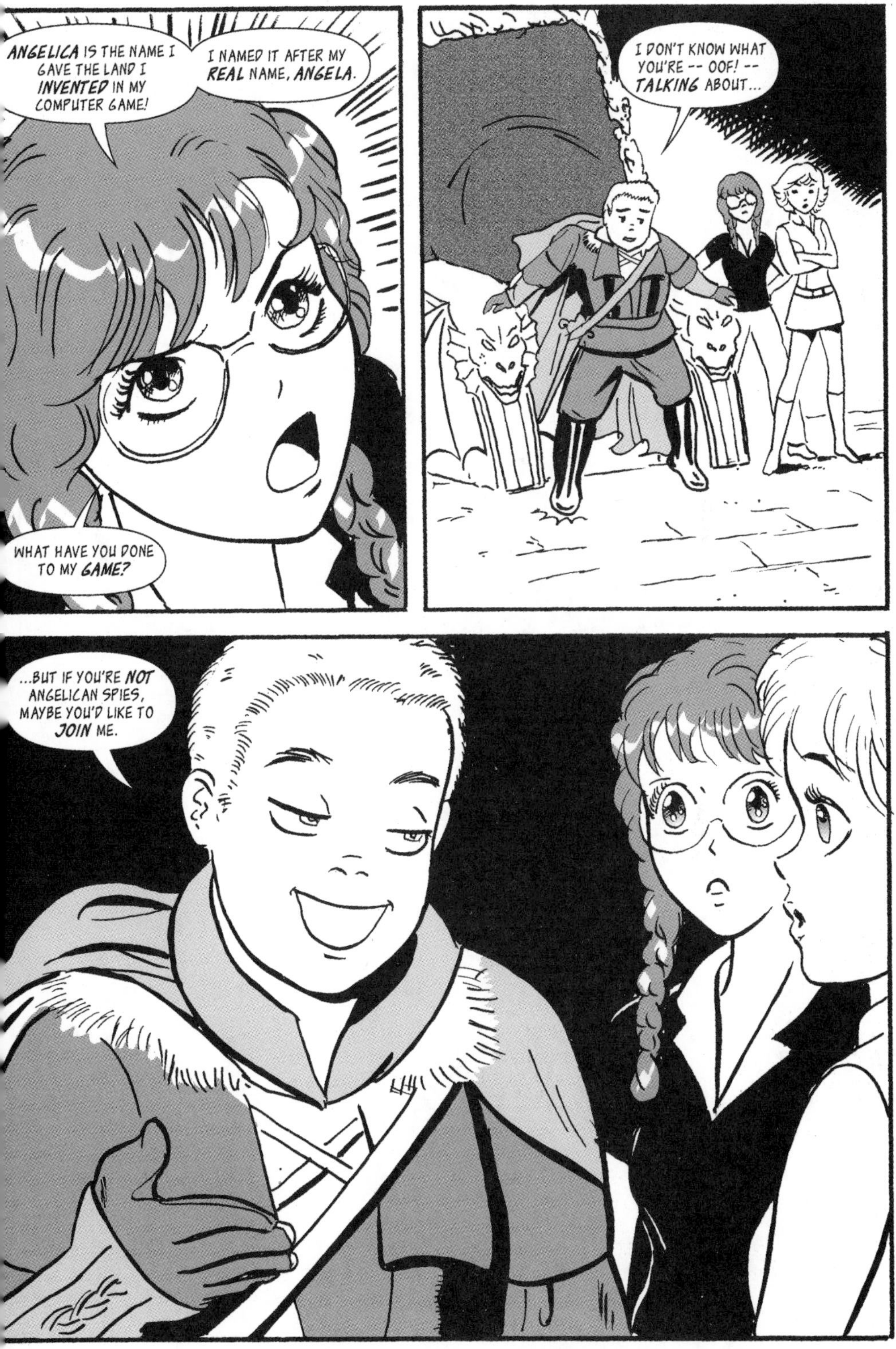
ANGELICA IS THE NAME I GAVE THE LAND I INVENTED IN MY COMPUTER GAME!
I NAMED IT AFTER MY REAL NAME, ANGELA.
WHAT HAVE YOU DONE TO MY GAME?
I DON'T KNOW WHAT YOU'RE -- OOF! -- TALKING ABOUT...
...BUT IF YOU'RE NOT ANGELICAN SPIES, MAYBE YOU'D LIKE TO JOIN ME.

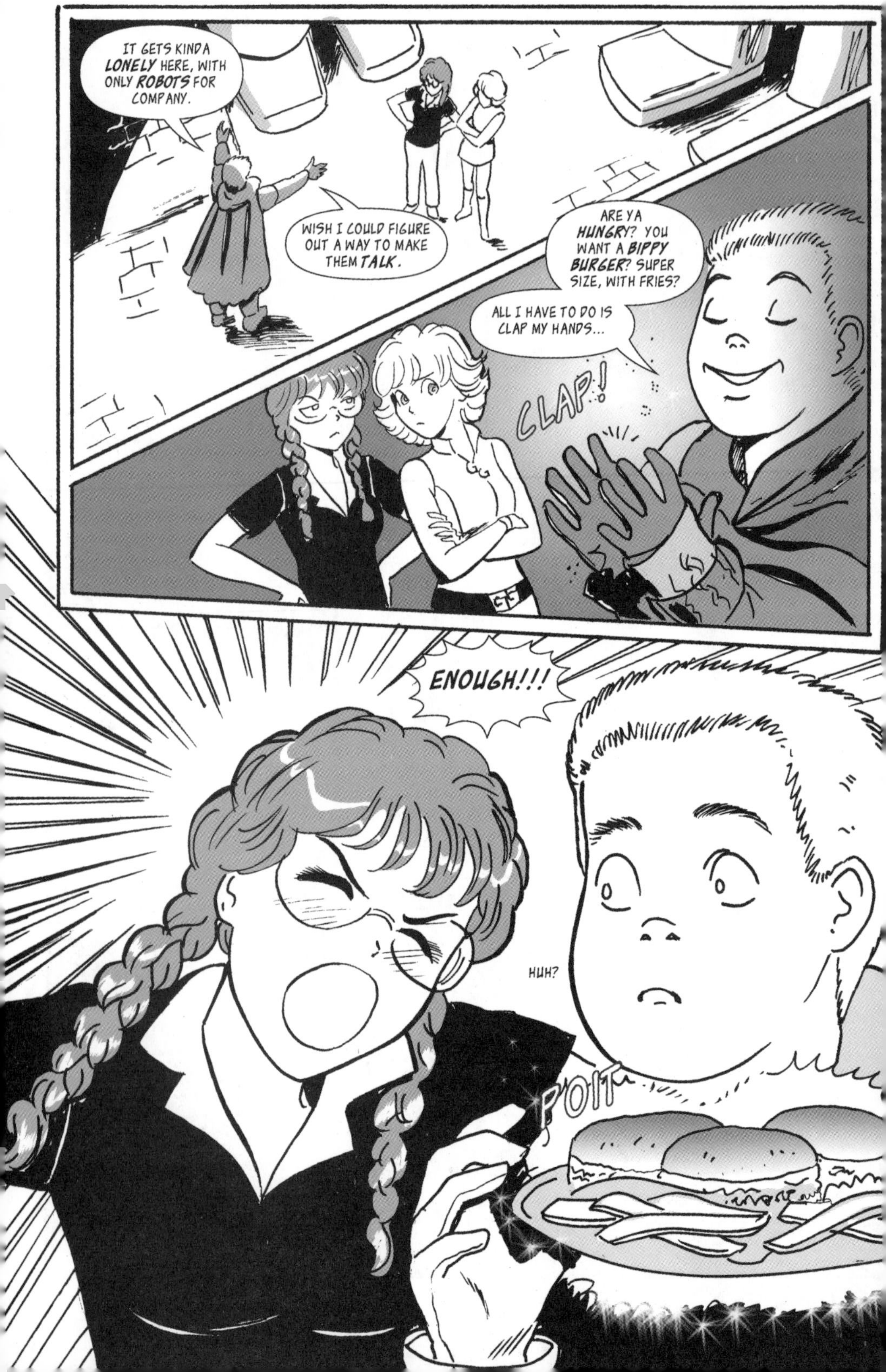
IT GETS KINDA LONELY HERE, WITH ONLY ROBOTS FOR COMPANY.
WISH I COULD FIGURE OUT A WAY TO MAKE THEM TALK.
ARE YA HUNGRY? YOU WANT A BIPPY BURGER? SUPER SIZE, WITH FRIES?
ALL I HAVE TO DO IS CLAP MY HANDS...
CLAP!
ENOUGH!!!
HUH?
POIT

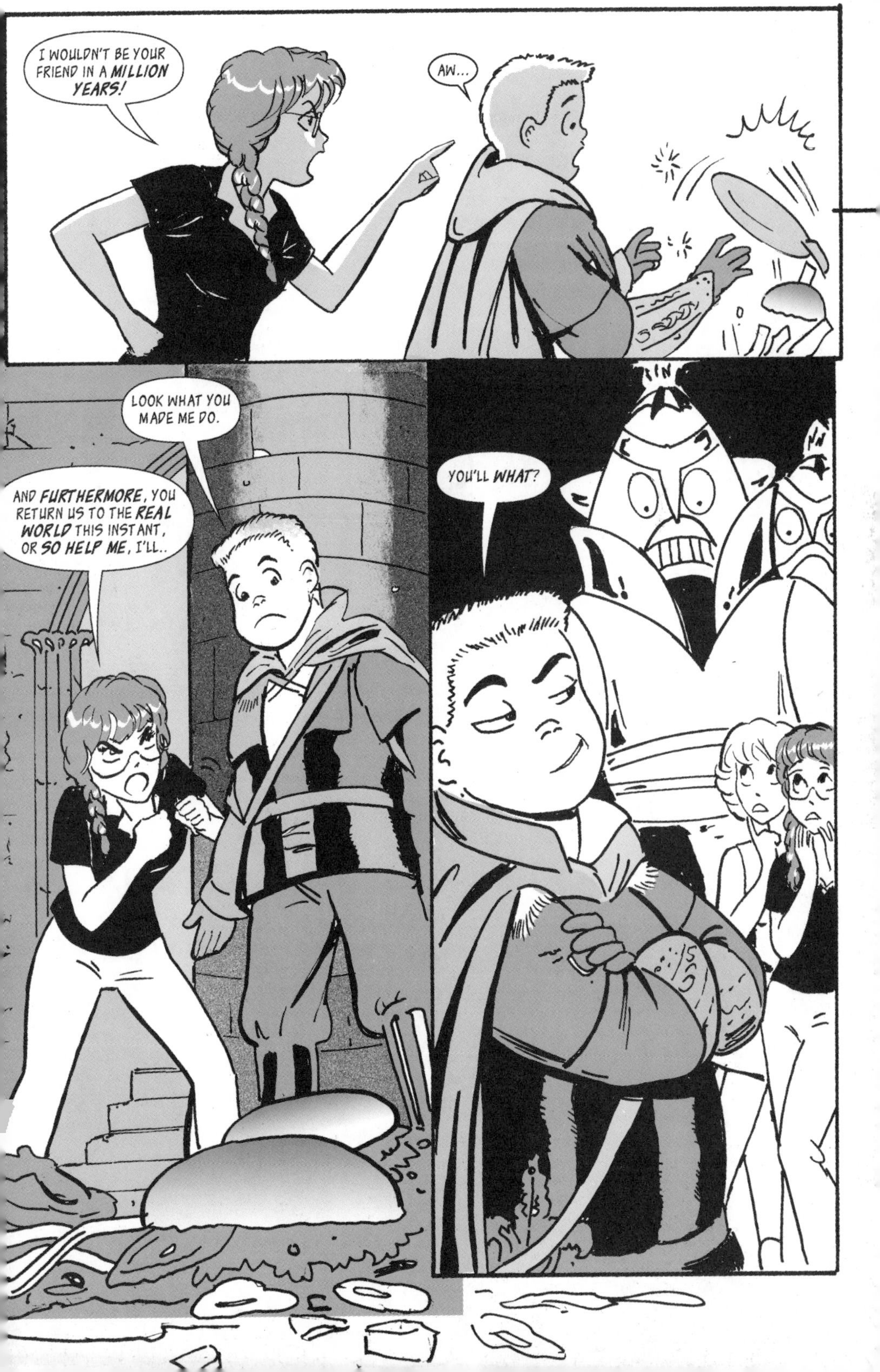
I WOULDN'T BE YOUR FRIEND IN A *MILLION YEARS!*
AW...
LOOK WHAT YOU MADE ME DO.
AND *FURTHERMORE*, YOU RETURN US TO THE *REAL WORLD* THIS INSTANT, OR *SO HELP ME*, I'LL..
YOU'LL *WHAT*?

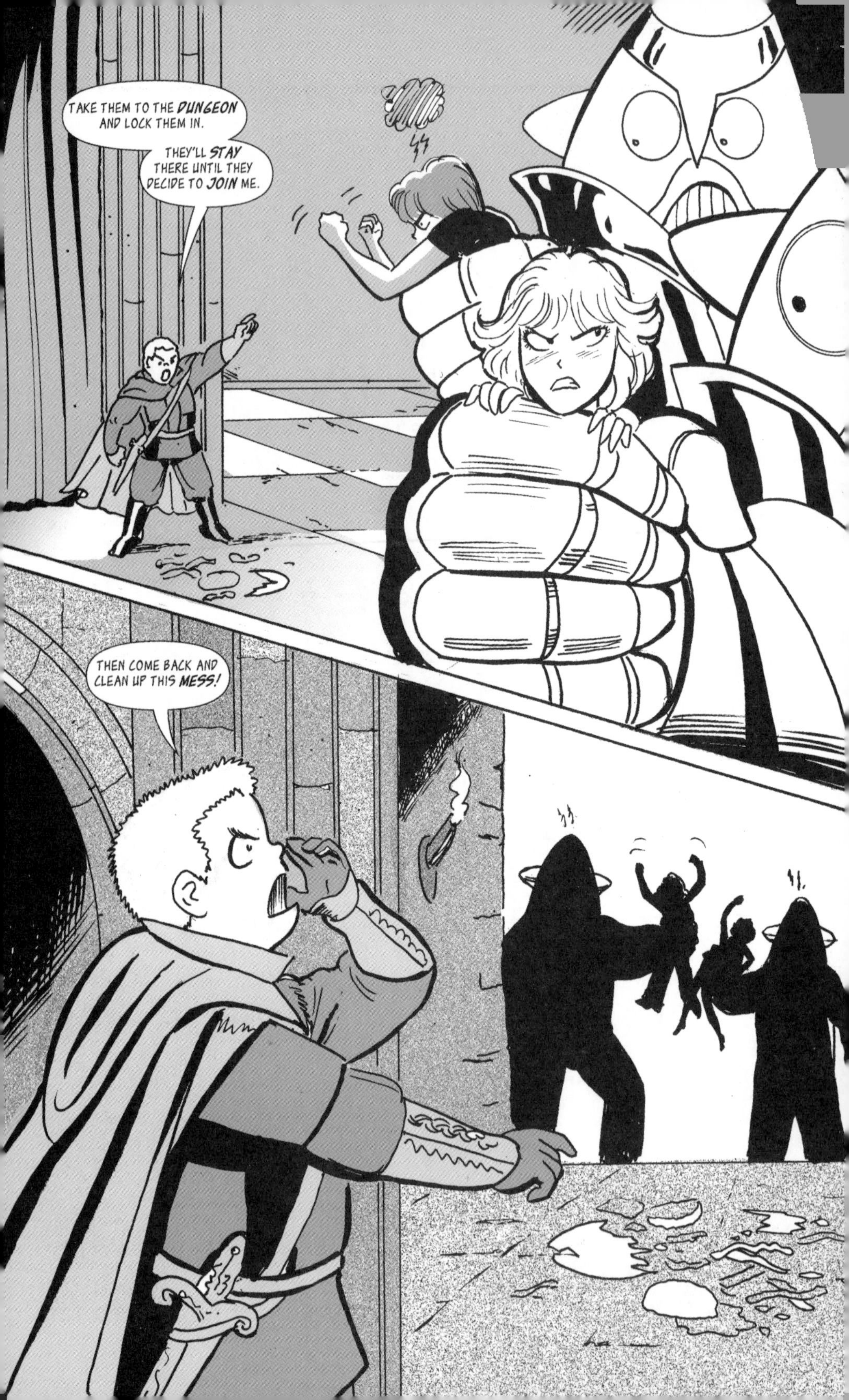
TAKE THEM TO THE DUNGEON AND LOCK THEM IN.
THEY'LL STAY THERE UNTIL THEY DECIDE TO JOIN ME.
THEN COME BACK AND CLEAN UP THIS MESS!

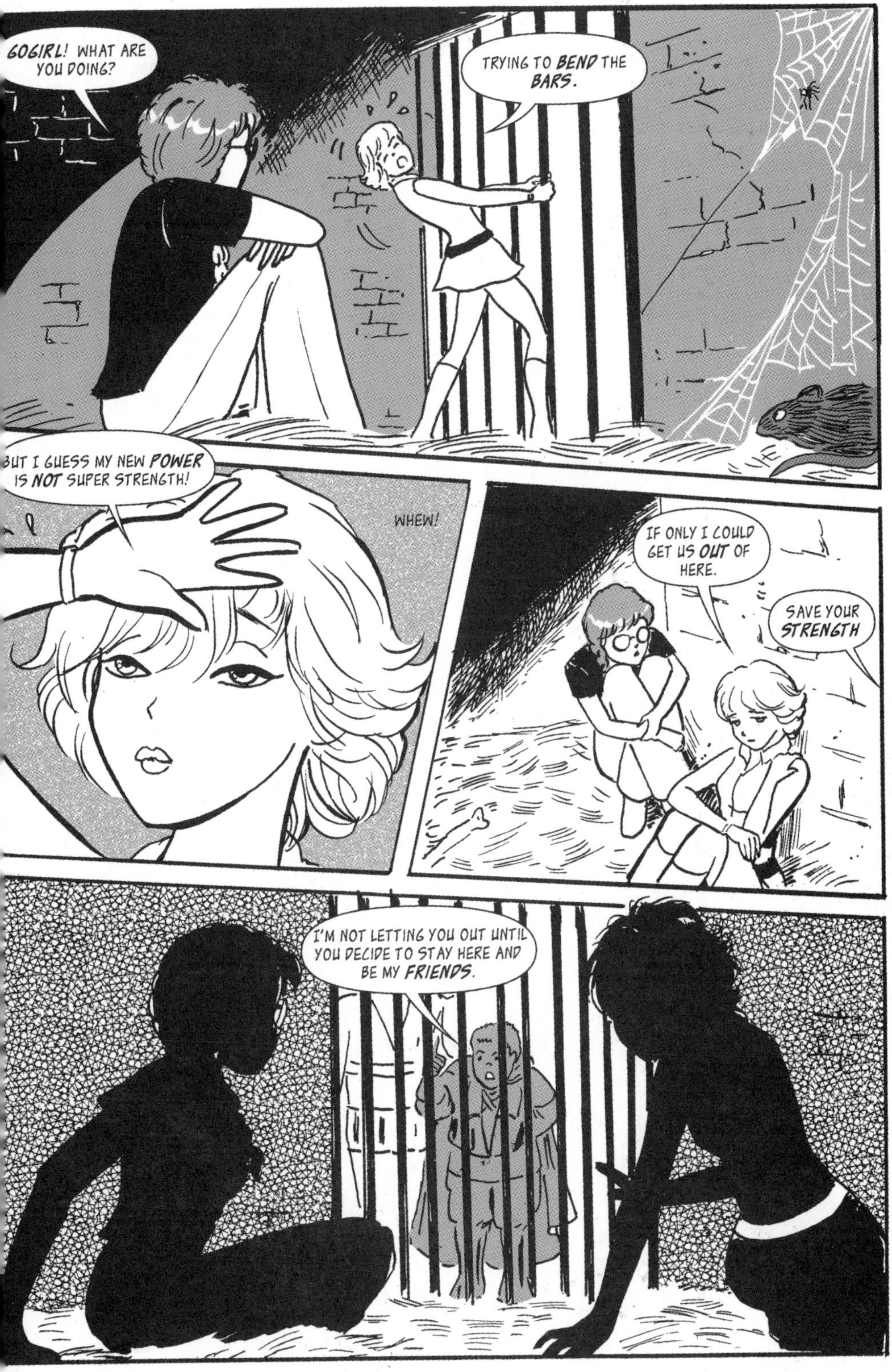
GOGIRL! WHAT ARE YOU DOING?
TRYING TO BEND THE BARS.
BUT I GUESS MY NEW POWER IS NOT SUPER STRENGTH!
WHEW!
IF ONLY I COULD GET US OUT OF HERE.
SAVE YOUR STRENGTH
I'M NOT LETTING YOU OUT UNTIL YOU DECIDE TO STAY HERE AND BE MY FRIENDS.

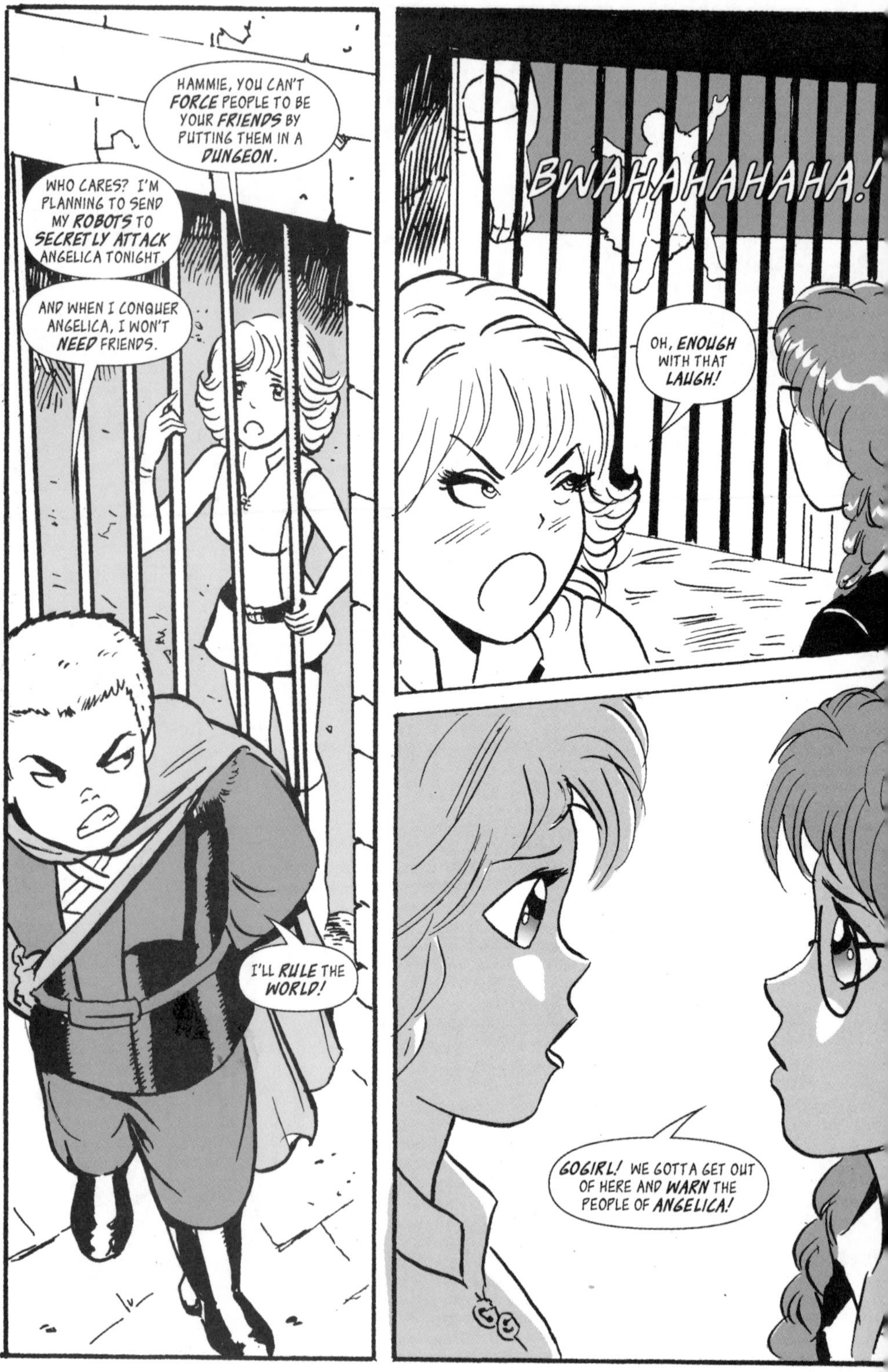
HAMMIE, YOU CAN'T FORCE PEOPLE TO BE YOUR FRIENDS BY PUTTING THEM IN A DUNGEON.
WHO CARES? I'M PLANNING TO SEND MY ROBOTS TO SECRETLY ATTACK ANGELICA TONIGHT.
AND WHEN I CONQUER ANGELICA, I WON'T NEED FRIENDS.
I'LL RULE THE WORLD!
BWAHAHAHAHAHA!
OH, ENOUGH WITH THAT LAUGH!
GOGIRL! WE GOTTA GET OUT OF HERE AND WARN THE PEOPLE OF ANGELICA!

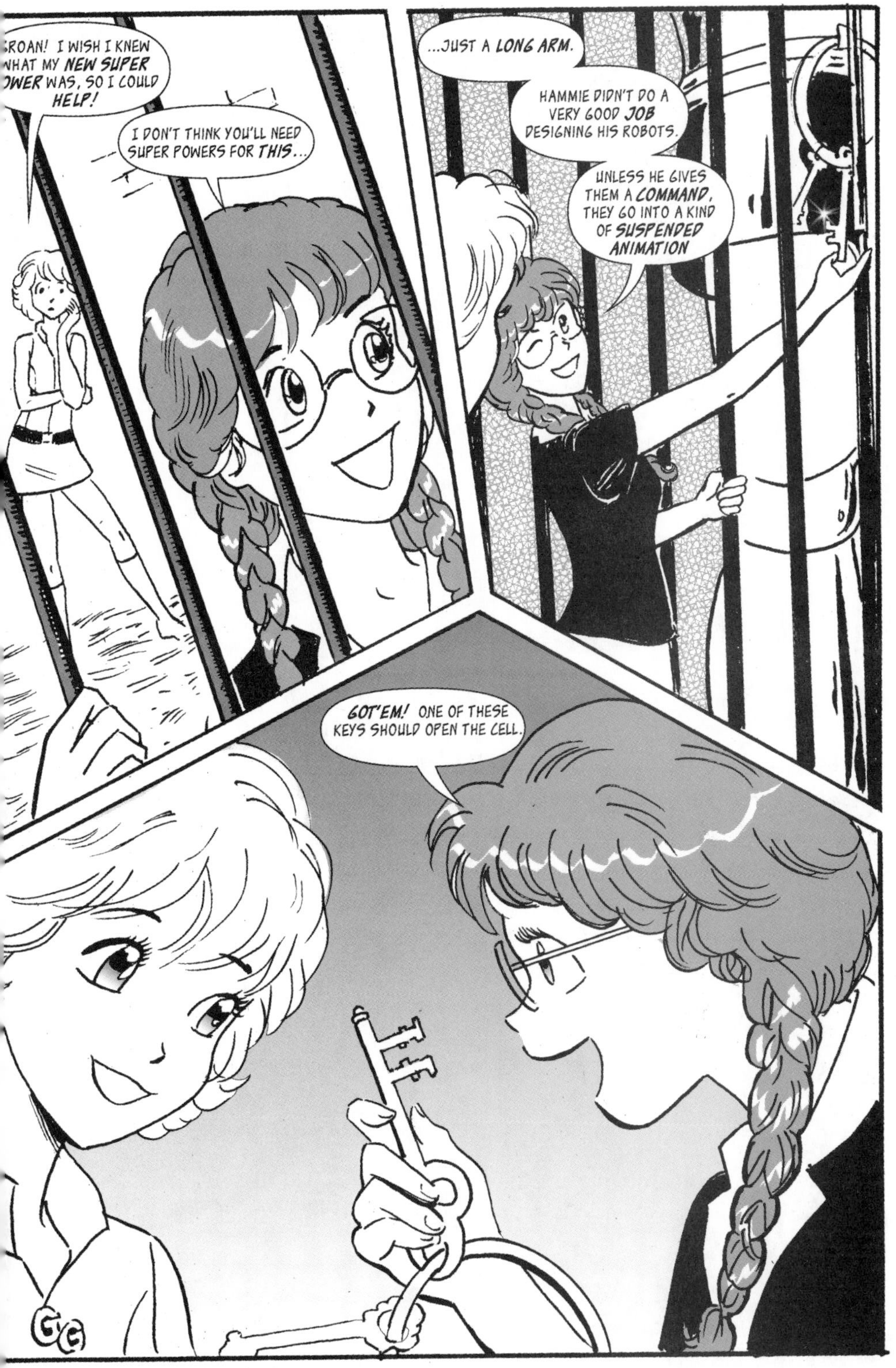
GROAN! I WISH I KNEW WHAT MY NEW SUPER POWER WAS, SO I COULD HELP!
I DON'T THINK YOU'LL NEED SUPER POWERS FOR THIS...
...JUST A LONG ARM.
HAMMIE DIDN'T DO A VERY GOOD JOB DESIGNING HIS ROBOTS.
UNLESS HE GIVES THEM A COMMAND, THEY GO INTO A KIND OF SUSPENDED ANIMATION
GOT'EM! ONE OF THESE KEYS SHOULD OPEN THE CELL.

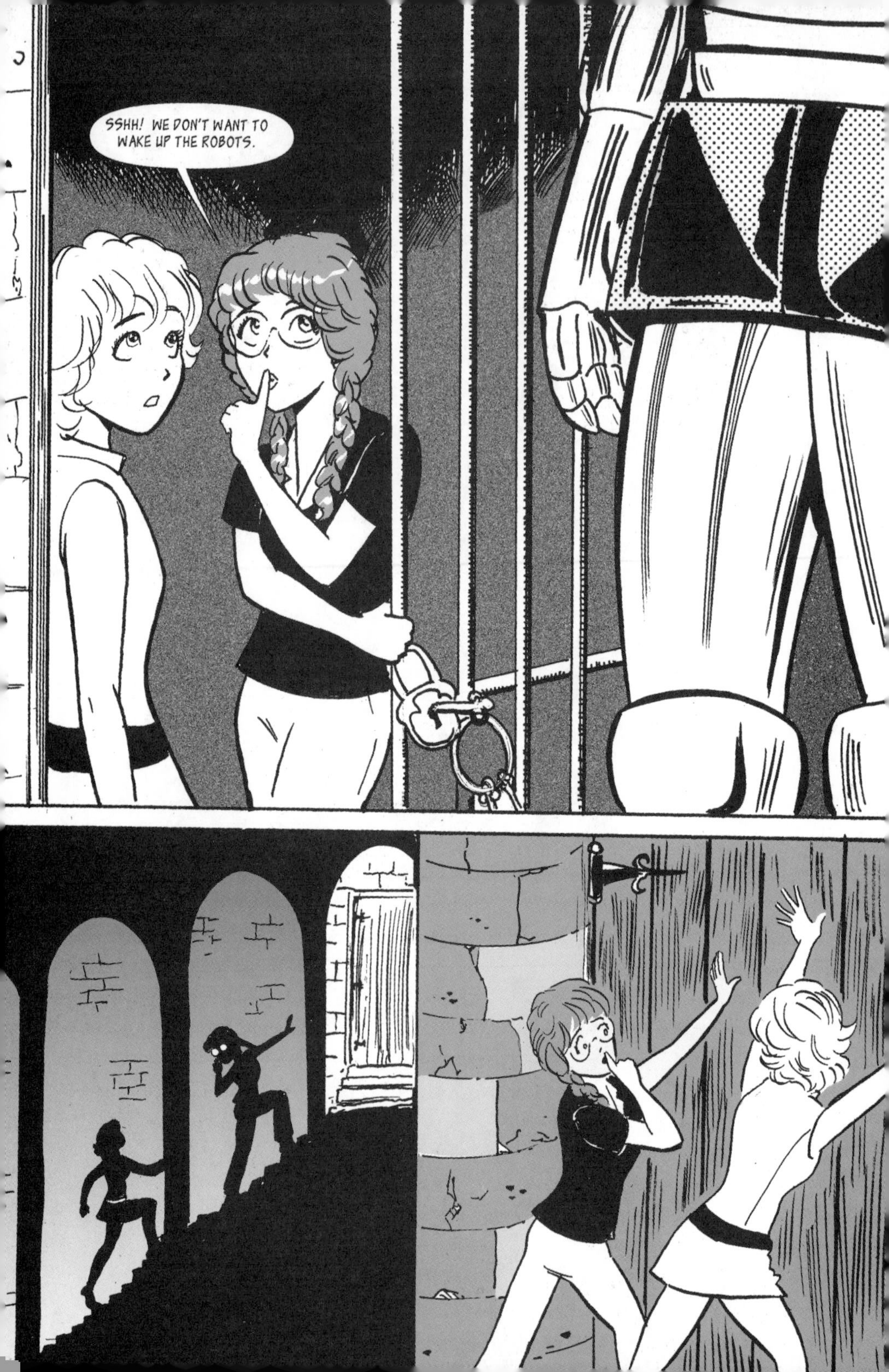
SSHH! WE DON'T WANT TO WAKE UP THE ROBOTS.

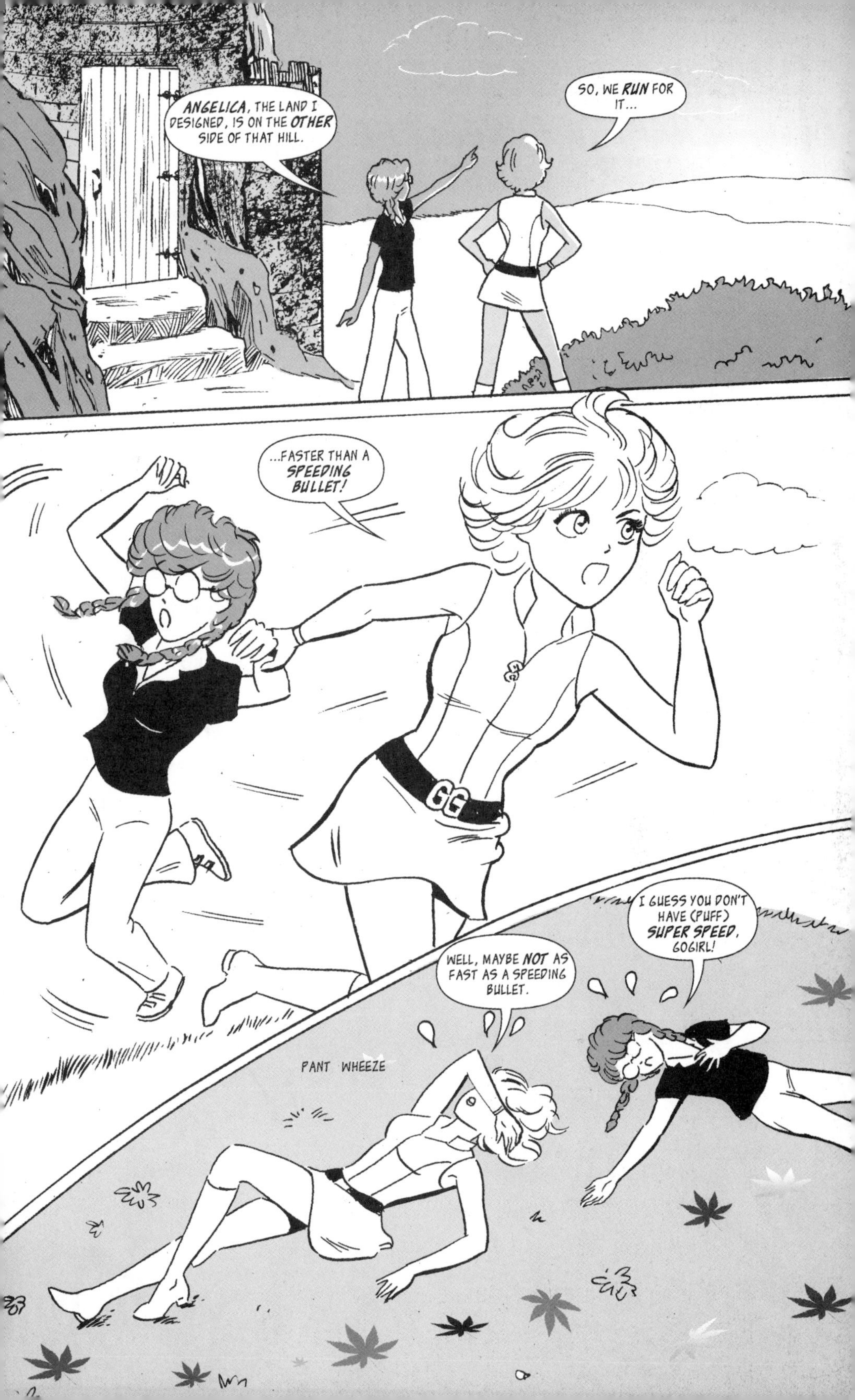
ANGELICA, THE LAND I DESIGNED, IS ON THE OTHER SIDE OF THAT HILL.
SO, WE RUN FOR IT...
...FASTER THAN A SPEEDING BULLET!
PANT WHEEZE
WELL, MAYBE NOT AS FAST AS A SPEEDING BULLET.
I GUESS YOU DON'T HAVE (PUFF) SUPER SPEED, GOGIRL!

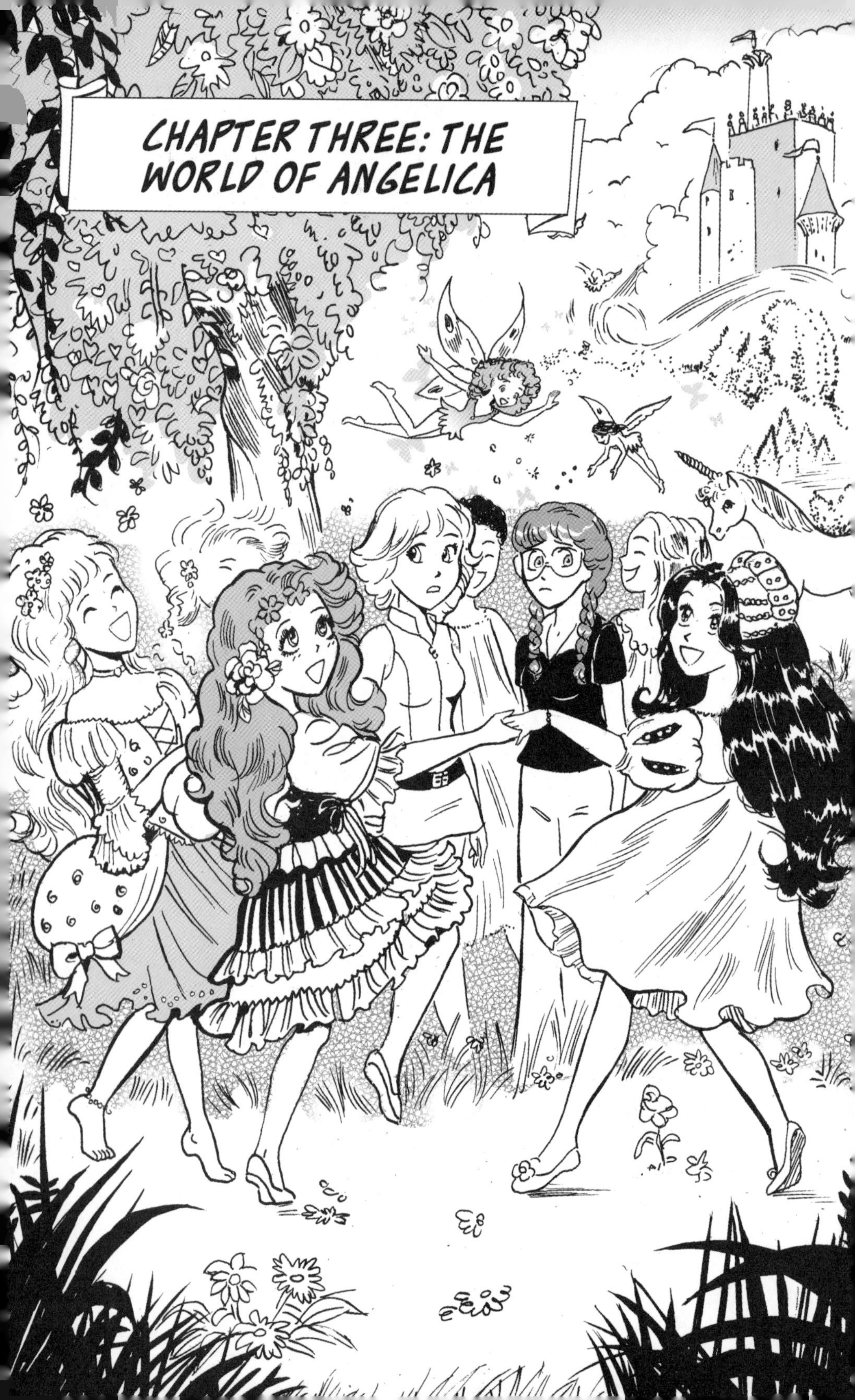
CHAPTER THREE: THE WORLD OF ANGELICA

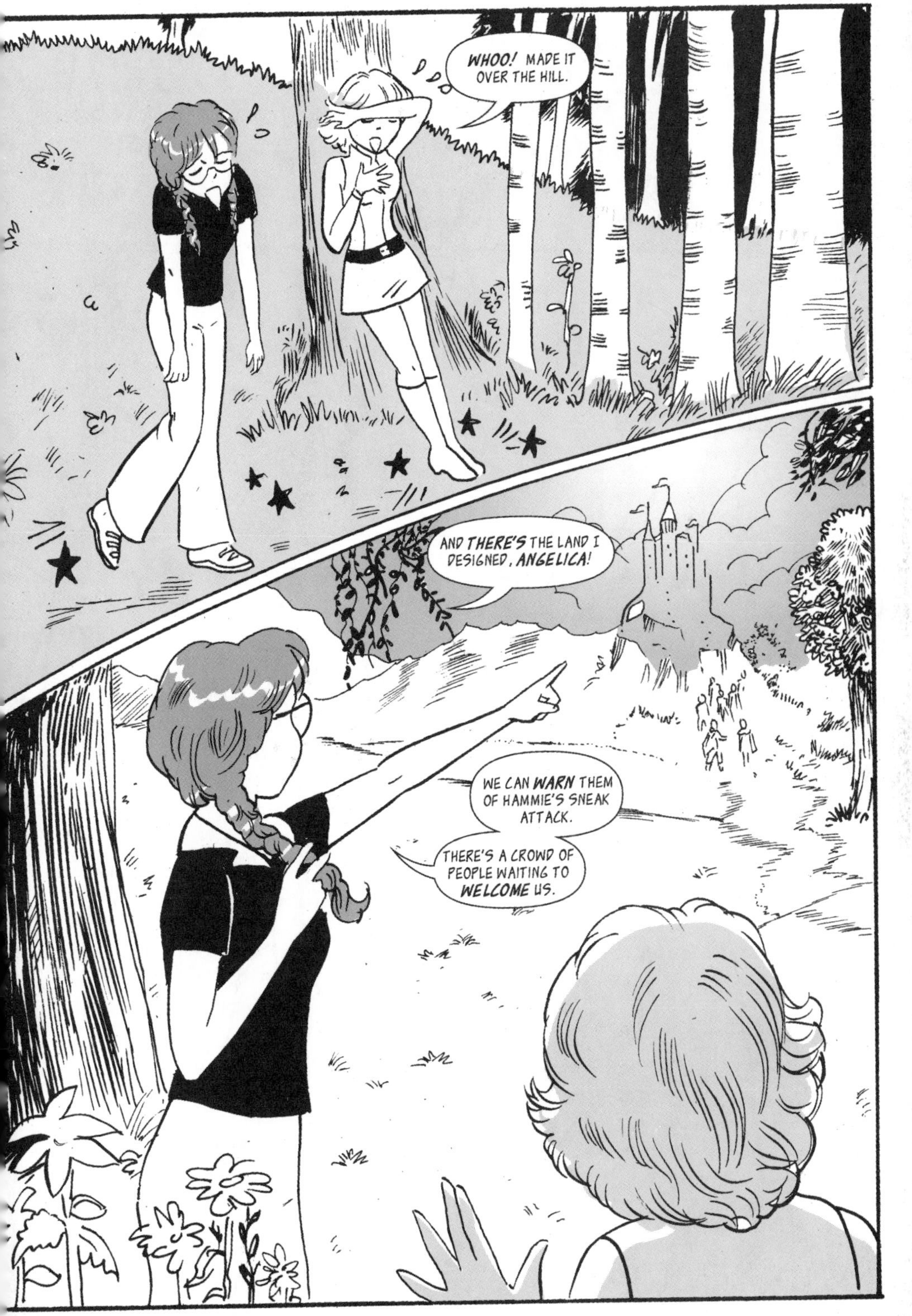
WHOO! MADE IT OVER THE HILL.
AND THERE'S THE LAND I DESIGNED, ANGELICA!
WE CAN WARN THEM OF HAMMIE'S SNEAK ATTACK.
THERE'S A CROWD OF PEOPLE WAITING TO WELCOME US.

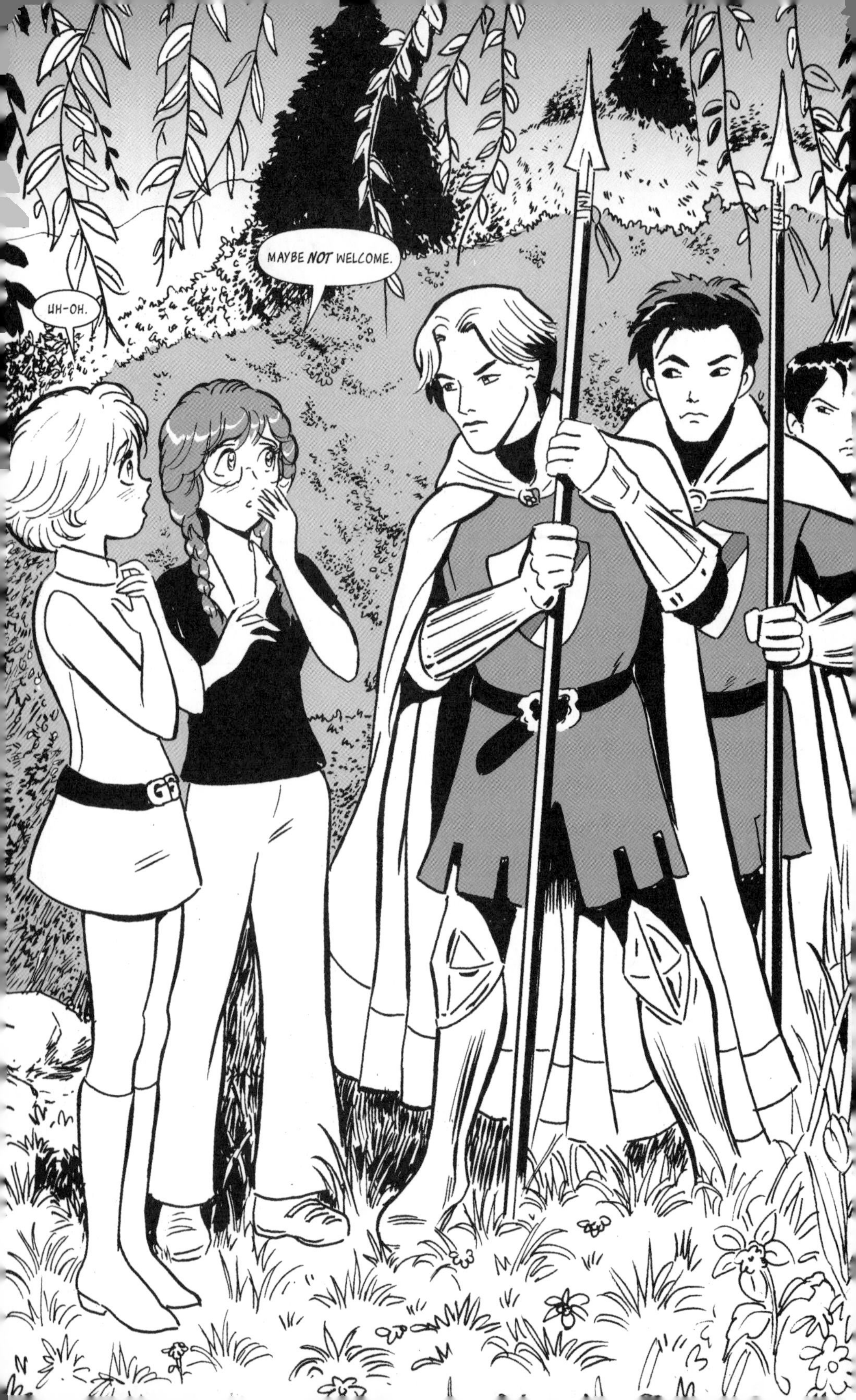
UH-OH.
MAYBE ***NOT*** WELCOME.

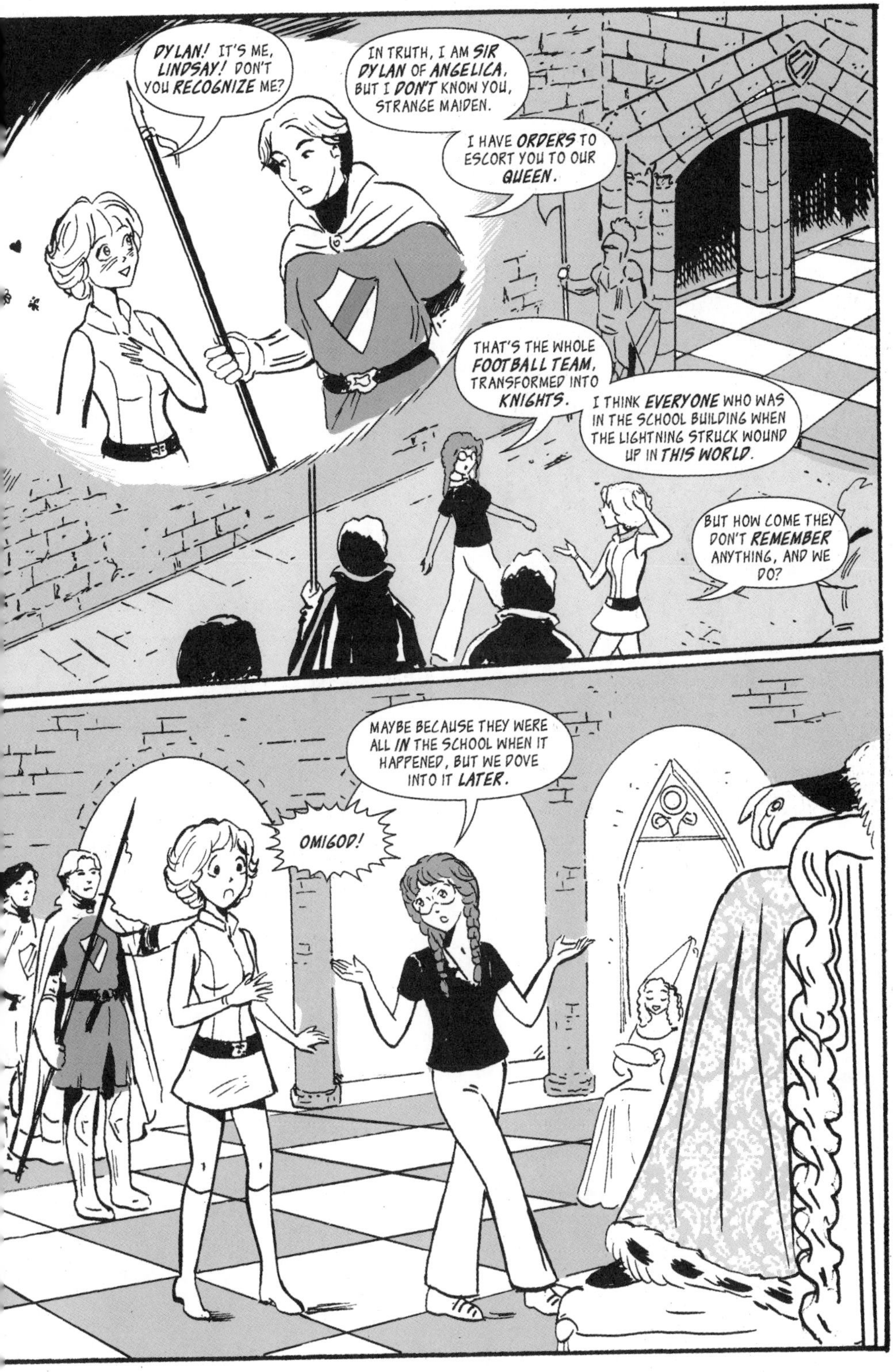
DYLAN! IT'S ME, LINDSAY! DON'T YOU RECOGNIZE ME?
IN TRUTH, I AM SIR DYLAN OF ANGELICA, BUT I DON'T KNOW YOU, STRANGE MAIDEN.
I HAVE ORDERS TO ESCORT YOU TO OUR QUEEN.
THAT'S THE WHOLE FOOTBALL TEAM, TRANSFORMED INTO KNIGHTS.
I THINK EVERYONE WHO WAS IN THE SCHOOL BUILDING WHEN THE LIGHTNING STRUCK WOUND UP IN THIS WORLD.
BUT HOW COME THEY DON'T REMEMBER ANYTHING, AND WE DO?
OMIGOD!
MAYBE BECAUSE THEY WERE ALL IN THE SCHOOL WHEN IT HAPPENED, BUT WE DOVE INTO IT LATER.

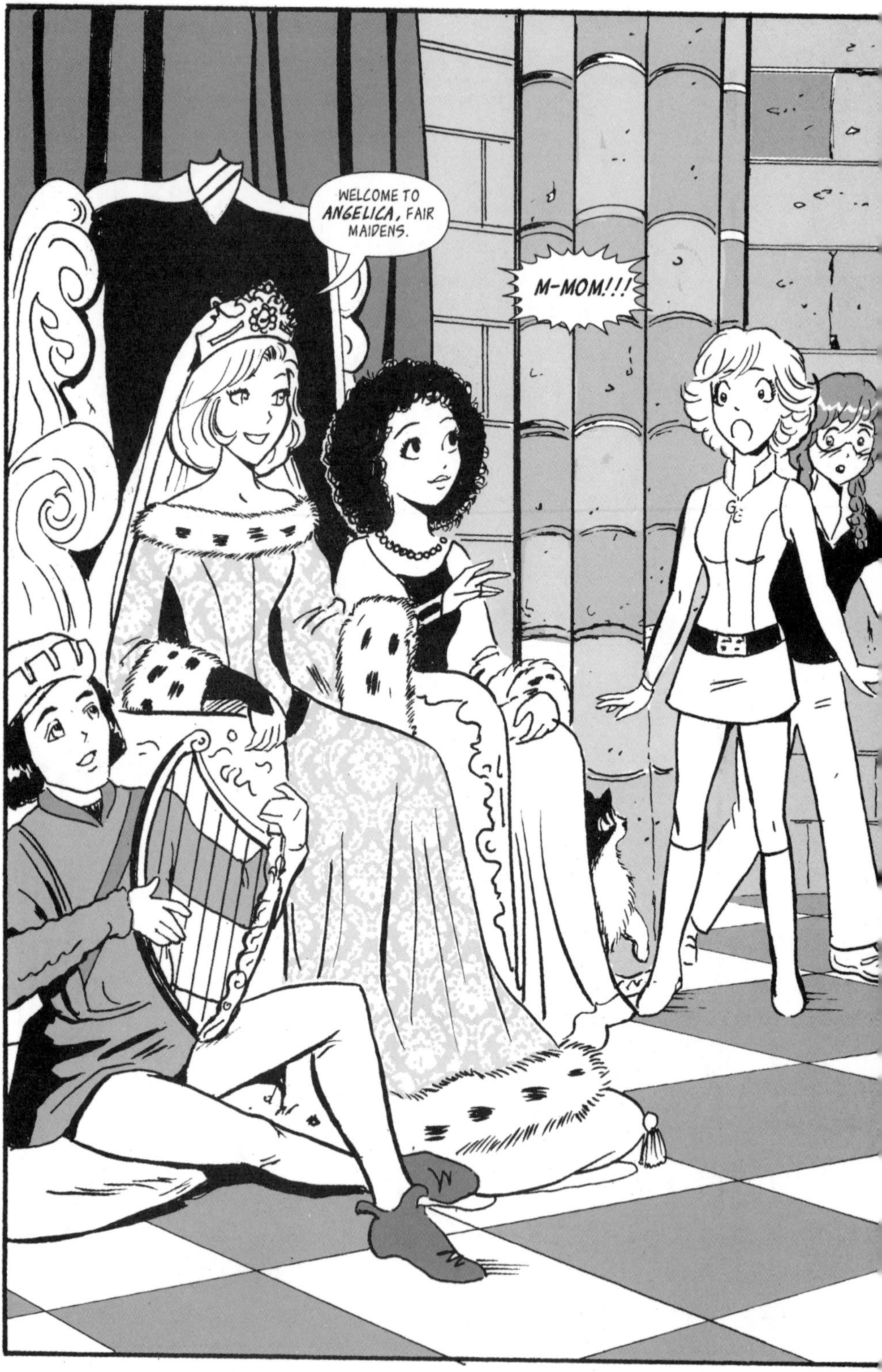
WELCOME TO ANGELICA, FAIR MAIDENS.
M-MOM!!!

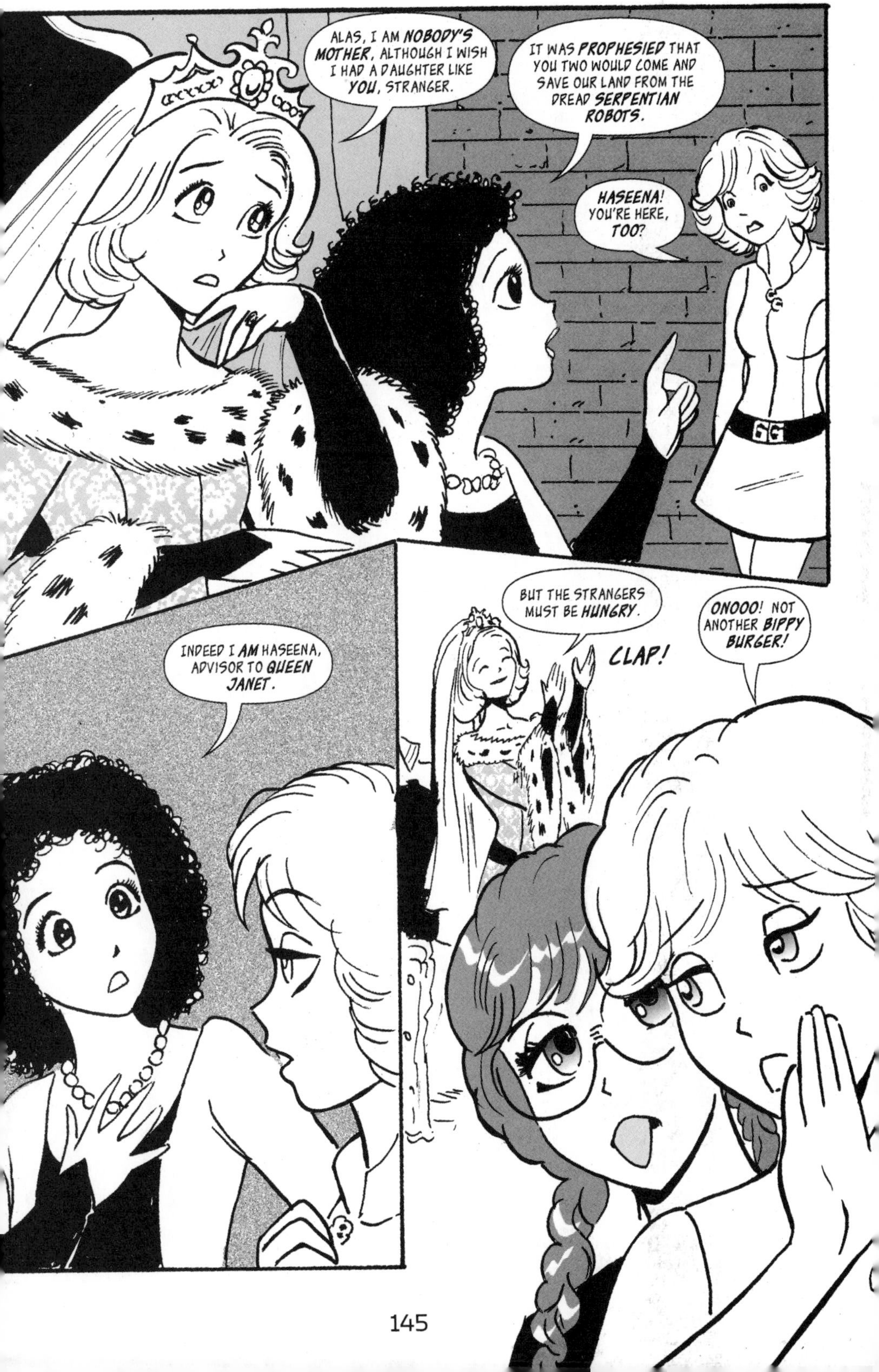
ALAS, I AM NOBODY'S MOTHER, ALTHOUGH I WISH I HAD A DAUGHTER LIKE YOU, STRANGER.
IT WAS PROPHESIED THAT YOU TWO WOULD COME AND SAVE OUR LAND FROM THE DREAD SERPENTIAN ROBOTS.
HASEENA! YOU'RE HERE, TOO?
INDEED I AM HASEENA, ADVISOR TO QUEEN JANET.
BUT THE STRANGERS MUST BE HUNGRY.
CLAP!
ONOOO! NOT ANOTHER BIPPY BURGER!

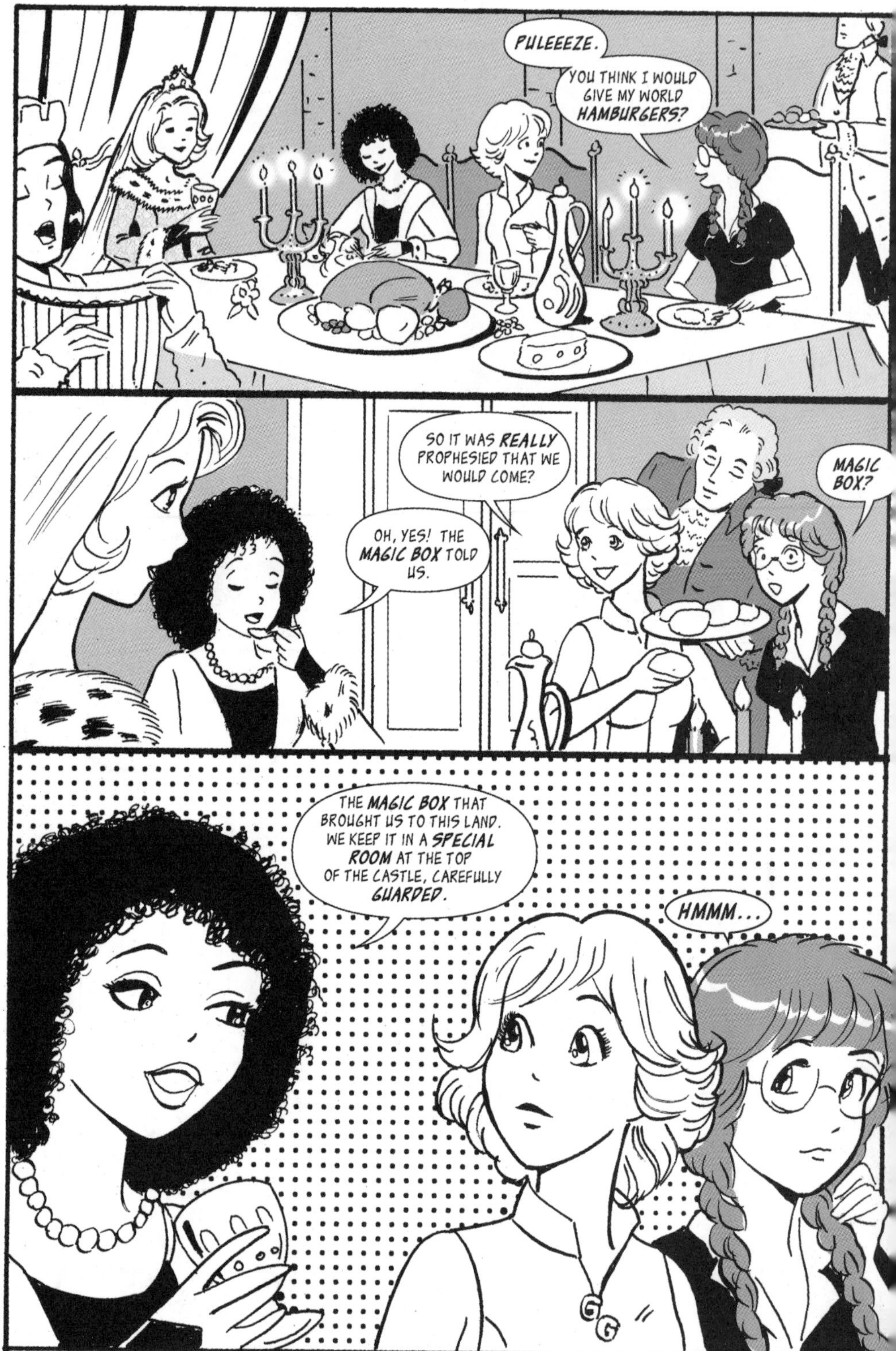
PULEEEZE.
YOU THINK I WOULD GIVE MY WORLD HAMBURGERS?
SO IT WAS REALLY PROPHESIED THAT WE WOULD COME?
OH, YES! THE MAGIC BOX TOLD US.
MAGIC BOX?
THE MAGIC BOX THAT BROUGHT US TO THIS LAND. WE KEEP IT IN A SPECIAL ROOM AT THE TOP OF THE CASTLE, CAREFULLY GUARDED.
HMMM...

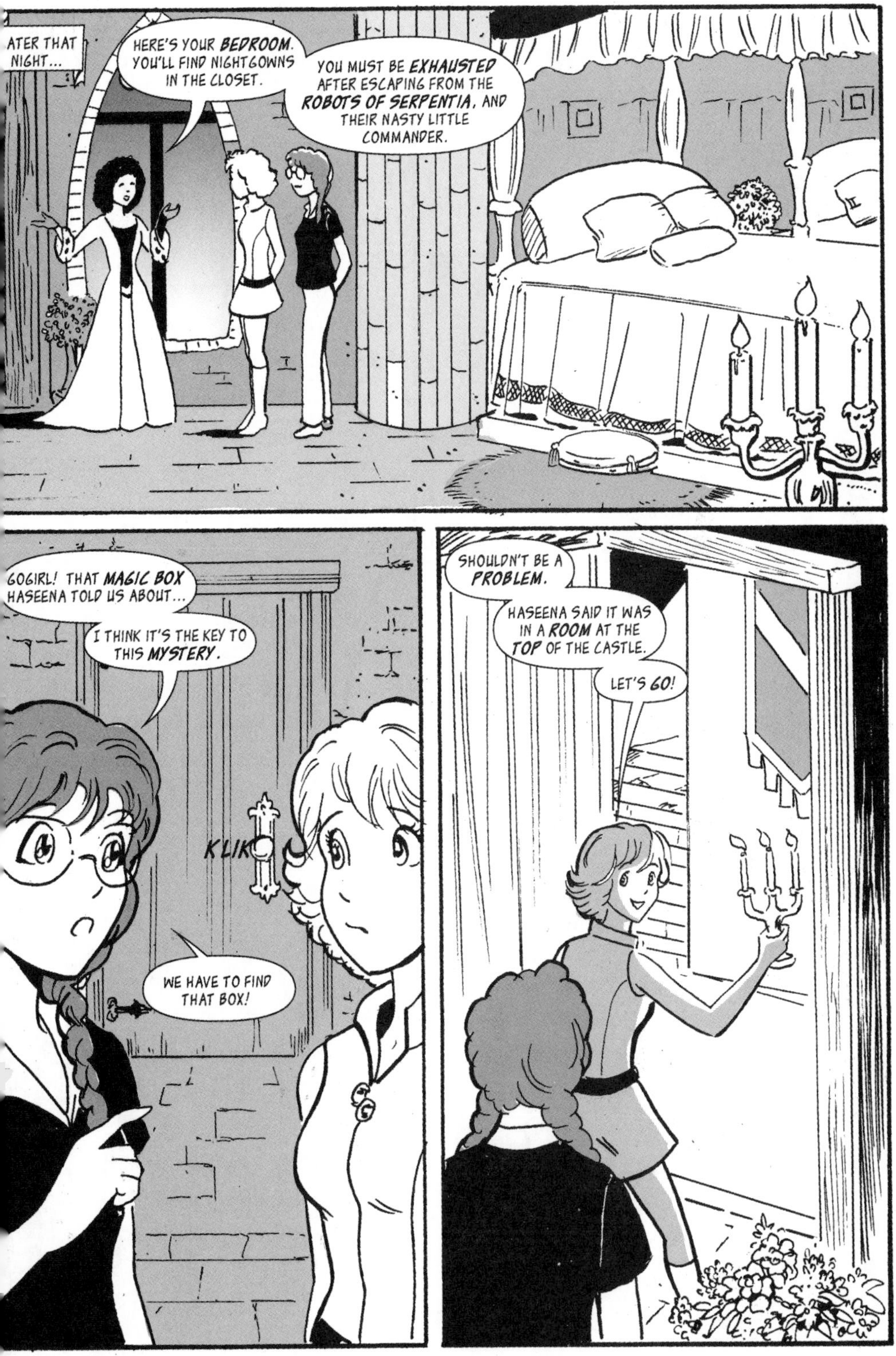
ATER THAT NIGHT...
HERE'S YOUR **BEDROOM**. YOU'LL FIND NIGHTGOWNS IN THE CLOSET.
YOU MUST BE **EXHAUSTED** AFTER ESCAPING FROM THE **ROBOTS OF SERPENTIA**, AND THEIR NASTY LITTLE COMMANDER.
GOGIRL! THAT **MAGIC BOX** HASEENA TOLD US ABOUT...
I THINK IT'S THE KEY TO THIS **MYSTERY**.
KLIK
WE HAVE TO FIND THAT BOX!
SHOULDN'T BE A **PROBLEM**.
HASEENA SAID IT WAS IN A **ROOM** AT THE **TOP** OF THE CASTLE.
LET'S **GO**!

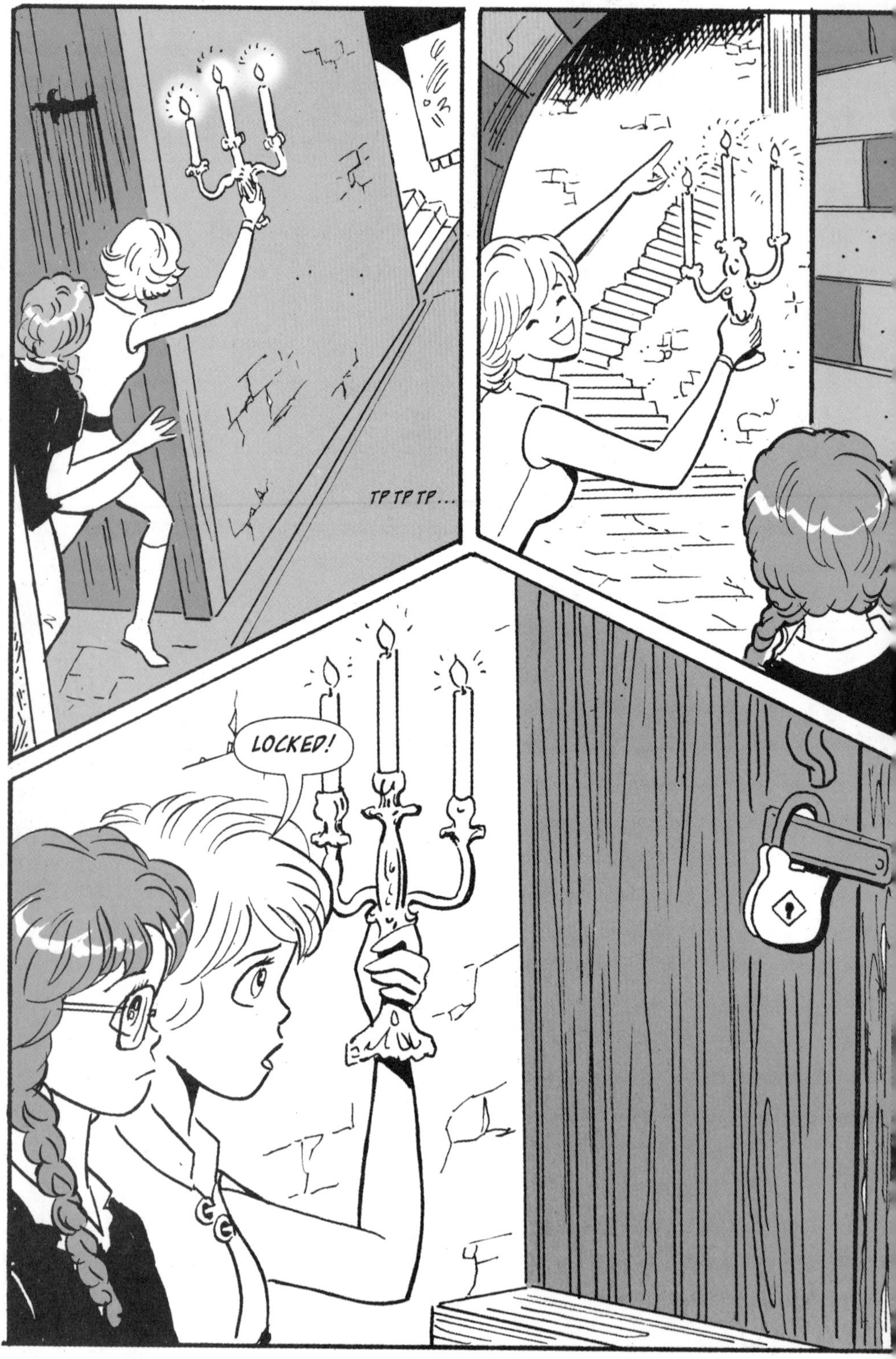
TP TP TP...
LOCKED!

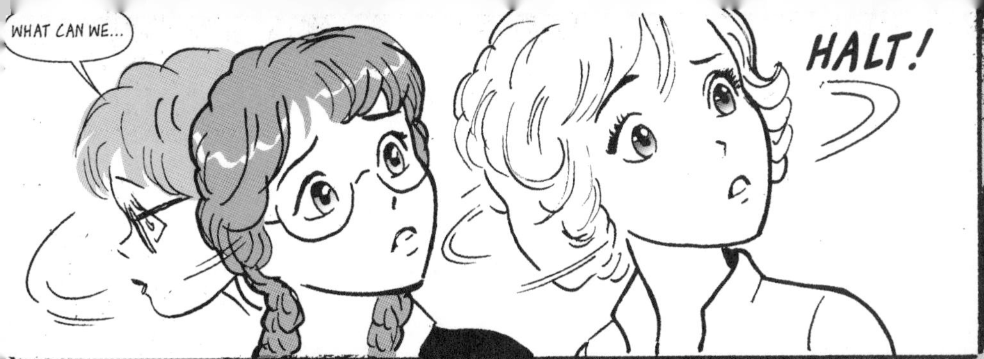
WHAT CAN WE...
HALT!
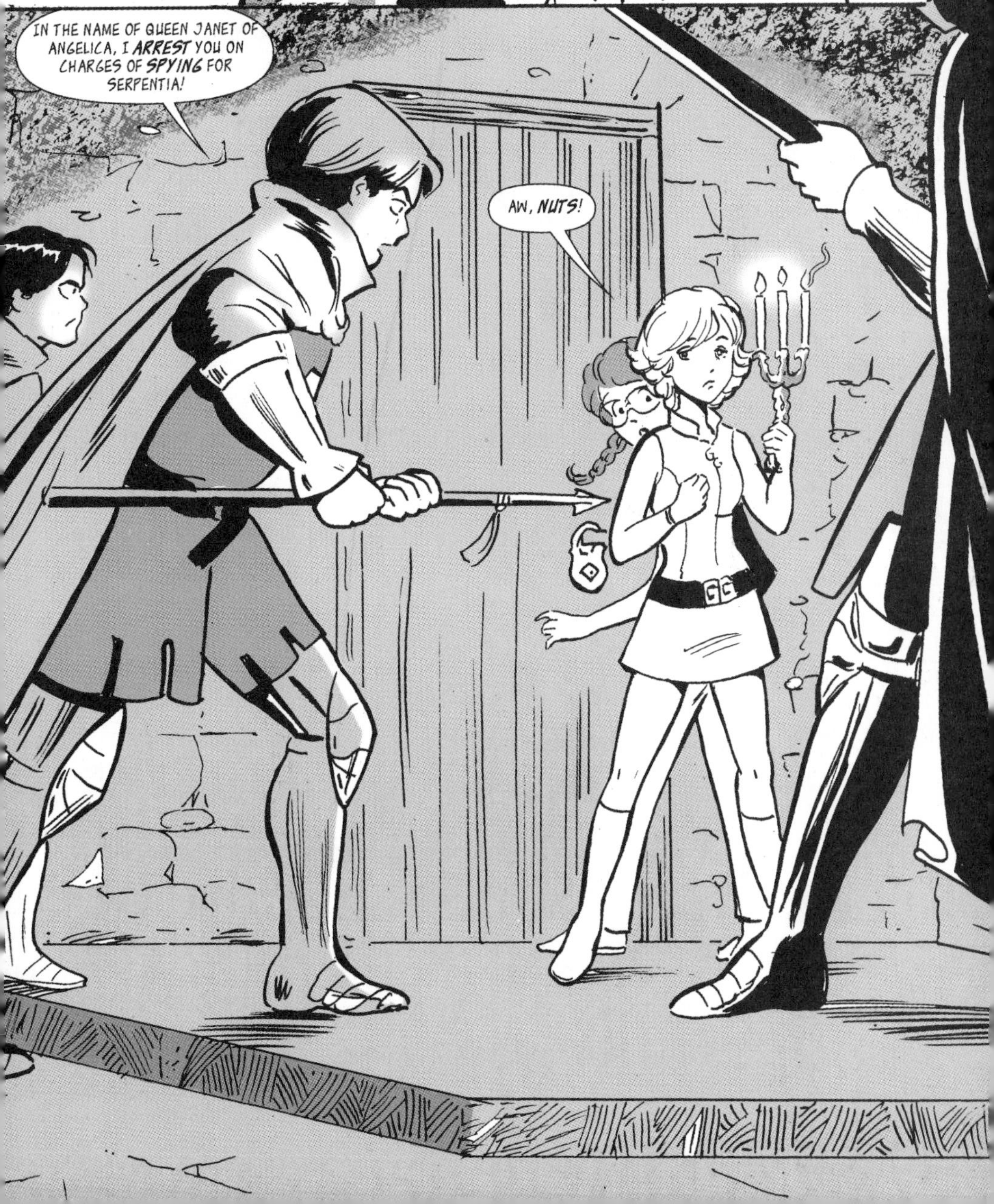
IN THE NAME OF QUEEN JANET OF ANGELICA, I ARREST YOU ON CHARGES OF SPYING FOR SERPENTIA!
AW, NUTS!

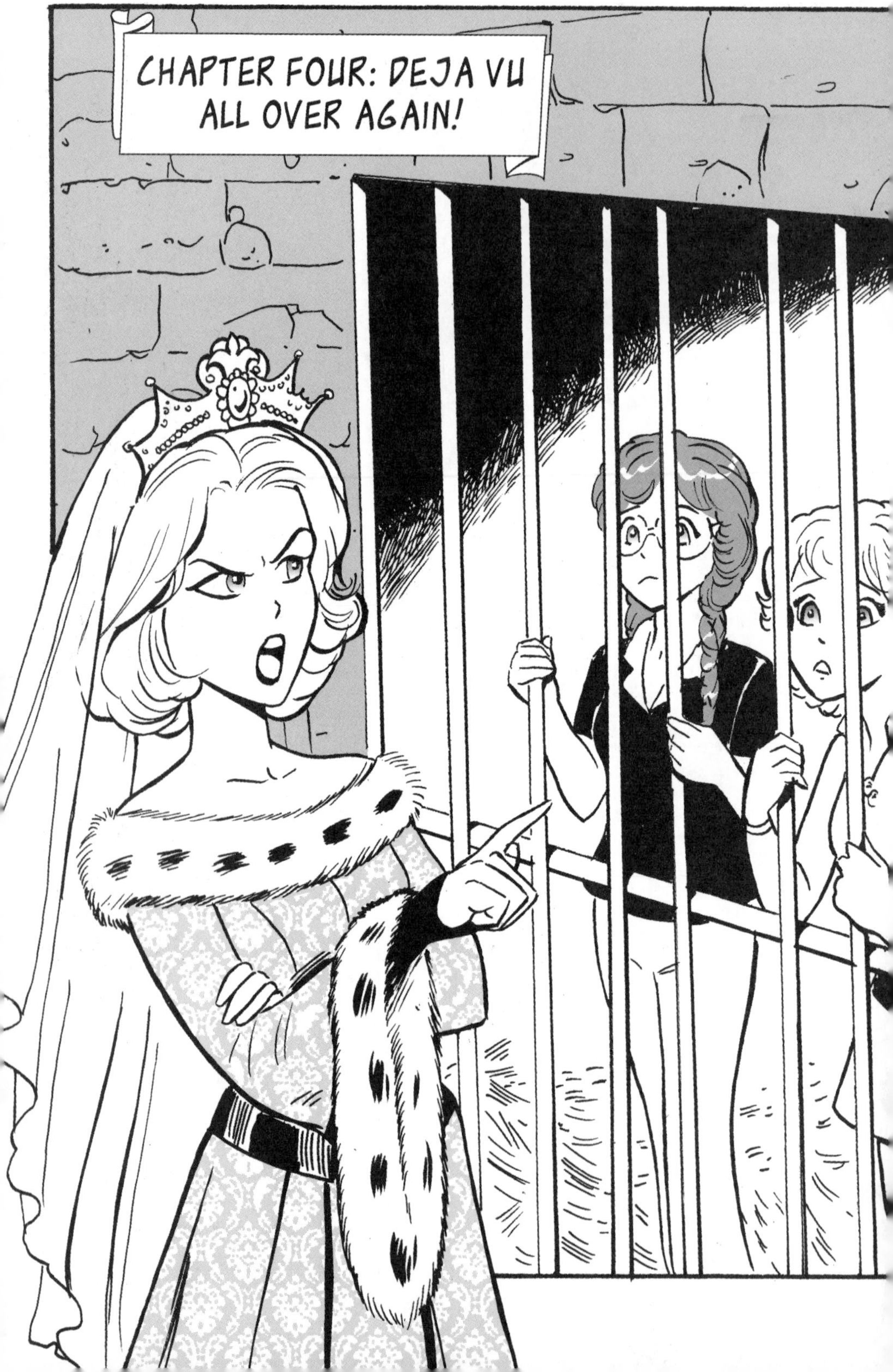
CHAPTER FOUR: DEJA VU ALL OVER AGAIN!

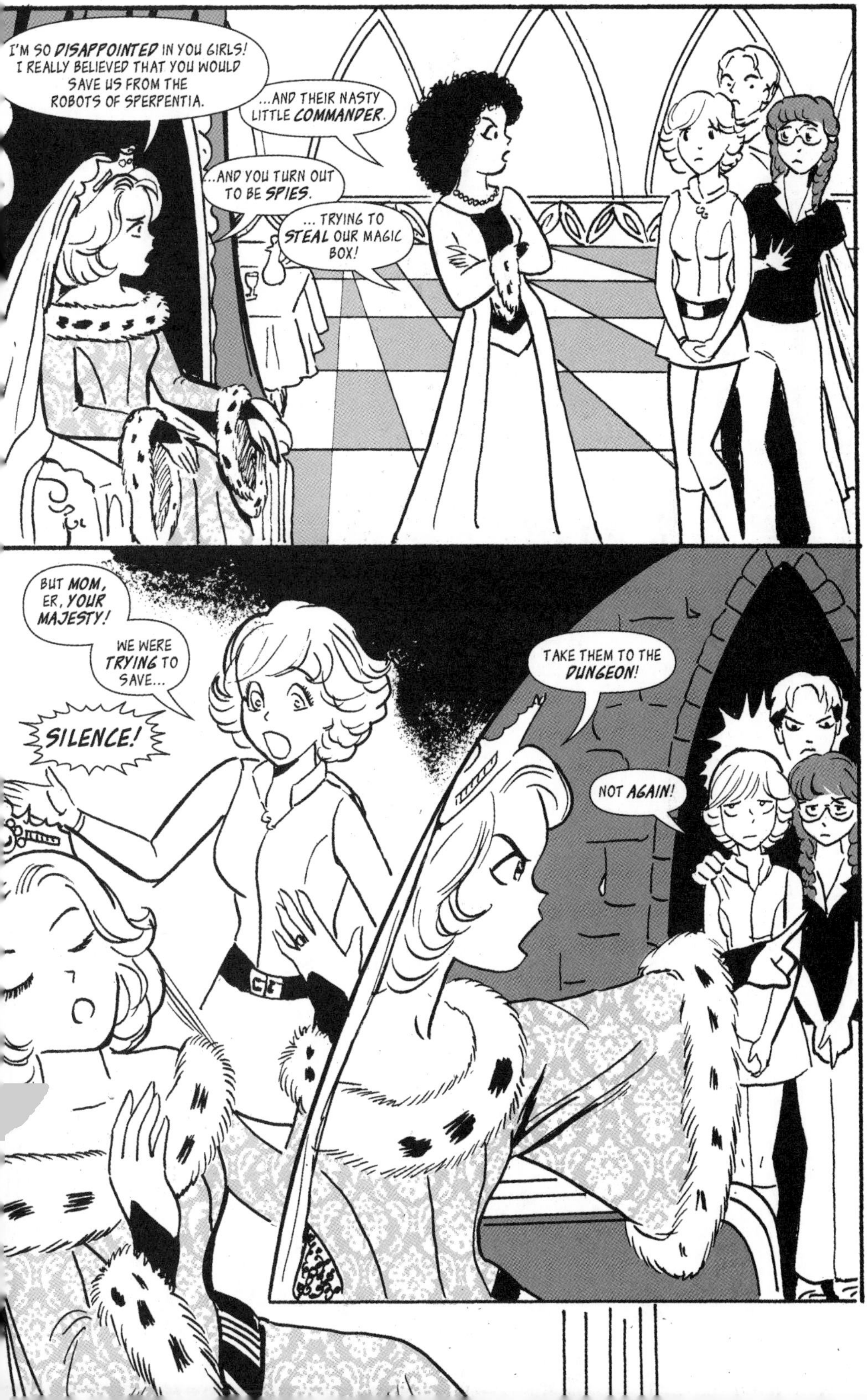
I'M SO DISAPPOINTED IN YOU GIRLS! I REALLY BELIEVED THAT YOU WOULD SAVE US FROM THE ROBOTS OF SPERPENTIA.
...AND THEIR NASTY LITTLE COMMANDER.
...AND YOU TURN OUT TO BE SPIES.
... TRYING TO STEAL OUR MAGIC BOX!
BUT MOM, ER, YOUR MAJESTY!
WE WERE TRYING TO SAVE...
SILENCE!
TAKE THEM TO THE DUNGEON!
NOT AGAIN!

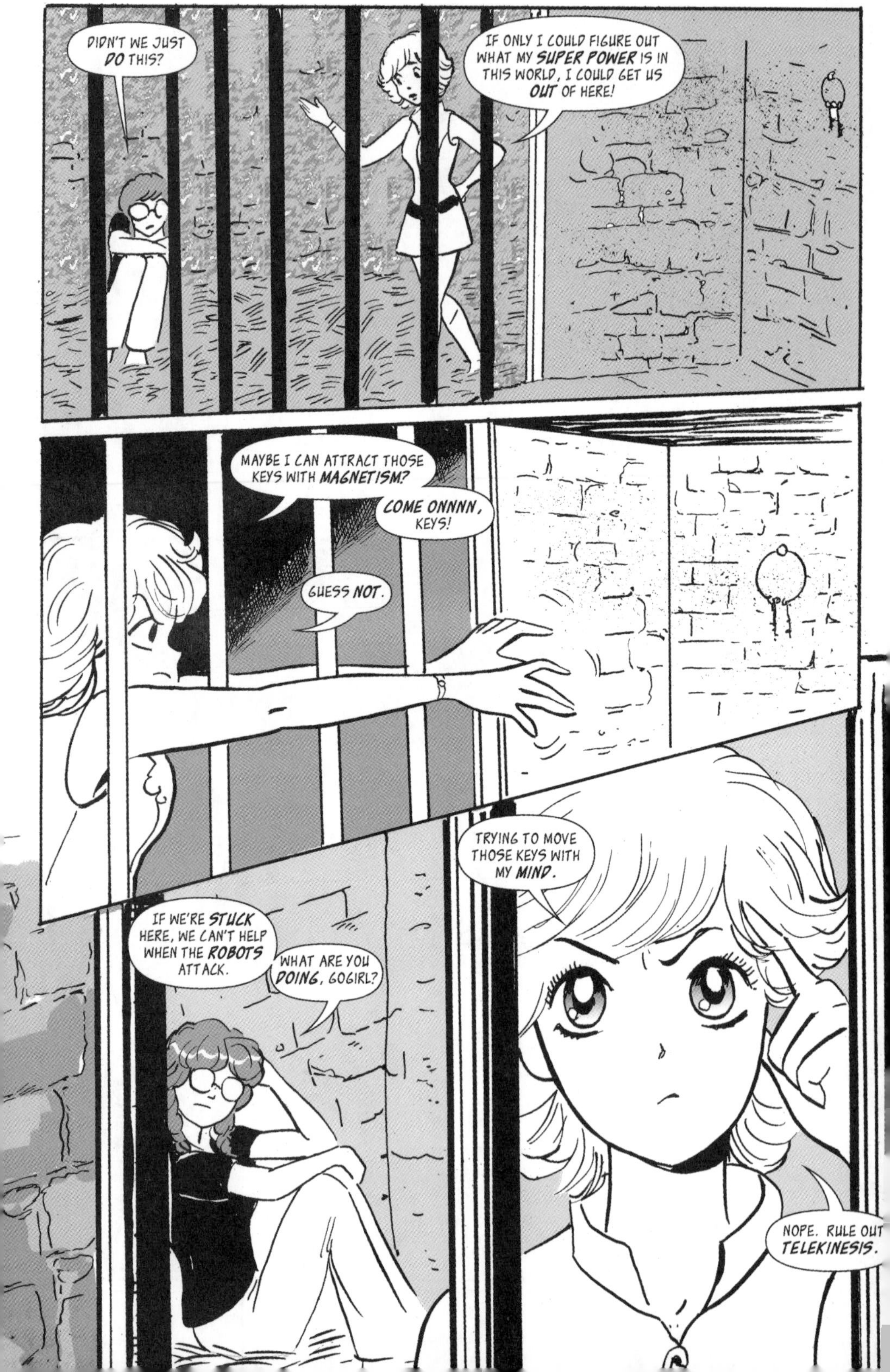
DIDN'T WE JUST DO THIS?
IF ONLY I COULD FIGURE OUT WHAT MY SUPER POWER IS IN THIS WORLD, I COULD GET US OUT OF HERE!
MAYBE I CAN ATTRACT THOSE KEYS WITH MAGNETISM?
COME ONNNN, KEYS!
GUESS NOT.
IF WE'RE STUCK HERE, WE CAN'T HELP WHEN THE ROBOTS ATTACK.
WHAT ARE YOU DOING, GOGIRL?
TRYING TO MOVE THOSE KEYS WITH MY MIND.
NOPE. RULE OUT TELEKINESIS.

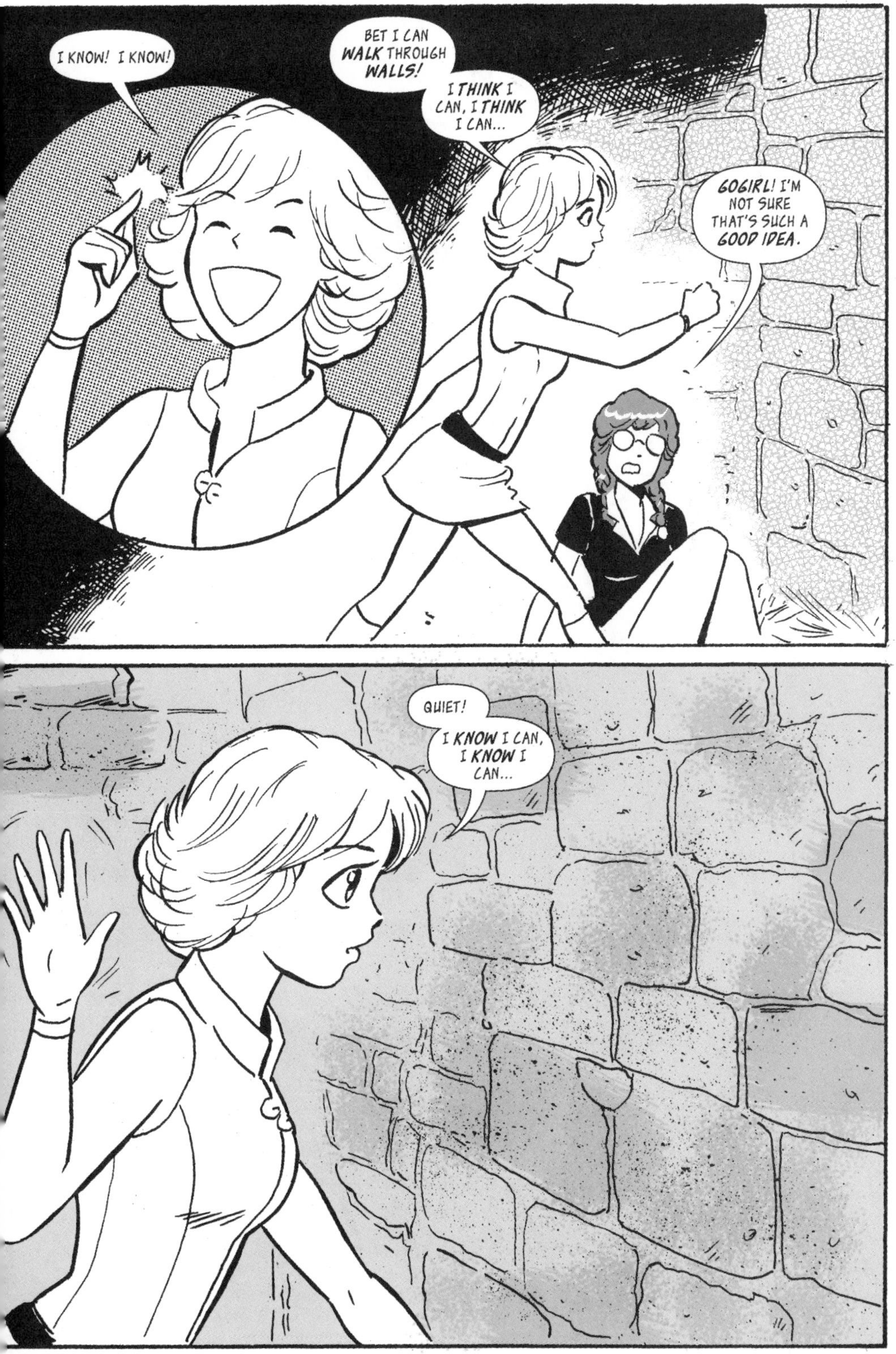
I KNOW! I KNOW!
BET I CAN WALK THROUGH WALLS!
I THINK I CAN, I THINK I CAN...
GOGIRL! I'M NOT SURE THAT'S SUCH A GOOD IDEA.
QUIET!
I KNOW I CAN, I KNOW I CAN...

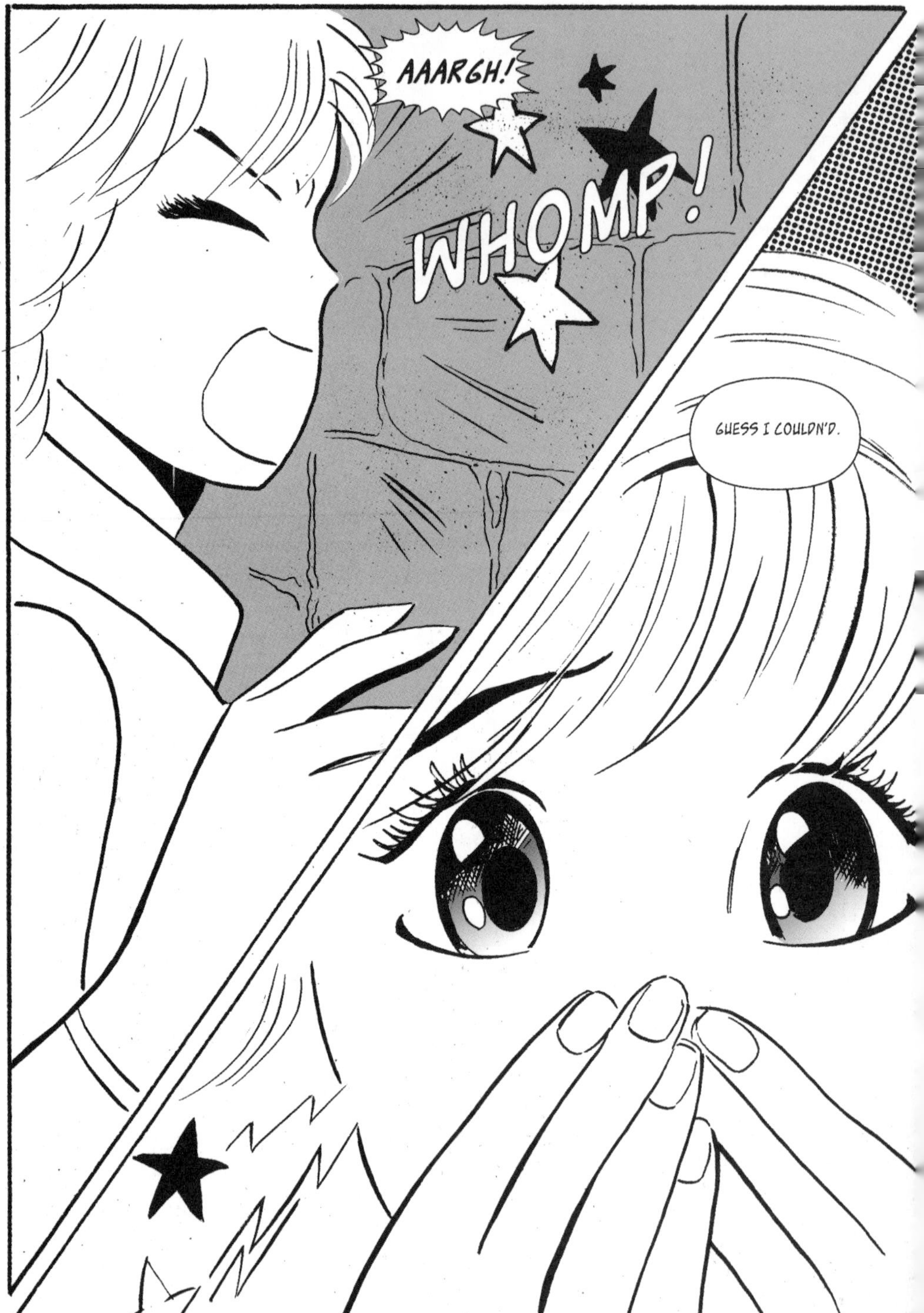
AAARGH!
WHOMP!
GUESS I COULDN'D.

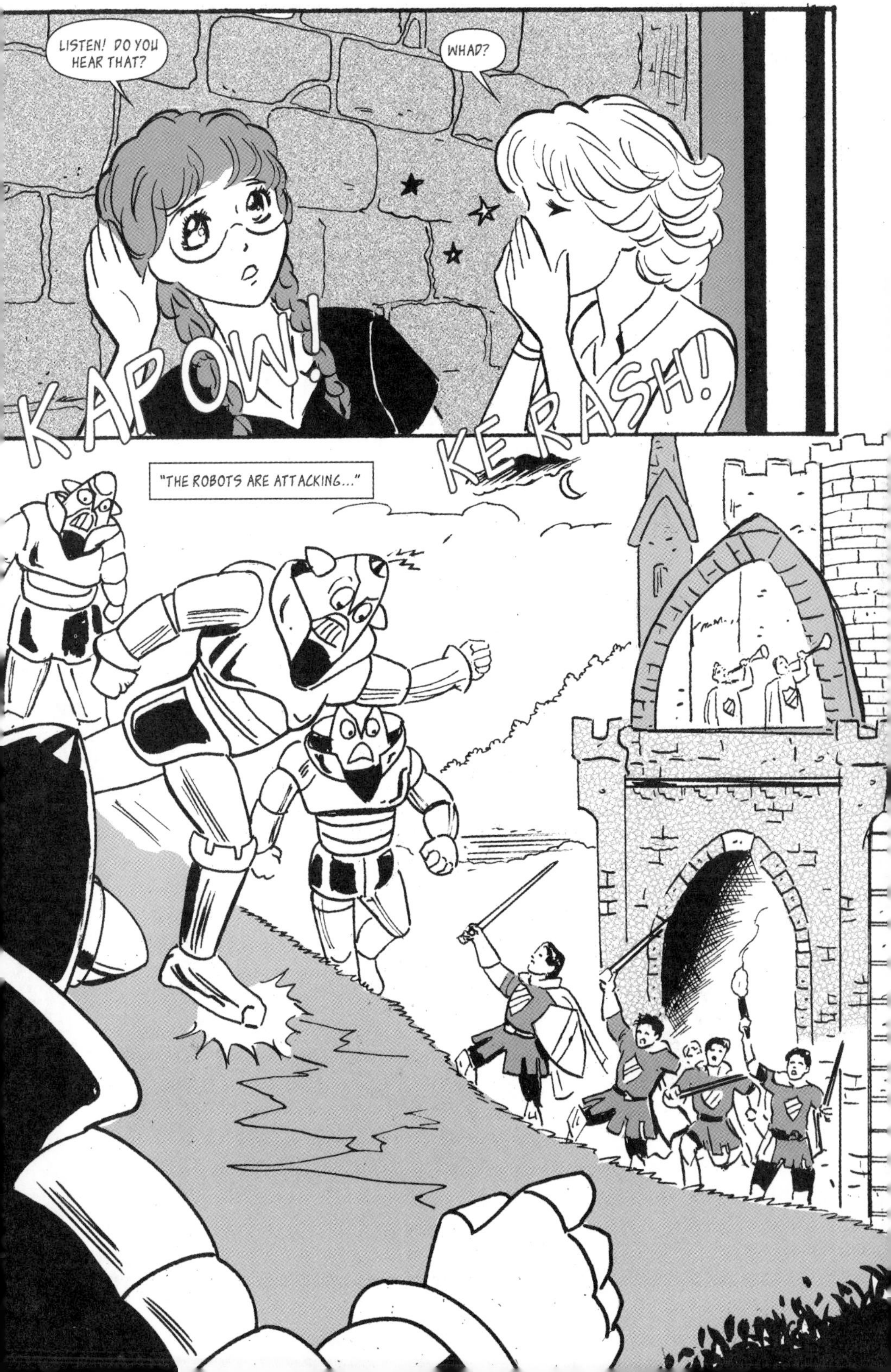

LISTEN! DO YOU HEAR THAT?
WHAD?
KAPOW!
KERASH!
"THE ROBOTS ARE ATTACKING..."

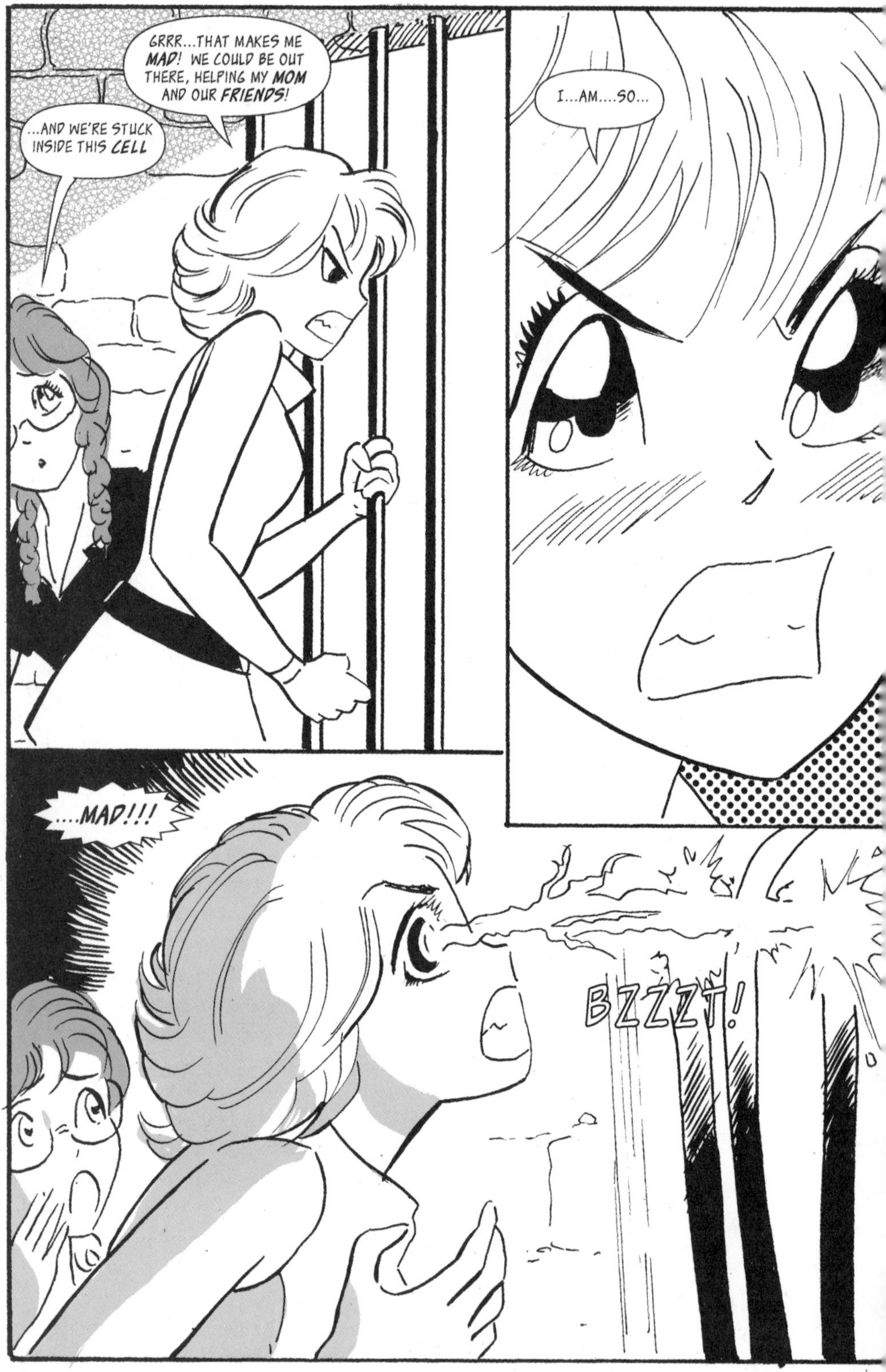
GRRR...THAT MAKES ME MAD! WE COULD BE OUT THERE, HELPING MY MOM AND OUR FRIENDS!
...AND WE'RE STUCK INSIDE THIS CELL
I...AM....SO...
....MAD!!!
BZZZT!

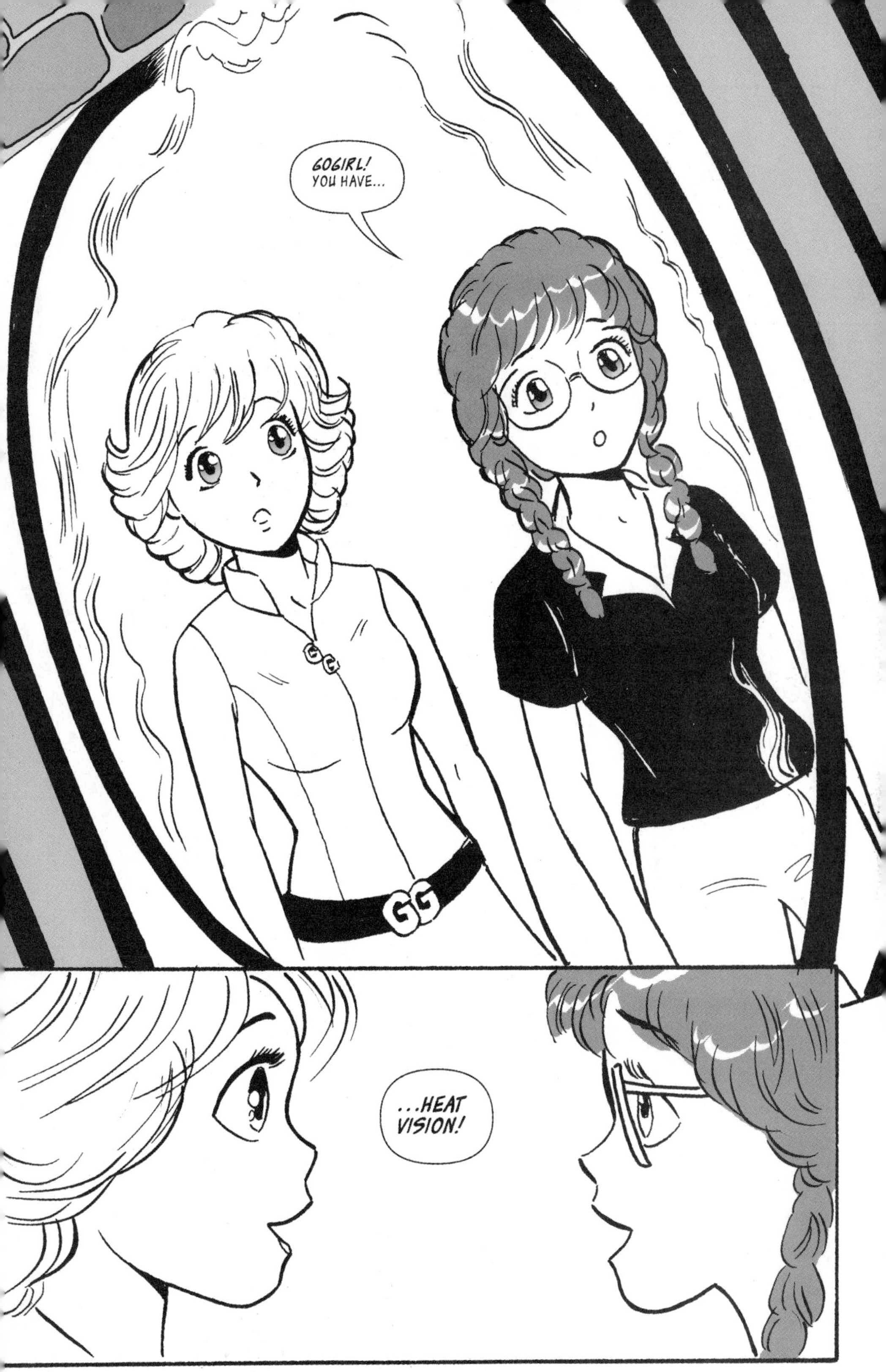
GOGIRL! YOU HAVE...
...HEAT VISION!

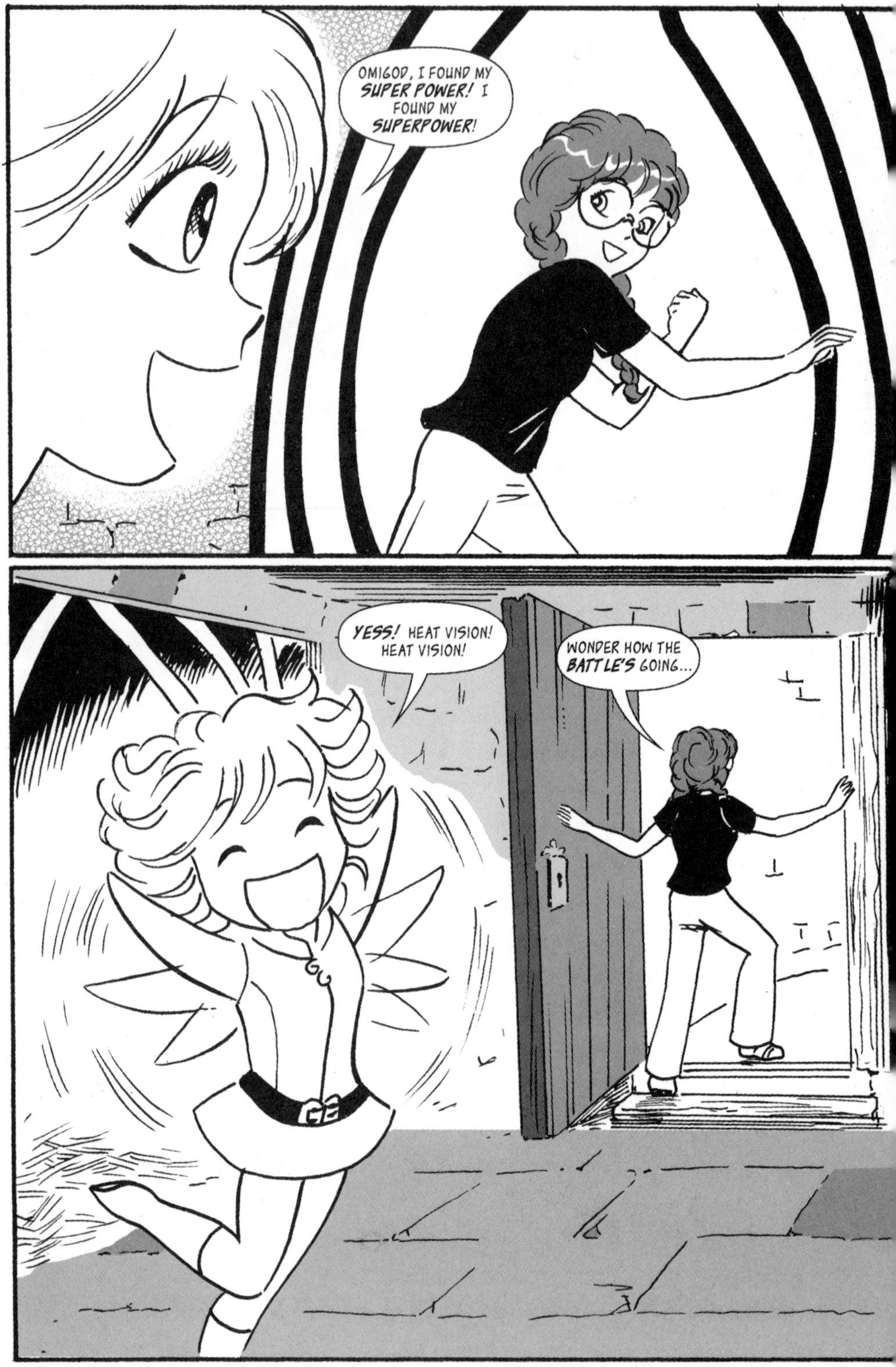
OMIGOD, I FOUND MY SUPER POWER! I FOUND MY SUPERPOWER!
YESS! HEAT VISION! HEAT VISION!
WONDER HOW THE BATTLE'S GOING...

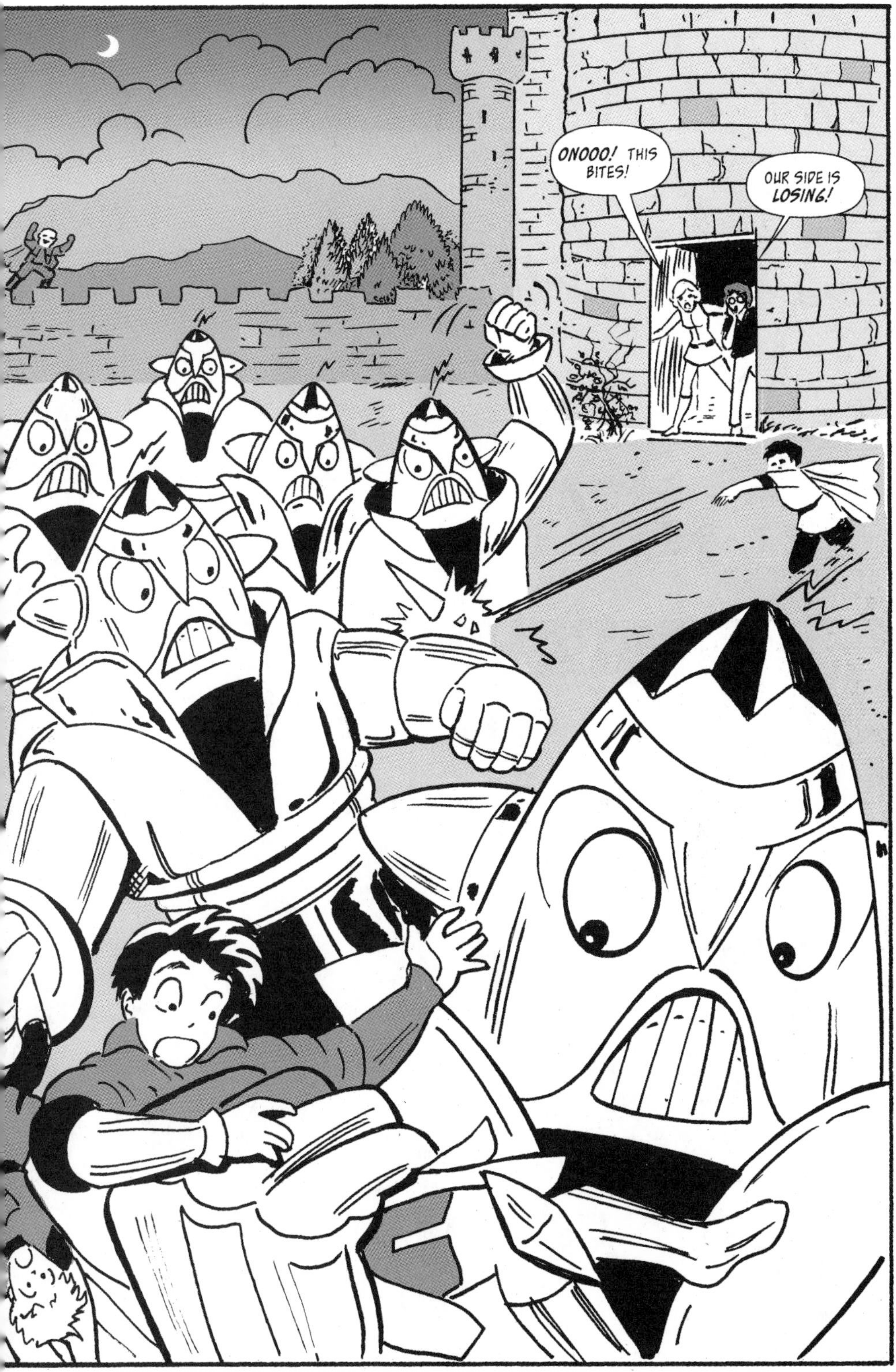
ONOOO! THIS BITES!
OUR SIDE IS LOSING!

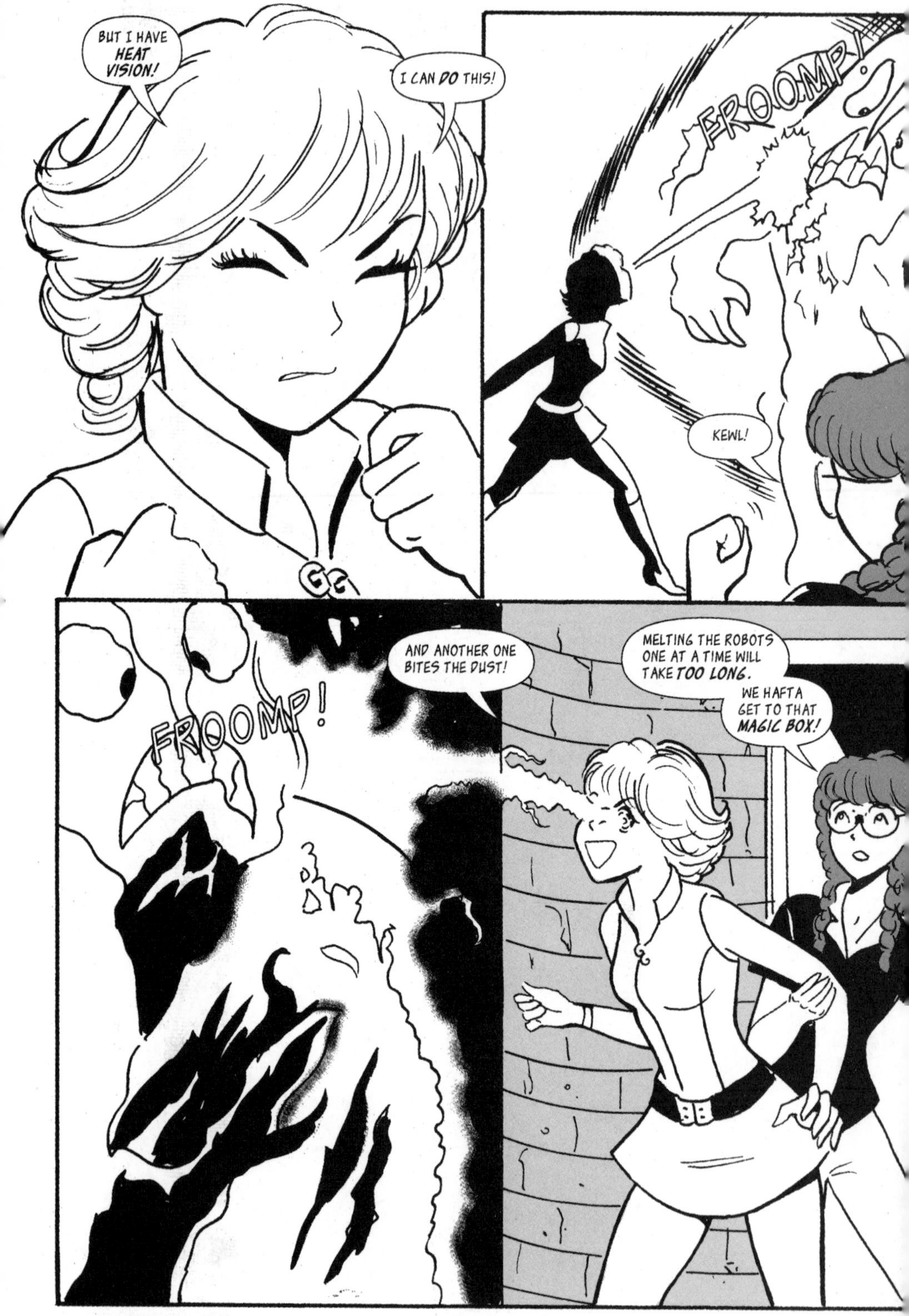
BUT I HAVE **HEAT VISION!**
I CAN **DO** THIS!
FROOMP!
KEWL!
AND ANOTHER ONE BITES THE DUST!
FROOMP!
MELTING THE ROBOTS ONE AT A TIME WILL TAKE **TOO LONG.**
WE HAFTA GET TO THAT **MAGIC BOX!**

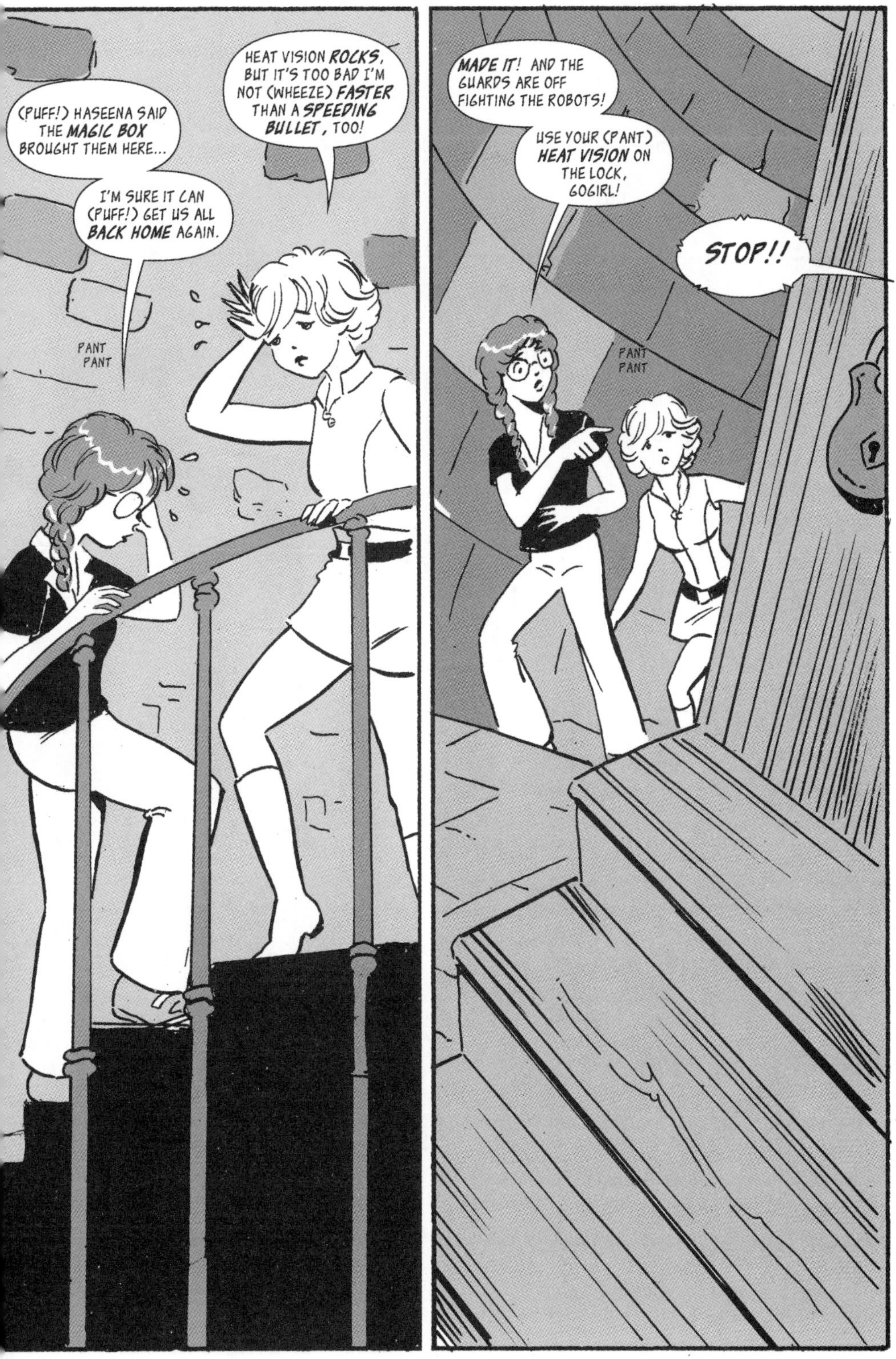
(PUFF!) HASEENA SAID THE MAGIC BOX BROUGHT THEM HERE...
I'M SURE IT CAN (PUFF!) GET US ALL BACK HOME AGAIN.
PANT PANT
HEAT VISION ROCKS, BUT IT'S TOO BAD I'M NOT (WHEEZE) FASTER THAN A SPEEDING BULLET, TOO!
MADE IT! AND THE GUARDS ARE OFF FIGHTING THE ROBOTS!
USE YOUR (PANT) HEAT VISION ON THE LOCK, GOGIRL!
PANT PANT
STOP!!

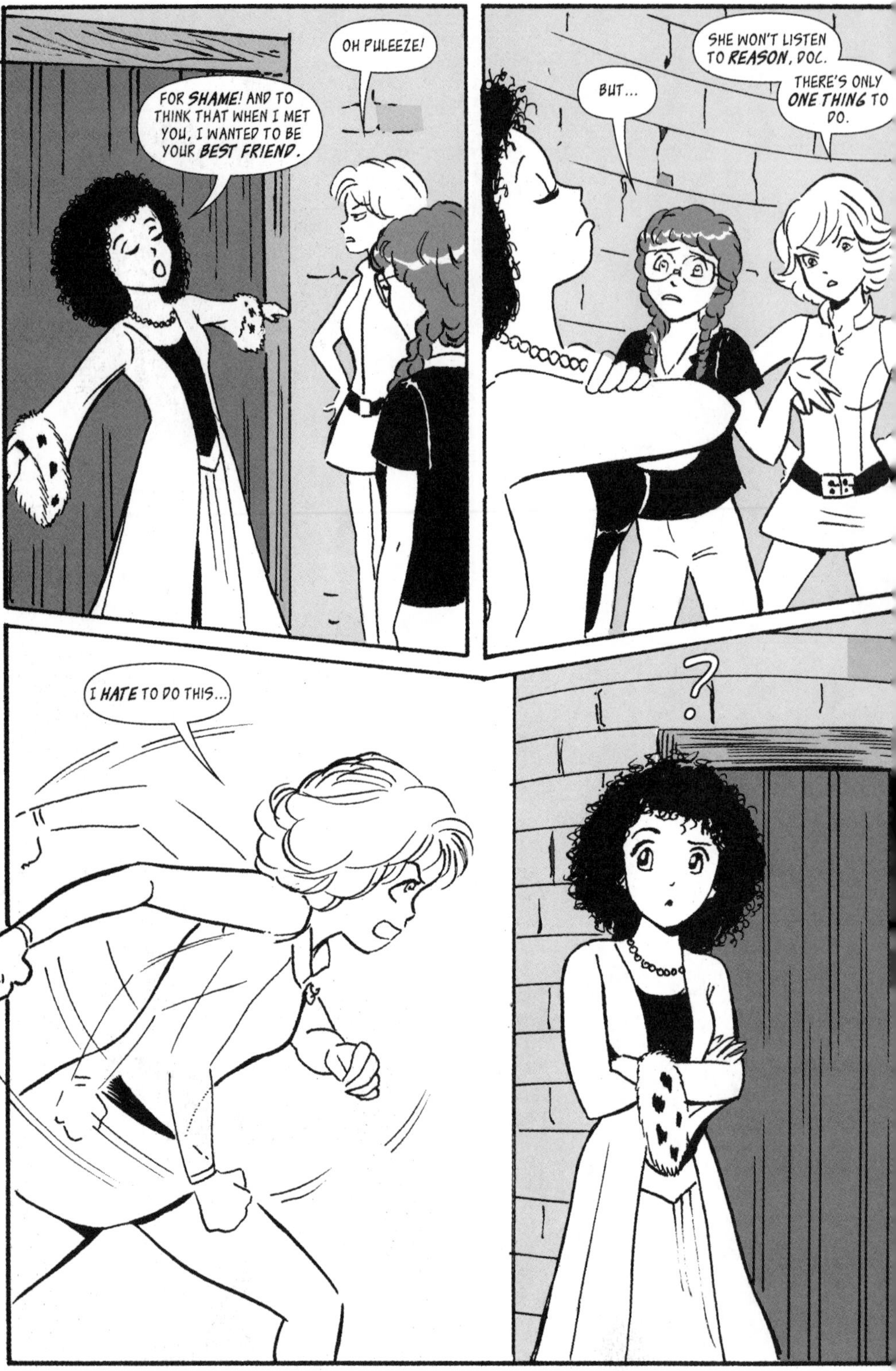
FOR **SHAME**! AND TO THINK THAT WHEN I MET YOU, I WANTED TO BE YOUR **BEST FRIEND**.
OH PULEEZE!
BUT...
SHE WON'T LISTEN TO **REASON**, DOC.
THERE'S ONLY **ONE THING** TO DO.
I **HATE** TO DO THIS...
?

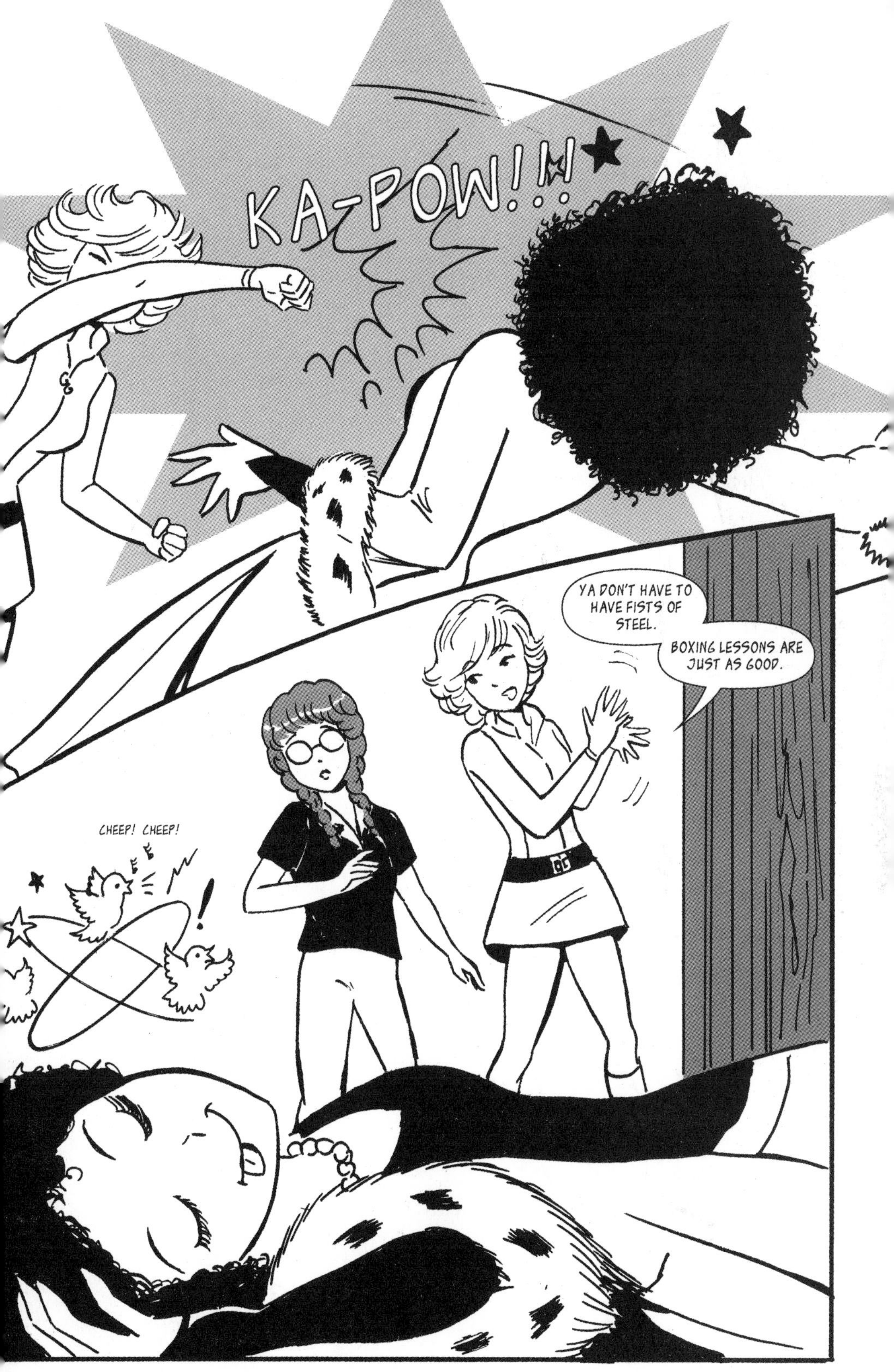
KA-POW!!!
YA DON'T HAVE TO HAVE FISTS OF STEEL.
BOXING LESSONS ARE JUST AS GOOD.
CHEEP! CHEEP!

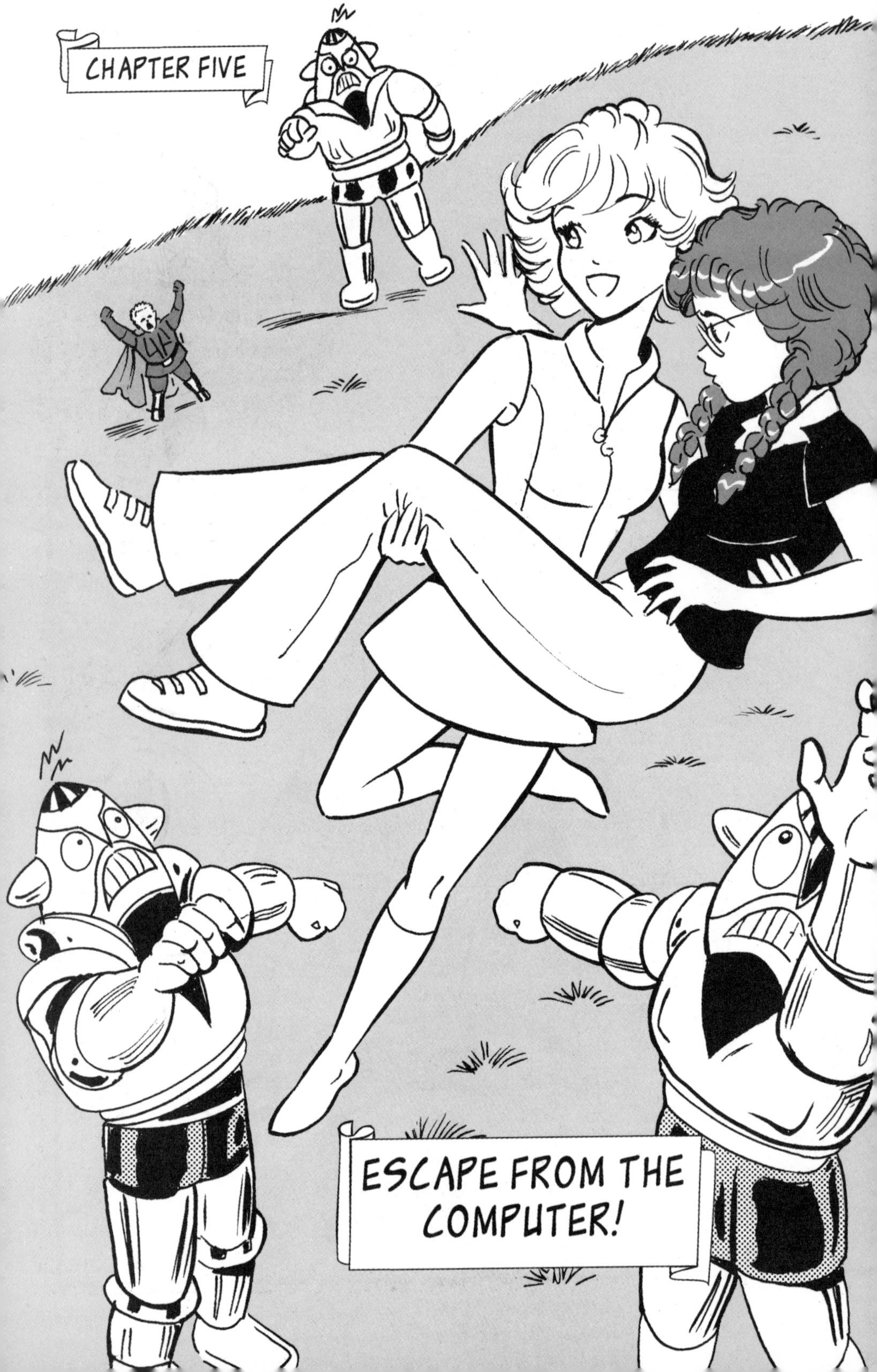
CHAPTER FIVE
ESCAPE FROM THE COMPUTER!

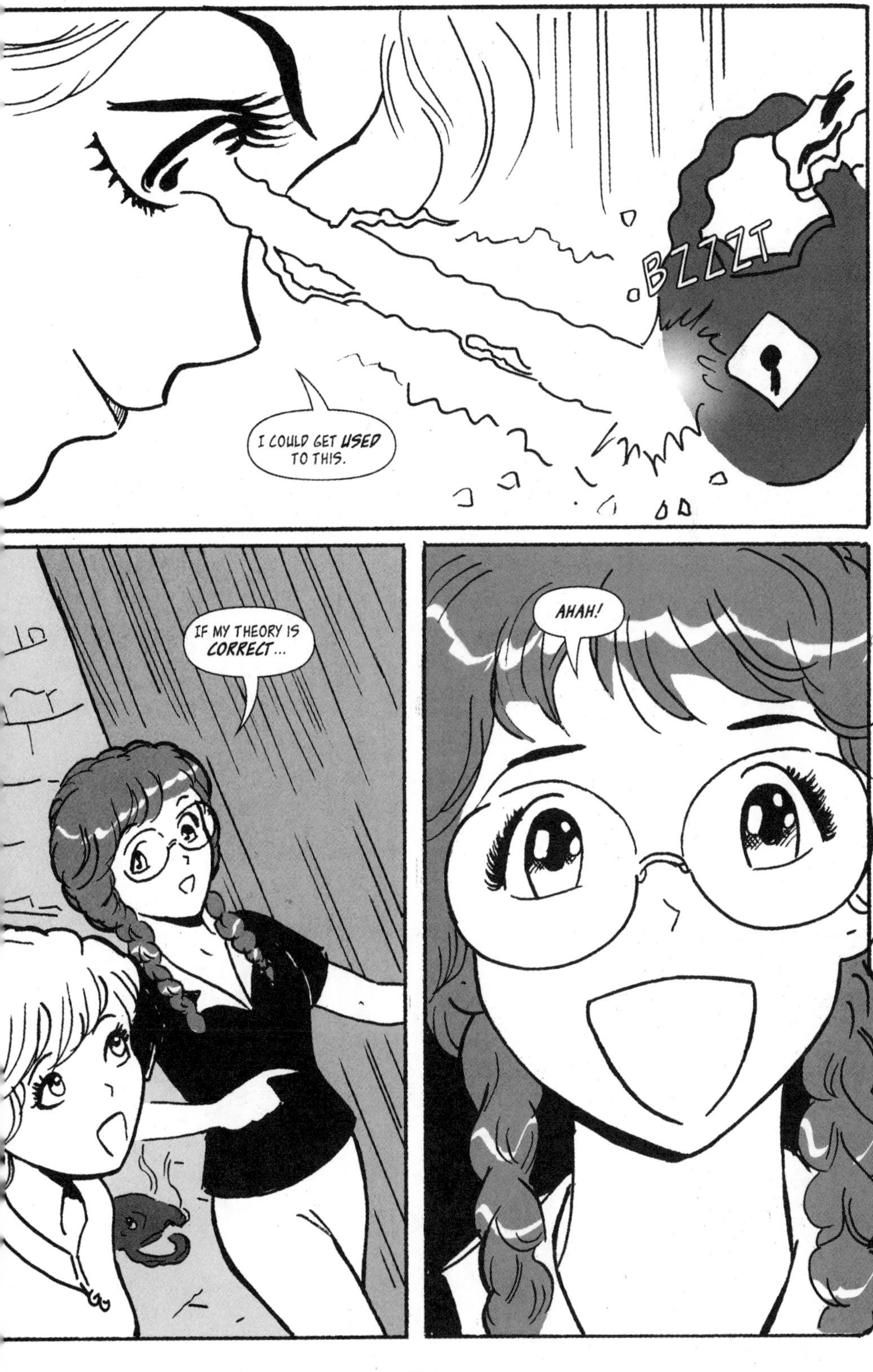
BZZZZT
I COULD GET USED TO THIS.
IF MY THEORY IS CORRECT...
AHAH!

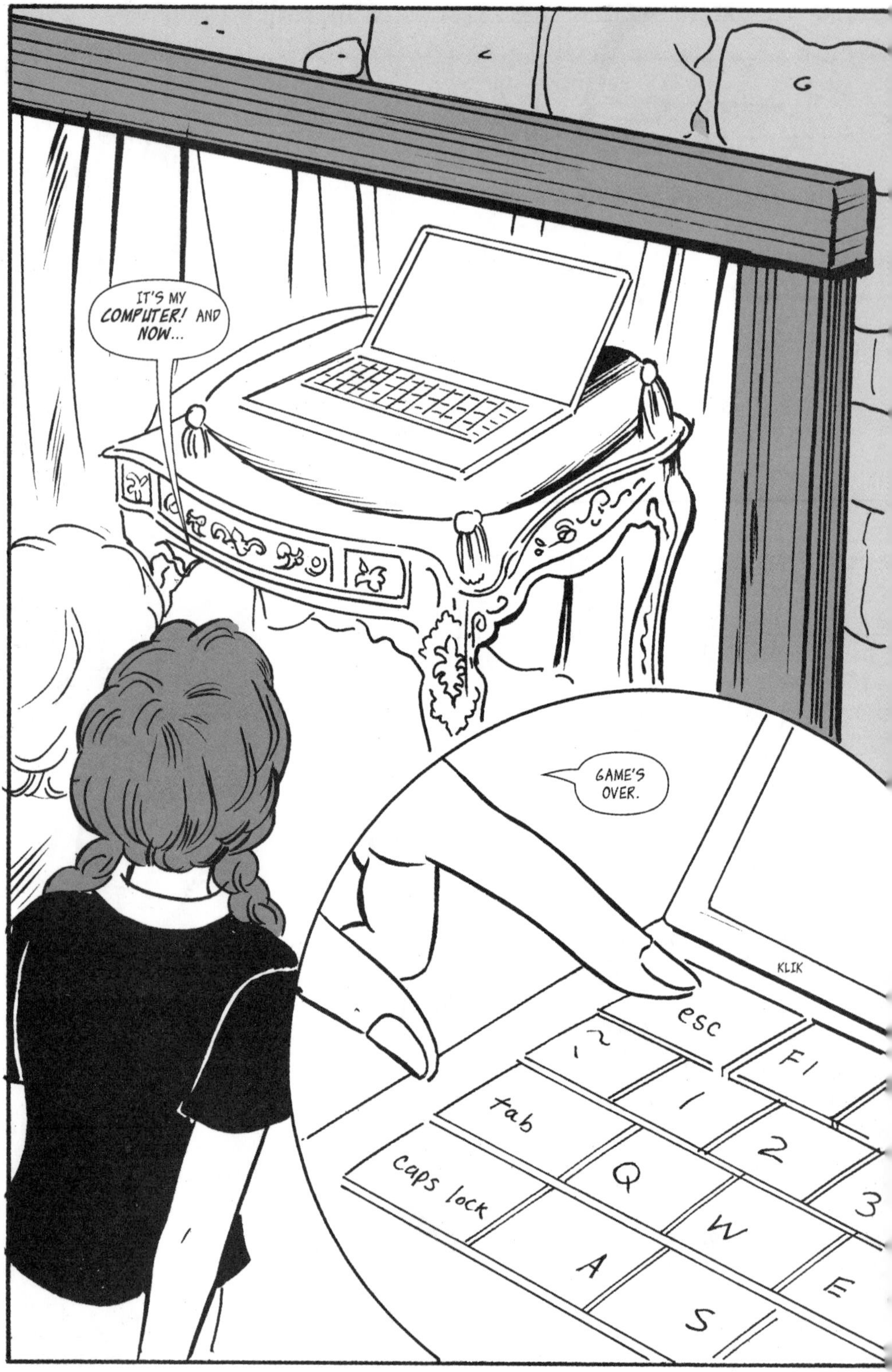
IT'S MY COMPUTER! AND NOW...
GAME'S OVER.
KLIK
esc
F1
tab
1
2
caps lock
Q
3
W
A
E
S

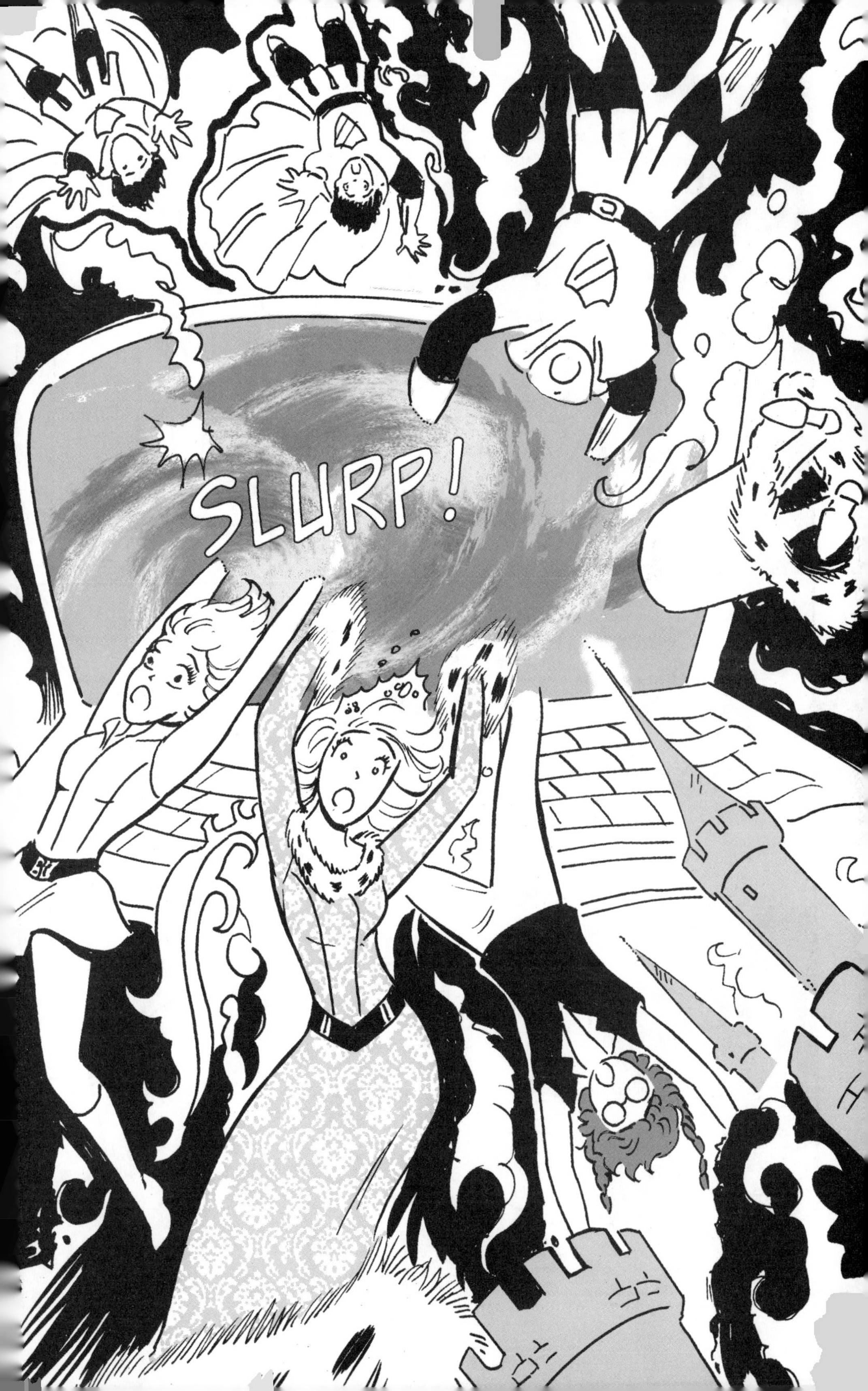
SLURP!

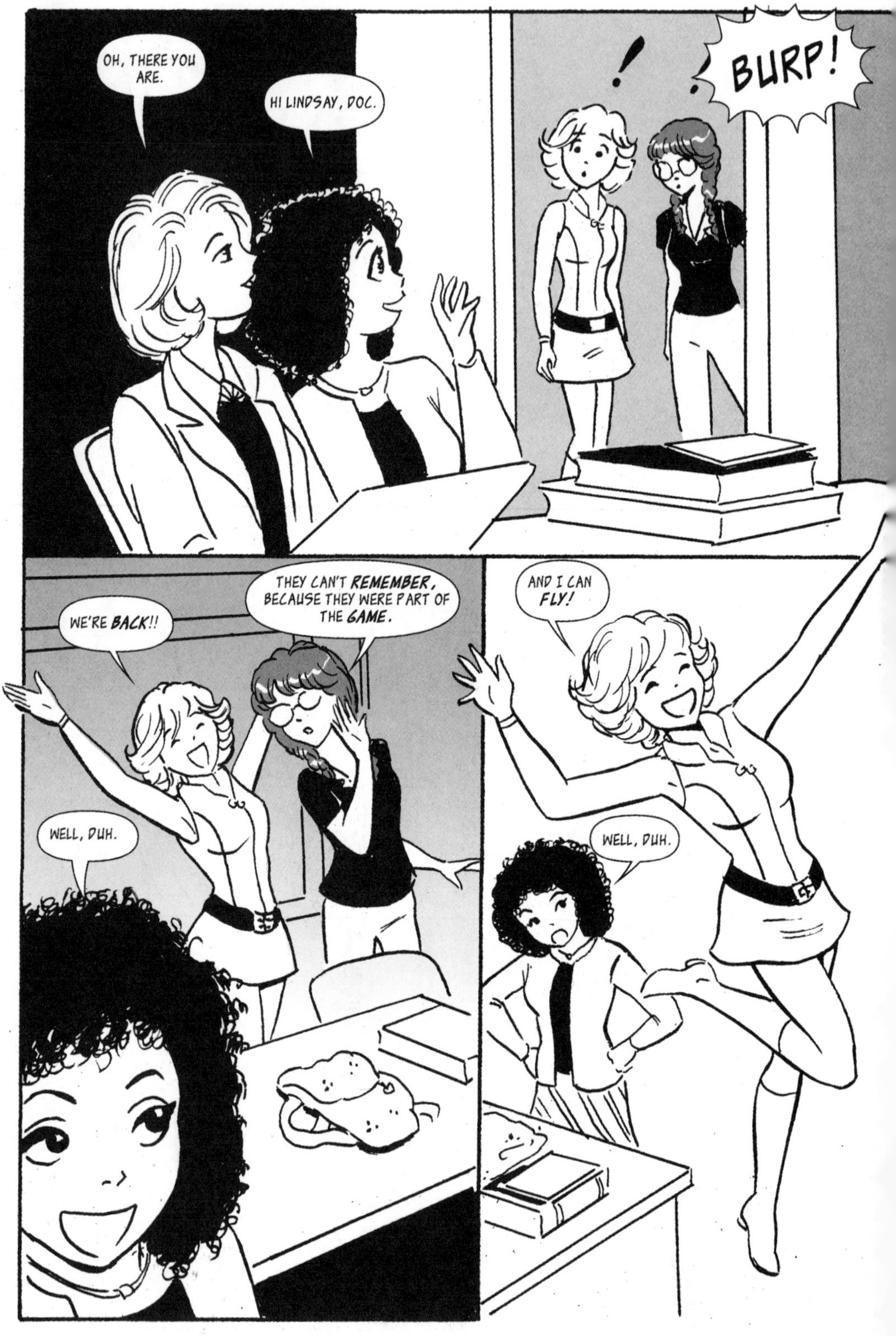
OH, THERE YOU ARE.
HI LINDSAY, DOC.
!
!
BURP!
WE'RE BACK!!
THEY CAN'T REMEMBER, BECAUSE THEY WERE PART OF THE GAME.
WELL, DUH.
AND I CAN FLY!
WELL, DUH.

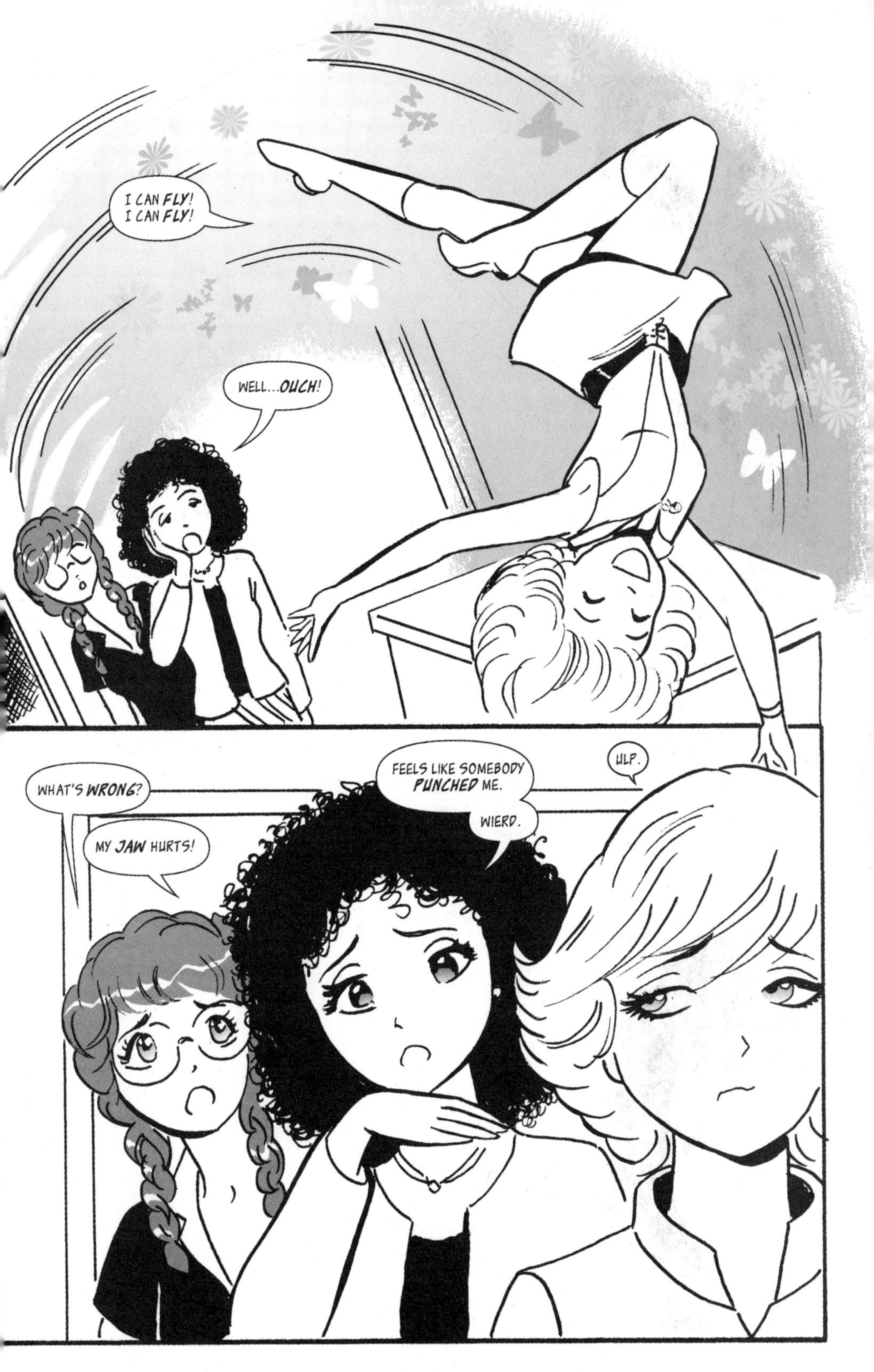
I CAN FLY! I CAN FLY!
WELL...OUCH!
WHAT'S WRONG?
MY JAW HURTS!
FEELS LIKE SOMEBODY PUNCHED ME.
WIERD.
ULP.

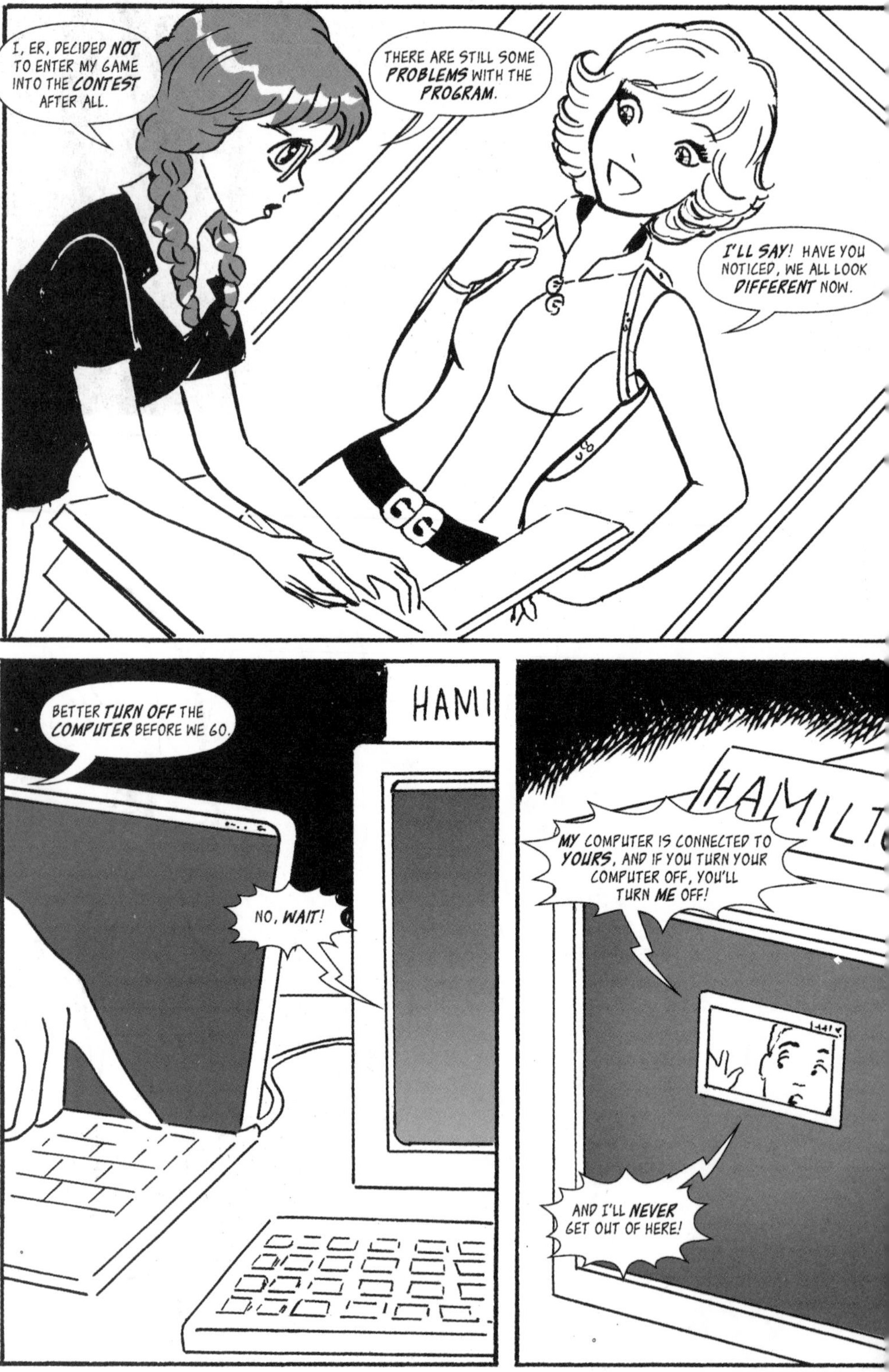
I, ER, DECIDED NOT TO ENTER MY GAME INTO THE CONTEST AFTER ALL.
THERE ARE STILL SOME PROBLEMS WITH THE PROGRAM.
I'LL SAY! HAVE YOU NOTICED, WE ALL LOOK DIFFERENT NOW.
BETTER TURN OFF THE COMPUTER BEFORE WE GO.
HAMI
NO, WAIT!
HAMILT
MY COMPUTER IS CONNECTED TO YOURS, AND IF YOU TURN YOUR COMPUTER OFF, YOU'LL TURN ME OFF!
AND I'LL NEVER GET OUT OF HERE!

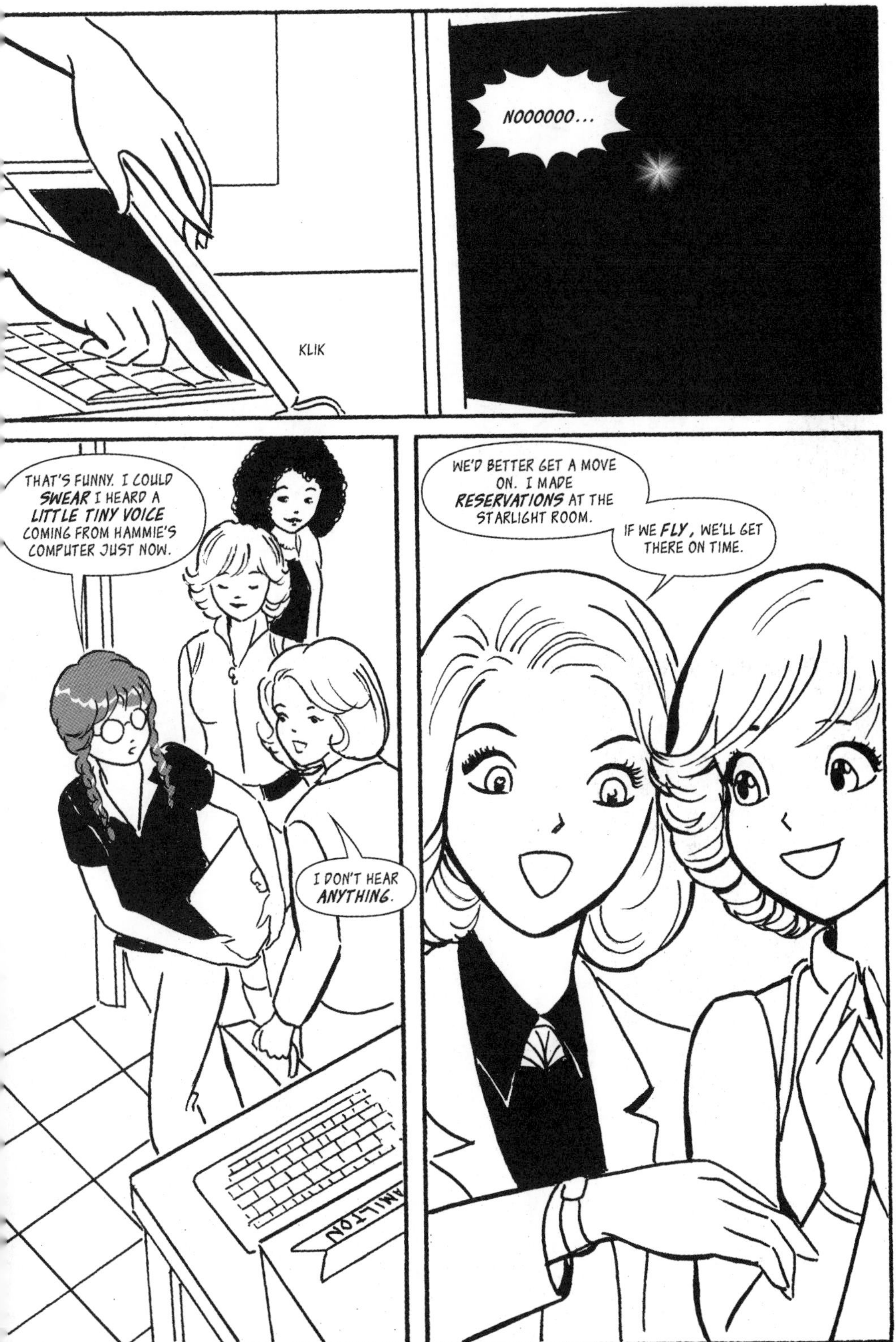
KLIK
NOOOOOO...
THAT'S FUNNY. I COULD SWEAR I HEARD A LITTLE TINY VOICE COMING FROM HAMMIE'S COMPUTER JUST NOW.
I DON'T HEAR ANYTHING.
WE'D BETTER GET A MOVE ON. I MADE RESERVATIONS AT THE STARLIGHT ROOM.
IF WE FLY, WE'LL GET THERE ON TIME.

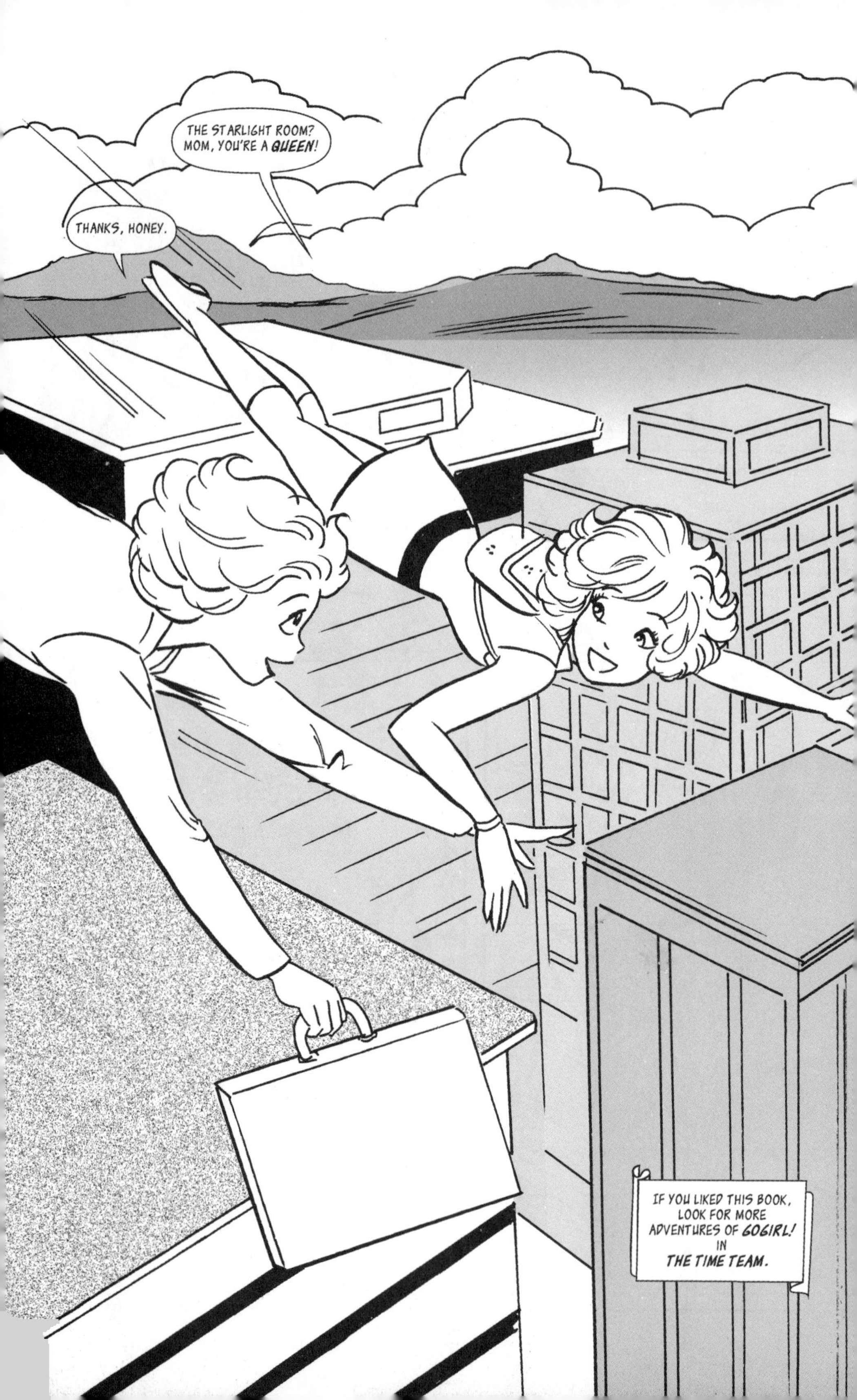
THE STARLIGHT ROOM? MOM, YOU'RE A QUEEN!
THANKS, HONEY.
IF YOU LIKED THIS BOOK, LOOK FOR MORE ADVENTURES OF GOGIRL! IN THE TIME TEAM.

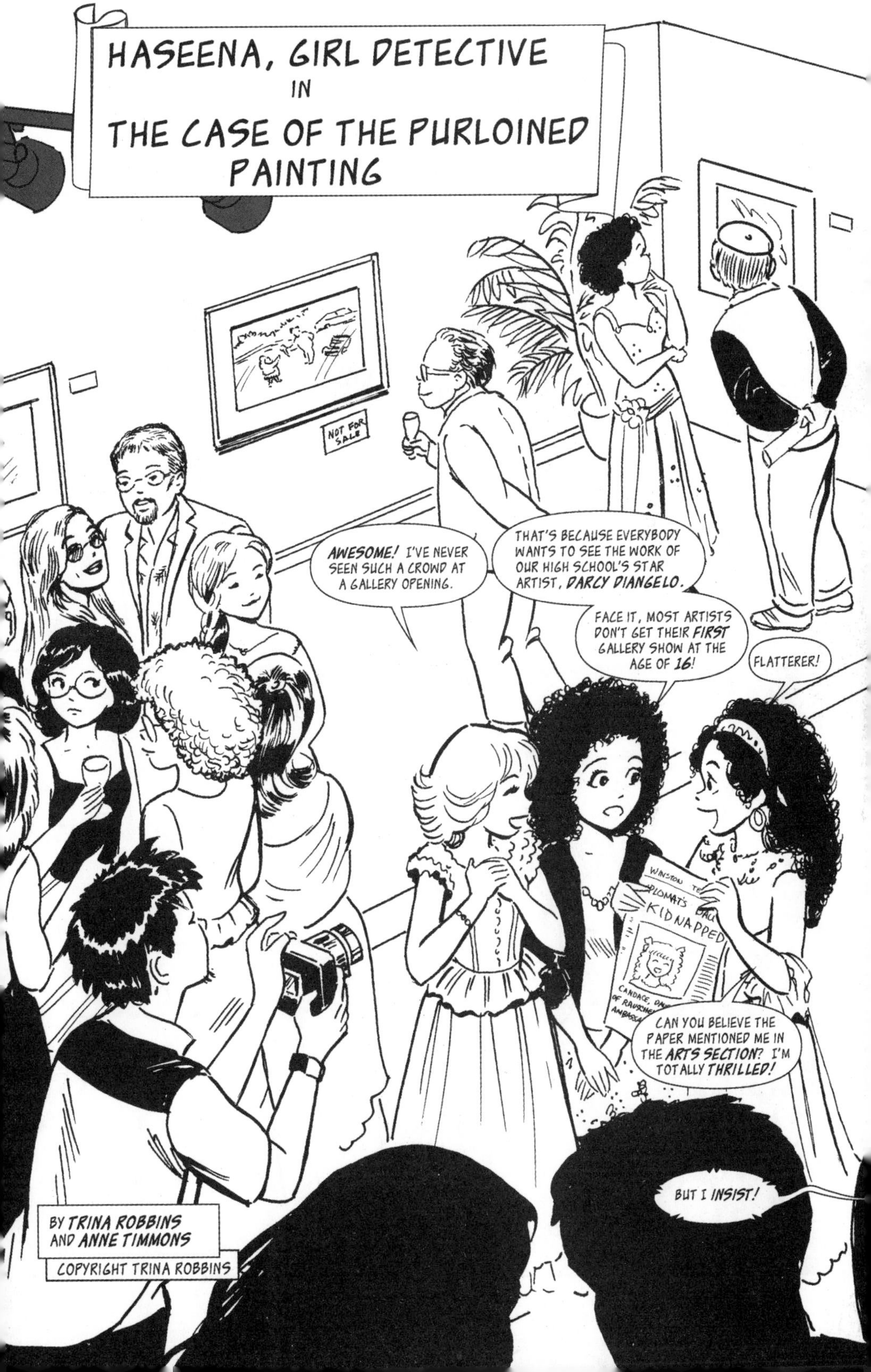
HASEENA, GIRL DETECTIVE IN THE CASE OF THE PURLOINED PAINTING
NOT FOR SALE
AWESOME! I'VE NEVER SEEN SUCH A CROWD AT A GALLERY OPENING.
THAT'S BECAUSE EVERYBODY WANTS TO SEE THE WORK OF OUR HIGH SCHOOL'S STAR ARTIST, DARCY DIANGELO.
FACE IT, MOST ARTISTS DON'T GET THEIR FIRST GALLERY SHOW AT THE AGE OF 16!
FLATTERER!
KIDNAPPED
CAN YOU BELIEVE THE PAPER MENTIONED ME IN THE ARTS SECTION? I'M TOTALLY THRILLED!
BUT I INSIST!
BY TRINA ROBBINS AND ANNE TIMMONS
COPYRIGHT TRINA ROBBINS

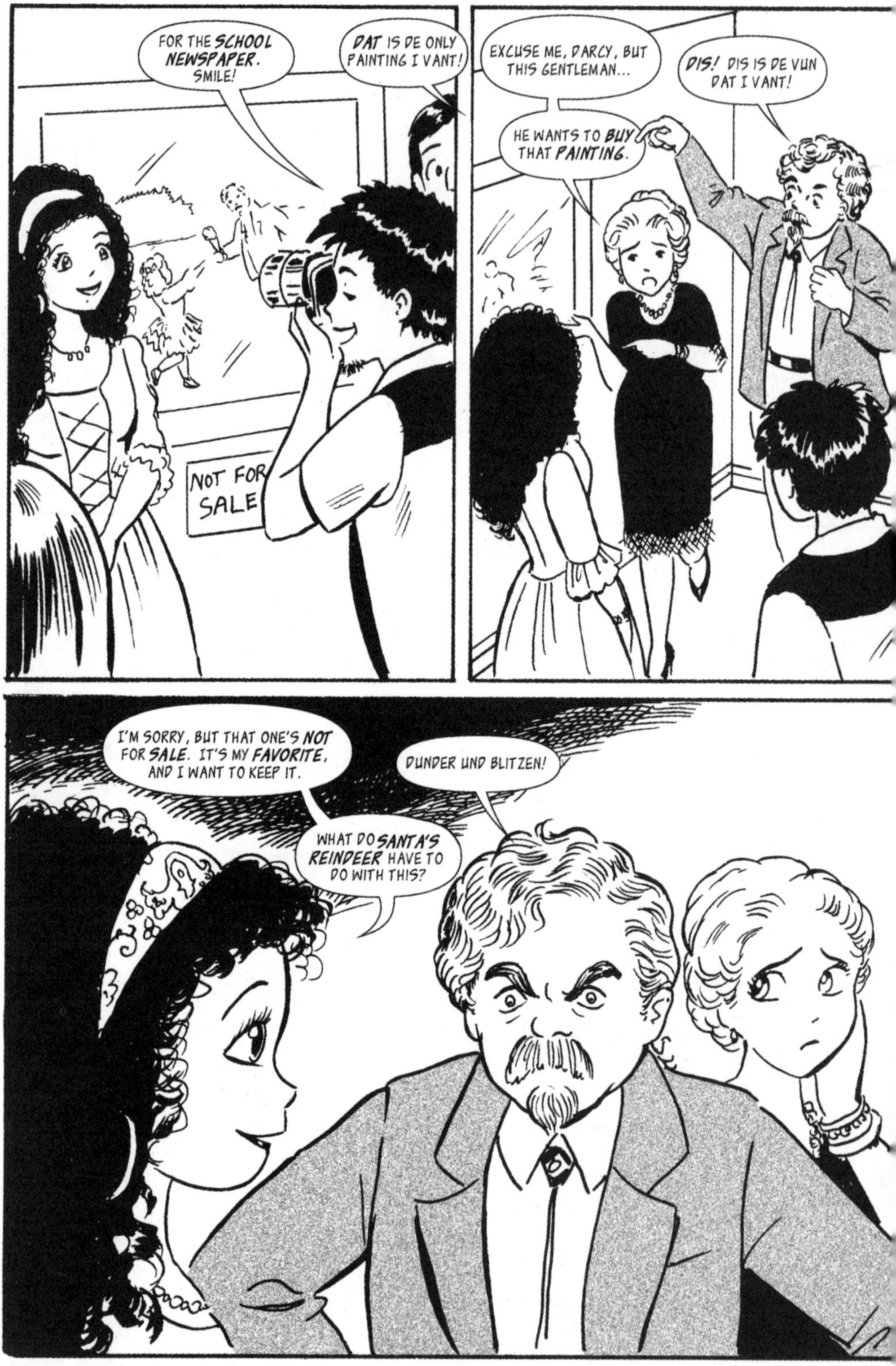
FOR THE SCHOOL NEWSPAPER. SMILE!
DAT IS DE ONLY PAINTING I VANT!
NOT FOR SALE
EXCUSE ME, DARCY, BUT THIS GENTLEMAN...
HE WANTS TO BUY THAT PAINTING.
DIS! DIS IS DE VUN DAT I VANT!
I'M SORRY, BUT THAT ONE'S NOT FOR SALE. IT'S MY FAVORITE, AND I WANT TO KEEP IT.
DUNDER UND BLITZEN!
WHAT DO SANTA'S REINDEER HAVE TO DO WITH THIS?

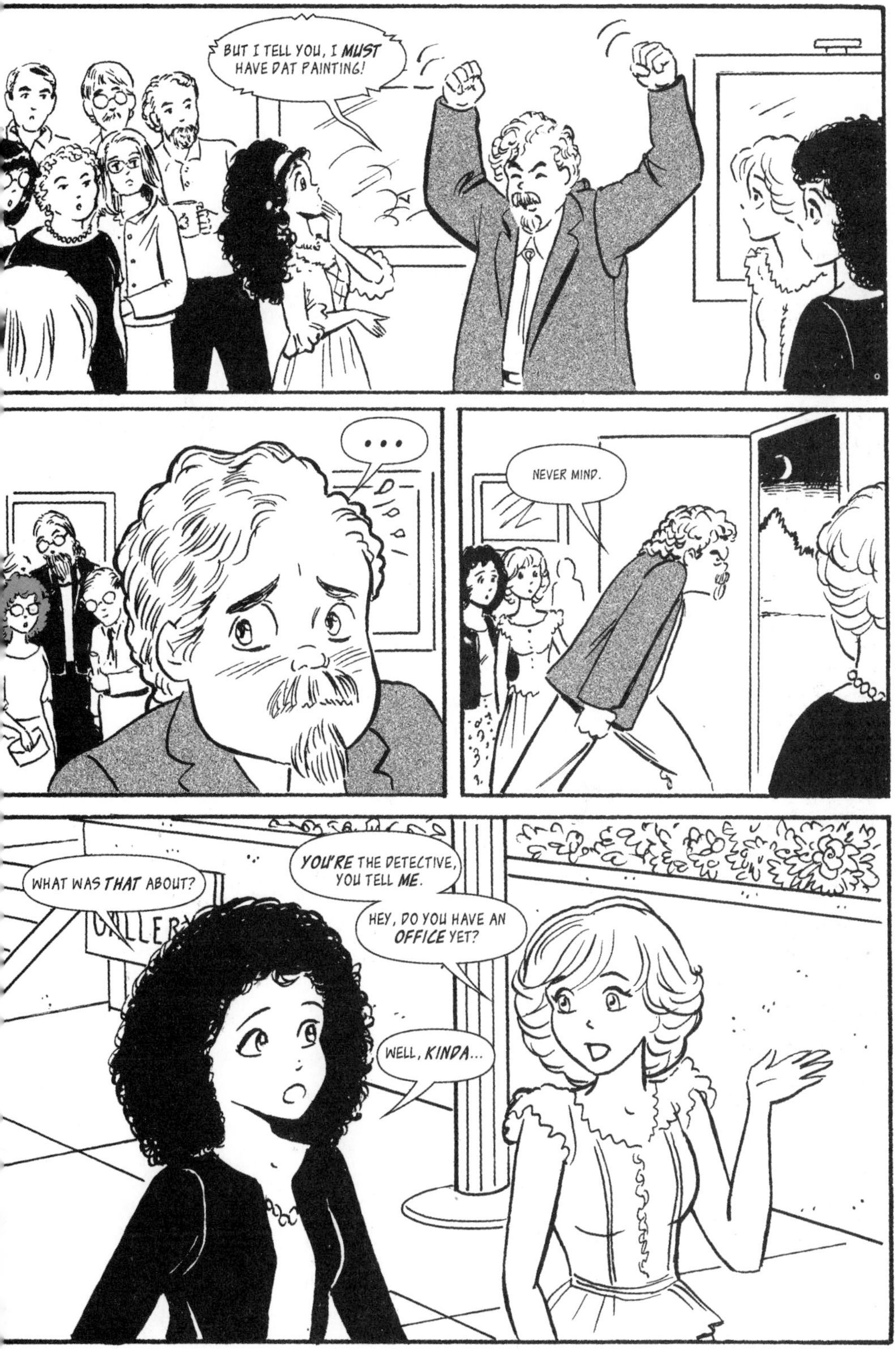
BUT I TELL YOU, I *MUST* HAVE DAT PAINTING!
...
NEVER MIND.
WHAT WAS *THAT* ABOUT?
*YOU'RE* THE DETECTIVE, YOU TELL *ME*.
HEY, DO YOU HAVE AN *OFFICE* YET?
WELL, *KINDA*...
GALLERY

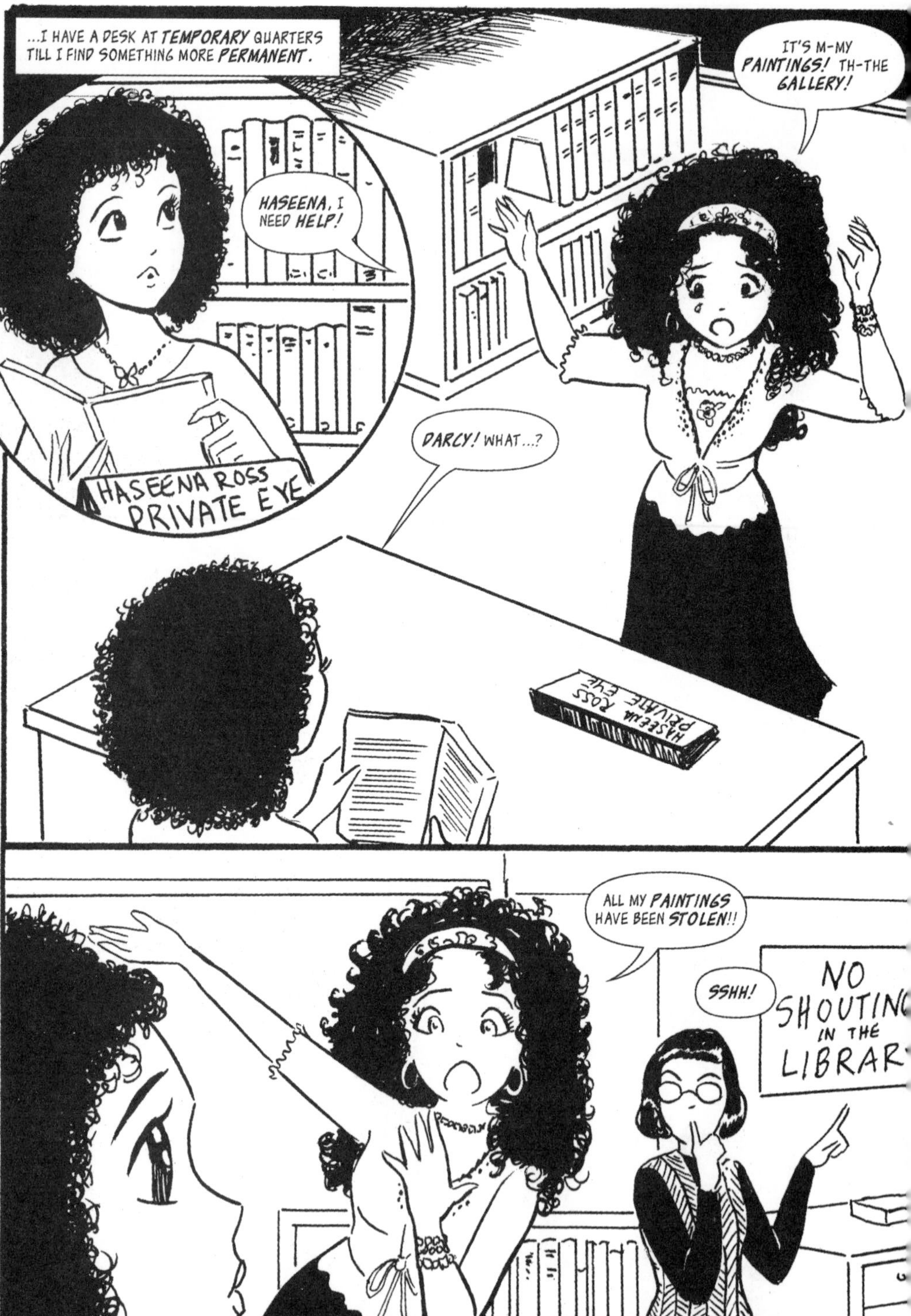
...I HAVE A DESK AT TEMPORARY QUARTERS TILL I FIND SOMETHING MORE PERMANENT.
HASEENA, I NEED HELP!
HASEENA ROSS PRIVATE EYE
IT'S M-MY PAINTINGS! TH-THE GALLERY!
DARCY! WHAT...?
HASEENA ROSS PRIVATE EYE
ALL MY PAINTINGS HAVE BEEN STOLEN!!
SSHH!
NO SHOUTING IN THE LIBRAR

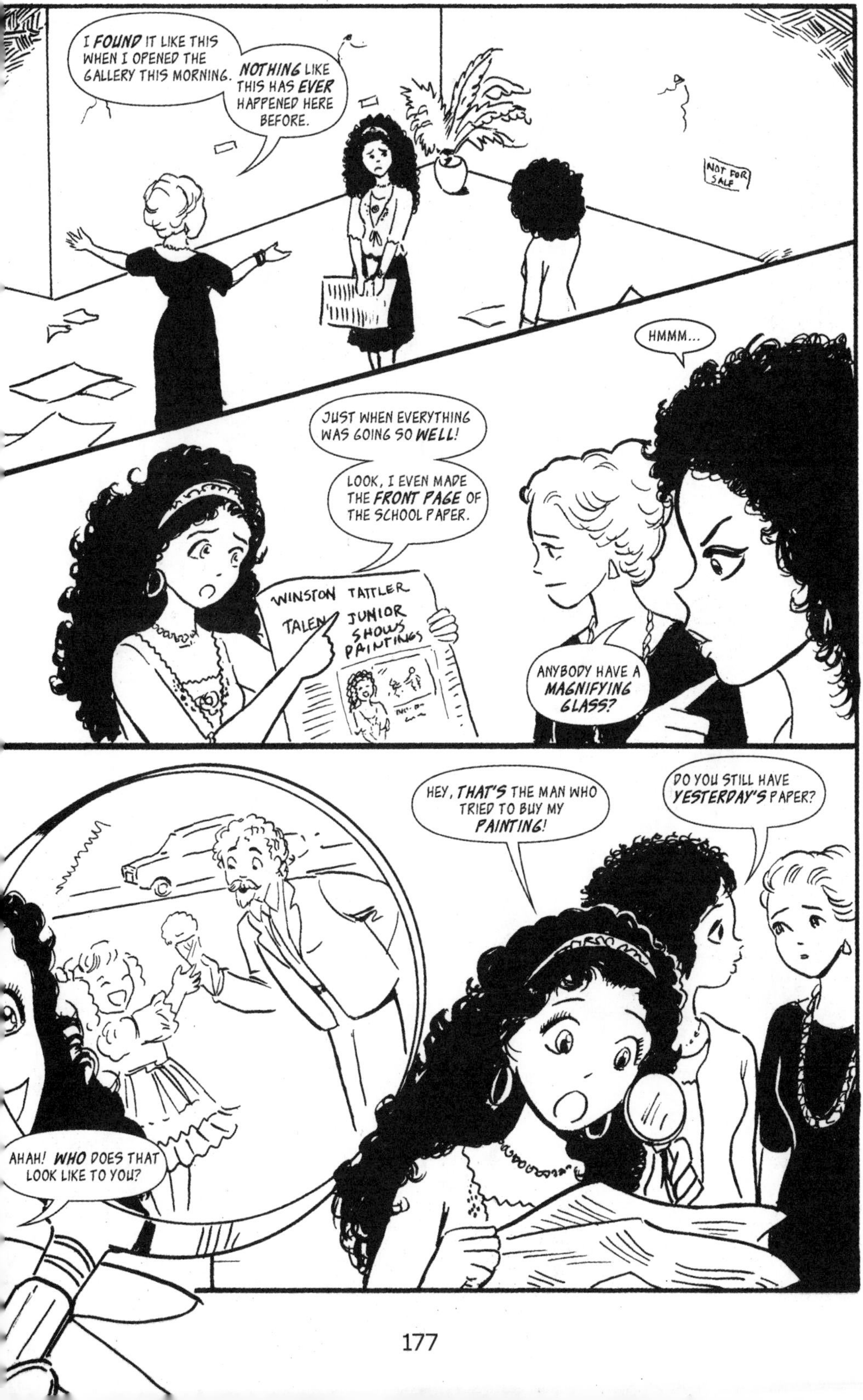
I FOUND IT LIKE THIS WHEN I OPENED THE GALLERY THIS MORNING.
NOTHING LIKE THIS HAS EVER HAPPENED HERE BEFORE.
NOT FOR SALE
HMMM...
JUST WHEN EVERYTHING WAS GOING SO WELL!
LOOK, I EVEN MADE THE FRONT PAGE OF THE SCHOOL PAPER.
WINSTON TATTLER
JUNIOR SHOWS PAINTINGS
ANYBODY HAVE A MAGNIFYING GLASS?
HEY, THAT'S THE MAN WHO TRIED TO BUY MY PAINTING!
DO YOU STILL HAVE YESTERDAY'S PAPER?
AHAH! WHO DOES THAT LOOK LIKE TO YOU?

AND THAT LITTLE GIRL IS THE *MISSING* DAUGHTER OF THE AMBASSADOR OF RAUSCHENBURG.

NO DOUBT YOU PAINTED THE KIDNAPPING IN *PROGRESS*, DARCY!

OMIGOD, YOU'RE *RIGHT!* HOW DID YOU FIGURE IT OUT, HASEENA?

WINSTON TAT
TALENTED JU
SHOWS
PAINTING

WINSTON TELEC
DIPLOMAT'S DAUGHTE
KIDNAPPED

CANDACE, DAUGHT OF RAUSCHENBU AMBASSA DO

ELIMENTARY.

IT SAYS HERE THAT RAUSCHENBURG IS A SMALL PRINCIPALITY ON THE BORDER BETWEEN FRANCE AND GERMANY, AND THAT PART OF THE COUNTRY SPEAKS *FRENCH* AND THE *OTHER* PART SPEAKS *GERMAN*.

I BET THAT'S THE KIDNAPPER'S *CAR* IN THE PAINTING. IF WE COULD ONLY READ THE *LICENSE PLATES...*

WORLD ATLAS

WE CAN!

WOW, YOU CAN READ THE *LICENSE PLATE!*

THERE IT IS, *CLEAR AS DAY.*

I *PAINT* WHAT I *SEE.*

TRBLZ

178

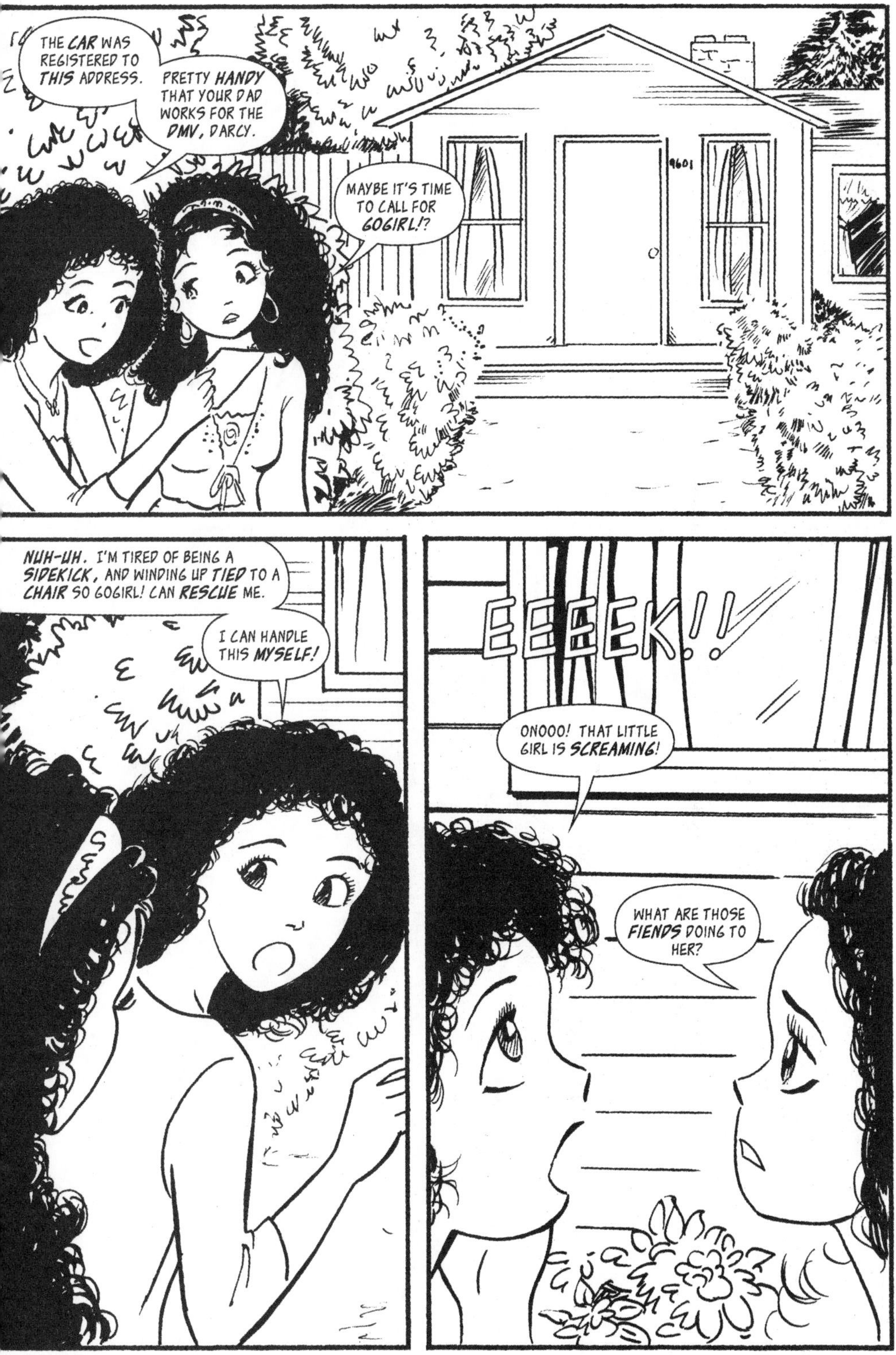
THE CAR WAS REGISTERED TO THIS ADDRESS.
PRETTY HANDY THAT YOUR DAD WORKS FOR THE DMV, DARCY.
9601
MAYBE IT'S TIME TO CALL FOR GOGIRL!?
NUH-UH. I'M TIRED OF BEING A SIDEKICK, AND WINDING UP TIED TO A CHAIR SO GOGIRL! CAN RESCUE ME.
I CAN HANDLE THIS MYSELF!
EEEEK!!
ONOOO! THAT LITTLE GIRL IS SCREAMING!
WHAT ARE THOSE FIENDS DOING TO HER?

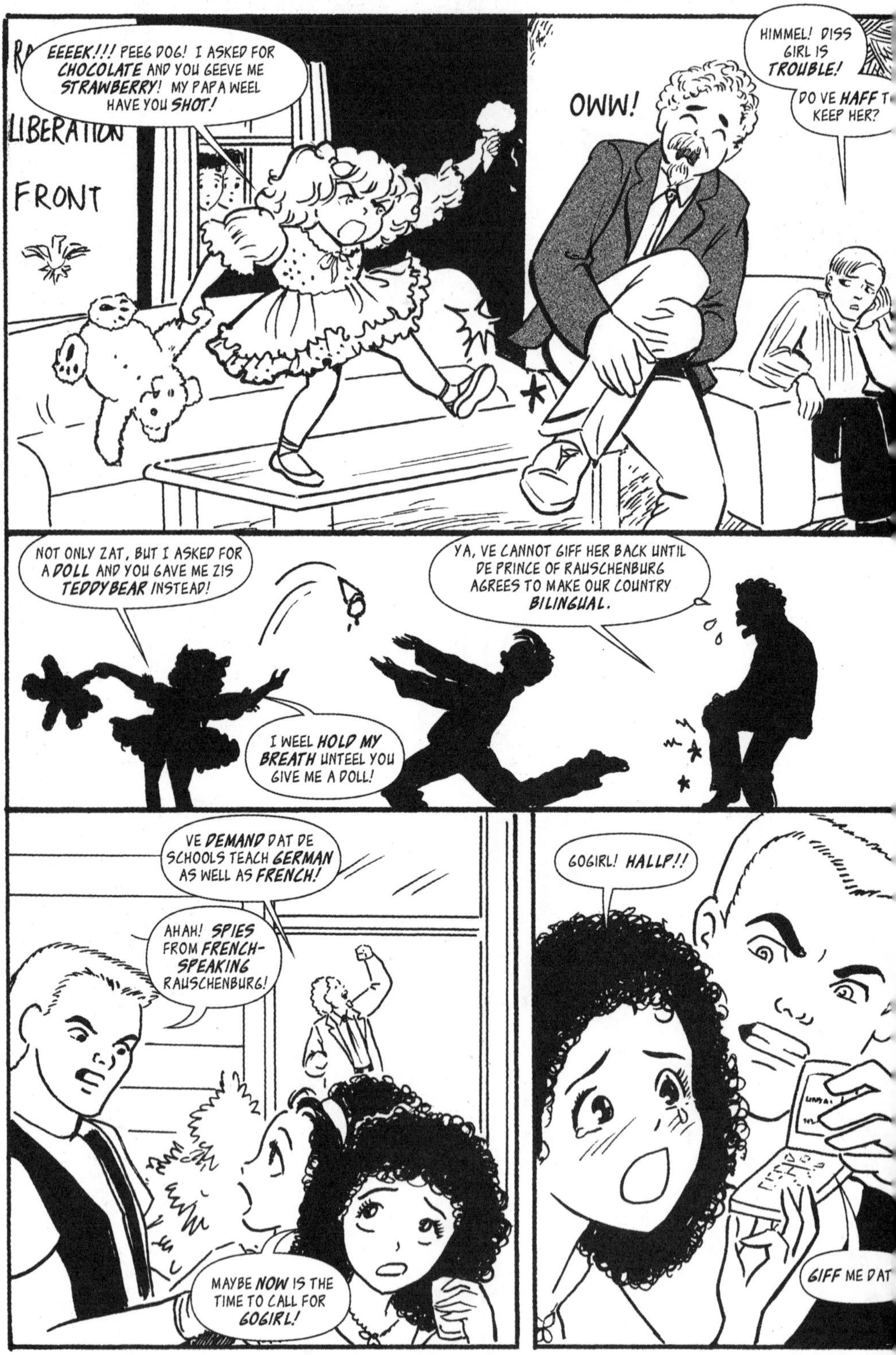
LIBERATION
FRONT
EEEEK!!! PEEG DOG! I ASKED FOR CHOCOLATE AND YOU GEEVE ME STRAWBERRY! MY PAPA WEEL HAVE YOU SHOT!
OWW!
HIMMEL! DISS GIRL IS TROUBLE!
NOT ONLY ZAT, BUT I ASKED FOR A DOLL AND YOU GAVE ME ZIS TEDDYBEAR INSTEAD!
I WEEL HOLD MY BREATH UNTEEL YOU GIVE ME A DOLL!
YA, VE CANNOT GIFF HER BACK UNTIL DE PRINCE OF RAUSCHENBURG AGREES TO MAKE OUR COUNTRY BILINGUAL.
VE DEMAND DAT DE SCHOOLS TEACH GERMAN AS WELL AS FRENCH!
AHAH! SPIES FROM FRENCH-SPEAKING RAUSCHENBURG!
MAYBE NOW IS THE TIME TO CALL FOR GOGIRL!
GOGIRL! HALLP!!

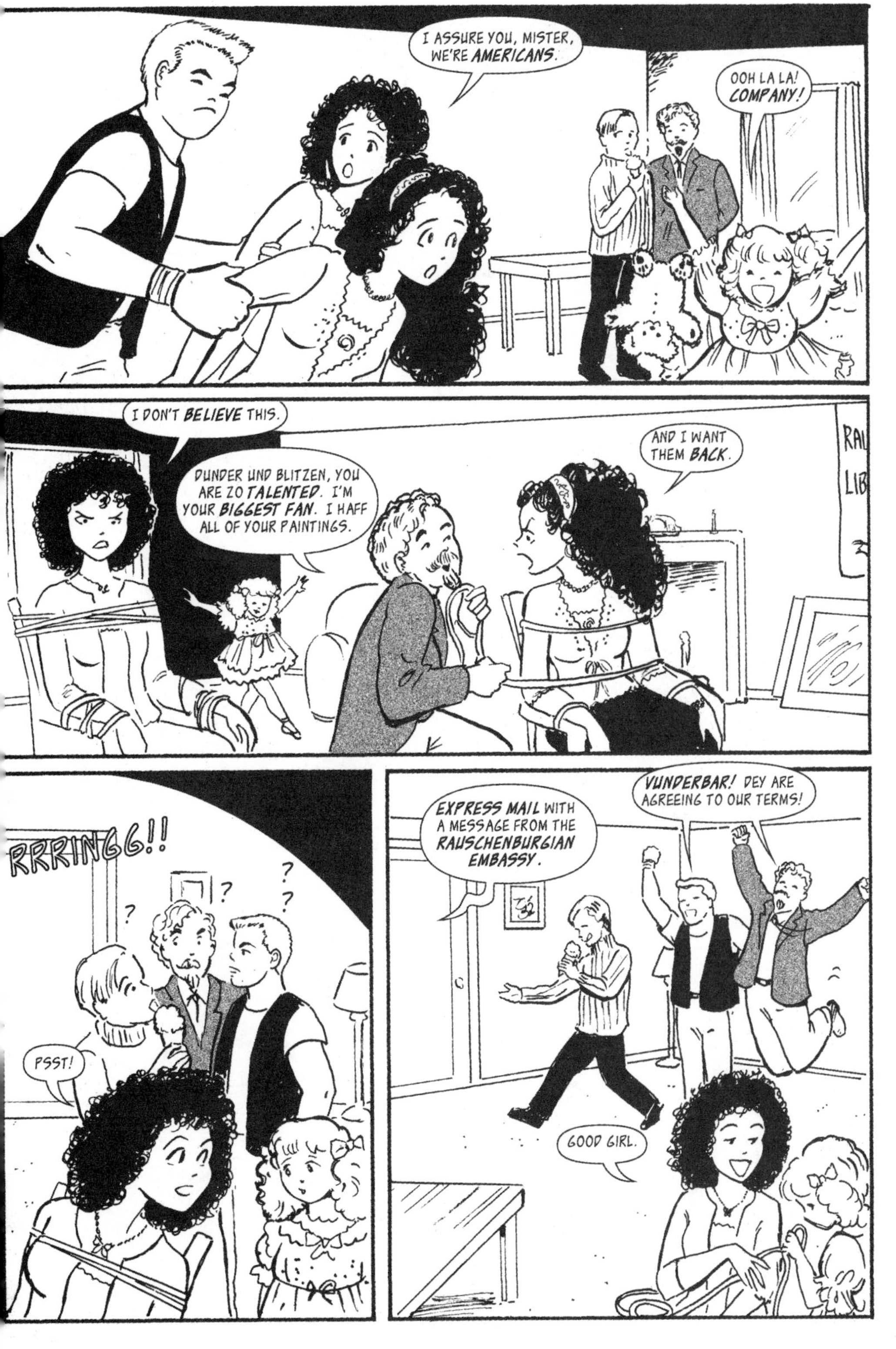
I ASSURE YOU, MISTER, WE'RE AMERICANS.
OOH LA LA! COMPANY!
I DON'T BELIEVE THIS.
DUNDER UND BLITZEN, YOU ARE ZO TALENTED. I'M YOUR BIGGEST FAN. I HAFF ALL OF YOUR PAINTINGS.
AND I WANT THEM BACK.
RRRINGG!!
? ? ?
PSST!
EXPRESS MAIL WITH A MESSAGE FROM THE RAUSCHENBURGIAN EMBASSY.
VUNDERBAR! DEY ARE AGREEING TO OUR TERMS!
GOOD GIRL.

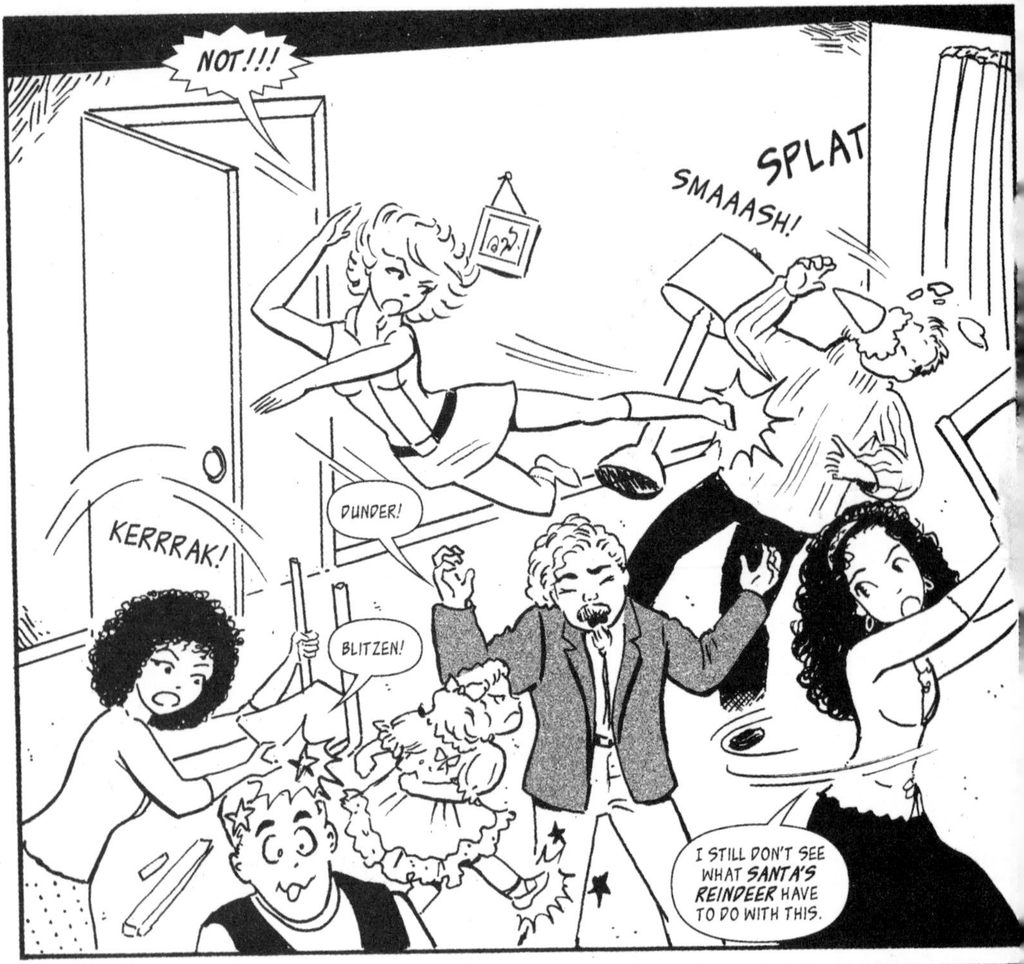
NOT!!!
SPLAT
SMAAASH!
KERRRAK!
DUNDER!
BLITZEN!
I STILL DON'T SEE WHAT SANTA'S REINDEER HAVE TO DO WITH THIS.

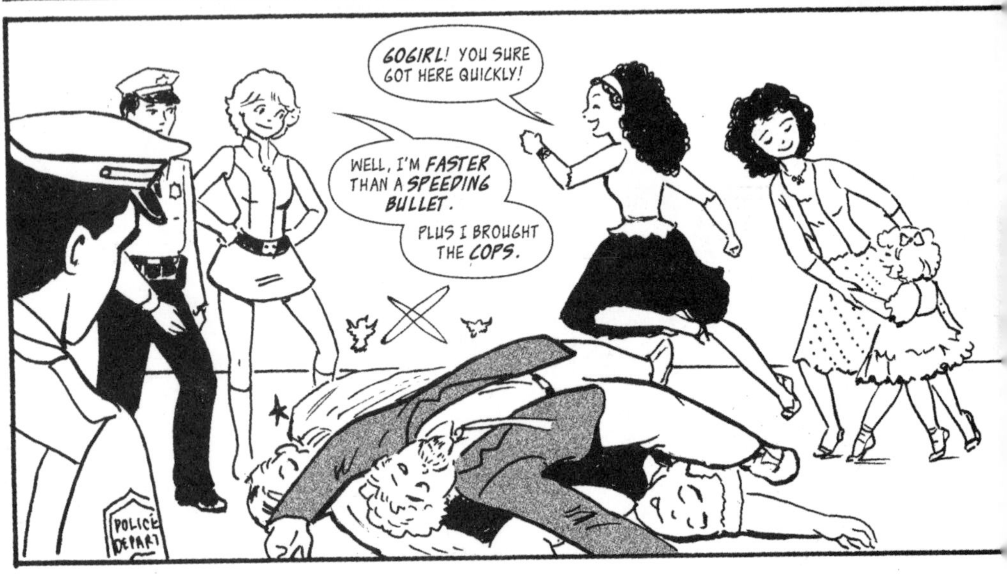
GOGIRL! YOU SURE GOT HERE QUICKLY!
WELL, I'M FASTER THAN A SPEEDING BULLET.
PLUS I BROUGHT THE COPS.
POLICE DEPART